## About the author

Saul David is the author of several critically acclaimed history books, including *The Indian Mutiny: 1857* (short-listed for the Westminster Medal for Military Literature), *Zulu: The Heroism and Tragedy of the Zulu War of 1879* (a Waterstone's Military History Book of the Year) and, most recently, *Victoria's Wars: The Rise of Empire*. He is currently working on a history of the British Army.

An experienced broadcaster, Saul has presented and appeared in history programmes for all the major TV channels and is a regular contributor to Radio 4. On 21 February 2009 he presented 'Queen Elizabeth's Lost Guns' for BBC2's flagship history series, *Timewatch*.

In 2007–8, Saul was Visiting Professor of Military History at the University of Hull. He is now Professor of War Studies at the University of Buckingham, and Programme Director for Buckingham's new London-based MA in Military History from September 2009.

# SAUL DAVID

HODDER

First published in Great Britain in 2009 by Hodder & Stoughton
An Hachette UK company

This paperback edition first published in 2009 by Hodder & Stoughton

10

A CIP catalogue record for this title is available from the British Library.

B format ISBN 978 0 340 95364 8
A format ISBN 978 0 340 99796 3

Map drawn by Martin Collins

Typeset in Sabon by Hewer Text UK Ltd, Edinburgh
Printed and bound by Clays Ltd, St Ives plc

Hodder & Stoughton policy is to use papers that are natural, renewable
and recyclable products and made from wood grown in sustainable
forests. The logging and manufacturing processes are expected to
conform to the environmental regulations of the country of origin.

Hodder & Stoughton Ltd
338 Euston Road
London NW1 3BH

www.hodder.co.uk

For my darling Nell

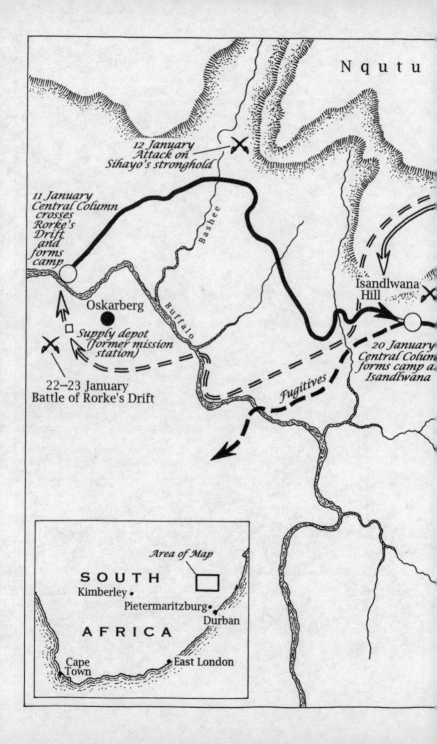

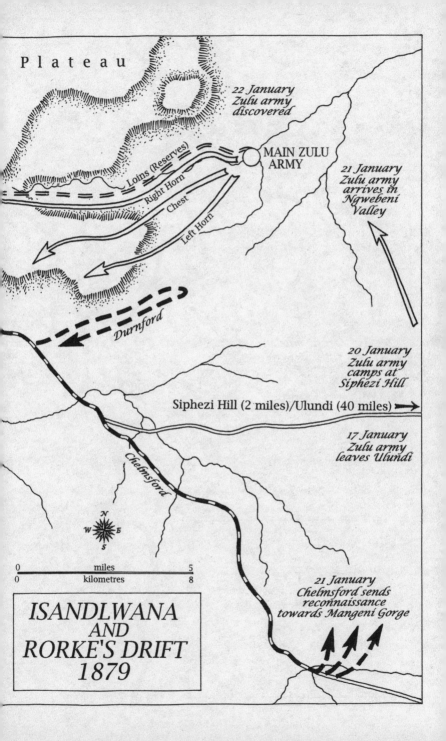

Plateau

22 January
Zulu army
discovered

MAIN ZULU
ARMY

Loins (Reserves)

Right Horn

Chest

Left Horn

21 January
Zulu army
arrives in
Ngwebeni
Valley

Durnford

20 January
Zulu army
camps at
Siphezi Hill

Siphezi Hill (2 miles)/Ulundi (40 miles) →

17 January
Zulu army
leaves Ulundi

Chelmsford

N
W · E
S

0          miles       5
0    kilometres    8

ISANDLWANA
AND
RORKE'S DRIFT
1879

21 January
Chelmsford sends
reconnaissance
towards Mangeni Gorge

# Prologue

## Dublin, 1 October 1859

I shall never set foot in a theatre again, vowed the tall, well-dressed occupant of the hansom cab as it drew up in front of No. 27 Connaught Square. Casting his eyes up to the warmly illuminated windows of the elegant town-house, he drew a deep, determined breath. Ever since meeting his wife Louisa twenty years earlier, he had had a penchant for actresses. But a liaison was one thing, a bastard quite another. Fully resolved to keep the child's existence a secret, he opened the cab door and stepped down to the pavement. 'Wait here,' he told the driver, perched high above the cab.

The shiny black door was opened by a liveried footman. 'Good evening, sir. Miss Hart is expecting you. She's upstairs in the drawing room.'

He handed the footman his Chesterfield overcoat, top hat and cane, and strode up the sweeping staircase to the first floor. He paused before a gilt mirror to straighten his white neckcloth. It was unfashionably broad and worn with a high collar. The latest style was for small bows and low collars, but he had never been one to follow trends, and the rest of his evening dress said as much, with its traditional black tails, white waistcoat with embroidered borders, black trousers and pumps. Though his boyish handsomeness was marred slightly by his receding hair-line, he still cut a dashing figure in the mirror with his impressive moustache and whiskers. Not bad for forty, he thought, before continuing on to the drawing room.

'Hello, darling,' said a female voice as he entered. 'Come and meet your son.'

She was standing in front of the fireplace, a broad smile on her radiant face, a tiny baby clutched in her arms. Her curly raven hair was piled high on her head, her full figure enclosed in a tight-fitting green velvet gown that matched her flashing eyes. She was even more beautiful than he remembered. 'Hello, Emma,' he responded, nodding at the baby. 'Is he well?'

'He is. And *he* has a name: George Arthur, named for you and the Iron Duke. For now, my surname will have to suffice.'

He walked over, kissed her cheek and peered down at his sleeping son. The boy's features were regular, the hair glossy black, and the skin much lighter than his mother's milk-coffee tone. 'He's perfect,' he said. 'But I can never acknowledge him.'

Emma's smile faded. 'Why ever not? It's not as though he's your first bastard, nor I your first mistress.'

'No. But I married your predecessor. And, as you well know, she doesn't take kindly to rivals.'

'Any rivals?' she spat. 'Or just those who are younger, more beautiful and more talented?'

'Sarcasm doesn't become you, Emma. You must realize I have no choice. Louisa is insanely jealous if I even so much as look at a pretty girl, and this would break her heart. Nor would Her Majesty regard it with any more favour.'

'The queen has accepted the bastards you bred with your wife before you married her. Why not this one?'

He sighed and walked towards the window overlooking the square, his hands clasped behind his back. 'The queen has never even mentioned them. As far as she's concerned, my wife and children do not exist, which is why I'd be a fool to reopen old wounds. An injudicious marriage is bad enough, but infidelity she would never forgive. You know what sticklers she and Albert are for moral propriety.'

'Indeed,' said Emma with contempt. 'But that's never discouraged you, has it? Are you sure there isn't another reason? Like the colour of his skin?'

He turned sharply. 'That has nothing to do with it. The boy's no darker than our good Mr Disraeli. And don't think I'm trying to shirk my responsibilities. As long as you keep quiet about his provenance, you'll receive an annuity of three thousand pounds. But it will cease on his eighteenth birthday, by which time I'll have arranged a commission for him in my old cavalry regiment. From then on he's on his own. He'll have to live on his army pay.'

'And what if I don't want him to become a soldier?'

'How could you object? A more honourable profession does not exist.'

'It's not the nature of the profession I'm concerned with, George, but the obvious truth that not everyone is suited to war. Surely you know that as well as anyone.'

3

'*I?*' he said indignantly. 'What *exactly* are you getting at? I did my duty in the Crimea and only came home on a medical certificate.'

'Of course, but . . .'

'But *what*?'

She was about to mention the adverse reaction by the press to his early return, but thought better of it.

After a pause he continued, 'I've told you my terms. If you renege on them, I'll stop the annuity and *still* deny he's my son. But I'm prepared to offer an additional induce-ment: if you allow him to enter the army and he achieves certain goals by a certain age, then he'll receive from my solicitor a series of substantial payments.'

'What goals?'

'I have yet to decide. But all will be revealed on his eighteenth birthday.'

Looking down at her baby, she said in a low voice, 'So that's your plan: to blackmail your son into becom-ing a successful soldier? Why him? Why not your other sons?'

'Thus far my elder sons have shown little aptitude for the military. I don't know why. Maybe I've indulged them. But the truth is they're far more interested in drinking and gambling than taking their profession ser-iously. In short, they lack ambition, like a lot of young men today. He won't. Life in the army will toughen him up and give him something to work for.'

She snorted and shook her head. 'I don't think you've thought about this enough. George is the bastard son of a half-breed actress. He wouldn't survive five minutes in the army.'

'I never said it would be easy. That's part of the challenge. But to make life simpler I suggest you tell him he's of Maltese blood and that his father died when he was an infant.'

She shook her head. 'No, I'm sorry. I can't do that.'

He stared at her coldly for a while, nodded at the child in her arms and said, 'You can and you will, for his sake if not your own. Your time on the stage is limited. Your beauty will fade. Then how will you provide for your son? I can do that, but my identity must remain a secret – even to him.'

She turned away to hide her tears. When she turned back, he'd gone.

# I

*Harrow School, Michaelmas Term 1873*

'Hart, you lazy bastard, where the devil are you?' came a cry from outside the dormitory.

George flinched at the sound of his tormentor's voice and continued buffing the large black shoe in his hand. He had been working on it for a good ten minutes, and the result was a shine so clear he could see his reflection in it. Yet he knew from experience that his fagmaster, Percy Sykes, would find fault with the smallest blemish.

'Hart!' The call was angry now. 'You've got twenty seconds to produce my shoes. I'm counting.'

A last vigorous rub and George was done. He grabbed the shoe's twin from the floor and hurtled out of the dormitory, along the corridor, up a flight of stairs and came to a halt in front of Sykes's study. The door was open.

'Twenty-two seconds,' said Sykes, pocket-watch in hand. He was sitting in an armchair and, apart from his stockinged feet, was immaculately turned out in his Sunday best of top hat and tails. 'Shame. Shoes, please.'

George handed over the gleaming footwear.

'Not bad, not bad at all,' said Sykes, turning them over.

'We'll make a valet of you yet. But I can't abide lateness. Report to the gym after lunch for your punishment.'

George knew the gym meant another beating. He had had enough.

'No.'

'What did you say?'

'I said no. I was only two seconds late.'

Sykes stood up and approached George menacingly. He was tall for his seventeen years and stockily built. 'You dare to say no to *me*?'

George said nothing, prompting Sykes to lower his face to within inches of his fag's. 'I'm going to teach you some manners, Hart. Forget the gym. Meet me in the long field at six – and don't be late.'

George knew he had gone too far. The long field was the venue for fist-fights, or 'affairs of honour', as the boys chose to call them, the means by which most quarrels at Harrow were settled. George thought back to the two bouts he had already fought and won against boys his own age. Neither had been a pleasant experience. But the bigger and stronger Sykes was a very different proposition. His instinct was to decline and take his punishment in the gym. But where would it end? No, he decided, it was far better to stand up to Sykes and his kind in an open fight, even if it meant a pummelling.

'I'll be there,' he said, with more confidence than he felt.

News of the fight spread rapidly, and a large crowd had gathered by the time George and his second, a pale youth called Watson, reached the long field at a few minutes to six. They pushed their way through the excited throng to find Sykes in the centre of the field, stripped to the waist

8

and shadow-boxing with one of his cronies. The sixth-former acting as referee was also there.

Sykes raised his eyebrows at George's arrival. 'Didn't think you'd show,' he said with a sneer. 'And you'll soon wish you hadn't.'

'Enough!' said the referee. 'Time to let your fists do the talking. You both know the rules: three minutes a round, sixty seconds to recover from a knockdown and you fight until one or other of you has had enough. Any questions?'

They both shook their heads.

'Come together, then.'

George stripped off his shirt and handed it to Watson. He was much slighter than Sykes, causing the crowd to howl with laughter as the two fighters stepped up to the mark: one tall, white and muscular; the other dark and scrawny.

The referee dropped his hand. 'Round one!'

Sykes came rushing forward, a straight right and a swinging left both narrowly failing to connect with his opponent's face. George countered with a jab that caught Sykes flush on the chin and rocked his head back. The crowd roared its approval, delighted they would see a contest after all.

'You'll pay for that,' said Sykes, spitting blood from a split lip.

But as the fight wore on it became clear that George's superior technique was every bit a match for Sykes's size advantage. Each time the older boy tried to close and bring his strength to bear, George ducked and danced his way out of trouble. He was like a matador with a bull, and by round five a wheezing Sykes was getting desperate. He ploughed forward again and straight on to George's right hook. The crack as fist connected with bone cartilage could be heard by latecomers fifty yards away. As Sykes staggered and fell, his nose streaming blood, George clutched his injured right hand.

The crowd was shocked into silence, as bewildered by the smaller boy's extraordinary courage as they were by his lightning hands. They sensed, too, that he was badly hurt.

'You all right, Hart?' asked Watson.

'No. I think I've broken a bone in my right hand, but for God's sake don't let on.'

Watson looked across at Sykes. He had been helped into a sitting position by his second, who was sponging his face. 'I don't think he'll make it. But if he does, you have to concede. You can't fight with one hand.'

'I won't concede.'

With only seconds of his minute's grace remaining, Sykes stumbled forward to the mark, his face groggy and his arms hanging limply by his sides.

'All right to go on?' asked the referee.

Sykes nodded, fury in his eyes.

George continued as before, keeping his opponent at bay with well-aimed jabs. His fluid movement over the ground gave little away to the crowd, but it quickly became apparent to Sykes that he was reluctant to land any blows with his previously fearsome right hand. This knowledge brought a smile to Sykes's battered lips. He feinted with his right hand and landed a crunching left hook on George's undefended right ear, stunning his opponent but not felling him.

George stumbled backwards, trying to clear his head, but Sykes could smell blood and was on him in an instant, landing two more swingeing lefts to the side of the smaller boy's head. The baying crowd groaned as George fell awkwardly to the ground, his face bruised and bleeding.

'Give it up, Hart,' hissed Watson, as he sponged away the blood. 'Walk away now, while you still can!'

George heard these words through the buzzing in his right ear, but far from causing him to see sense, to give in to this thug, their effect was quite the opposite. He had been bullied long enough; it was time to make his stand. As he walked slowly back to the mark, distantly recalled episodes, some horrid and violent, others quite banal, rushed uninvited to the forefront of his mind, like the time Sykes and his cronies had forced his head down a lavatory before pulling the chain. The sense of injustice seemed to flow into his broken right fist. Before he could stop himself, he had driven that fist with all his strength into the point of Sykes's chin.

He must have blacked out with the pain, because when he came to, Watson was hovering above him again, concern etched on his face. 'Are you all right, Hart?'

George nodded, though his right hand felt as if it was on fire.

Watson gestured towards the prostrate Sykes. 'I don't think he can carry on, Hart: you've won.'

George grimaced with the pain. As he staggered to his feet, a familiar voice shouted, 'Out of my way, you bloody fools!'

The crowd parted to reveal the tall, thin figure of Mr Hardy, George's housemaster. 'Back to school, all of you!' he roared. 'Now!'

As the crowd scuttled away, Hardy walked over to Sykes and examined his battered face. 'Not a pretty sight. You'll need that nose reset, and when Matron's done with you, report to my study for ten strokes of the cane. You're also demoted from prefect.'

'But, sir,' implored Sykes.

'But nothing. Fighting a boy three years your junior? What were you thinking? You might have killed him. It happened to a boy at Eton in the twenties. Lord Shaftesbury's son, if memory serves. Just be thankful I'm not sending you down.'

Hardy turned to George. 'You all right, Hart?'

'I think my hand's broken, sir.'

'Off to the infirmary with you, then, and Hart . . .'

'Yes, sir?'

Hardy's craggy face broke into a half-smile. 'That was a plucky effort, lad, very plucky. But don't let me catch you fighting again.'

## Summer 1877

George clenched his fist and winced. Almost four years had elapsed since the fight; his broken bones had long since knitted, yet he could still remember the pain as if it were yesterday. It had been worth it, though. His gallant showing had been the talk of the school, with Sykes cast in the role of pantomime bully; small wonder that he and his cronies had kept a low profile thereafter.

It would have made his life easier, of course, if his mother had not been an actress, a most unusual profession for a woman of allegedly gentle birth (for she had always insisted her father was an Irish-born army officer and her mother a Maltese lady); and even more so if he had not been born out of wedlock and his father had survived his infant years. But such was fate, thought George, and hopefully the bad times were in the past.

He had got through Harrow, excelled at Sandhurst, and was about to join one of the finest cavalry regiments in the British Army. His appointment to the 1st King's Dragoon Guards – or KDG, as it was generally known – was, he had to confess, something of a mystery. Its officers were typically very rich or very well connected. He was neither, and had put this choice posting down to the potential he had shown as a gentleman-cadet. He was determined to fulfil that potential, even if it meant curbing his fiery temperament. But tonight he could be himself. It was his eighteenth birthday and, to celebrate, his mother had arranged a grand dinner party for their closest friends. He could hardly wait.

George rose from his dressing table and peered at himself in the full-length mirror. His evening-dress suit had cost him a sizeable portion of his private allowance, but even he had to admit he looked well in it. It helped that he was over six feet, with broad shoulders and a narrow waist, a natural clothes-horse. It helped, too, that his black tailcoat was of the finest twilled cashmere, with a low velvet collar and silk lapels. As he adjusted his white bow tie, he regretted again the inadequacy of his thin black moustache. He had only been shaving for a year, and his bristles were not yet thick enough to produce the necessary growth. The only other flaw in his classically handsome face, with its large hazel eyes and even white teeth, was a slightly crooked nose, the legacy of another fight. But that was no bad thing, he thought, as it gave his fresh-faced looks a mildly piratical air.

A knock on the door brought colour to his cheeks, as if his self-satisfied contemplation had been witnessed. 'Come in!' he said.

It was Manners, the old family retainer who had served his grandfather. 'Begging your pardon, Master George, but your mother would like to speak to you before you go down.'

George sighed. The guests would be here soon. Couldn't it wait?

'All right, Manners, I'll be down presently, and less of the "Master George", if you please. I'm eighteen and a commissioned officer in the British Army. "Mr Hart" will suffice.'

Manners raised his eyebrows. 'As you wish, Master . . . um . . . Mr Hart.'

George heard the door close and took a moment to try and smooth the unruly black curls at his temples; but no amount of water, patted on with his fingers, seemed to do the trick. He gave up and followed Manners down to his mother's sitting room on the second floor, entering without knocking.

His mother was seated on the sofa in quiet contemplation. As he bent down to embrace her, George marvelled again at her ageless beauty. Clad in a gorgeous off-the-shoulder blue velvet gown, complete with train and elaborate overskirt, she seemed to him more striking than ever. Yet her expression was pained, as if she had something unpleasant to say. 'What is it, Mother?' he asked.

'Sit down, Georgie,' she said, patting the sofa beside her. 'Now that you're eighteen, there's something I must tell you. Before I do, I want you to know that the day you were presented with the sword at Sandhurst was the proudest of my life. I never wanted you to join the army, but I made a promise years ago, and I've stood by it.'

'What promise and to whom?'

'To your father. Darling, what I'm about to tell you will come as quite a shock. Try not to be angry with me.'

'I could never be angry with you, Mother. Just tell me.'

She took a deep breath. 'You know I've always told you that your father and I never married and that he died at sea. Well, the first part is true, but not the second. He's very much alive.'

George's jaw dropped. 'Are you being serious? My father *alive*! Why would you keep this from me?'

'I had my reasons, darling, please believe me.'

'What reasons?'

'He made me promise, shortly after your birth, that in return for his anonymity I would receive money for your upkeep and, when the time came, he would arrange for you to become an officer in a cavalry regiment. I kept that promise. If I had not, he would have cut us off without a penny. Who do you think paid for your education?'

'You, of course: you're a famous actress.'

'I *was* a famous actress, Georgie, but not any more. I'm thirty-six, for goodness' sake, and well past my prime. I haven't played a leading role for more than three years. It's your father's money that's been keeping us afloat, but that stops on your eighteenth birthday – today. From now on we're on our own.'

15

'Mother, stop!' said George, raising his hands, palms outwards. 'This is too much to take in. You say I have a father who refuses to acknowledge me. Why? What sort of man abandons his infant son?'

'The sort that's married,' sighed his mother.

'Mother. I despair of your judgement sometimes.'

'That's not fair. I've had lovers, and have never denied it, but my priority has always been you. I'm sorry I lied about your father, but I really had no option. I've always wanted the best for you, and only he could provide it.'

'Have you any idea, Mother, how hard it was for me at Harrow and Sandhurst? The fatherless bastard with a touch of the tarbrush, that's what they called me. Now you tell me my father is alive but won't see me. That's almost worse. But it explains one thing that's been bothering me: why a crack regiment like the KDG would accept a social misfit like me. My father must be a man of considerable influence.'

'He is. I can't say any more than that. If it had been up to me you would never have known of his existence. But there's another reason why I let you become a soldier, and why I'm telling you now. It's because your father held out the promise of a sizeable legacy if you made a name for yourself. I don't know the details, but if you want to find out what they are, I suggest you read this.' She handed him a small cream envelope she had been holding. 'It arrived this morning.'

The envelope was addressed to 'George Arthur Hart, Esq.'. George broke the seal and withdrew a single sheet of writing paper. It came from a firm of solicitors in the

City of London that George had never heard of and its message was brief:

*Dear sir,*

*My client, who has chosen to remain anonymous, has assigned you a considerable sum of money. Before any of this money can be made over to you, you must fulfil certain conditions laid down by my client. I can only reveal the nature of those conditions in person. I would be grateful, therefore, if you could reply by return to arrange a personal interview.*

*Please accept my congratulations on reaching your majority.*

*I am your humble and obedient servant,*
*Josiah Ward*

George handed the letter to his mother. 'What can he mean? What conditions?'

'I don't know, Georgie. Your father said something about you achieving various goals by a certain age. What they are I've no idea.'

'But why? Why not just leave me the money?'

'He fears you won't take your career seriously. He has other sons in the military, and they've all disappointed him.'

'So I have half-brothers?'

'Yes. But don't ask me about them. I promised your father I would keep his identity secret, and I intend to honour that promise. He's not a man to cross, Georgie, even if you are his son.'

'So I'm supposed to ignore the fact that I have a father and brothers living, and go along with this charade?'

His mother nodded.

'Damned if I will,' spat George.

'Georgie, please, for me. I've been reliant on your father's money, and now he's stopped paying your annuity I don't know what I'll do. I'm already overdrawn at the bank, and if something doesn't turn up soon I'll be forced to sell the house. So please go and see the lawyer. Hear what he has to say.'

George stood up and walked over to the fireplace, resting his hand on the mantel. He remained there for some time with his back to his mother. His thoughts were confused. He had no wish to please a father he had never known, who had all but abandoned him, yet he was curious to know his identity. Moreover, he had enjoyed his military training thus far and did not require bribes to give of his best; if anything, they might cause him to do something foolish and send him to an early grave. Yet his beloved mother clearly needed some urgent financial support to save her house, and how could he manage that on his army pay?

At last he turned. 'No good can come of this, Mother, but for your sake I *will* see this pen-pusher. You never know, Father's conditions might be easy to comply with and we'll both be rich. Now can we say no more on the subject, and enjoy one last evening of fine food and wine before the purse strings are tightened?'

His mother rose and embaced her son. 'Of course, darling,' she whispered in his ear. 'Thank you.'

George had always loved London, and he revelled in the bustling sights and sounds of the greatest urban centre in the world as his cab took him back in time from the vaulted splendour of Brunel's Paddington Station to the Jacobean elegance of Gray's Inn Square in the City of London. It was still early, with little horse-traffic on the streets, and the driver was able to take the more direct, but usually busy, northern route along Marylebone and Euston roads, down Gray's Inn Road and into the square through an arched entrance topped with the image of Pegasus.

'Whoa!' shouted the driver, causing the cab to come to a jerky halt. 'Number One, sir, as you requested.'

George was confronted by a beautiful red-brick town-house, the first of a terrace. To the right of the front door was a small brass plaque that read, 'Ward & Mills, Solicitors-at-Law'. A prosperous law firm if ever I saw one, thought George as he rapped on the door with his cane. It was answered by a stooped old cove in a dark suit and starched collar.

'Yes?'

'My name's George Hart. I'm here to see Mr Ward.'

'Do come in.'

The old man led the way down a dark corridor and into a spacious, oak-panelled office. George handed his hat, coat and cane to the man, expecting him to leave and fetch his master. Instead he hung George's things on a coat-stand near the door and sat down behind the large desk.

'Do sit down,' he said.

George's brow furrowed. 'Will Mr Ward be long?'

'I am Mr Ward. Please, take a seat.'

'But I thought you were . . .'

'An understandable mistake,' said the lawyer, nodding, his lined features easing into a slight smile. 'After all, it's not every day the senior partner of a respected City law firm answers his own door. No indeed. And why today?' Ward tapped the side of his nose. 'Confidentiality, Mr Hart. My client has impressed upon me the delicacy of this matter, and has insisted upon absolute secrecy, as is his right. He is – how can I put it? – a man of considerable rank and influence. Our most valuable client, if you like, and we do all we can to retain his confidence, which is why I've given the rest of the firm the morning off.'

'Very sensible,' said George, glancing at his pocket-watch. 'But I don't have long. I've got a train to catch to Manchester in under two hours. I'm expected at my new regiment at four in the afternoon and my commanding officer is not the type of man to be kept waiting.'

'May I ask the name of the regiment?'

'The First King's Dragoon Guards.'

'A fine corps with an illustrious history, Mr Hart. My congratulations on your appointment.'

'Thank you. Now can we get on?'

'Of course.' Mr Ward picked up a manilla envelope from the desk. 'This envelope was handed to me by my client almost eighteen years ago. My instructions were to reveal its contents to you, and only you, on or soon after your eighteenth birthday. I should add that, once read, the letter is to remain in my possession. Shall I continue?'

George snorted and shook his head. 'This is a rum business, Mr Ward. But I'm here now, so proceed.'

Clutching an ivory paper knife in his thin, bony hand, the lawyer deftly opened the envelope and handed George the single sheet of thick, watermarked paper. The handwriting was untidy, sloping slightly to the right, and there was no heading or signature to identify the author. It read:

> *To my son George Arthur Hart, Esq.,*
>
> *To encourage you in your early military career, I have put aside the sum of £30,000. But it will only be made over to you, in the amounts mentioned, if you manage to comply with the following conditions before your twenty-eighth birthday, a lapse of ten years:*
>
> 1. *Marry respectably, that is to a lady of gentle birth – £5,000.*
> 2. *Reach the substantive rank of lieutenant colonel in the British Army – £5,000.*
> 3. *Be awarded the Victoria Cross – £10,000.*
>
> *If you comply with all three conditions within the time allotted, you will receive an additional sum of £10,000. This money is in the safekeeping of my solicitor, Josiah Ward of Ward & Mills, and will be disbursed by him once reasonable proofs of compliance have been provided.*

George read the note a second time and snorted. 'My father has an interesting sense of humour, don't you think?' he said, handing the letter to the lawyer.

Mr Ward peered closely at the note through his half-moon spectacles. 'I am not sure I understand your meaning, Mr Hart. It all seems quite straightforward to me.'

George frowned. 'Straightforward? I can see, Mr Ward, you have no experience of the military. Victoria Crosses are only awarded for, and I quote the Royal Warrant, "signal acts of valour or devotion to their Country". They require a level of conspicuous courage that few can hope to attain at any age, let alone in their twenties. As for achieving the substantive rank of lieutenant colonel by twenty-eight, it's well-nigh impossible. A young officer is lucky to make the step up to captain in that time, and most won't get further than lieutenant. I would need four promotions in ten years! The only condition that's achievable is to marry well. But there's a sting in the tail there too, because, as I'm sure my father's well aware, it is not the done thing in the army to marry young. Few colonels will give their permission, on the grounds that wives are seen as an encumbrance to junior officers. So I might earn five thousand, but I can wave goodbye to my career.'

The old lawyer took off his spectacles and began to polish them with his handkerchief. 'These are large sums of money, Mr Hart. You father obviously intends that you should earn them.'

'I am no stranger to hard work, if that's what you're implying,' said George testily. 'But these terms of my father's are far too steep. You'd have to possess the qualities of a young Napoleon to win the money. Now, if you'll excuse me, I have a train to catch.'

George rose and began to gather his belongings from the coat-stand.

'What should I tell your father, Mr Hart? That you refuse his challenge?'

George turned, his eyes flashing. 'I've never refused a challenge in my life. This isn't a challenge; it's a recipe for self-destruction. Tell my father he can keep his money; I owe him nothing. If I do well in the army it will be to satisfy my own ambition, and not to please a parent I don't even know. Good day to you.'

'As you wish,' said Ward, 'but the bequest will still be here if you change your mind.'

As George left the building, and his temper cooled, he wondered if he had been a bit hasty. It was, after all, not *impossible* for a young officer to be awarded the Victoria Cross by the age of twenty-eight; nor was complying with the other conditions completely out of the question. His anger, he realized, was not so much with the terms of the bequest, but rather because his absent father was trying to manipulate his career. What right did he have? None, as far as George could tell.

He began to walk up Gray's Inn Road more determined than ever to make his own way in the world. He knew it would be a struggle, now that he had his mother to support, but he was used to that. All his life he had been swimming against the current.

He turned and hailed an appoaching cab. 'Where to, guv'nor?' asked the driver from his high perch behind the passenger's compartment.

'Euston Station, please. As fast as you can.'

# 2

## Manchester, 5 September 1877

George paused before the heavy oak door marked 'Commanding Officer'. He had heard much of Lieutenant Colonel Sir Jocelyn Harris, Bart., and none of it good. Possessed of a vast fortune and a large estate in Gloucestershire, Harris was said to be a harsh disciplinarian, a snob and worse, given George's sallow skin, a rabid xenophobe. George took off his heavy brass helmet with its '1 KDG' badge and red horsehair plume, and tucked it under his left arm. Taking a deep breath, he knocked twice, the hard wood stinging his knuckles.

'Enter!' sounded an irritated voice within.

George stepped into a large, sparsely furnished room, empty save for a couple of easy chairs and a mahogany desk, behind which sat a tall, elegantly dressed figure that could only be Harris. Stopping the regulation six paces from the desk, George came to attention and saluted. 'Cornet George Hart reporting for duty, sir.'

Harris continued writing. At last he looked up, scanning George's uniform for flaws. There were none. The handsome young officer was immaculate in his scarlet tunic with blue velvet collar and cuffs, gold-striped dark blue breeches and shiny black leather boots. From his gold-lace sword-belt hung a regulation 1856-pattern heavy cavalry sword in its stainless-steel scabbard. His turnout was impeccable.

Harris spoke at last. 'Glad to see you're wearing the regulation breeches, Hart. Too many of my officers cling to their leathered overalls, a full three years after they were discontinued. I won't stand for it, and the next officer to appear on parade improperly dressed will be arrested.'

George breathed a sigh of relief that *his* appearance had not been criticized. Yet the man before him hardly looked the ogre of repute, with his thin, finely boned face, aquiline nose, blue eyes and fashionable mutton-chop whiskers. His golden hair, while thinning at the temples, contained no trace of grey. Only his lips, thin and curled, betrayed a slight hint of cruelty.

Harris's voice brought him out of his reverie. 'And there's another thing I won't stand for, Hart. I won't have unsuitable officers like you foisted on my regiment. You may have finished top of your class at Sandhurst, but that holds no sway with me. When I joined the army in the fifties, you had to buy your commission. It was a way of ensuring that only gentlemen of property, men with a vested interest in the status quo, became officers. But since Cardwell, and the abolition of purchase, any Tom, Dick or Harry can get a commission. Meritocracy be damned. It's a bloody disgrace.'

George wisely said nothing and kept his eyes fixed on the regimental photograph behind Harris. 'We've learnt to put up with change in the King's Dragoon Guards, Hart. We've even accepted the odd officer whose money comes from trade. But in the illustrious one-hundred-and-ninety-year history of this regiment, the officers have never been asked to share a mess with a tawny Irishman of unknown paternity.'

The colour rose in George's cheeks.

'Tell me if I'm wrong,' said Harris with a sneer, 'but is not your mother an actress, a profession little removed from a street girl? As for your father, well, bar your mother, and possibly not even her, nobody knows his identity. He could be anyone.'

Stony-faced, his fists clenched, George took a step forward.

'Stand still!' bellowed Harris. 'You dare to approach me without leave, I'll have you cashiered.'

George could contain himself no longer. 'Sir,' he said through gritted teeth, 'I must protest in the strongest terms. I've endured many taunts on account of my birth. But I cannot stand silent while you insult my mother.'

'Can you not, Hart? Glad to hear it. Our acquaintance is going to be even shorter than I'd hoped. But let me spell it out for you in case you're confused. I did not approve your appointment. I was not even consulted. Instead I was informed by the military secretary, no less, that you would be joining us on such and such a date. When I protested that I knew nothing about you, he waved my objections aside. Clearly you have friends in high places. Well, so do I, and I've made enquiries. I know you were a bit of a loner at both Harrow and Sandhurst, that you had few friends and that you're prone to settling arguments with your fists.'

'Sir,' said George, trying hard to keep his voice level, 'I have only ever fought in defence of my person and my mother's honour.'

Harris grimaced. 'Honour, you say. Can a common actress have honour?'

'Her father, my grandfather, was an officer and a gentleman.'

'He was a captain in the Twenty-Seventh Inniskilling Fusiliers – hardly the same thing. But I digress. The point is, no cavalry regiment in the British Army would have accepted an officer like you by choice. I certainly wouldn't have. And yet here you are. So we'll try and make the best of it. If you learn your duties well, and prove to me that you have the makings, if not the breeding, of an officer, then all will be well. But if you step of out line, even so much as an inch, then your time here will be brief indeed.' Harris waved his hand dismissively. 'Now get out!'

George was still seething as he strode across the barrack square to the headquarters office of E Troop, the sub-unit to which he had been assigned. His mind wandered back to the early days of torment at Harrow: to the taunts of 'Fenian bastard' and 'oily blackguard'; to the endless fagging and the constant terror of being hauled from his bed and tossed from a blanket until he had struck the low ceiling the requisite number of times, a favourite Harrow ordeal. The fight with Percy Sykes had put a stop to the physical bullying, but not the taunts. They had continued during his military training at Sandhurst, and his only solace had been his friendship with Jake Morgan, the son of a Welsh colliery owner and another outsider.

Determined to outdo their haughty classmates, they had drilled and studied hard, even during free weekends when most gentleman-cadets fled Camberley for the fleshpots of

London. And the work paid off. George had passed out first of the summer class of 1877, Jake second. George remembered the elation he felt as he accepted the General Proficiency Sword from General Lawrence: surely now, he had thought, he would be judged by what he did, not where he came from. Harris had proved him wrong.

'You must be Hart?' said a voice, as George entered E Troop's small, cluttered office. A smiling officer came over and shook his hand. 'I'm Dick Marter. Your troop commander.'

George took in the gold-braided double Austrian knot on Marter's sleeve, denoting the rank of captain. He also noted the livid red scar above his left eyebrow, and the two campaign medals – the Crimea and China – on his left breast. Marter was clearly a veteran.

'And that's Corporal White, my orderly,' said Marter, nodding towards the only other occupant of the room, a large red-faced man hunched over a ledger.

'Pleased to meet you both,' said George, surprised by the warmth of Marter's reception.

'How did you get on with the colonel?' asked the captain.

'Not well, I'm afraid. He made it quite plain that I'm not welcome in the regiment.'

'Did he, by God? He never gives new blood an easy ride, does he, White? But that's harsh, even for him. What exactly did he say?'

'He insulted my country and, even worse, my mother.' Marter let out a silent whistle. 'If duelling hadn't been outlawed,' continued George, 'I'd have called him out. Commanding officer or no.'

Marter could tell George had been badly shaken by his first meeting with Harris, and wanted to offer him some words of comfort. But the troop office was too public for such a discussion, so he arranged to see him for a drink in the officers' mess that evening.

'There are one or two things you need to know about the colonel,' he began when they met up later, lowering his voice. 'First off, he's never seen action. He joined the regiment after the Crimea and shortly before the Mutiny of fifty-seven, when, as I'm sure you know, we were confined to police operations in the south of India while Campbell's Bays got all the glory at Lucknow. In China in sixty we *were* in the thick of it, routing the Tartar cavalry before the gates of Peking – it's where I got this.' He tapped his scar. 'But poor Harris caught dysentery before we sailed from Madras and missed the entire campaign. After that, nothing. We've been home since sixty-six and the only excitement we've had is breaking a few Fenian heads in Ireland. So you see, Harris is desperate to prove himself and emulate his father. *He* charged with the Household Brigade at Waterloo, you know. And when Harris does get his chance, he's determined his regiment won't let him down, which is why he drills us incessantly and is such a stickler for the regulations. He's even harder on us than the men, and rarely a week goes by without at least one officer being confined to his quarters. The army hasn't seen Harris's like since the late Lord Cardigan.'

'Why do you put up with it?' said George, slowly shaking his head.

Marter snorted. 'Because he's our commanding officer and we have no choice. He has his favourites, mind:

Captain Bell, the adjutant, for one. And some of us suspect that he's tasked the RSM, Roberts, with secretly making notes of conversations to use as evidence against us. How else could he have confronted Captain Ponsonby with a written record of a previous conversation? When Ponsonby complained, Harris had him arrested, and only the intervention of the district commander secured his release. Most of the officers are good fellows, though, as you'll see. We're *all* waiting for Harris to tire of northern garrison life and send in his papers. He complained enough when we were first posted to Manchester last year. But he's still with us.'

George pointed to the yellow and sky-blue ribbon on Marter's chest. 'I see, sir, that you served in the Crimea, which means you joined the regiment before Colonel Harris. How, then, did he manage to gain promotion before you?'

'Simple, Hart: money. Before seventy-one, when commissions were bought, money talked. A rich officer could bribe his less well-off seniors not to purchase a vacancy, so enabling him to do so. Of course it got expensive. But what did Harris care? Only that he kept rising in rank. And didn't he just? From cornet to colonel in ten years. I, on the other hand, with twenty-three years' service, am still only a captain. It's better now, with talent and length of service counting for something, but influence still matters. Harris is an ADC to Queen Victoria and has good connections at Court. He'll surely rise higher, despite his lack of active service. He is a dangerous man to cross.'

'I'll remember that, sir. Thank you.'

'Don't mention it,' said Marter, rising to shake George's hand. 'Just keep out of his way and you'll do fine.'

George woke with a start. The first streaks of daylight were just visible through a gap in the window shutters. He glanced around the unfamiliar room, his eye taking in the washstand and basin, heavy wardrobe and easy chair. Not exactly the Ritz, he mused. But on his meagre army pay of £95 a year, 10 shillings a week for lodging was all he could afford. His landlady, Mrs Arkwright, seemed friendly enough, if a little gruff, and her boarding house was well placed, just three streets away from the cavalry barracks on Hulme Street.

He glanced at his fob-watch on the side table and saw to his horror the time: 5.15 a.m. Reveille had sounded fifteen minutes earlier; Stables began at 5.30, and it would not do to be late. Not with a commanding officer like Harris. He dressed and shaved as quickly as he could, buckled on his sword and took the stairs two at a time. In the hall stood the formidable bulk of Mrs Arkwright, barring his way to the door. 'Will you be wanting tea, Mr Hart?'

'Not today, thank you. I'm in a fearful hurry,' said George, as he edged past his landlady, one hand on his sword pommel, the other holding his helmet.

'I've just made a pot.'

'No time!'

George pounded down the street, his boots echoing on the cobbles, and was still a couple of hundred yards shy of the entrance to the barracks as the clock struck the half-hour. He shot past the startled sentry on the gate and, breathing hard, entered the troop stable-block, where he was met by Marter and his troop sergeant, a solid fellow with a fine pair of ginger whiskers.

'You're cutting it a bit fine on your first day!' admonished Marter.

'I know, sir. I'm sorry. It won't happen again.'

'It had better not. This is Sergeant Tomkinson, by the way. He'll show you the ropes.'

For the next hour or so, George and Tomkinson toured the stable-block, talking to the troopers as they groomed their horses. With Stables almost over, he looked in on his own mount, Emperor, a sturdy sixteen-hand Irish hunter in the care of his orderly, Trooper Murphy. He had been introduced to Murphy the night before, and took to him immediately. A dark, wiry man from County Carlow, to the south of Dublin, Murphy had been raised on a smallholding and knew more about horses than people. George was no slouch on a horse, having ridden since the age of three, but caring for them was a different matter. And in Murphy he had found just the man.

George opened the door to the stall and found Murphy hard at work with a body brush. 'How's he today?' he asked, nodding towards the chestnut gelding eating hay.

The horse responded first to the familiar voice, raising its head and snorting. 'Just fine, sir,' added Murphy. 'If a little skittish. 'Spect he needs some exercise.'

'Well, it won't be long now.'

As if on cue, a bugle signalled the end of Stables. 'Time for breakfast, sir,' said Murphy. 'Riding Drill's at seven forty-five. See you then.'

Marter and a handful of officers were already seated at the long mahogany table, tucking into assorted dishes, when George entered the officers' mess. 'Gentlemen,' said Marter, 'meet our latest recruit, Cornet George Hart.'

George smiled. A couple of officers nodded in response. No one spoke. Unconcerned, George served himself scrambled eggs and devilled kidneys from the sideboard, and sat down next to Marter.

'Not there,' said Harris, who had just entered the room with Adjutant Bell, a thin, weasel-faced officer. 'Subalterns sit at the bottom of the table. We adhere strictly to rank in the King's Dragoon Guards.'

'My apologies, sir,' said a chastened George. 'I didn't know.'

'Well, the sooner you learn our ways, the better,' replied Harris, taking his own seat at the head of the table.

George reddened. With no one to talk to, he ate in silence. Even at the more populous end of the table, conversation was kept to a minimum. Once Harris had taken his leave, however, the atmosphere relaxed and Marter turned to George. 'Don't mind the colonel, Hart. He's a terror for precedence and abhors banter during breakfast. Now, I don't think you've met our second-in-command, Major Wingfield.'

Marter was gesturing towards a tall, slightly balding officer near the head of the table.

'Pleased to meet you, Major,' said George.

'You too, Hart,' said Wingfield. 'Welcome to the KDG. I hope you don't regret your choice.'

'Thank you, Major. I'm delighted to be here. But I didn't get to choose a regiment. I was simply informed by the Horse Guards that I had been accepted by the KDG and told when to report!'

'Is that so? No matter, you're here now.'

'Gentlemen!' interrupted Harris's voice from the doorway. 'If it isn't too much trouble, Riding Drill begins in five minutes. I don't need to remind you that the inspector-general of Cavalry will be attending our field day on Thursday, and I would not like him to find fault with *any* aspect of the regiment.'

An hour in and George was beginning to enjoy Riding Drill. The eight troops of the regiment – 320 sabres in all – had already completed a number of complicated manoeuvres without a hitch. They had moved from a closed column of troops, four riders abreast, to the looser open column, and from open column to line. George knew from Sandhurst that a cavalry regiment would always arrive on the battlefield in column formation, either closed or open, depending on the terrain, and then attack in a single line, two ranks deep, with the officers slightly to the fore and the bugler signalling the change in pace from walk to trot, gallop and finally charge. As the KDG swept across the field that morning, hooves drumming and swords pointing the way, it had seemed to an excited George that nothing could stand in the way of that wall of horseflesh. But with no opposition it was hard to tell.

Once the charge had been accomplished to Harris's satisfaction, the regiment reverted back to an open column of troops, one behind the other. Harris was scrutinizing each troop as it rode past, and when E Troop came level, he barked, 'Hart! Carry your sword, sir. Can't you carry your sword properly?'

George quickly checked the position of his sword. As per regulation, it was in his right hand at 'the slope', pointing upwards and leaning against his right shoulder, while his left hand controlled Emperor's reins. He was mystified by the criticism, and chose to ignore it; but as soon as Riding Drill was over, he rode up to Harris and asked him what he had done wrong. 'Your sword hand was too low. Make sure it doesn't happen again.'

'That, sir, was the position I was taught at Sandhurst.'

'Well, you're not at Sandhurst now. You're in the King's Dragoon Guards, and we do things properly here. You may look the part, Hart, with your easy smile and natty uniform. But you and I know what you really are, or rather what you're not. And that, sir, is a gentleman.'

George could feel the familiar red mist beginning to descend. The last time it had happened, at Sandhurst, he had knocked down a fellow cadet who had been taunting him. His intention now was just as violent. He nudged Emperor closer to Harris, but before he could strike, a hand grabbed his bridle and led him away. It was Marter's.

'Not a good idea,' said Marter, as they rode away. 'Unless, that is, you *want* to be cashiered.'

Harris watched them until they were out of sight. He then turned to Adjutant Bell and said, 'Did you see that? He was within an inch of attacking me! Damn Marter for interfering.'

For the next week or so George kept out of Harris's way. But the bad feeling between them was palpable and it came to a head during musketry practice at the Hilton Firing Range in the Peak District, sixteen miles due east of Manchester. Sergeant Tomkinson was in bed with influenza, and in his absence George had been put in charge of the troop's thirty newest recruits. His task, as relayed to him by Adjutant Bell the previous evening, was to work the men until they were capable of firing four aimed rounds a minute, which meant hitting a target known as a butt, twelve inches in diameter, at a range of 200 yards. The time allotted for this training was just three hours, because at noon Colonel Harris would arrive for a demonstration by a random soldier of his choice. And failure, Bell stressed, was not an option. Soldiers from the King's Dragoon Guards had won the last three annual inter-cavalry shooting competitions. The reputation of the regiment was at stake.

Given that the basic proficiency level for all cavalrymen was to achieve a rate of fire of seven aimed rounds a minute, the task did not appear to George to be that onerous. Moreover the weather conditions at the picturesque range – a lush meadow surrounded by craggy peaks – were perfect: light cloud, no wind and good visibility. On the other hand, George had little experience of the carbine his men would use, and they had even less. To compensate, he had spent the previous evening mugging up on the weapon's characteristics.

'Now, pay attention, men,' said George, as he held up the short-barrelled weapon for all to see. 'This is the Martini-Henry carbine. It has the same falling-breech mechanism as the infantry's rifle, but with a shorter barrel so that it can be stowed in the leather bucket attached to your saddles. It fires a heavy .45-calibre hardened lead bullet with a muzzle velocity of 1,350 feet per second. That's enough firepower to stop an elephant or tear the limb off a man. It's sighted up to 1,000 yards and extremely accurate at half that range. You're only required to hit targets at 200 yards. How hard can that be?'

George looked along the line of recruits facing him in their scarlet stable jackets with blue facings. They were mostly in their teens with the fresh-faced, ruddy look of the rural poor. One or two stood out on account of their height, but the majority seemed below the cavalry minimum of 5' 5", a good half a foot shorter than George himself. He scanned their faces, waiting for a response; nothing, beyond the odd inane grin and sideways glance.

'Very wise,' said George at last. 'Truth is, the Martini-Henry's a fine weapon in experienced hands; but for novices it takes some getting used to, particularly its recoil, as you're about to discover. And it's not without its defects: it has a tendency to jam, either because sand and dust gets into the breech mechanism or because prolonged firing melts the thin brass of its empty cartridges, making them difficult to extract; also the rifling in the barrel has a tendency to foul, producing a kick even more vicious than usual. The trick is to keep it clean at all times and you won't have any problems.'

George handed the carbine to Trooper Murphy, who was standing at ease alongside him. 'Murphy will show you how it's done. The more observant of you will have noticed that he's wearing on his lower sleeve the crossed rifles of a marksman. That means he's capable of hitting ten bull's-eyes out of ten at 400 yards. Your task is much easier. The only difficulty is that you've got to repeat the feat four times in a minute. All right, Murphy, the loading procedure first.'

Murphy stepped forward a pace, the carbine cradled across his body. 'You load like this,' he said, pulling down the lever behind the trigger guard with his right hand. This dropped the breechblock, so enabling Murphy to insert a cartridge, which he extracted from a pouch on his belt. He then closed the breech by raising the lever to its original position. 'It's now ready to fire.'

'Thank you,' said George, before turning back to the men. 'And don't forget: there's no safety; as soon as you close the breech, the gun is cocked. So mind where you point it. Carry on, Murphy.'

His orderly turned back towards the targets in the distance, knelt down on one knee and fired off three rounds in the space of twenty seconds. Each shot made a surprisingly loud boom, jerking the barrel of the rifle and shrouding the muzzle for a second or two in thick white smoke. The air was heavy with the acrid smell of gunpowder. A runner reported back two bulls and an inner ring.

'So you see,' said a grinning George to the recruits, 'even a marksman has his off days. And you'll have noticed that, while it's easier to shoot straight on a still day, you have to wait longer between each shot for the smoke to disperse. On a windy day it's blown away almost immediately. And that's just the effect of one soldier firing. Imagine the smoke that's generated by a troop firing volleys. But we'll come to that. For now just concentrate on loading, aiming and firing independently.'

And they did – for two whole hours, at the end of which time the recruits were a sorry-looking bunch, their ears ringing, their shoulders sore and their faces grimed with soot. About a third of the group had reached the necessary level of competence and was told to fall out.

'The rest of you,' George told them, 'are going to have to do better. You're either hitting the target but are taking far too long to load and aim or you're firing too soon and missing. We need to split the difference.'

George looked at his pocket-watch. It was five past eleven and Harris was due at noon. Nowhere near enough time, but they had to try. 'You've got just under an hour. Get on with it.'

As the firing resumed, George walked slowly along the line, ready to offer advice where needed. He stopped behind one recruit, a freckled-faced redhead of medium build, and watched him loosing off one wild shot after another. 'What's your name, Trooper?'

'Penhaligon, sir.'

'And where're you from?'

'Near Redruth in Cornwall, sir.'

'Well, you're the first Cornishman I've met with a tendency to rush. Take your time. When you've got the target lined up, take a deep breath and hold it. Then gently squeeze the trigger.'

The trooper did as he was bidden. Crack, sounded the next shot, followed by an imperceptible shudder of the straw target.

'High on the right, if I'm not mistaken. Try again.'

Penhaligon reloaded and took even more time. This time the bullet struck the outer ring.

'Well done,' said George, patting him on the shoulder. 'You see the reward for a bit of patience? Keep at it.'

George continued his pacing, encouraging the good shots and correcting the bad. With the time almost up, he asked Murphy how the men were doing. 'Pretty well, sir,' came the reply. 'Most can manage four in a minute. Fingers crossed the colonel doesn't choose one of the others.'

'Luck be damned. Let's reduce the odds by putting the poor shots at either end of the line. Colonel Harris is bound to choose one of the men in the centre: it's human nature.'

'Good thinking, sir. I'll do just that.'

The sound of hoof beats announced the arrival of Harris, Major Wingfield and Adjutant Bell. Harris dismounted and, with the others in his wake, strode up to George. 'Good morning, Hart. I trust your men are up to scratch.'

'They're almost there, sir.'

'Almost there, nothing. If they can't manage five hits in a minute after a morning's instruction, they're not fit to serve in the KDG.'

'Excuse me, sir,' said George, frowning. 'Did you say five strikes? The adjutant assured me that your requirement, at this early stage of the recruits' training, was only four aimed shots a minute.'

'Four? Nonsense. Even a child could manage four. No, I certainly said five.'

'That's as may be, sir. But the adjutant must have misheard you because he definitely said four to me.'

Harris snorted and turned to Bell. 'Did you say four or five to Cornet Hart?'

'I most assuredly said five, sir.'

'There you are, Hart. We both said five, so five it is. Carry on with the demonstration.'

'Sir, I must protest. Adjutant Bell's memory is faulty. If he *had* said five to me, I would not have spent the morning trying to achieve a lesser rate of fire.'

Harris looked angry now. 'Are you calling the adjutant a liar?'

'No. But he is mistaken.'

'On the contrary, Hart, it is you who are mistaken. Now carry on.'

George looked at Wingfield, imploring him to intervene, but the second-in-command had no wish to face Harris's ire and he averted his gaze. George was on his own. 'Yes, sir,' he said after a pause. 'Would you care to select a soldier?'

'That one will do,' said Harris, pointing towards Trooper Penhaligon, who was standing among the average-to-good shots between the centre and the end of the line. Like the rest of the recruits, he was doing his best not to attract attention; his freckles must have singled him out. George breathed a sigh of relief: his ruse had worked. Penhaligon was not the best shot, but he was far from the worst, and had improved out of sight thanks to George's instruction.

'All right, Penhaligon,' said George. 'Five hits in a minute, if you please.'

Penhaligon looked puzzled. 'Did you say five hits, sir?'

'I did.'

'Very well, sir. I'll do my best.' Penhaligon settled into the prone firing position, legs spread behind him, the barrel of his carbine supported by the palm of his left hand. In easy reach of his right hand he placed a pile of cartridges. George crouched down beside him and whispered, 'Do your best, Penhaligon. And remember to take your time. Better to have four hits than five misses.'

Penhaligon nodded.

'When you're quite ready,' said Harris. 'Adjutant Bell will time you.'

Bell stepped forward, fob-watch in hand. 'Trooper, you have one minute, starting from . . . now!'

Penhaligon pulled the lever to open the breech and reached for the first cartridge, but he was too hasty and fumbled it before grabbing another and stuffing it into the breech. When he tried to raise the lever, it refused to go. The bullet was not sitting squarely in the breech, and he wasted precious seconds realigning it. By now he had lost all composure and his hurried shot was high and wide.

'Don't worry,' encouraged George. 'Plenty of time.'

Penhaligon reloaded, took careful aim and fired. A hit, followed by three more. As he reached for the sixth cartridge, Bell called time.

'A gallant effort,' said Harris to George, 'and a shame about that first shot. But there's no place in the KDG for substandard soldiers. All the other recruits are confined to barracks until they've attained the required musketry standard. The trooper who failed the test is discharged forthwith.'

'Discharged?' spluttered George, looking from Harris to the bewildered Penhaligon and back again. 'For missing a single shot in five? He reached the standard asked for by Adjutant Bell yesterday. If I'd been told to achieve five aimed shots in a minute, I'd have said it was impossible. These are raw recruits, for heaven's sake.'

'Nothing's impossible, Hart. Try to remember that. And if you persist in calling the adjutant a liar, I'll have no option but to put you under arrest, pending a court martial.'

'I never used the word liar, sir. I simply say the adjutant's memory is playing him false.' George turned towards the smirking Bell. 'Will you swear on your mother's life that you said five rather than four?'

Bell hesitated, prompting Harris to intervene. 'He will do no such thing. Your behaviour is insubordinate, Hart. Take your men back to barracks while I decide on your punishment.'

George was shaking with fury. He had been set up, he was sure of that. And the end result: his men had been unfairly punished and, worse, a promising young soldier had been turned out into the street. Harris, he realized, was capable of just about anything, and he would have to tread extremely carefully in future. He was about to salute and take his leave when he suddenly remembered one crucial detail. He had made a note of Bell's instructions in his pocket book.

'One moment, sir. Might it help to refresh the adjutant's memory if I showed him a written record of our conversation last night?'

'What are you talking about?' said Harris.

George took the pocket book from inside his tunic, opened it at the relevant page and showed it to Harris. It specifically referred to 'four aimed shots a minute' and was dated the previous day.

'Well, you must have misheard the adjutant,' said Harris, less sure of himself now, 'because I told him five aimed shots.'

'Sir, I made this note as soon as Bell left the room. I could not have confused "four" for "five".'

Harris turned to Bell. 'Can you explain this?'

43

'Sir . . . I . . . I'm certain I said five.'

George interjected. 'Sir, perhaps you're right and we should let a court martial decide. I'd be happy to produce the notebook as evidence.'

Harris considered the likely outcome of a trial, and decided not to risk it. 'No,' he said at last, through gritted teeth. 'That won't be necessary. Return to barracks, if you please. We'll discuss this later.'

'What about Penhaligon, sir? Is he still to be discharged?'

'No. He can remain with the regiment.'

'Thank you, sir,' said George, saluting before leading the recruits over to the picket line where they had tethered their horses.

Bell looked apologetic. 'I'm sorry, sir. How was I to know he'd make a record of our conversation?'

'He's a sharp one, all right, and is going to be a harder nut to crack than I'd imagined.'

'Sir, I know you're keen to see the back of Hart as soon as possible, but can I make a suggestion?'

'Please do.'

'Instead of tackling the problem head on, wouldn't it be better to take a leaf out of Sun Tzu's book and play on Hart's weaknesses?'

'Go on.'

'Well, according to a cousin of mine who was with him at Sandhurst, he has at least two . . .'

# 3

## Westbury Park, Gloucestershire, 23 January 1878

'Hart, how good of you to come!' said a smiling Sir Jocelyn Harris as he shook George's hand in the doorway of his huge Palladian mansion. Given the rancour of their first meeting nearly five months earlier, the last thing George had expected was an invitation to Harris's country seat. Yet their day-to-day relationship had improved dramatically since the confrontation at the firing range, with Harris complimenting him on his steady progress at drill, and George had decided it would be churlish not to accept the proffered olive branch. So here he was, shaking Harris's hand and marvelling at the graceful proportions of the mansion's great hall, a welcoming fire burning in the grate to George's left.

'Delighted to be asked, sir,' said George. 'What a beautiful house you have.'

'Isn't it?' replied Harris, turning and beckoning to a waiting footman. 'Andrews will show you to your room. We're meeting for drinks in the drawing room at seven. See you then.'

George followed Andrews up one side of the sweeping double staircase to a charming set of rooms: a bedroom complete with four-poster bed, a bathroom and even a dressing room, and all with magnificent views of parkland studded with oaks. As Andrews was leaving, George asked him if he knew the identity of the other houseguests.

'I know that Lord and Lady Fitzmaurice are expected,' said Andrews. 'Also Captain Bell, Colonel Alexander of the Seventeenth Lancers and a young lady called Mrs Bradbury. She's in the suite next to yours.'

As George lay in a bath so hot it reddened his skin, he tried to remember where he had heard the name Mrs Bradbury. Then it came to him. She was the beautiful young widow who had only been married six months when her Old Harrovian husband, a captain in the Royal Artillery, was killed in battle during General Wolseley's victorious war against the Ashanti of the Gold Coast in '74. It had been the talk of the school. It was a bit odd, he thought, for a widow to be staying with a man like Harris, a committed bachelor with a reputation as a ladies' man. Then again, with a rake like the Prince of Wales setting the social agenda, what could you expect?

He entered the bedroom, with only a towel wrapped round his waist, to find a young chambermaid unpacking his clothes. She did not notice George at first, giving him a chance to admire a curvaceous figure that not even her drab black uniform and white apron could disguise.

'What's your name?' asked George, as he reached for his Paisley pattern dressing gown.

The girl jumped at the sound of his voice and turned. She was extremely handsome, with green eyes and alabaster skin, her lovely oval face framed by a few wisps of curly chestnut hair that had escaped from her white cap.

'Begging your pardon, sir,' she said, bobbing. 'My name's Lucy Hawkins.'

'Pleased to meet you, Lucy Hawkins. Where are you from?'

'Devon, sir.'

'And your family? What do they do?'

'My father's a farrier and my mother's in service, as are my two sisters.'

George nodded, desperately trying to think of a way to keep the conversation going, and prevent this vision of loveliness from leaving. 'How old are you?' he said at last.

'Eighteen, sir.'

'Same age as me. Oh, and don't call me sir. My name's George, George Hart.'

'I know, sir. We're given a list of all the guests' names.'

'Of course you are. Tell me, Lucy, do you enjoy working for Colonel Harris?'

The girl raised her eyebrows. 'That's an odd question. Why do you ask?'

'Oh, no reason in particular. It's just that most of the officers serving under the colonel, myself included, find him a little temperamental.'

'Cornet Hart, I appreciate your condescension, but I really don't think it's my place to discuss my employer with a man I've never met, even one as affable as you.'

George chuckled. The girl obviously had beauty, spirit *and* vocabulary, a dangerous combination. 'Thank you for the compliment, and please accept my apologies. Of course you mustn't indulge in tittle-tattle about your master. Whatever next? But I think I can surmise, even from your guarded response, that the colonel has his moments.'

'You can surmise what you like,' said Lucy, as she hung George's smoking jacket in the wardrobe. 'I prefer to hold my tongue.'

'Clever girl. You'll go far,' said George, laughing. 'Don't bother with the rest,' he said, gesturing towards his clothes. 'But if I need you later, will you be available?'

'I'm on duty all night, sir. Just ring the bell by the bed.'

'I'll do that. Thank you.'

George had never been shy around women. He knew they found him attractive, and some of the young ladies he had met while at Sandhurst had all but thrown themselves at him. And yet his only two sexual partners to date had been a kitchen girl at Harrow and a Haymarket prostitute. He often asked himself why. And the best answer he could give was that he feared awkward questions about his background; the sort of questions that lower-class girls like Lucy were unlikely to ask. He was intrigued by Mrs Bradbury, though, and looked forward to meeting her. It promised to be quite an evening.

With seven fast approaching, he dressed hurriedly in black evening dress and white bow tie, and made it to the drawing room before the clock struck the quarter-hour. It was a high-ceilinged, beautifully proportioned room with heavy silk drapes covering three picture windows that overlooked the front and side of the house. The furniture was Louis XVI, as was the large crystal chandelier that dominated the centre of the room.

'Ah, Hart,' said Harris, catching sight of George, 'come and meet the other guests.'

They were grouped in a small knot around the large Adam fireplace, some on sofas, others standing. Harris himself was leaning against the mantelpiece, a glass of champagne in his hand. Addressing the group, he said, 'I would like to present Cornet George Hart, the newest member of my officers' mess.'

Harris then introduced George to each guest in turn. 'Of course you know Bell,' he said of the penultimate guest. 'And, last but not least, Mrs Bradbury.' A pretty blonde gazed up from the sofa, her eyebrows rising ever so slightly. She was wearing a low-cut dinner dress of pale blue satin that matched her eyes, offset by a train of ruby velvet. Her hair she wore up in a chignon, with the odd ringlet falling to the nape of her neck. 'It's a pleasure to meet you, Cornet Hart,' she said, extending a shapely hand in George's direction.

'The pleasure,' said George, admiring her upturned nose, 'is all mine.'

At dinner George was seated next to Mrs Bradbury on one side and Lady Fitzmaurice, a portly matron, on the other. He talked to her ladyship for the first course, and then turned and monopolized Mrs Bradbury. Her name, he discovered, was Sarah. She came from a respectable northeast farming family and had married at the age of seventeen in 1873, which meant she was only four years George's senior. Her late husband had not been wealthy, and after his death she had found work as a governess for Lady Charlton's children, at whose house she had met Colonel Harris. The colonel had been 'very kind', she told George, who thought it best not to enquire further. But one thing was obvious: she could not have afforded her dress on a governess's salary.

After the ladies had retired, port and cigars were brought out and the conversation eventually turned to cards. 'Fancy a game of baccarat later, gentlemen?' asked Harris.

'Don't mind if I do,' said Lord Fitzmaurice, a large florid-faced man. Colonel Alexander and Captain Bell also assented.

'What about you, Hart?' asked Harris, a smile on his lips.

'I can't say I've ever played baccarat, sir. We preferred chemin de fer at Sandhurst.'

'There's very little difference. You're still aiming for a points total of nine, preferably in two cards, but in baccarat the banker deals three hands rather than two. Other than that the rules are virtually the same. Interested?'

George hesitated. 'The thing is, I lost rather a lot of money gambling . . .'

'If you're worried, we'll keep the stakes low,' Harris said. 'How about a maximum bet of a guinea?'

'All right by me,' said Lord Fitzmaurice.

They both looked at George. He was desperate to say yes, not least because he loved gambling, and did not want Harris to think him priggish, not now they were getting on so well. Yet since the bombshell about his father and the stopping of his allowance, he could not afford to risk even a few pounds. Then again, what if he won? The money would certainly come in handy. He was in a dilemma. 'Perhaps I could watch the first few hands, and maybe join in later?' he said without conviction.

'Look, Hart,' said an exasperated Harris, 'if money's a bit tight, I'm happy to lend you some.'

'I appreciate the offer, sir, but I'd prefer not to get into debt.'

'Suit yourself. Well, gentlemen, I think we've kept the ladies waiting long enough. Shall we?'

George cut a tormented figure as he followed his host to the drawing room. He knew his refusal to play had disappointed Harris, and he feared the consequences; but he also knew that gambling was a pleasure he no longer had the means to indulge.

'You look pensive,' said Mrs Bradbury, as he approached the fireplace. 'Penny for your thoughts?'

'The colonel's suggested a game of baccarat. Most times I'd jump at the chance, but I thought it best to decline.'

'Why?'

George sat down next to her. 'Let's just say,' he said with a smile, 'I haven't always enjoyed the greatest fortune at cards.'

'So you've lost money. Everyone does. The good news is your luck's about to change.'

'Really,' said George. 'How can you be certain?'

'Because *I* always win at cards, and I'll be your lucky charm.'

'I'd love to take up your offer, but I have to confess I'm a little out of pocket this month.'

'It happens to us all! Tell you what,' said Mrs Bradbury, grinning. 'I'll bankroll your first ten pounds' worth of losses. I can't say fairer than that.'

'I can't let you do that.'

'You can and you will,' she said, grasping George's hands in hers. 'Sir Jocelyn won't let ladies play on their own, so you're my only hope.'

George looked up into the roundest, brightest pair of

blue eyes he had seen. They seemed to be imploring him to say yes. The effect of that look, allied to Mrs Bradbury's subtle perfume and sensual touch, was utterly bewitching. All thought of placating his mother vanished from his head. How could he say no? 'You've found yourself a partner.'

She had been as good as her word, thought George, as yet another hand went his way. He glanced down at his growing pile of chips and estimated his winnings at around £30. And they had only been playing for an hour. If he kept this up, he would be able to move into more salubrious lodgings *and* have a few pounds to spare for his mother. 'I told you so,' said a happy Mrs Bradbury, seated on a chair behind his left shoulder.

He smiled back, and wondered for the umpteenth time that evening who he found more appealing, Mrs Bradbury or Lucy. The widow was clearly the more experienced and sophisticated of the two, but Lucy had all the allure and innocence of bright-eyed youth. It was a close call.

'Sorry to interrupt your pleasant musings, Hart,' said Harris, tight-lipped. 'Are you placing a bet on the next hand?'

'Of course. How much is the bank's stake?'

'Ten shillings, as before.'

'Well, I'll match it.'

'Banco, eh?' said Captain Bell on George's left. 'Probably best to make hay . . .'

'What do you mean by that?' said George, turning.

'Only that you've had a good run. It never lasts.'

'We'll see.'

Harris, the banker, dealt three closed hands of two cards each: one to the players on his left, George and Bell; one to the players on his right, Fitzmaurice and Alexander, and one to himself. George looked at his cards: a four and a king. With picture cards scoring zero, his total was four. He needed a five to give him the strongest hand, and only a six to a nine would weaken his hand. The odds were with him, but just to be sure he conferred with Mrs Bradbury, who advised taking another card. '*Carte*,' he said to Harris.

It was a four, giving him a total of eight. He turned to Mrs Bradbury and winked.

Fitzmaurice had a total of five and decided to take another card. It was a nine. 'Damn,' he said, realizing his new score of fourteen was rounded down to four.

That just left Harris, who turned over an ace and a five. Should he take another? he asked himself. Why not? He revealed another ace. 'Six,' he declared.

'Too good for me,' said Fitzmaurice, throwing in his cards.

'But not for me,' crowed George, showing his cards.

Harris shook his head and handed over two crowns.

And so it continued, with George winning at least two hands out of every three. The only sour note was when Harris queried the size of one of George's losing bets. 'I thought your stake was ten shillings?' said Harris.

'No, a crown, as you can see.'

'I could've sworn it was more. Must have been mistaken.'

A few hands later, after yet another win for George, Harris again questioned the amount he had bet. 'Surely it was half a crown?'

'You can see that it's a crown,' said George, his brow furrowing.

'It's a crown *now*.'

'What are you trying to say?'

'Nothing. Forget it.'

George put Harris's odd behaviour down to sour grapes and the fact that they'd all consumed a fair amount of champagne, wine, port and brandy during the course of the evening. He had, in any case, other matters on his mind. 'Gentlemen,' he said, as the clock struck two, 'I hope you will excuse me. It's been a long night and I think it's time to turn in.'

'What?' said Harris. 'And deprive me of a chance to recoup some of the bank's losses?'

'I'm afraid so, sir, though I'll gladly put my winnings on the line tomorrow night.' In truth George knew that his luck was bound to change, and he had no intention of risking his windfall. He needed the extra money badly, but that was hardly something he could admit to Harris.

'Hmm, well, if you must go,' came the grudging response.

George rose unsteadily to his feet, kissed Mrs Bradbury's hand and held her gaze a fraction longer than necessary. He was desperately hoping she would take the hint and follow him up. But she was too cool to give anything away, so he bade the others goodnight and climbed the stairs to his bedroom. He undressed, poured a last glass of whisky from the decanter on the side table and got into bed.

\* \* \*

As he lay there, flushed with alcohol and success, he did not feel like sleeping. He was suddenly anxious for female company, and found himself thinking of both the alluring, but very different, young women he had met that day. Were they thinking of him? Should he call for Lucy, who as a servant was bound to come, or wait to see if Mrs Bradbury paid him a visit? After a while, though, the alcohol got the better of him and he fell asleep undecided – or at least thought he had.

A soft click woke him. He could hear the door closing and the swish of skirts as a shadowy figure approached the bed. 'Who's there?' he whispered.

An index finger pressed against his lips. 'Who do you think, silly?'

The clipped tones were those of a lady, and that could only mean Mrs Bradbury. George could hear her undressing, then felt the soft warmth of a body climbing in beside him. 'Darling,' he murmured, 'I thought you'd never come.'

She answered with a greedy kiss. George pulled her close; her body felt muscular, yet velvety smooth. She moaned as he caressed her breasts. Fortified by drink and lust, and inexperienced as he was, George dispensed with the niceties and manoeuvred himself on top of her. Giggling at his eagerness, she guided him in with her hand. But the frantic nature of his lovemaking soon caused her to chide him. 'Slow down,' she whispered, 'you're like a bull at a gate.'

He did as he was told, but not for long. Soon she, too, had abandoned herself to the frenetic pace, and his only concern now was the steadily increasing volume of her cries and the rhythmic tapping of the four-poster against the wall. He deadened one sound with his hand, the other with a pillow, but the telltale creak of the bed was still audible. It was a relief in more ways than one when he could hold himself back no longer, his pleasure intensified by a sharp pain as she bit into his hand. 'Ouch!' he yelped, before falling away to his side of the bed, and, despite his best intentions, collapsing in an exhausted heap.

As he drifted off to sleep, he felt a hand stroking his face. A voice was murmuring, 'I'm sorry . . .' or so he thought, but he could not drag himself back to consciousness to find out what had necessitated an apology.

George woke alone with a splitting headache, a dry mouth and a dull pain in his right hand. On both sides of the heel of his palm was a neat imprint of teeth, the skin not broken but badly bruised. He remembered and laughed. With winnings of £63, topped by an accommodating bedfellow, it had been a good night. He hummed a ditty as he shaved, confident that the evening to come would bring more of the same.

The other guests, bar Mrs Bradbury, were already seated when he reached the breakfast room. Their response to his cheery good morning was a stony silence. 'Is something wrong?' asked George.

'I think you'd better ask Sir Jocelyn,' said Lord Fitzmaurice, trying to avoid eye contact. 'He's waiting for you in the library.'

George's heart was thumping as he approached the library. His lovemaking must have been overheard, he reasoned, but was that reason enough for such a frosty reception at breakfast? He suspected not, and opened the door with mounting apprehension. Harris was seated at a bureau, his back to the door. He turned and beckoned George over. 'Take a seat, Hart. You're going to need one. What I have to say is not pleasant, so I'll just get on with it. Two serious allegations have been made against you: first that you cheated at cards, and second that you entered Mrs Bradbury's room uninvited and tried to force yourself on her. What have you got to say for yourself?'

George stared open-mouthed. This cannot be happening, he told himself. 'I . . . I utterly refute both charges,' he said at last. 'Who made these claims?'

'The first charge is not in dispute. I myself thought you were altering your bets, increasing them when you won and reducing them when you lost, and mentioned it at the time, if you recall. After you departed for bed, I was confirmed in my suspicions by both Lord Fitzmaurice and Captain Bell. As for the second charge, that was of course made by Mrs Bradbury. Do you dare deny it?'

'Of course I deny it. I never went near Mrs Bradbury's room last night . . .' He was tempted to tell the truth; however ungentlemanly it might sound, it was better than being accused of attempted rape. But it quickly dawned on him that it was his word against Mrs Bradbury's. He decided not to elucidate, but said instead: 'As for cheating at cards, that's ridiculous. I announced my bet before each hand.'

'Yes, but what's to stop you altering it to suit the outcome of the hand? Bell claims he saw you doing it.'

'Well, he's a liar.'

'And he's prepared to sign a sworn statement to that effect, as is Lord Fitzmaurice. Mrs Bradbury has already done so.' Harris handed him a piece of paper with five lines of writing on it.

'But it's in your hand,' protested George.

'So it is, but dictated and signed by her. And you'll note that she mentions biting your hand as you tried to stifle her cries. I see you have just such a bite mark on your right hand.'

George read the note with mounting horror. Why, he asked himself, would she make such falsehoods? And then, creeping over him like damp fog came the horrible realization that he had been set up. By coming to his room and sleeping with him, Mrs Bradbury had made it impossible for him to deny he had assaulted her. It was clear to him now that all Harris's affability over the previous few months had been a sham to lull him into letting down his guard. And it had worked. He had allowed himself to be lured on to Harris's territory, among Harris's friends. And together they had trapped him.

'I know what you're up to,' said George with more equanimity than he felt. 'And you won't get away with it.'

'Let's cut to the chase, shall we, Hart?' said Harris, a glint of triumph in his eye. 'Three separate witnesses are prepared to swear they saw you cheating at cards. That crime alone brings with it the punishment of professional disgrace and social death. But not content with one enormity, you commit another by trying to force yourself upon a defenceless widow. She too will stand by her claim. The question now is what's to be done with you. My duty is to prevent the regiment from being dragged into this sordid affair, and to that end I'm prepared to offer you a deal. If you agree to resign your commission immediately, and of course return the money, we'll say no more about last night. I have spoken to the others and we're all in agreement.'

'And if I refuse?' said George.

'Then I'll have no option but to report your behaviour to both the Horse Guards and the local constabulary. Either way you'll lose your commission. But if you accept my offer, at least you'll retain your freedom *and* your honour, such as it is.'

George was shaking with fury. He was close to losing control, and knew it. 'You dare to talk of honour,' he said loudly. 'Nothing could be more dishonourable than the underhand way you've treated me. I was a fool to believe you could change. I suppose I wanted to. Only now you show your true colours. I will resign, because you and your creatures have left me no option. But don't for a minute think you've won. Some day, somehow, I will have my revenge.'

And with that he flung the money from his pocket and strode from the library.

Returning to his room to pack, he found Lucy making the bed. 'Good morning, sir,' she said with a broad smile.

'Is it?' replied George, his temper barely abated. 'I wouldn't know. And don't bother with that. I'm leaving as soon as I've packed.'

'I'll do that, sir,' she said, fetching his leather suitcase from the wardrobe. 'But why are you leaving? I thought you were staying until tomorrow.'

As George's anger gave way to shock he found himself telling the pretty maid what had happened.

'I was. But thanks to your employer and his lady friend Mrs Bradbury, I've been forced to resign from the regiment.'

Lucy looked shocked. 'Resign? Why?'

'Because he's a vindictive man who could not bear having an officer of dubious social standing like me foisted upon his regiment. Unfortunately he has his wish, thanks to a combination of my gullibility and his scheming.'

'I'm sorry, sir,' she said, pausing from her packing, 'but none of this makes any sense. Why would Sir Jocelyn invite you here if he didn't like you?'

'To set me up for a fall – and he seems to have succeeded.'

'And you say Mrs Bradbury was involved?'

'Yes.'

'How exactly?'

George blushed. 'I don't want to go into details, but she was certainly party to the scheme.'

'I'm shocked, I truly am. She seemed the perfect lady to me, but I won't deny Sir Jocelyn has a curious hold over her. She adores him and would do anything for him.'

George raised his eyebrows. 'Quite. But it's as well you know the real Sir Jocelyn. He's a dangerous man who will stop at nothing to get his own way.'

'I already know that,' said Lucy quietly. 'When you asked me about him yesterday, I didn't feel I knew you well enough to speak my mind. But the truth is, I'm afraid of him. He has often tried to kiss me – without succeeding. And each time I reject him he becomes angrier still, telling me I should be flattered by his attention. He swears he will have me sooner or later, which is why I'm so desperate to leave his service.'

'Then why don't you?'

'It's not as easy as that. Anyway, where would I go?'

'Does it matter? Surely anywhere would be better than here?'

Before Lucy could answer, the door was opened by Andrews, the butler. 'Sir,' he said, 'the carriage is ready to take you to the station.'

'Thank you. Take my suitcase. I'll be down presently.'

Once Andrews had left the room, George turned back to Lucy. 'I'm sorry. I have to go. I wish I could offer you a post myself, but without money or a career I'm in no position to do so. But I'll think of a way to get you out of here and will write in a day or two when my plans are a little clearer. Will you be all right until then?'

'Of course. Sir Jocelyn leaves me alone when Mrs Bradbury is in the house, and she's staying until next weekend.'

'Goodbye, then,' he said, pecking Lucy on the cheek.

She reddened and lowered her eyes. 'Goodbye.'

# 4

*South Wales, 24 January 1878*

George's instinct was to head straight for Dublin and tell his mother everything. But he knew how important she now regarded his military career to be, and how shocked she would be by the news, for financial reasons as much as anything, and so he chose to travel first to Brecon, where his best friend, Jake Morgan, was stationed with his new regiment, the 2nd Battalion of the 24th Foot.

At Sandhurst, George had ribbed Jake mercilessly for preferring the infantry – 'the footsloggers' – to the more mobile and glamorous cavalry, and had tried on a number of occasions to make him change his mind and join the KDG. Jake, however, had been adamant. His father had fought with the 24th Foot at Chillianwala in 1849, when the regiment had lost thirteen officers and more than half its strength in a matter of minutes, and he was determined to follow in his footsteps. Literally, thought George at the time, given that Jake was a poor rider and much happier on his own two feet than four hooves.

As his train chugged slowly towards Brecon through the rugged splendour of the Black Mountains, George's mind wandered back to their first meeting on the opening day of the new term at Sandhurst. Jake had been given punishment drill for taking issue with an instructor's mockery of his Welsh accent, and was doubling round the parade ground in full kit, a slight figure almost dwarfed by his pack. The sun was beating down remorselessly and after an hour the instructor took pity on him and said he could stop if he apologized. Jake refused and the ordeal continued until nightfall. When it was over, and George was helping this tough young Welshman to a cup of water, he asked him why he had been so obstinate. 'Because,' said Jake, coughing, 'if I hadn't made a stand now, the jokes would have continued.'

The words had struck a chord with George, and since that day the pair had been inseparable. They could hardly have been more different: George a tall, dark Irishman of unknown paternity and fresh-faced good looks; Jake an unassuming Welshman, the son of a wealthy colliery owner, small and lean, with red hair, freckles and a crooked smile. But opposites attract and the two had developed a bond of friendship that, they had promised each other, time and distance would never break. George had always trusted Jake's advice. Now he needed it more than ever.

The walk from the railway station to the new red-brick barracks on the outskirts of Brecon took George about ten minutes. At the guardhouse he asked to speak to Second Lieutenant Morgan and was told to wait. Within minutes the door opened and in walked Jake, looking extremely dapper in his new scarlet tunic with green facings, Sam Browne belt and blue cloth helmet.

'George!' he said, slightly taken aback that his friend was wearing mufti. 'To what do I owe this unexpected pleasure? Don't tell me your regiment has been ordered overseas and you've come to say goodbye?'

'No, nothing like that. Is there somewhere we can talk in private?'

'Of course. Let's go to the Red Lion across the street. I'm not on duty again until six.'

The pub was a gloomy affair, all sawdust and stale beer, with only a couple of working men propping up the bar. Jake bought two pints of cider and led George to a secluded table in the saloon.

'Your health,' said Jake, raising his glass and taking a large gulp. 'Just what I needed. Now are you going to tell me why you're here?'

'It's hard to know where to start. But the bombshell my mother dropped on my birthday is, I suppose, as good a place as any.'

'What bombshell?'

George told him everything: about his father and the deal his parents had done; the visit to the lawyer and the ridiculous terms of his father's bequest; and the series of run-ins with his commanding officer, Colonel Harris, culminating in the set-up at Westbury Park. When he had finished, Jake was speechless. He sat there open-mouthed, slowly shaking his head. At last he spoke. 'George, if I didn't know you better, I'd say you've been at the drink already. What an extraordinary tale. Poor you! As if finding out the truth about your father and his disgraceful machinations was not enough, you have your career ended by a man who sounds every bit as unpleasant. The question is, what can we do about it?'

'Not we, Jake – I. I won't have you jeopardizing your career for my sake. It's too late anyway.'

'It's never too late. Your father, whoever he is, clearly has influence at the Horse Guards. Why don't you appeal directly to the military secretary, or the commander-in-chief, even? You've been wronged, George, surely they'll see that?'

George put his hand on Jake's sleeve. 'I admire your spirit, but there's no way back for me now. Harris has witnesses who will testify to my cheating at cards, not to mention that vixen Mrs Bradbury, who claims I tried to dishonour her. It's my word against theirs. Who do you think a jury's going to believe: an eighteen-year-old officer or a "respectable" widow? In any case, I gave my word to Harris that, in return for his silence, I'd resign from the KDG. He's kept his side of the bargain; I've got to keep mine.'

'But you haven't done anything wrong!' said his friend, banging the table with his fist. 'It's madness to stay silent. That way Harris wins.'

'Either way Harris wins, because if I speak out, I'll face social ostracism and a probable term in prison. No, I have to face facts. My time in the army is over. But look on the bright side,' said George, smiling in a vain effort to lighten the mood. 'At least there's no longer the temptation for me to put my life on the line to win my father's bequest.'

Jake sighed. 'Those sort of sums are not to be sniffed at. I know winning a VC by the age of twenty-eight is not going to be easy, but nor is it impossible. And bear in mind that you don't have to be an officer in a British regiment to win a VC; just under British command. We've recently been warned for service in South Africa against the Kaffir tribes of the Cape frontier. If you go out under your own steam, you might be able to join one of the irregular units already in action. Probably not as an officer, but at least you'd be back in the military. You're a born soldier, George, and don't let anyone tell you different.'

'And you're a good friend. But I've had my fill of the army and officers like Harris and Bell. I've a mind to try something different, and now that you mention it, South Africa might just be the place. Didn't they find diamonds in the Cape a few years ago?'

'Yes, along the Orange and Vaal rivers, if memory serves. But they've made more discoveries since, particularly at Kimberley, where the diggings are dry and the diamonds the size of gulls' eggs. It's said you can go from pauper to prince with one find. If you're lucky, that is. Most aren't.'

'You're such an old pessimist, Jake. It sounds just the ticket. What have I got to lose?'

'I suppose you're right. And if it doesn't work out, which it won't, you can always join up. But don't wait too long or the war will be over and the opportunity gone.'

'There'll never be a shortage of wars to fight, Jake, of that we can be certain. The main thing is we're agreed on my course of action: to take the next ship to South Africa.'

'Aren't you forgetting one thing?' said Jake, draining his glass.

'Am I? What?'

'Your mother.'

'Ah, yes. My mother. She won't be happy, of course. But then she's partly responsible for getting me into this mess in the first place.'

'How so?'

'By her poor choice of men, for one.'

'That's hardly fair, George.'

'I know, please ignore my remarks. I'm just upset. I don't really blame her; how could she know how things would turn out? The real culprit is Harris. But for him I'd be enjoying my time in the army. He has a lot to answer for, and mark my words, one day he will.'

'I don't doubt it, George. And if I can help in any way, I will. Do you need money?'

'Yes, I'm afraid so.' George didn't see any point in beating about the bush with his wealthy friend. He knew that Jake trusted George to stand by him if their positions were reversed.

'How much?'

'Two hundred should do it.'

Jake sucked in air. 'Crikey, that much? I don't have that in cash. I'll have to wire it to your bank in Dublin.'

'Thank you. You'll get it back. Every penny. Oh, and there's one more favour I have to ask of you.'

'Ask away.'

'Would your father consider employing an acquaintance of mine? At present she's a chambermaid at Westbury Park, Harris's seat, but has good reason to seek another position.'

'A maid? An acquaintance of yours? Is there something you're not telling me, George?' queried Jake, one eyebrow raised.

'It's nothing like that,' said George, affronted. 'Though I won't deny she's a highly attractive girl, which is part of the problem. Harris has taken a liking to her and won't be denied.'

'I understand,' said Jake, tapping the side of his nose. 'I'll have a word with Father and see what I can do.'

George shook his hand. 'You're a good friend.'

'I know.'

## Dublin, 27 January 1878

Three days later George found himself in a hansom cab in the familiar surroundings of Dublin's Sackville Street. As the driver whipped up, coaxing a little more speed from his tired-looking nag, George knew that time was running out. His mother's house in Connaught Square was just round the corner.

He was let into the house by Manners. 'Good morning, *Mr* Hart,' said the old butler pointedly. 'Your mother is in the sitting room. Shall I let her know you've arrived?'

'That won't be necessary, Manners. I'll go straight up.'

He took the stairs two at a time, but halted at the door to the sitting room, his hand hovering above the door-knob. Taking a deep breath, he entered to discover his mother reading quietly on the sofa. 'Hello, Mother,' he said with a frown.

'Georgie darling!' she cried, putting down her book. 'You didn't tell me you were coming, and you're not in uniform. Is something the matter?'

As she rose to embrace him, her shiny hair loose about her shoulders, George's heart sank. He had been dreading this meeting since leaving Harris's house, and every minute of the long train and boat journey to Dublin had been spent wracking his brains over how best to break the news.

They sat down on the sofa, his mother taking his hand. 'Georgie, please tell me what's wrong.'

After a pause, George said, 'I don't know how best to say this so I'm just going to say it. I've resigned my commission.'

Emma's mouth gaped. 'You've done what?'

'I've left the army.'

'Why? I know you're upset about your father and his clumsy attempt to bribe you, but you would have achieved great things as a soldier without his help. You finished top of your class at Sandhurst, for heaven's sake. I imagined a brilliant military career for you. Why would you throw it all away?'

George loosened his mother's grip, rose and walked towards the nearest window. He could see a wet nurse pushing her charge along the gravel path of the square's well-kept garden, mostly given over to lawn and shrubs. As a child he had spent many a hot summer's day in that garden. He turned to face his mother. 'I was going to lie and tell you the army was no longer for me. But I know there's no point. I never could lie to you.'

Instead he told the whole truth of his ill-starred association with Sir Jocelyn Harris, from their early clashes in the regiment to the denouement at Westbury Park. 'So you see, Mother,' he concluded, 'I was partly responsible for my own downfall.'

Emma stayed silent for some time, her eyes fixed on her son. At last she spoke. 'You were foolish to gamble, but you don't deserve to lose your career, your only means of earning a living, as a consequence. I'll write to your father.'

'What good will that do? I've discussed this with Jake and we both agree that Harris has me over a barrel. If I complain, he'll use the witnesses against me. No, my only course of action is to make a fresh start.'

'With what exactly? You have neither a salary nor an allowance.'

'Jake has agreed to lend me two hundred pounds.'

'That's very generous of him. But what do you propose to do with this money?'

'Travel to South Africa and try my luck in the diamond mines at Kimberley. People are making fortunes overnight. Why not me?'

'Have you lost your reason? You know nothing about South Africa and even less about mining diamonds!'

'That, Mother, is where you're wrong. Since discussing the matter with Jake, I've been reading up on the subject. It's really quite straightforward. You turn up at Kimberley, stake your claim, buy the necessary equipment and get on with it.'

'As easy as that?'

'Yes. There's no guarantee you'll strike it rich, of course. Prices are high and most prospectors run out of money before they find a diamond worth selling. But don't you see, Mother? If you aren't in the race you can't win the prize. And as things stand I have nothing to lose.'

'Apart from Jake's money.'

'Apart from that. Please try to understand that I'm doing this as much for your benefit as I am for my own. I know you'll lose this house if I don't make some money soon, and I don't want that to happen.'

'And I don't want you to leave on a fool's errand because of me.'

'It's not a fool's errand,' said George irritably, 'and I'm not going *because* of you. But I do want to help you out and South Africa might afford me the opportunity.'

His mother stood and began to pace the room. She stopped by the fireplace, turned and said, 'So your mind's made up? You're going to South Africa, come what may?'

George nodded.

'Well, there's something you need to know before you go. It may alter your plans.'

'Go on.'

'You have family in Natal.'

'*Family?*' said George, a baffled look on his face. 'What family?'

His mother bit her lip, as if loath to continue. After a lengthy pause, she said quietly, 'You have an uncle, my half-brother, Patrick. He lives on a farm near Pietermaritzburg that was left to both of us by my father. Half of it is rightfully yours.'

George stared wide-eyed. 'An uncle and a farm! You can't be serious? Why didn't you mention this before?'

'Because I haven't heard from Patrick in years. But if you're going to South Africa you can look him up. It's got to be a better bet than prospecting for diamonds.'

George stood there, shaking his head. 'You never cease to amaze me. Not content with one bombshell, you drop two. Are you sure there isn't anything else I should know?'

His mother looked rueful. 'As it happens there is, but please try to understand that I've kept all this quiet for your sake.'

'Kept what quiet?'

Again she hesitated, as if weighing up the damage her latest revelation would cause. George could see in her tortured expression the mental struggle she was going through.

'Kept what quiet, Mother?' he asked again.

Unable to keep it a secret any longer, she blurted out, 'That my mother, your grandmother, was the daughter of a Zulu chief.'

George looked stunned, his face a mask of disbelief. 'What are you talking about? You told me your mother was Maltese.'

'That's what your father wanted me to tell you. He didn't want you to grow up with the stigma of having African blood. I suppose he wanted to make it as easy as possible for people in the army to accept your Mediterranean looks. But you're not in the army now and it's as well you know the truth. You were bound to find out from your uncle, in any event.'

George slowly shook his head. 'I can't believe I'm hearing this. It's just too much to take in. Forgive me, I need some air.'

'Georgie, wait!' said his mother, plaintively.

He ignored her and left the house. For an hour he wandered the streets, trying to make sense of these latest revelations. Why didn't she tell me before? he asked himself, again and again. How could she bring me up as a Christian gentleman, educated at Harrow and Sandhurst, when in truth I'm nothing more than an illegitimate half-breed who's been abandoned by his father? What was she thinking of? And where does that leave me? Am I civilized or a savage? Desperate for answers, he returned to Connaught Square.

He found his mother where he had left her, tears streaking her face. For a long time he just stared in silent reproach. At last he spoke: 'I wish you'd told me all this before.'

'I was trying to protect you.'

'Well you failed. Look at me, brought up a gent, wearing the latest fashions.' He gestured towards his stylish double-breasted Cambridge coat and dark blue whipcord trousers. 'But it's all a sham. I've obviously got foreign blood and everyone knows it.'

His mother was angry now. 'So you have. But don't you dare feel sorry for yourself. Can you imagine how hard it was for me growing up in Dublin with brown skin and no mother? And yet I survived and made a living. So must you.'

'You think I don't know that? Why do you think I raised the subject of Africa in the first place?'

'I know. I'm sorry. But you must admit it's quite a coincidence you choosing to seek your fortune in the country of my birth.'

'I don't believe in coincidence,' said George, calmer now. 'It must be fate.'

'Possibly.'

'So tell me about your mother.'

'Her name was Ngqumbazi. She was the daughter of a Zulu chief called Xongo kaMuziwento. You have *heard* of the Zulus?'

'I think so. Wasn't King Shaka a Zulu?'

'He was.'

George remembered back to long, drowsy summer afternoons at Sandhurst, listening to the history lecturer drone on about the early nineteenth-century military genius who, in less than a decade, had revolutionized tribal warfare and transformed an insignificant Bantu tribe into the dominant power in southeast Africa. 'So where does your mother fit in?'

'I'm coming to that. As you probably know, Shaka was murdered in eighteen twenty-eight by his half-brother Dingane, who was toppled in turn by another brother, Mpande. My mother's family were followers of Mpande and were with him during his brief exile in Natal in eighteen thirty-nine. While there she met my father, who was stationed with his regiment in Durban. By the time Mpande returned to Zululand to defeat his brother Dingane, early the following year, Ngqumbazi was already pregnant with me. Her family would never have accepted her back with a half-white baby. So she stayed in Natal until I was born, handed me over to my father and then left. I never saw her again.'

'What about my uncle? Is he part Zulu too?'

'No. Patrick's the son of a Basuto servant girl who worked for us until my father returned to Ireland with his regiment in forty-six.'

'Taking you but leaving your brother?'

'Yes. I had no mother; he did. We left them on the farm.'

'Do you know what happened to *your* mother? Could she still be alive?'

'It's possible, though we heard nothing after she returned to Zululand. If she is still alive, she'd be in her sixties.'

'Well, if I do make it to Natal, I'll try and find out.'

'So you've decided to go to Natal rather than Kimberley?'

'To begin with, yes. I've a mind to meet this mystery uncle and claim my share of the inheritance. But if it doesn't work out I'll give the diamond mines a go.'

His mother stared at him for some time. At last, a tear in her eye, she said, 'Wait here. I've got something for you.'

She returned a few minutes later and gave George an oilskin packet tied with string. He opened it and discovered two items: a small gold signet ring and an ancient muzzle-loading five-shot revolver, the metal dulled and the wooden handle scarred. 'They were my father's.'

George tried the ring on the little finger of his right hand; it fitted perfectly.

'That was given to him by his father,' Emma added. 'The gun saved his life in the Crimea. I hope it does the same for you. Africa's a dangerous country.'

'Thank you, Mother,' said George, turning the pistol over in his hands. 'I'll keep them with me always.'

That evening, before dining with his mother for the final time in heaven knew how long, George wrote his promised letter to Lucy Hawkins, the chambermaid who had so captivated him at Westbury Park. It was good news:

*Dear Lucy,*

*Today I received a message from my best friend, Jake Morgan. He writes that his father, Thomas Morgan of Tredegar Park in Monmouthshire, is willing to offer you the position of Mrs Morgan's lady's maid. It is a step up from your current employment and, more importantly, will provide a solution to your difficulty. I have forwarded your details to Mr Morgan and you should be hearing from him presently.*

*For my part, I am going to seek my fortune in South Africa and leave by the Plymouth mail packet next Thursday.*

*I much enjoyed our brief acquaintance and hope we will meet again when I return to Britain.*

*I am, etc.,*
*George Hart*

Having sealed and addressed the envelope, George rang for Manners. 'Make sure this goes by first post tomorrow morning.'

'Yes, Mr Hart.' Manners stood there awkwardly.

'Anything the matter?'

'Begging your pardon, sir, but the mistress happened to mention you were starting your journey to Africa tomorrow, and I just wanted to wish you, on behalf of all the staff, the best of luck with your travels.'

'Thank you, Manners,' said George, a tear coming suddenly to his eye. 'You and some of the older servants have been like a family to me. I'll do my best to return in one piece.'

So recently he had stood before the old man with a fine military career in front of him, an officer and a gentleman. Now he didn't know who he was.

# 5

## *The Angel Inn, Plymouth, 30 January 1878*

George stared at his food. It was his favourite dish – beef stew and dumplings – and, having eaten little that day, he should have been wolfing it down. But now that it had arrived, brought to him by a jolly serving girl with bad teeth and an ample bosom, he found he had no appetite. He felt queasy, and put it down to the strain of the previous few days and the nerves that were natural when embarking on a long and uncertain journey. When the sickness passed, he took another swig of his glass of claret, toasting Jake's generosity in the process, and looked appreciatively around the cosy, low-beamed private room that the innkeeper had set aside for his dinner. The room was silent but for the gentle crackling of the wood fire in the grate.

A sharp knock and the door opened. 'Begging your pardon, sir,' said the serving girl, 'there's someone here to see you.'

George's brow furrowed. '*Me?* Impossible: no one knows I'm here.'

'It's a young woman, sir. She asked for you by name.'

'Well, you'd better show her in, then,' said George, none the wiser, but curious all the same.

Moments later a small figure appeared in the doorway, her features concealed by the hood of a black cloak glistening with rainwater. She was holding a small portmanteau. 'Hello, sir.'

The voice sounded familiar. 'Lucy? Is that you under there?'

She pulled back her hood to reveal a pretty, tear-stained face and dishevelled hair. Her lower lip was swollen and she was shivering.

'It is you,' he said, rising from his seat. 'You poor thing, you're soaked. Take off your wet things and warm yourself by the fire.'

She stood there motionless, so George helped her out of her cloak and sat her by the fire. When the flames and a glass of whisky had brought some colour back to her cheeks, he asked her what had happened.

'Last night he came to my room,' she said in a dull monotone.

'Who came?'

'Sir Jocelyn. It was late and the other servants were already in bed. He asked me about the letter I'd received from Ireland, and whether it was from you. I said no, but he didn't believe me. He demanded to see it.'

'And did you let him?'

'I had no choice. It put him into such a fury. He asked me what I'd done to encourage you to write to me. I said nothing, but he didn't believe me. He said that if you, a lowborn foreigner, were good enough for me, then he certainly was. He tried to kiss me again but I wouldn't let him. When he persisted, I slapped him.' The memory of what happened next caused the tears to

78

flow anew, great rivulets of sorrow that sparkled in the firelight.

George feared the worst, but he needed to know. 'What did Harris do?'

'He hit me,' she said, putting her hand to her battered lip. 'Then he told me to take off my nightdress. I refused and he punched me in the stomach. I couldn't breathe, it was horrible. He threatened to hit me again if I resisted, so I didn't. I just wanted it to be over.'

Great waves of fury were breaking over George. 'Did he . . . ?'

He left the sentence unfinished, but his meaning was obvious.

'No, but he would have if Mrs Bradbury hadn't intervened. She was looking for Sir Jocelyn and heard my cries.'

'*She* stopped him?' asked George, scarcely able to believe that one of the agents of his downfall had saved Lucy's honour.

'Yes. He'd locked my door, but she demanded that he open it, and eventually he did. She found me sobbing, naked on the bed, saw at once what he was about and shouted at him to get out. After he left she burst into tears, saying she hadn't thought him capable of such a despicable act and that she wanted nothing more to do with him. She also said she was determined to leave his house that very night and that she was happy to take me with her. I was only too glad to accept. She gave me a little money, which I used to get here.'

'Well, thank God for Mrs Bradbury,' said George, in a voice so low it was barely audible. 'She's gone at least some way to making amends for her perfidy. But we can't let Harris get away with this. Where is he now?'

'Still at Westbury Park, I imagine.'

'Have you told anyone else about this?'

She shook her head.

'Why not? You should have gone to the police.'

'That's what Mrs Bradbury suggested. But what good would it do? He's a baronet and a magistrate; I'm a servant. They're hardly likely to take my word over his.'

George knew she was right, and it made him angrier still. 'He deserves to die for the way he's treated us.'

Lucy was silent.

'I've taken a room upstairs,' said George, rising. 'You can sleep there. I'll be back as soon as I can.'

'Where are you going?'

'To Gloucestershire.'

'Please don't. No good can come of it. If you kill him you'll certainly be hanged.'

'I don't care.'

'Well I do. I won't have your blood on my hands.'

A loud knock sounded on the door.

'What is it?' said George loudly.

'Only me, sir,' said the serving girl, peering round the door. 'Would your guest like some refreshments? We're about to close the kitchen.'

'Would you?' he asked Lucy. 'You should.'

She shook her head.

'No, thank you,' said George to the girl. 'That will be all.'

The girl bobbed her head and left. Her interruption had cooled George's anger a little and allowed him to think.

Murder was not the solution. There had to be another way to make Harris pay. 'I could call him out,' he said after a long pause.

'He won't accept. He can't: he'd lose his commission. And even if he did, you might die rather than him.'

'What, then, would you have me do?'

'There is something you can do for *me*.'

'What?'

'Take me with you to South Africa, where we can both start again.'

Of course, thought George. That was why she had come. She knew from his letter that he was due to leave the following morning on the weekly mail packet. She must have visited countless inns in the town before finding him. But it changed nothing. How could he take her with him? He had already spent much of Jake's money on clothes suitable for South Africa and his boat ticket. He needed the rest to survive. And much as he liked Lucy, he hardly knew her. No, he decided, he would stick to his original plan.

'I can't take you with me.'

'Why?'

'Because I have no fixed plans beyond visiting my uncle in Pietermaritzburg. I might go on to Kimberley to try my luck in the diamond fields. I just don't know. In any case, I intend to travel light. I'm taking my horse and a minimum of kit. You'd only slow me down.'

'I won't slow you down. I can ride, you know. I learnt as a young girl.'

'I'm sorry, Lucy. I've made my decision and it's final. Besides, you've got a perfectly good job to go to in

Monmouthshire, as I told you in my letter. They're good people and will treat you well.'

Lucy began to cry. 'I'm sure they will, and I'm very grateful to you for finding me a new position. But I can't stay in Britain,' she sobbed. 'Sir Jocelyn might find me. He lent my father money in lieu of my wages and I've yet to pay it back.'

George walked over and held her close. He did not want to take her with him. The last thing he needed was another mouth to feed. But nor was he prepared to leave her to Harris's tender mercy. He settled for a compromise. 'Now stop your crying. You can come to South Africa; I'll buy you a ticket. But to Cape Town, not Durban, and from there you're on your own. And you'll go second class, not first class. It's all I can afford.'

Lucy looked up at him and smiled. 'You won't regret it, sir.'

'I hope not – and don't call me sir. George will do.'


It was still dark when they left the inn the following morning. The rain had stopped but the cobbles were slick with water. 'Watch your step,' said George. 'These wet streets can be lethal.'

They walked down Lockyer Street towards Citadel Road, intending to catch a horse-drawn tram to the Great Western Docks about a mile distant. But as they neared the end of the street, a bulky figure in a top hat and cape appeared from a side road and blocked their path.

'Excuse us,' said George, stepping off the pavement to avoid the obstacle. But as he did so, Lucy following, the man moved to intercept them, using his cane as a barrier.

'Not so fast, Mr Hart,' he said in a voice with traces of Cockney.

'Who are you?' said George, stopping.

'My name's Thompson. I'm a private detective working for Sir Jocelyn Harris. You've got something of his,' he said, nodding at Lucy, 'and he wants it back.'

'Kindly inform your master that Miss Hawkins has left his employ. Any money owed will be paid in full.'

The man's round, flat face broke into a sneer. 'I think not. I've been told to return the young woman to Westbury Park and that's what I intend to do. What Colonel Harris has in store for her I wouldn't like to say.'

'Why you bloody—'

'Temper, temper,' taunted Thompson. 'Seems the colonel's not the only one with a soft spot for the girl, and I can see why. But that's no concern of mine. Just hand her over and you can leave in one piece.'

'Please don't, George!' cried Lucy.

George took in Thompson's size – at least 6' 4" and heavily built – and decided his only hope of besting him was surprise. 'Look,' he said, putting down his bags and reaching into his pocket for money, 'I'm sure we can come to some arrangement. I've got about a hundred pounds here. Will that do?'

He held out the notes in his left hand, and as Thompson leant forward greedily to take them he caught him flush on the chin with a right cross. There was a loud thud as fist met flesh and bone, causing Thompson to stagger like a drunk. But he stayed on his feet. My God, thought George, he's even tougher than I thought; I'd better finish this quickly.

George moved forward with both fists raised, in classic pugilist style, but his opponent was a street fighter from the East End of London who would use anything to hand. 'Watch out, he's got a sword-stick!' shrieked Lucy as Thompson unsheathed a rapier blade from his cane, the street gaslight glinting on its shiny surface.

He slipped on the cobbles as he thrust at George with the point, missing his midriff by inches. George responded with two quick punches, a right and a left, that both caught Thompson in the face and again failed to down him. 'You'll have to do better than that, boy,' he said, wiping blood from his mouth.

George thought about flight. He knew he could outrun the bigger man, but that would mean abandoning Lucy, who was crouching in fear behind him. 'Run, Lucy, now!' he shouted over his shoulder. 'I'll meet you at the docks.'

'What about you?'

'I'll be all right. Just go!'

As Lucy set off up Lockyer Street, her bag bumping against her legs, Thompson came on again, forcing George to retreat until his left heel bumped against something solid. It was his kitbag. In one fluid motion he crouched down to grab the bag, keeping his eyes all the while on his assailant. Thompson seized his opportunity and lunged forward, the point of his blade entering not flesh but the thin canvas of the bag that George had, in the nick of time, raised for protection. In struggling to free the blade, Thompson lost balance and staggered backwards. It gave George a few crucial seconds to pull the drawstring on the bag, reach inside and grasp his grandfather's revolver.

'Don't move,' shouted George, levelling the pistol at Thompson's breast, 'or I'll shoot!'

Thompson saw the pistol and laughed. 'I haven't seen one of those ancient pieces for years. It's probably not even loaded.'

'I assure you it is. Don't make me prove it.' George turned to Lucy, who had stopped halfway up the street. 'Keep going!'

A movement caught his eye. Thompson had seized on the momentary lapse in concentration and was lurching towards him again to run him through. George swung round. A loud boom sounded from the pistol and flame leapt from its muzzle. The heavy lead ball tore into the right side of Thompson's chest, spinning his body round as he crumpled to the ground, his sword-stick ringing on the cobblestones. A shocked George looked at the revolver in his hand, then down at his victim. He was lying on his front, a large crimson stain spreading on the cobbles beneath him. As he gasped for breath the gaping exit wound on his back made a curious sucking sound; from his lips dribbled frothy bubbles of pink blood. George felt sick.

'Will he die?' asked Lucy, who had run back down the street on hearing the shot.

'I don't know . . . probably. I think he's been hit in the lung. My God, what have I done?'

'It's not your fault, George. You had no choice. But all the same we should get help.'

George glanced up. 'Have you gone insane? If he dies I'll swing for sure.'

'But it was self-defence.'

'Yes, but it was hardly a fair fight. I had a pistol to his sword-stick. How do you think I'm going to explain that?'

'You were protecting me.'

'I know, but they'll never believe us. I'll be charged with manslaughter at the very least; Harris will see to that. No, Lucy, the only thing to do is make ourselves scarce. In a few hours we'll be clear of England forever. And don't feel sorry for him. He's a goner, I'm certain of that, and good riddance.' George picked up his bag. 'Let's go.'

Lucy hesitated. 'We can't just leave him.'

'He tried to kill me, for heaven's sake! Now come on.'

Reluctantly she followed.

An hour later and George was still in shock. The nausea had gone, to be replaced by a cold sweat and the shakes. Did I need to pull the trigger? he kept asking himself, and each time the answer was yes.

He shivered and turned up the collar of his quilted pea-jacket as a biting wind blew across the dockside. Looming above him was the silent bulk of the SS *American*, a hybrid steam-sail vessel that for five years had been ferrying mail and passengers to South Africa for the Union Steamship Company. She did not look particularly swift with her stubby centre funnel, twin masts and a poopdeck that reminded George of a Spanish galleon. Yet the month she would take to cover the 6,800 nautical miles that separated Plymouth from Durban was, George had been assured by the ticket office, faster than any other form of transport.

Lucy was already on board, snug in her second-class cabin. George had remained on shore to await the arrival of his horse, Emperor, from the nearby livery stable. A clatter of hooves signalled his wait was over.

'Cutting it a bit fine, aren't you, Pickering?' said George to the groom who was holding Emperor's lead rein.

'Sorry, sir, but he didn't want to leave his stable.'

'Never does, lazy blighter. Well, get him stowed. We don't have much time.'

'Sir,' said Pickering, with a nod, as he led Emperor up the gangway and on to the ship's main deck. There he was placed in a small wooden horsebox and lowered by a derrick into the bowels of the ship. Once below deck, Emperor was put into a narrow stall, a canvas sling beneath his belly to prevent him from falling in bad weather. Cinders were spread beneath his hooves to give him grip, and carbolized powder scattered as a disinfectant. Lastly he was watered and fed, the groom mixing a spoonful of nitre with his bran and oats to ward off seasickness. George supervised the whole operation, soothing the frightened horse with quiet words of assurance. He was surprised to see so many neighbouring stalls empty, and asked Pickering the reason.

'Oh, that's because the troops on board are mainly infantry, sir,' replied Pickering. 'All the horses you can see are the property of officers.'

'Is that so?' said George. 'Well, look after Emperor. I'll check on him at evening stables.'

Back on deck, George was welcomed by the purser and allocated a first-class cabin on the starboard side of the ship. He found it cramped but comfortable with a bunk, desk and small fitted wardrobe. He paid the porter and was sorting out his gear when a horn signalled the ship's imminent departure. George peered out of the porthole at Plymouth docks and wondered for the hundredth time whether he had made the right decision. What would Africa hold for him? And when, if ever, would he see Britain's shores again?

George was still lost in thought when a tall, sandy-haired officer poked his head round the half-open door. 'Hello,' said the officer. 'As we're going to be neighbours, I thought I'd better introduce myself. I'm Captain Matthew Gossett.'

'George Hart. Pleased to meet you.'

The two shook hands.

'So where are you heading for?' asked Gossett.

'Durban.'

'Business or pleasure?'

'Both, I hope. I've got family near Pietermaritzburg. And you?'

'Oh, definitely business. I'm an aide-de-camp to General Thesiger, the new commander-in-chief in South Africa. We're off to fight the Kaffir tribes of the eastern Cape. The war's been dragging on since last September and we're going out to see if we can put an end to it. You do *know* there's a war on?'

George nodded. It was a reasonable question, with the press devoting most of its foreign coverage to the Russo-Turkish War and the possibility of Britain entering on the side of the Turks to protect Constantinople. But he had discovered, hidden away in *The Times*, a small article about Thesiger and his predecessor, Sir Arthur Cunynghame. For five months Cunynghame had tried and failed to bring the war against the Galeka and Gaika tribes – the so-called

Ninth Kaffir War – to a successful conclusion. Now it was somebody else's turn. The only surprise was that Thesiger had been chosen ahead of Sir Garnet Wolseley, Britain's foremost fighting general, and a man with extensive experience of African warfare and politics. Thesiger had neither, though he had served on Napier's staff during the Abyssinian Campaign of 1868. His advantage over Wolseley was that he was very much an Establishment man: an aide-de-camp to Queen Victoria and a traditionalist when it came to reform. Wolseley was a man of action *and* ideas, and his championing of change had gained him the enmity of both the conservative Duke of Cambridge and his cousin the queen.

George could not resist asking his neighbour's opinion of Thesiger's prospects.

'I have no worries about General Thesiger's ability, if that's what you're getting at,' replied Gossett. 'I've been with him for six months, and you'd be lucky to meet a kinder-hearted man or a more efficient soldier. No, what concerns me is the quality of the troops available to him. You've only got to look at the soldiers on board. Most are barely out of short trousers and few have even completed a recruit's course of musketry. It's an absolute scandal and, in my opinion, the inevitable consequence of Cardwell's decision to introduce short-service soldiering. In the old days, when soldiers could serve twenty years and more, a regiment would be packed with veterans. Now that the term is six years with the Colours and six with the Reserve, greenhorns are the order of the day.'

George was in complete agreement, telling Gossett that during his limited time with the King's Dragoon Guards the youth and inexperience of the troopers had been the talk of the officers' mess.

'You were in the army?' asked Gossett, eyebrows raised. 'Why ever did you leave?'

'Oh, various reasons. I didn't get on with my CO.'

'I'm sorry to hear that,' said Gossett. He looked as if he was about to ask another question, then seemed to think better of it. 'Well, I must be off. The general will probably want his bed turned down, or some such nonsense.'

'The life of a personal staff officer, eh?' said George in a jocular tone.

'Quite.'

As Gossett was about to leave, he caught sight of the revolver on the desk. George had left it out to clean away all traces of the shot he had fired at Thompson; but had not had an opportunity to do so.

'Where on earth did you get that old pistol?' asked Gossett.

George flinched. How could he have been so stupid? 'It was my grandfather's,' he replied, trying to sound nonchalant.

'Does it still work?'

'I think so.'

'Mind if I have a look?' asked Gossett, reaching his hand out to pick the pistol up.

'Actually I do!' said George sharply, placing his own hand on the gun. 'It's a little fragile.'

Gossett looked surprised. 'Fair enough. It's a Colt, isn't it? We mostly use Adams and Webleys today,' he added, tapping his leather holster. 'Much more reliable.'

\* \* \*

That evening, as the ship entered the often stormy seas of the Bay of Biscay, George went to check on Emperor and found him quietly eating his evening ration of hay. His mind at ease, he made his way to the saloon on the main deck, where the first-class passengers were about to sit down to dinner with the captain of the ship, a jovial gentleman by the name of Wilson. The civilian passengers included a judge and his wife, the Cape attorney-general, a member of the Legislative Assembly, a Port Elizabeth businessman and George; the rest were British officers.

'I'm afraid you're slightly outnumbered on this trip,' said Captain Wilson after George had introduced himself. 'General Thesiger has commandeered most of the best cabins for himself and his staff.'

George followed the line of Wilson's gesture to a tall, bearded officer in a blue patrol jacket, of the type favoured by senior officers and staff. Though surrounded by his subordinates, Gossett among them, Thesiger had an air of restless unease, his dark eyes flitting back and forth across the room. 'I don't mind a bit,' said George, his eyes still on Thesiger but warming to Wilson's tone. 'I used to be an officer myself.'

'Did you, by God,' said Wilson. 'You hardly look old enough. Who were you with?'

'The King's Dragoon Guards. I resigned after five months.'

'I won't say I'm surprised,' commented Wilson. 'It can't be much fun serving under Colonel Harris.'

'Do you know him?'

'Not personally. But I've read plenty about him in the papers. Wasn't he reprimanded by the Horse Guards for spying on his own officers?'

'Yes, he was,' said George. 'But that's not the half of it. I could tell you stories about Harris that would make your hair curl.'

'Do go on,' said Wilson, but before George could speak they were interrupted by a steward who handed the captain a note. 'Well, I'll be damned,' exclaimed Wilson, as he finished reading it.

'Trouble?' asked George.

'You could say that. I've just received word from another ship about the shooting of a private detective in Plymouth this morning. A young couple were seen fleeing from the scene of the crime towards the commercial docks and we've been asked to keep an eye open for them. You joined us at Plymouth. Did you notice anything suspicious?'

'Not a thing,' said George, his heart racing. 'Did the victim survive?'

'No, he died in hospital. Apparently the gunman was pretty handy with his weapon and the police suspect he has military training.'

'Do they? Well, that narrows the field a little. Do the police have a description of the couple?'

'There's no mention of any description.'

George breathed an inward sigh of relief.

'Excuse me, Captain Wilson,' interjected Gossett. 'Could I borrow young Hart for a moment? I'd like to introduce him to General Thesiger.'

'Of course,' said Wilson.

Thesiger was polite enough, asking George his destination, but hardly seemed to listen to the response. Until, that is, George mentioned his brief time in the army. 'I can't understand,' said Thesiger, frowning, his bushy black eyebrows almost knitted, 'why anyone would leave the army after just five months, Colonel Harris or no. None of my business, of course, but it's a damn shame.'

George replied that he did not want to go into the details, but that he had been left no option but to resign. What he had seen of the army, he had enjoyed very much.

'How did you do at Sandhurst?' asked Thesiger.

'I passed out first.'

'So we lose one of our most promising young officers because he doesn't see eye to eye with his CO! It happens all the time, Hart. The solution is not to resign but to exchange regiments, as I myself did when I left the Rifle Brigade for the Grenadiers.'

'Quite right, General,' interrupted the officer to Thesiger's right, a short, haughty-looking major with impressive whiskers. 'The only honourable way to leave the service is in a coffin or a bathchair.'

'See, Hart,' said Thesiger, gesturing towards the officer who had spoken, 'even my military secretary, Major Crealock, agrees with me on this point, and that doesn't happen often.'

George ignored Crealock's put-down. 'As I said before, General, it was out of my hands.'

'So you say. I wish you luck with your ventures in Africa, whatever they may be. We soldiers have the small matter of a war to attend to.'

Before George could respond, the gong was rung for dinner.

\* \* \*

The meal passed slowly for George, stuck as he was between a judge's humourless wife and a Natal trader called Laband who was convinced that the solution to South Africa's woes was to extend white rule throughout the region. 'Mark my words,' he said for the umpteenth time, 'a confederation of white colonies is the only way.'

George was too distracted by the news of Thompson's death, and the subsequent manhunt, to do anything more than nod vaguely in agreement. He was desperate to talk to Lucy, but felt he had to wait at least until the pudding course had been served before he could make his excuses. Then he hurried down the steel staircase to the deck that held the second-class cabins and, having checked he was not being observed, knocked on Lucy's door.

'Who is it?'

'George.'

The door opened to reveal Lucy in a nightdress, her curly chestnut hair loose on her shoulders. 'Thank God you've come. I can't get the memory of that poor wounded man out of my head.'

George raised a finger to his lips and shooed her back into the cabin. 'I know how you feel. But you must be careful what you say because that poor wounded man is now dead.'

'How can you be sure?'

George repeated what Captain Wilson had told him. 'Luckily it was still dark,' he added, 'so they don't know what we look like.'

'But they know we're a couple and that we made for the docks,' said a wide-eyed Lucy. 'Thank God you gave me money to buy my own ticket. If we'd gone in to the ticket office together we'd certainly have been caught.'

'Yes, so from now on we must avoid each other's company as much as possible. They're looking for a couple. We must make it seem like we've never met.'

'I'm scared, George,' said Lucy, 'I don't want to be alone.'

George noticed her dilated pupils. Of course, he thought, she's also in shock: first the attempted rape, then the shooting. It would take time for both of them to recover, but now was not the moment to take risks. 'I'd like to stay but I can't,' he said tenderly. 'Imagine if I was seen leaving your cabin in the morning. I'll call again as soon as it's safe to do so.'

'When will that be?'

'Soon.'

Back in his own cabin, George spent a fitful night regretting his caution. He lay awake for hours, tormented by images of the dying man gasping like a fish on a block; and when he finally did get to sleep he dreamt of Lucy, her body naked, her hair fanned out on the pillow beneath her.

George woke with a start. It was 6.30 a.m. and time to check on Emperor. On his way down to the horsedeck, he heard raised voices. He entered an open hatchway to investigate and found himself in a dark, cavernous room, festooned with hammocks and packs. The room was deserted but for three men to the left of the hatchway. Two of them had their backs to George and were pinning the other man up against the bulkhead, their spare hands raised in fists. Their victim, fair-haired and a good six inches taller than either, looked strangely unconcerned.

'What's going on here?' said George in his best parade-ground voice.

The shorter of the aggressors glanced round, decided George was not an officer, and replied, 'It's not your concern, so bugger off.'

George's anger flared. 'Well, I'm about to make it my concern. Now let him go or I'll—'

'You'll what?' said the same soldier, a dark wiry man with a distinctive Welsh accent.

George took a step forward and planted a right hook into the soldier's stomach, causing him to double up in pain.

'Now salute, damn you,' said George, 'or is that no longer the fashion in the Twenty-Fourth?' Though all three were wearing the anonymous sea kit of blue serge issued to soldiers in transit, he had spotted the tell-tale '24' badge on their woollen caps.

Both aggressors snapped to attention and saluted, their victim following suit but with less precision. 'Begging your pardon, sir,' said the soldier he had punched. 'I didn't know you was an officer, like.'

George ignored him, addressing the tall soldier instead. 'Why were they threatening you?'

'I wouldn't like to say, sir,' said the soldier softly, with only a hint of a Welsh lilt.

'Would you not? Well, we'll see about that. Come with me!' George had enough experience of ordinary soldiers to know they never blabbed. His question had put the tall man in an impossible position and he regretted it at once.

Far better, he knew, to quiz him in private, so George made his way down to the horsedeck, the tall soldier in his wake.

There was no sign of Pickering and, from force of habit, George entered Emperor's stall and took up a body brush and a currycomb. Emperor's coat was immaculate, and hardly needed grooming, but George knew that a good rub-down would keep his muscles warm.

'What's your name?' he asked the soldier, as he ran the brush in rhythmic strokes from Emperor's forelock to his withers, removing the accumulated hair with the currycomb.

'Private Thomas, sir.'

'Not your rank, your Christian name.'

'Owen, sir.'

'And don't call me sir. I'm not an officer.'

'But you said—'

George interjected. 'I simply asked whether it was still the fashion in your regiment to salute. I at no time declared *myself* an officer.'

'You implied—'

'That I may have done, it's true.' Having finished brushing Emperor's neck, George moved on to his flank. 'What about you? I'd hazard we're close in age, so you can't have been in the army long.'

'I'm nineteen years and took the shilling last September.'

George smiled at the coincidence, for he had joined his regiment that very month. 'Where are you from?'

'Monmouthshire.'

'I know Monmouthshire. Have you heard of the Morgans of Tredegar Park? They own a colliery.'

'I have, sir. I hail from Raglan, but some of my cousins work in the Tredegar colliery. They say old Mr Morgan is a fair employer.'

'I'm glad to hear it. His son Jake is a friend of mine. He's an officer in the Second Battalion of the Twenty-Fourth. Are you bound for the First or Second Battalion?'

'The Second.'

'Well, who knows, you may be assigned to his company.'

'That I may,' said Thomas.

George gestured with his head towards the deck above. 'So what was that all about?'

'Oh, nothing, a bit of harmless chat. They're the Davies brothers from Trewern, and difficult to tell apart, so I call them Tweedledum and Tweedledee. They aren't amused.'

'I'm sure they aren't. If you don't mind me saying so, Thomas, you don't strike me as a typical army recruit. You seem far too sensible.'

Thomas grinned. 'All thanks to my mam. She kept me at school when my pa wanted me to work with him in the fields.'

'So you can read and write?'

'That I can.'

'Well, that's more than most of the NCOs in the King's Dragoon Guards can manage. So why enlist? It can't be for the ten shillings a week. You could do better than that.'

'No, it's not for the money. I enlisted for adventure. My mam hoped I'd become a schoolteacher, but I want to see the world.'

'As good a reason as any, I suppose. But how do you put up with barrack-room life?'

'It's not too bad, and certainly no worse than growing up in a big family. I'm one of ten and had to share a bed with three brothers. In the army I get my own bed, clean sheets once a month and a new straw mattress every quarter. And I get enough to eat, as well, though bread and meat can get monotonous, and we have to pay for our vegetables.'

'How do you get on with the other men? Do you have anything in common?'

'A lot of us come from the Welsh borders. And if I've more learning than most, I'm not the only one who can read and write, and we try to help the others with their letters. A few, like the Davies brothers, are a bit rough and ready. But overall they're not a bad bunch.'

'Do you know anything about the Kaffir tribes you're being sent out to fight?'

'Only that they fight with spears and won't stand against a bayonet charge.'

George stopped brushing. 'Is that what they told you? And what about the Zulus, have you heard of *them*?'

Thomas shook his head.


A week into the voyage and George had spoken, at one time or another, to all but two of the first-class passengers. The exceptions were both middle-ranking officers – a lieutenant colonel and a major – who, like him, had joined the ship at Plymouth. They could not have been less alike. The colonel was short and bald, with doleful eyes and a large, unruly beard; the major tall and powerfully built, a luxuriant moustache sprouting from under his long patrician nose.

As they were about to sit down for dinner, George asked Gossett the major's name. 'Oh, that's Redvers Buller, one of our special service officers. Impressive, isn't he? He was Wolseley's intelligence chief during the Ashanti campaign and is tipped for great things. We're lucky to have him.'

George was intrigued. 'It sounds like it. But why would one of Wolseley's protégés volunteer for service in Africa when a war in Europe is a strong possibility?'

'Good question. And you could ask the same of Colonel Evelyn Wood over there, our other "special". He's also a member of the Wolseley "Ring", and a VC-winner to boot.'

Gossett was nodding in the direction of the colonel. He looked so nondescript that George had paid him little heed. 'That's Wood?' asked George, the astonishment evident in his voice. '*The* Wood, who fought in the Crimea as a sixteen-year-old midshipman, switched to the army and promptly won a Victoria Cross during the Mutiny?'

'The very same.'

George shook his head. 'I'll say this, he's a most unlikely looking hero.'

'They often are,' said Gossett. 'Would you like to meet him?'

George said yes and was placed next to Wood at dinner. It was a bizarre experience, not helped by the colonel's apparent deafness. Fortunately Wood did most of the talking, regaling George with a stream of amusing anecdotes, including the time he tried to ride a giraffe for a bet and had his nose broken as a consequence. On a more serious note, he spoke passionately about the army's need for more staff-trained officers – he himself had graduated from the Staff College in the 1860s – and a Prussian-style general staff to plan and execute war.

'Take the recent Franco-Prussian War,' said Wood. 'Nobody expected the Prussians to win so easily – so why did they?'

Remembering a Sandhurst lecture on the war, George muttered something about the Prussian needle-gun and their excellent Krupp artillery.

'What's that?' said Wood, cupping a hand to his ear. George repeated his point, but much louder this time.

'Yes, yes, but bear in mind the French had the Mitrailleuse, a machine gun not unlike the Gatling, and that their own rifle had twice the range of the Dreyse. No, the key advantage for the Prussians was their general staff, which enabled them to mobilize and deploy with a speed and efficiency the French could not match. The sooner we follow their example, the better. But there's little chance of that with a stick-in-the-mud like the Duke of Cambridge at the head of the army. He opposed both the abolition of purchase and the intro-duction of short-service soldiering. Now I ask you, would such a dyed-in-the-wool conservative ever agree to limit his own power by creating a British general staff? I don't think so.'

Next morning, George came across Lucy taking the air on the main deck. He knew it was foolish to be seen with her, and was about to walk past, when she beckoned him over. 'Look,' she said, pointing to a large island away to the east. 'Isn't it beautiful? The steward assures me it's Palma, the most westerly of the Canary Islands.'

George raised the telescope he was carrying to his eye. It was a fine sunny day, and he could make out houses in the hills and snow on the peaks. 'You're right, it's very beautiful. Would you like a closer look?'

She accepted the telescope. 'I wonder what it's like to live there,' she murmured. 'I'm almost tempted to jump ship.'

'No chance of that, I'm afraid. But try not to worry. All mention of Thompson's death has ceased. I think we're in the clear.'

'I pray that's the case. Does that mean we can see more of each other?'

'No,' said George. 'It's better to be safe than sorry. I shouldn't really be talking to you now.'

'Hello, Hart,' said a voice behind them, causing George to turn sharply. It was Major Crealock, Thesiger's military secretary, who had not spoken to George since the first evening on board. 'Aren't you going to introduce me to your charming companion?'

'You are mistaken, Major. She's not my companion. I was just lending Miss Hawkins my telescope so that she could see the island of Palma a little better.'

'Ah, yes, it's a fine sight. I've half a mind to paint it. Well, sorry for the interruption,' said Crealock, bowing. 'I hope to see you again, Miss Hawkins.'

Lucy nodded in acknowledgement.

'You see what I mean?' said George, once Crealock was out of earshot. 'People are likely to make assumptions if they see us together. I'd better go. If you need to talk to me in future, send a message to my cabin. We mustn't take any more chances until we're safe on African soil.'

# 6

## SS American, *Atlantic Ocean*, 13 February 1878

George stared at the ceiling above his bunk. His naked body was covered with a thin film of sweat, the sheet damp beneath him. He had been tossing and turning all night, but it was too hot to sleep. He swung his legs off the bunk, padded over to the washstand and splashed water on his clammy face. Would this torturous journey never end? he asked his unshaven reflection in the mirror. They had been at sea for two weeks now, and each passing day seemed to bring a rise in temperature. But the heat was the least of his worries: until he disembarked, he would run the constant risk of being exposed as Thompson's killer.

An hour later, dressed simply in blue serge trousers, a white cotton shirt and a straw boater, George made his way down to the horsedeck. He found Pickering shovelling Emperor's droppings into a wooden bucket.

'How is he?' asked George.

'A little off colour, Mr Hart,' said the groom, pausing in his labours. 'He's hardly touched his breakfast.'

George leant over the rail of the stall and saw for himself the untouched mixture of bran and oats. Emperor was standing motionless in his sling, his head bowed, seemingly oblivious to George's presence.

'Not like him at all,' observed George. 'It must be the heat. It's bad enough on deck, and must be unbearable down here.'

George left the stall and returned, a minute or two later, with a damp cloth and a sponge soaked in vinegar. He used the sponge to moisten Emperor's quivering nostrils, a tried-and-tested remedy for seasickness. The cloth he placed over the horse's head to keep him cool.

'Does that make any difference?' asked George, nodding in the direction of a nearby canvas tube that, attached to a wind sail, was meant to bring fresh air to the horsedeck.

'Sometimes,' said Pickering with a grimace. 'But only if there's a breeze.'

George got his meaning. When the wind was up, the ship fairly flew along, powered as it was by both sail and steam; but as they approached the equator the wind had died away, leaving them on steam power alone.

George stroked Emperor's muzzle. 'Good boy. Not long to go now.'

In truth they were still a fortnight from Durban. But George's words of reassurance seemed to soothe Emperor and the horse whinnied in reply.

'I'll be back after breakfast,' said George.

'Begging your pardon, Mr Hart, but will you not be attending the flogging?'

'What flogging?'

'Haven't you heard? A private of the Twenty-Fourth was caught stealing grog. He's to be flogged after breakfast.'

George had missed dinner the night before with an

upset stomach, and this was news to him. 'Do you know his name?'

'Thomas, I think.'

'*Owen* Thomas?'

'I think so, sir.'

George stared open-mouthed. He had liked Thomas from the off and, since their initial meeting, had spoken to him on a number of occasions, discussing Africa and learning the gossip from the ranks. They were both out-siders, in their different ways, and George had nothing but admiration for Thomas's zest for life. For him to have committed an offence worthy of flogging was scarcely credible.

'There must be some mistake,' said George at last. 'It's probably another Thomas.'

'No mistake, I can assure you,' said Major Crealock, looking up from the small desk in his cabin. 'He was caught red-handed in the quartermaster's store, drunk as a lord.'

This was the first time that George had had occasion to speak to Crealock since their encounter on deck with Lucy. Gossett had told him that the major was a clever, fiercely ambitious officer who would stop at nothing to get what he wanted, and George had resolved to keep out of his way. But having discovered that Crealock was president of Thomas's court martial, and therefore chiefly responsible for the severity of his punishment, George had felt compelled to confront him.

'That's as may be,' said George curtly, 'but how can it merit a flogging?'

Crealock put down his pen and leant back in his chair. 'Hart, can I speak plainly? This is a military matter and you are no longer a soldier. The sentence of the court was confirmed by General Thesiger, who, as a teetotaller, has little sympathy for drunkards. It's not your concern.'

'I *know* Private Thomas. He's not a troublemaker, far from it. He's a quiet, sensitive fellow and has it in him to become a first-class soldier. Flogging him will do more harm than good.'

'So you say, but in my experience a short, sharp lesson is the only way to discourage reoffending.'

'I thought,' said George, changing tack, 'that flogging had been abolished in peacetime.'

'And so it has,' replied Crealock with a sneer. 'But we're not at peace, are we? We're on our way to a theatre of war, which means we're on active service. As things stand, Thomas's sentence is lawful, and there's nothing you can do about it.' Crealock looked at his pocket-watch. 'Now, if you'll excuse me, I'm required on deck. Will you be joining us?'

George was torn. He had seen all too many soldiers flogged during his short time with the KDG. But he felt he owed it to Thomas to share his suffering. 'Lead the way.'

They left the cabin and joined the other officers and gentlemen on the poopdeck. Captain Wilson was there, looking suitably grave. General Thesiger appeared less concerned and was sharing a joke with Gossett. George stood apart, his hands on the rail above the main deck. Down below him, formed into a hollow square, stood row upon row of red-faced, sweating soldiers. Despite the fierceness of the equatorial sun, they had been ordered to don their full dress uniforms of scarlet woollen tunic, dark blue Oxford trousers and black leather boots. A garb less suitable for the tropics was hard to imagine. The only item of a soldier's kit that seemed to take account of the African sun and heat was his cloth-covered cork helmet, complete with a peak to shield the eyes and a tail to protect the neck.

'Bring out the prisoner,' shouted a dapper officer with a waxed moustache. The collar and cuffs of his scarlet dress tunic were the unmistakeable light green of the 24th Foot; in place of a cork helmet he wore a peaked forage cap with a sphinx and the number '24' prominent on its front. The crown on his shoulder and single bar of lace on his cuff identified him as a lieutenant.

Leaning forward, George could see a defiant-looking Thomas emerge from a hatch. Stripped to the waist and flanked on either side by an armed marine, he was led to the centre of the hollow square.

'Private Thomas,' said the lieutenant of the 24th in a loud, clear voice, 'a court martial has found you guilty of theft. The sentence is twenty-five lashes. Secure the prisoner.'

A wooden ladder had been attached to the rigging, and to this the marines tied Thomas's wrists above his head with leather thongs, leaving his white scrawny back exposed. Two burly drummers then took their positions on either side of Thomas. They both held a cat o'nine tails, comprised of a foot-long wooden handle and nine lengths of knotted whipcord.

'On my command,' bellowed the lieutenant. 'One!'

The drummer to Thomas's left drew back his right

hand and swung the cat in a vicious arc, shifting his weight as he did so from his right foot to his left. As the blow struck, Thomas gave a low moan, the sound muffled by the cloth gag in his mouth.

George winced. The cat had left a livid welt that ran obliquely from Thomas's right shoulder to his left hip.

'Two!'

Another blow fell.

'Three!

'Four!' The welts had merged into a thick stripe.

'Five!'

Now it was the second corporal's turn, using his left hand.

'Six!' A new welt appeared on Thomas's other shoulder.

'Seven!'

And so it went on. After the thirteenth stroke, blood began to flow from the mangled flesh, dripping in rivulets down Thomas's back. George felt physically sick. From the ranks arose a murmur of discontent.

'Silence!' roared the lieutenant.

'Fourteen!'

'Fifteen!'

George tried to intervene. 'Surely he's had enough,' he urged Crealock. 'Can't you ask the general to put a stop to this?'

'Of course I can't.'

'At least ask the doctor to examine him.'

'No,' said Crealock, tight-lipped.

'Sixteen!' shouted the lieutenant.

'Seventeen!'

George turned away.

By the time the twenty-fifth and last stroke had been administered, Thomas was hanging limply by his arms, his back disfigured by a bloody 'X'.

'Cut him down and douse his wounds with salt water.'

George gagged. The sickly-sweet smell of blood and antiseptic was almost overpowering, and it took a while for his eyes to accustom to the gloom of the sickbay. Thomas was lying face down on a makeshift bunk, his back the colour of raw steak. George felt a surge of anger at the pointless brutality of it all. How could the most advanced nation in the world, he wondered, treat its soldiers as if they were mere beasts of burden, to be thrashed when they got out of hand? He shook his head.

'How is he?'

'A little feverish, which is to be expected,' said the ship's surgeon, his white apron stained with blood. 'But his pulse is strong, which is the main thing.'

'How long has he been unconscious?'

'Since they brought him in, and he's likely to remain that way for some time. Come back later if you need to talk.'

'I'll stay, if you don't mind,' said George, pulling up a chair.

Sitting there, staring at Thomas's lacerated back, George felt for the first time a sense of relief that he was no longer a soldier. Harris aside, he had loved his time in the King's Dragoon Guards. The comradeship of his fellow officers had given him a sense of belonging that he had never known before. Yet the British Army, even in its reformed state, was still far from ideal. Too many of its officers were ignorant snobs who expended more energy on the hunting field than in learning their profession. They made little effort to know, still less to understand, their men, and were far too quick to flog them for minor infractions. Thomas was a case in point. No, he decided, it was no longer a world he wanted to be part of.

He would forge a new career for himself. He thought of his mother, and all she had been through: born in Africa, removed from her mother at birth, a painful childhood in Dublin, a succession of unsuitable or unavailable lovers. No wonder she reserved her love for her son, and had been so distraught at their parting. He had let her down once; it would not happen again. But how to make her proud and, more importantly, ensure she did not want for money?

A groan made George start. Thomas's eyes flickered open. 'Ah, back with us at last,' said George. 'How're you feeling?'

Thomas was silent.

'A stupid question. Would you like some water?'

Thomas nodded. George held the tin cup to his chapped lips. The awkward angle caused much of the water to spill on the sheet.

'Thank you,' croaked Thomas.

'How could you be so foolish?' said George gently. 'Surely you knew the penalty?'

Thomas turned his head slightly, his pale cheek pinched with pain. 'Tweedledum dared me,' he whispered. 'I had to do it.'

At dinner that evening, George said little. It irked him that his fellow passengers were behaving as if nothing had happened; even Captain Wilson, who had seemed so affected at the time, was joviality himself as the port did the rounds.

'Yes, it's all true, Lieutenant Melvill,' said Wilson, addressing the dapper officer who had presided over the flogging. 'I did once mistake the lights of the Channel fleet for the coast. My exact words, if I remember rightly, were, "Hard-a-port! We must be running into Brighton, but I never knew they had so many chemist shops there." My junior officers have never let me forget it.'

Of those in earshot, only George failed to laugh. He could bear the merriment no longer and, addressing Melvill opposite him, blurted out, 'How can it be right to disfigure a man for life for stealing an extra ration of rum?'

Melvill looked at George with a mixture of pity and contempt. 'It may seem harsh,' he responded, 'but most of the soldiers on board are young recruits and it's important to set an example.'

'Surely a period of confinement would have sufficed?'

Crealock, who was sitting next to Melvill, responded, 'The members of the court considered it. But when we discovered that the ship's prison was far from secure, with a ventilation slit that allowed beer to be passed through, we settled for flogging. Some men prefer it, you know.'

'I find that hard to believe,' said George. 'How can you hope to win the men's trust if they're in constant fear of the lash?'

Crealock snorted. 'You've got a lot to learn. If you don't mind me asking, Hart, how long did you serve?'

'Five months.'

'Well, I've been a serving soldier for more than twenty years, which makes me slightly better qualified to talk about discipline than you. Most soldiers join the army as a last resort. They're the dregs of society, and the only way to keep them in order is to make them fear authority. To mollycoddle them is the worst thing you can do.'

'Poppycock,' said a voice from further up the table. George turned to look and was met by Major Buller's steely gaze. 'Proper discipline,' continued Buller, 'depends upon mutual respect. It can only be achieved by force of personality and not by coercion. There's no place for the lash in a modern professional army. The sooner it's abolished, the better.'

Crealock was about to respond, but so emphatic was Buller's statement, so self-assured his manner, that he held his tongue. At that moment George revelled in Crealock's discomfiture. Thinking about it later, however, he realized how foolish he had been to draw attention to himself. He resolved to keep a lower profile and not to make any more enemies.

A couple of days after the flogging, while taking a turn on deck, deep in thought, George walked straight into a fellow passenger. Caught by surprise, the man stumbled and fell. 'Please excuse me,' said George, helping the man to his feet. 'I wasn't looking where I was going.'

Their eyes met. 'Major Buller!'

'Have we met?'

'Not exactly, sir. But you were kind enough to take my side in the flogging debate at dinner the other night.'

'Of course,' said Buller, his gaunt face breaking into a smile. 'Think nothing of it. It makes my blood boil to hear anyone defend flogging. The battlefield is a bloody, horrific place to be. It's bad enough having to face that, without the additional threat of barbaric punishments hanging over you off the field as well. People imagine war to be an honourable affair fought by gentlemen, but it's not. A point that will be amply illustrated in Colonel Wood's talk, I don't doubt.'

'Which talk is that?' asked George.

'He's giving a lecture in the saloon at three. Strictly speaking it's only for officers, but I'm sure the general will make an exception.'

George was less certain, and was pleasantly surprised when Gossett brought word that Thesiger was happy for him to attend. At the appointed hour, George made his way to the saloon, where an impromptu lecture theatre had been set up at one end of the room, with a blackboard facing three rows of chairs. Around a dozen officers were present, including Thesiger.

The lecture was a fascinating résumé of South African history, delivered in Wood's typical jaunty style. He used an expertly drawn map to trace the story of European encroachment, pointing out that while the Portuguese had rounded the Cape of Good Hope as far back as 1488, the Dutch had been the first to settle, landing at Table Bay in 1652. They were later joined by German and Huguenot settlers, and together these early Boers were able to dominate the indigenous population of small, semi-nomadic, yellowish-black people known as Hottentots, who had themselves supplanted the even smaller and more primitive Bushmen. Until, that is, the arrival of two new threats: the Bantu and the British.

The Bantu were a taller and stronger race of black tribesman – called 'Kaffirs' by Europeans – who drifted down from the north. The British came from the sea, capturing Cape Town from the Dutch in 1806. By the 1830s, to avoid being caught between the hammer of hostile Bantu tribes and the anvil of British colonial authority, more than 15,000 Boers left the Cape Colony in their ox-drawn wagons and trekked north in search of new territory. This brought them into conflict with yet more Bantu tribes, notably the Zulu, and the British settlers in Natal, where, for a brief time in the early 1840s, the Boers proclaimed the 'Free Province of New Holland'. These same Boers helped Prince Mpande overthrow his brother Dingane and become King of the Zulus in 1840. When the British responded by annexing Natal in 1842, the Boers simply moved north to their other independent territories, later known as the Transvaal and the Orange Free State. But this uneasy situation could not last and, in 1877, just a year before George set off for Africa, Britain annexed the Transvaal.

Seeking out Wood after the lecture, George asked the significance of this recent annexation.

'Well, the excuse they gave,' said Wood, 'was that the Transvaal government was bankrupt and couldn't defend itself against hostile blacks, particularly the Zulu. But that was just a smokescreen. What the British government really wants is a self-governing confederation of South Africa, which would both save money on imperial defence and keep the whole of the region within Britain's sphere of influence. The annexation of the Transvaal is just another step along that road. But there's still a long way to go.'

'Surely,' said George, 'African tribes like the Zulus will never agree to confederation.'

'Of course not. Which is why, sooner or later, they'll all be conquered.'

George bristled. A few weeks earlier he would not have thought twice about the fate of an obscure African tribe. But his mother's confession had changed all that, and he now felt oddly protective towards his Zulu kin. Not that that made him, in his own mind, any less European. He certainly didn't *feel* African, and was only too aware of the need to keep his Zulu links hidden if he wanted to masquerade as a British gentleman. But nor could he any longer see the British Empire – and her African colonies in particular – from a strictly white perspective.

Wood sensed his unease. 'I can see you're not convinced. Can I suggest you read some of the material the War Office has provided us with? If nothing else, it will help to pass the time.'

That afternoon, George returned to his cabin to find a neat stack of books and pamphlets on his desk. It included War Office blue-books, Silver's *Guide to South Africa*, Galton's *Art of Travel*, a number of Xhosa and Zulu dictionaries, and a précis from the Intelligence Department on the manner and customs of the South African tribes. Over the course of the next week George read them all, but gave particular attention to the Zulu dictionary.

He could speak passable French and German, having excelled in his language exams at Harrow and Sandhurst, and was determined to learn a smattering of Zulu before he landed. To speed up the process he persuaded the Natal trader Laband, who had travelled extensively in Zululand

and spoke the language fluently, to teach him the rudiments of Zulu grammar. The sessions went well, but Laband made no attempt to conceal his contempt for the Zulus, a prejudice George found hard to stomach.

'What exactly have you got against the Zulus?' asked George, after one particularly vituperative jibe.

'Got against them?' said Laband, a look of surprise on his craggy face. 'Why, only that they're violent savages who stand in the way of progress.'

'I don't understand.'

'It's quite simple, really. All right-thinking people agree that the long-term economic wellbeing of South Africa depends upon the establishment of a confederation of white, self-governing colonies. This won't happen until the Zulus have been conquered, partly for reasons of security and partly because they're a simple people with no interest in developing the trade and mineral potential of their land.'

George frowned. 'I'm not sure your government would agree. According to the blue-books, it's been on friendly terms with the Zulus for years. Why, it even sent an official to preside over King Cetshwayo's coronation in seventy-three.'

'That's true, but times change. When it suits our politicians to make enemies of the Zulus, they won't hesitate, and if they need a pretext for war, they'll find one. Mark my words.'

'And if it does come to war?'

'We'll win, of course. But the Zulus will be a much tougher nut to crack than people imagine. They might not have sophisticated weapons, but they're superb physical specimens, incredibly disciplined and, most importantly, will be fighting on their home turf.'

George felt an odd mixture of pride and apprehension. He appreciated Laband's generous assessment of the Zulus' fighting prowess, but feared for their future. They were, after all, a relic of pre-colonial tribal Africa and stood little chance of thwarting the seemingly inexorable spread of white rule. And if it did end in war, particularly a war fought for such cynical motives, where would he stand?

With the end of the long run to Cape Town in sight, disaster struck. The shift in the weather was barely noticeable at first, but as the barometer continued to fall, and the wind rose accordingly, the crew feared the worst. First the sails were dropped, then the decks were cleared, and finally the hatches were battened down. By nightfall the ship was at the mercy of one of the worst southeast gales Captain Wilson could remember, a mountainous sea with waves a hundred feet high. To save the ship, Wilson altered course so that he could run before the wind. But while this had the effect of minimizing the yawing motion from side to side, it exaggerated the ship's speed as it plunged through and down each successive wave.

To George it felt as if the ship was hurtling towards the very bottom of the ocean, only to brought up short as the lowest point of the trough was struck with a sickening jolt. He lay on his bunk with legs and arms braced, to prevent him from being flung to the floor, where he had long since deposited his dinner. Hour after hour the storm raged on. George eventually fell asleep exhausted, and when he woke it seemed as if the howl of the wind was a little less shrill. Though still dark, he decided to risk leaving his cabin to check that Lucy was all right, and soon regretted his foolishness as the ship surfed down the face of yet another huge wave, sending him crashing into the door of the opposite cabin. Shaken but unhurt, he carried on his precarious way, clinging to the rail that ran alongside the stairs.

He eventually found his way to Lucy's door and knocked twice. No response. He tried the handle and found it unlocked. Lucy was lying face down on the bunk, wearing nothing but a petticoat, her skin a sickly green. In normal circumstances the sight of a scantily clad beauty would have set George's pulse racing. But these circumstances were anything but normal.

'It's me,' he said. 'Are you all right?'

She groaned in response. 'George, thank God you've come. I've never felt so ill. Please, sit with me a while?'

He sat on the bed next to her, holding her clammy hand. 'I can't stay for long. Someone might come and, in any case, I need to check on Emperor before the storm worsens.' He felt her grip tighten as if she would never let go. 'All right,' he conceded. 'I'll stay for a short time. Close your eyes and try and get some sleep.'

She looked so vulnerable lying there that, for a brief moment, George considered changing his mind about not taking her with him to Natal. But it would be hard enough making his own way in a strange land; Lucy was an encumbrance he could not afford. He stayed there, stroking her hair, until the evenness of her breathing told him she had fallen asleep. He gently loosened her grip and left the cabin. As he did so he heard the sound of footsteps at the end of the corridor.

He froze in the doorway, silently praying that the person would pass by without glancing in his direction. No such luck. 'Hart?' said Major Crealock. 'What are you doing here?'

'I've, um . . . I've been visiting a friend.'

'I didn't know you had any friends on board, and in second class too.'

George knew he was in a tight spot and tried to stay calm. 'She's . . . er . . . a recent acquaintance.'

'Not that girl I saw you talking to on deck?'

'Yes. I was just making sure she was all right.'

'Of course you were,' said Crealock, a knowing look on his face. 'None of my business, of course.'

'No. Well, if you'll excuse me,' said George, squeezing past Crealock on to the main stairway, 'I've got to check on my horse.'

As he continued down into the bowels of the ship, George cursed his bad luck and prayed that Crealock had swallowed his line about an on-board dalliance and was none the wiser. Had he, though?

From the main mess deck came the sound of men moaning and a smell George would never forget: a repulsive mixture of burning oil from the lamps, bilge water and vomit. George hurried by and soon found himself in the dark, fetid atmosphere of the horsedeck. The animals were whinnying piteously; all except Emperor, who was standing wide-eyed, trying desperately to keep his feet. The groom was at his side, adjusting the sling.

'Everything all right?' asked George.

'He's fine, Mr Hart,' said the groom. 'But we've already had to destroy one animal that fell and broke his leg, so I'm just tightening the sling to be sure.'

'Well done. And don't forget to give him regular doses of vinegar. Seasickness is the biggest killer.'

His duty done, George retraced his steps, each ten yards a hazardous procedure. The wind had risen again, and the passageways were empty but for a couple of green-looking crew members. George felt only relief as he at last regained his cabin and slumped wearily into his bunk. The ordeal, however, had just begun.

The gale lasted for two more days, and even when it was over, the traumatized passengers took some time to emerge from their respective billets. George was among the first to dine, his appetite merely sharpened by so long without food. And as he ate, with only a handful of the ship's officers for company, his thoughts turned to Lucy. How was she feeling? Would she forgive him for not returning to check on her? He had wanted to, more than once. But the chance encounter with Crea-lock had shaken him and left him unwilling to risk a repeat.

At dinner the following evening, with almost all the first-class passengers now well enough to attend, Captain Wilson announced that they would reach Cape Town on the morrow, and that if anyone wanted to see the famous Table Mountain they would need to be up at daybreak, because the early morning mist would obscure it for much of the day. George at once thought of Lucy, who would be disembarking when they docked, and realized it was his last opportunity to say goodbye to her. Was it worth the risk? He decided that it was.

He made it to her cabin unobserved and, sitting by her on the bunk, proceeded to declare his admiration for her as a person and his sadness that they would soon be parted. Fighting back tears, Lucy thanked him for all his support and wished him luck in Africa. 'But given the bond between us since the unfortunate shooting,' she added, 'I don't understand why we can't pool our resources and travel together.'

George repeated his old argument about needing to travel light, and not wanting to be encumbered by a woman, but even he sounded unconvinced. 'I'll be honest with you, Lucy,' he said at last. 'We've been through a fair bit together, and I owe you that. Truth is, I only have enough money to keep myself. I know it sounds selfish, but there it is.'

'It is selfish. I won't be a financial burden to you, if that's what you're worried about. I can earn my own keep.'

'I'm sure you can. But there are things I need to do alone. Things connected to my past.'

'What things?'

'It's a very long and . . . involved story.'

'I'm not in any hurry.'

'All right,' said George after a pause, 'but I must leave before sun-up.'

George was reticent at first, and gave only the barest outline of his childhood and time at Sandhurst. But the more he talked about events since then, the more he realized there were issues he needed to resolve. Could he, for example, ever really forgive his mother for deceiving him? How did he feel about his Zulu blood? And did he really believe his military career was over?

Once again, Lucy showed an intelligence that belied her upbringing, quickly seeing George's dilemma. 'You talk about going to South Africa to claim your inheritance and make your fortune, and maybe you will. But from all you've said it's obvious that your real interest lies with the army. Why, your face lights up at the mere mention of a war.'

'I don't know about that,' said George, reddening. 'Anyway, that's all in the past. My only plan now is to meet my uncle and see which way the land lies in Natal. What about you? Have you thought about what you'll do?'

'Well, first I'll see if I can get a job in Cape Town,' she said, 'and if that goes well, and I manage to save some money, I might see what Kimberley has to offer.'

'Good idea. There are bound to be opportunities for a woman with beauty and resource like you. And, you never know, we might meet again in Kimberley.'

'I hope so,' said Lucy, a thin smile on her face. 'Now you'd better go. It's almost dawn.'

George leant forward to kiss her cheek, but she turned at the last and their lips met. There was something about the urgency of the kiss that made him think again about leaving her, but he convinced himself there were things he needed to do alone.

Her eyes were still closed as he rose from the bunk. 'Goodbye, Lucy,' he said, holding the door slightly ajar.

She had buried her face in her hands and her reply, muffled by sobs, was almost inaudible.

That evening, after a little under four weeks at sea, the SS *American* steamed into Table Bay and dropped anchor opposite Cape Town. George had never seen a more spectacular setting for a port, its elegant seafront framed by the steeply sided, flat-topped peak known as Table Mountain. As bumboats swarmed around the ship, bringing supplies and news, he stood alone on the poopdeck, transfixed by the view; and there he remained until the red glow of the setting sun had receded behind the mountain.

In the morning a handful of passengers disembarked, Lucy and General Thesiger among them. The general and the rest of the soldiers were going straight to the front, and would leave the ship for good further up the coast at East London; but as the *American* was not scheduled to depart for another two days, Thesiger was taking the opportunity to call on Sir Bartle Frere, the Governor of Cape Colony, at his official residence on the outskirts of Cape Town.

George watched from the side of the ship as the lifeboat edged closer to the shore. He was desperate for Lucy to turn and acknowledge him one last time with a smile or a wave. But she did not, and he eventually lost sight of her amidst the bustle of the port.

'Such a shame,' said a voice beside him. He turned and found himself face to face with Major Crealock.

'What are you talking about?' said George sharply.

'You and your friend having to part. It's too sad.'

'I'm sure I don't know what you mean?'

'What I mean,' said Crealock, 'is that you and the young lady boarded separately at Plymouth and yet you obviously know each other. Quite a coincidence, don't you think, given that the authorities at Plymouth were looking for a young couple in connection with the murder of that private detective?'

George could feel the colour rising in his cheeks. 'We met on board.'

'So you say. I wonder what Captain Wilson would make of it all.'

'Now hold on a minute. You've got entirely the wrong end of the stick.'

'Have I? You're sure about that?' said Crealock, before stalking off. The note of menace in his voice had been obvious.

George's instinct was to get off the ship as quickly as possible. But the more he thought about it, the more he realized that Crealock did not actually *know* anything. Having seen George coming out of Lucy's cabin, he had put two and two together and come up with four. But where was the proof that either of them was involved in Thompson's death? Crealock did not have any. And with Lucy ashore it would be even harder to link them to the murder scene. The best course, George decided, was to ignore Crealock and continue with his trip as planned. Anything else would invite suspicion.

That evening, Thesiger returned to the ship; the news, as far as the officers were concerned, was far from welcome. After five months of trying, General Cunyng-hame had at last managed to clear the rebels out of the Perie Bush, a trackless terrain in the Eastern Cape, by using mixed columns of British troops, sailors, colonial volunteers, police and friendly natives. The rebel leaders were trapped; no further resistance was expected. That, at least, was the latest information from Cunynghame's headquarters at King William's Town.

Thesiger was unconvinced. 'Mark my words, gentle-men,' he announced to his staff at dinner. 'When a general says to his successor that the war is over and you needn't have bothered turning up, he's doing it to save face. Truth is, until Kreli, Sandilli and the other rebel leaders are actually in the bag, the fighting will continue. So don't look too glum!'

It was easier said than done, particularly for Captain Gossett. 'I can't believe I've come all this way and the fighting's as good as over,' he told George with a shake of his head as the ship weighed anchor the following morn-ing.

'That's not how your chief sees it.'

'No. But I fear it's wishful thinking. He's as determined as the rest of us to make a name for himself. I know it's hard to believe, but I haven't been on the warpath since the Mutiny. Twenty-three years a soldier and just a single step in rank. This might be my last opportunity to win a brevet.'

'I wouldn't fret. Colonel Wood seems to think the Zulus will be your next opponents.'

'Does he now?' said Gossett, his features brightening. 'That would be a war worth fighting. The Zulus are seen as the most formidable opponents in southern Africa.'

'Yes,' said George, 'and they're not called the Black Spartans for nothing. I'd be careful what you wish for.'

# 7

## East London, Cape Colony, 4 March 1878

The wind howled in the rigging as the helmsman fought to keep the ship from turning broadside to the high rollers that kept coming, at ever-shorter intervals, from the northeast. The sails had been furled, leaving the ship on steam power alone, but the combination of a south-west current and a southeaster breeze was rolling the ship so violently that it seemed only a matter of time before the yards went under.

'I'm sorry, General Thesiger,' said Captain Wilson, his double-breasted pea-jacket glistening with a fine sea spray. 'There's not a hope of landing you in this wind. We'll have to bear away until the weather improves.'

'You don't understand,' said Thesiger, peering anxiously through the saloon windows towards the white buildings of East London, less than half a mile distant. 'I must land today. The war's coming to an end and it wouldn't do to miss it altogether.'

'That's as may be. But there's a sandbank between us and the port and it's far too dangerous to cross it in these conditions. The surfboat is useless in high winds and I can't risk the lifeboat. You'd never make it.'

By morning the wind had dropped sufficiently for an

attempt to land General Thesiger and his military secretary, Crealock, by lifeboat. Captain Wilson was still against the idea, citing the strength of the current, but Thesiger insisted.

Sensing some drama, the ship's company gathered on the main deck to watch the two officers descend by the stern ladder to the lifeboat below. Before Crealock climbed over the side, he sought out George from the throng of onlookers. 'I just wanted to say,' murmured the major, 'that your secret's safe with me.'

George watched Crealock depart with a mixture of loathing and relief. He had never been more pleased to see the back of someone, and could not help wishing for some terrible accident to befall the man. It soon seemed as if he might get his wish. As the little boat approached the foaming line of water that marked the sandbar, its crew of rowers were fighting hard to keep it from turning side-on to the waves that followed each other in quick succession.

'They'll never make it,' muttered George with a shake of his head.

At that moment, just yards from the bar, the rudder slipped from the helmsman's grasp and the lifeboat turned broadside to the waves. 'Right yourself, you fools,' shouted Gossett. 'Before it's too late!'

They could see the crew, all hard-drinking, foul-mouthed men from the slums of Cape Town, pulling desperately on their oars to bring the boat around. Thesiger and Crealock were sitting towards the rear of the boat with shoulders hunched, powerless to avert the approaching calamity. The next wave was just feet away, a huge roller that threatened to swamp the flimsy craft. It struck the rear quarter of the lifeboat and sent it hurtling over the bar. His view obscured by the foam and spray, George held his breath. A part of him wanted the craft to sink, so that Crealock would be silenced for ever; but the others would die too, and he did not wish for that. So when, miraculously, the lifeboat bobbed back into view, its crew rowing hard for the shore, George joined the huge cheer that rose spontaneously from the watching passengers and crew. It died in his throat as Crealock celebrated his escape from danger with a dismissive wave of his hand.

With Thesiger and Crealock safely ashore, preparations were made to disembark the remaining soldiers and their kit by the safer, but more laborious means of the surfboat, an eighty-ton lighter with a central hatchway. Again George was a fascinated onlooker as the first batch of men and equipment was passed down the side of the ship, by means of the stern ladder and a derrick, and into the hold of the surfboat, amidst a hubbub of shouts and oaths. With its cargo safely stowed, the surfboat was towed by steam-tug to a buoy, where it picked up a hawser made from coconut husk, one end anchored inside the bar and the other out to sea. The hawser was then passed over sheaves in two posts on the deck, fore and aft, and secured with iron pins.

'Haul away!' hollered the surfboat's white skipper, and his ten-man crew, their naked black bodies shiny with sweat and spray, began to heave the boat towards the shore, hand over hand along the hawser. At the bar the surfboat seemed to stop with a jolt, as if it had struck sand. But the next wave swept it over into the smooth water beyond.

Among the last batch to disembark was Captain Gossett. 'Goodbye,' he said, giving George's shoulder a squeeze. 'I hope we meet again.'

'I'm sure we shall,' replied George.

Gossett waved as he disappeared over the side.

The sick were next: three cases of fever, a corporal with a broken arm and Thomas, his pale face and scrawny frame proof that he had yet to recover from the flogging. Despite this, he was in full uniform and carrying his pack and slung rifle.

'Need any help?' asked George.

'Thankee, Mr Hart,' said Thomas, using George's arm for support as he eased on to the top of the stern ladder. 'Much obliged.'

'Best of luck, Thomas, and don't forget to give my regards to Second Lieutenant Morgan.'

'I won't. Goodbye and God bless you for all your kindness.'

George had read somewhere that you could smell Africa long before you saw it. But only once, as the SS *American* was steaming in clear blue water off the West Coast of Africa, had the distinctive scent of palm oil and decayed vegetation wafted over the deck. Now, as the ship gently rose and fell in the evening swell off Durban, he detected a different smell: that of wood-smoke, from the hundreds of fires the natives of Natal had lit to cook their mealie porridge. It was a strangely reassuring odour and, like the vast canopy of sky above him, made him think, Yes, maybe this land is truly in my blood after all. He was anxious to get ashore, but, as at East London, the presence of strong currents and a sandbar meant that all passengers had to land by day. He consoled himself with the knowledge that, after a month at sea, one extra day was little hardship.

Next morning the sound of barked orders and scurrying feet woke George from a deep sleep. With the unloading of the final passengers and cargo clearly under way, he quickly dressed and made his way down to the horsedeck. Emperor welcomed him with a whinny. Despite the rigours of the long journey the horse looked surprisingly fit, his chestnut coat glowing with health. 'You've looked after him well,' George told the groom, handing him a crown. 'But we'll both be glad to see dry land. Can you get him ready for the derrick?'

'At once, Mr Hart.'

The groom led Emperor out of his narrow stall and under the open hatchway, where a canvas sling was dangling from the derrick. The other horses had already been dropped into a waiting lighter. Emperor was the last to go. The groom attached the sling and gave a signal to a sailor peering down through the hatchway. He, in turn, told the crew of the derrick to haul away. Slowly but surely, Emperor's limp form, his hooves almost touching, was raised out of the hold until it hung motionless above the deck.

George, meanwhile, had reached the poopdeck, from where he watched anxiously as the derrick swung Emperor over the side. Three times they tried and failed to lower him into the lighter's hold, the swell spoiling their aim. On the fourth they succeeded, though the lighter was rocking violently. George breathed a sigh of relief and returned to his cabin to collect his luggage and the revolver from under his pillow.

With everyone aboard, the lighter was towed by steam-tugs through a gap in the sandbar and on towards Durban Harbour, where it was tied to a wharf thronged with people. George marvelled at this first sight of Natal's multi-hued population: a white harbour official, in blue coat with brass buttons, waving his clipboard and shouting the odds; barefooted tars swarming over the various vessels; prostitutes of all colours, in various states of undress, hawking their wares from windows and door-ways; redcoats with even redder faces; and a host of half-naked black stevedores, some wearing tribal kilts, others rough trousers, but all jabbering away in a plethora of dialects as they carted goods to and fro. George was pleased to catch some words in Zulu, a reward for his study with the trader Laband.

With the sun already high in a cobalt-blue sky, and the heat oppressive, George retired to the shelter of a quayside bar. A glass of chilled porter in hand, he watched as a crane lifted the heavy cargo and horses out of the lighter. One horse panicked, its frightened kicks breaking the rear of the sling. Luckily the remaining canvas held long enough for it to reach solid ground. Emperor was next, and no sooner had he been deposited on the quayside, his flanks still trembling with fear, than George was there to soothe him. He had been advised not to ride the horse for at least twenty-four hours, to give him a chance to recover from the voyage, so instead he tacked him up and led him the mile or so into Durban proper.

After a sleepless night in the spectacularly misnamed

Grand Hotel on Smith Street – its only pretension to grandeur being the size of its cockroaches – George packed his kit into two saddlebags, collected Emperor from the nearby livery stable and, map of Natal in hand, began the fifty-mile ride inland to his uncle Patrick's farm near Pietermaritzburg. It was early, and few people were about as he left the environs of Durban at a trot. The road climbed steadily through rolling country, known locally as the Valley of a Thousand Hills, but Emperor kept a good pace, happy to stretch his legs after so long inactive. George was struck by the barrenness of the terrain, its red soil relieved here and there by tufts of yellow grass and the green and brown of the occasional acacia thorn tree.

At noon George stopped by the side of a stream to eat a lunch of bread and cheese, while Emperor grazed nearby. It was a beautiful shaded spot, nestled between high brown hills, and as he lay back, head on hands, George reflected on how relieved he was to be free of Crealock, the ship and all association with the dead private detective. But a nagging question remained: why had he refused to let Lucy accompany him beyond Cape Town?

He had his practical reasons, of course, like not having enough money and needing to travel light. Yet neither was insuperable. Was it not instead, he asked himself, a simple case of snobbery, viz. that he was embarrassed to be seen in the company of a former domestic servant, even in South Africa? And what about the term in his father's legacy that stated he had to marry respectably? Did that also play a part, in the sense that he knew if he fell in love with Lucy he might forfeit the only portion of the legacy he had a chance of winning? He feared it had; it would, he knew, be hard enough keeping his African blood a secret. This fleeting moment of self-knowledge made him ashamed. For one thing was not in doubt: he missed Lucy and thought about her often. There was, however, little to be done to make amends in the short term. He had no way of contacting her, and if they met again it would owe more to luck than design.

Preoccupied with such melancholic thoughts, George did not hear the silent approach of three black men, naked but for their monkey-skin loincloths. He had risen to his feet and was tightening Emperor's girth when he felt the slight prick of a bladed weapon in his ribs. 'Don't move, white man,' said a deep voice behind him.

George froze, his hands still on the girth. 'Who are you?'

The man behind him snorted. 'You hear that, boys? The white man wants to know who we are. You must be new to this country or you would know that all black men are called "Kaffirs", and not as a compliment. Most of us are Zulus and proud of it.'

George had read about the Natal Kaffirs, mostly political refugees from Zululand. The colony contained almost a quarter of a million of them, compared to just 20,000 whites, and to keep them under control the authorities had confined them in locations under their traditional chiefs. These men had obviously broken out and were planning to rob him, or worse.

'I too am Zulu,' said George in an attempt to find some common ground with his assailants.

'*You* – a Zulu?' said the man, laughing. 'I don't think so.'

'No, it's true,' said George, slowly turning round with his arms raised.

Facing him were three young warriors, each clutching an oval shield and a vicious-looking spear with a long, flat blade. The warrior closest to George, in the centre, was powerfully built with a chiselled, handsome face; he wore an elaborate headdress of leopardskin and widow-bird plumes, and was obviously in charge. 'So tell me, white man, how you came to have Zulu blood.'

'My maternal grandmother was the daughter of a chief called Xongo kaMuziwento.'

'Her name?'

'Ngqumbazi.'

'I know of her. She and her father accompanied Mpande into exile, as did my own grandfather. But unlike them, he never went back.'

'Why?'

'Because he quarrelled with Xongo over my grandmother and was warned never to return to Zululand. So, you see, your kin is directly responsible for my miserable existence in Natal, a despised Kaffir who will never set eyes on the land of his ancestors beyond the White Mfolosi River.'

George closed his eyes and sighed. *Of all the Zulu refugees in Natal, I have to bump into the one whose ancestor was an enemy of my own. Just my luck.*

'Check his horse for money,' barked the leader.

As one of the warriors began to rifle through his saddlebags, George realized he would have to act fast or he would lose everything. Slowly, he began to move his right hand towards his waist, where, beneath his shirt, he had secreted his grandfather's revolver.

The leader saw him, out of the corner of his eye, and shouted, 'Keep your hands up.'

George ignored him and made a grab for the gun. As his hand clasped the butt, the leader spun round and lunged with his spear, its flat blade penetrating a loose fold in George's shirt but missing his flesh.

George aimed his pistol and pulled the trigger. Nothing. It had misfired. By the time he had pulled back the hammer for another shot, the third warrior was upon him, a crashing blur of bone and steel and muscle. As he fell, George fired, the ball smashing into the warrior's chest and sending him spinning to the ground. He turned to face the leader but he and the other warrior had vanished into the wood. With adrenalin coursing through him, George loosed off another shot into the sky to speed them on their way. Then he checked the fallen warrior for signs of life. There were none. With the danger over, he looked down and saw that his pistol hand was shaking violently. Even killing in self-defence did not make it any easier.

He walked over to where Emperor was tethered. His ears were pricked, but otherwise he seemed unruffled, the benefit of having been trained to ignore the sound of firearms. George checked his saddlebags, the contents of which were strewn on the ground on either side of the horse. Everything was there apart from the pouch containing his money. 'No!' he howled, head in hands.

He needed that money. It was all he had in the world. How would he buy a stake in a diamond mine now? How would he eat? After all he had been through, it was too much to take and he sank to the ground, sobbing with frustration. Only gradually did it occur to him that it could have been worse. He still had his health and his horse, and an uncle not far distant who might provide food and shelter, and even some money if his share in the farm was still worth anything. It was in this more positive frame of mind that he covered the corpse as best as he could with earth and leaves, remounted Emperor, and continued up the road to Pietermaritzburg.

The sun was fast receding behind a flat-topped hill, its crown of red rocks glowing pink from within, as George covered the last half-mile of veldt that separated him from the isolated farmhouse. Watching him from the veranda that ran the length of the single-storeyed, brick-built dwelling was a lone man in an easy chair. It could only be his uncle, but George found it hard to make out the man's features in the failing light. He dismounted, tied Emperor to a hitching post and approached the veranda. 'Stay right where you are!' said the man.

George was close enough to see the black muzzle of a rifle, pointing right at him. He stopped and raised his hands, palm outwards. 'Don't shoot. My name's George Hart.'

'I don't know anyone of that name.'

'I'm Emma's boy.'

'Well, I'll be damned,' said the man, lowering the rifle. 'And to think I almost shot you. I'm sorry. But it's not a good idea to arrive at a farm unannounced. I've lost a lot of stock to thieves and you can't be too careful.'

'Of course. I understand.'

The man rose, leant the rifle against the wall and came down the steps to greet George.

'I'm your uncle Patrick,' he said, shaking his hand enthusiastically. 'It's good to meet you. Come inside and I'll get one of the boys to see to your horse.'

George retrieved his gear from Emperor's back and followed his uncle inside. The main room was spacious enough for both a kitchen and a sitting area, but its bare walls and basic furniture made the absence of a feminine touch all too obvious. 'You can use the spare room,' said Patrick. 'Supper's in twenty minutes.'

It was the first opportunity that George had had to study his uncle, albeit by the light of a paraffin lamp. They looked remarkably similar, though his uncle was noticeably darker and his hair a little wirier. He was also more heavily built, with flecks of grey in his hair and beard, and crow's feet at the corner of his eyes, the legacy of a lifetime squinting in the sun. But his uncle's amused response to his request for a lavatory – 'There's a spade by the door' – was proof enough they shared the same dry sense of humour.

Supper was eaten at a rough wooden table with benches on either side. It was a delicious beef stew, and George wolfed it down hungrily. Only when he had finished a second helping, washed down with a cup of maize beer, did his uncle ask him for details of what he was doing in Africa.

'It's a long story,' said George with a rueful smile. 'But suffice to say my African blood played its part. Would you believe that my mother only told me about it, and your existence, a few weeks ago?'

'Yes, I would. Emma was always embarrassed about her African relatives, even as a young girl. She and I were left this farm, but she's never shown any interest in it beyond asking for her share of the profits. Not that it's made any of those for a while. So if you've come here hoping to claim her inheritance, you can forget it.'

'Ah,' said George with a rueful expression, 'I was worried you might say that. Truth is, I've had quite a run of bad luck recently and, to top it all, I was held up by Kaffirs on the way here and relieved of what little money I had left.'

After George had explained, his uncle whistled and said, 'It's lucky you're so handy with Father's pistol. What did you do with the body?'

'I covered it with leaves and left it.'

'That's hardly going to discourage scavengers, but no matter. Probably best not to report it. You'll only get embroiled in legal matters, and I can't imagine his accomplices will make a fuss.'

'Is this sort of thing typical?'

'It's getting that way. The Kaffirs resent being confined to locations on the poorest-quality land, not above a tenth of the total, while the far less numerous white settlers own the rest. And the recent doubling of the hut tax, which applies to all dwellings occupied by blacks, has only increased the bad feeling. The white settlers, on the other hand, are terrified that one day the Kaffirs will rise and murder them in their beds.'

'How do you fit in?'

'Well, I'm exempt from the hut tax, if that's what you mean,' said Patrick, smiling. 'I try to keep my head down and stay out of politics. Even so, it's hard to get by. The farm was valuable once, but I've had to sell so much land just to balance the books that it's virtually worthless. I still graze a few cattle, as doubtless you noticed, but for much of the year I'm forced to work as a farmhand on other properties to make ends meet. You're welcome to stay here and help out for as long as you like. I can't pay you, though.'

'I appreciate your candour, Uncle. I won't say I'm not disappointed; I am. But it may be for the best. I'm not sure I'm cut out to be a farmer. I'd appreciate it, however, if you'd put me up for a short time while I find my feet. I intend, at some point, to head over to Kimberley and try my luck in the mines.'

His uncle frowned. 'I'm not sure I'd recommend that, George. A friend of mine went over there in seventy-two, just after word of the diamond-field discovery in Griqualand leaked out. Sold his house, packed all his belongings in an ox-cart and just took off. But, like thousands of other prospectors, he found nothing but flies, squalor and heartbreak. He stayed until his money ran out and he was forced to sell his three claims. With nothing to come back to, he blew his brains out.'

'I'm sorry to hear that, Uncle. But plenty of others have had better luck. I read about one penniless English prospector who found a stone worth thirty thousand pounds.'

'I'm not saying it's impossible. Just that the odds are against you. For every good-luck story there are thousands who leave the fields destitute, if they leave at all. I wouldn't want that to happen to you.'

George smiled thinly. 'Me neither. But it's not even an option until I've got some stake money together. In the meantime I've half a mind to visit Zululand and find out more about my grandmother and her family. Do you know if she's still alive?'

'I don't. But I know some of her brothers are. The eldest, Sihayo kaXongo, is a member of King Cetshwayo's council and one of his most trusted advisors. He rules a vast swathe of land on the left bank of the Buffalo River, beyond a ford known as Rorke's Drift. He's a man of considerable influence in Zululand.'

'Would it be possible to meet him?'

'I can't see why not, though you might have to wait until the Boundary Commission has drafted its report. It meets at Rorke's Drift in a few days and Sihayo is one of the Zulu delegates.'

'What is this Boundary Commission?'

His uncle rolled his eyes. 'I'm not the best person to ask. What I do know is that the commission has been set up by the Natal government to arbitrate on the border dispute between Zululand and the Transvaal. But given that the Transvaal is now a British colony, it's asking a lot to expect the Natal commissioners to be unbiased.'

'And Sihayo is advising this commission?'

'Yes. But if you want to know more, you need to talk to my neighbour John Colenso, bishop of Natal.'

'The same Bishop Colenso who wrote the Zulu-English dictionary?'

'The very same.'

'Well, I'll be damned. I studied the dictionary on the voyage over. I also read a bit about the bishop. Wasn't he forced to relinquish his pastoral duties for a time in the sixties?'

'He was indeed. He clashed with his superiors over doctrine. But he's a determined character and was eventually reinstated by the Privy Council in England. Quite right, too. He's done great work in the colony since arriving in the fifties.'

'Such as?'

'Well, for a start he's built five missions, including one in Zululand itself, and a church in every European settlement in the colony. And all the money to pay for it was raised by him in Britain. He's also a keen advocate for the rights of Africans in general, and Zulus in particular, and gets on well with King Cetshwayo. The Zulus call him "Sobantu", which means "Father of His People".'

'I can't imagine any of this makes him popular with his fellow white settlers.'

'No. He and his family are ostracized by most of the leading families, who regard him as a traitor. He's certainly a thorn in the side of the Natal government. Would you like to meet him?'

'Certainly.'

'Good. We'll ride over tomorrow.'

# 8

The short ride to Bishopstowe passed mostly in silence. The weather was crisp and clear, the dew still glistening on the grassy slopes that lay between George's uncle's house and the bishop's official residence. The track followed the base of Natal's own Table Mountain, and in the early morning light its rocky outcrop seemed to have taken on an aspect of deep ultramarine shadows, wreathed in white mists. George was entranced.

'Now you know,' said his uncle, 'why the bishop chose to build his house so far from his cathedral in Pietermaritzburg. And why he refuses to move his study to a quieter and more convenient part of the house that doesn't have a view of the mountain.'

As they crested the next rise, Bishopstowe came into view. It was a substantial two-storey brick-built house with a steeply pitched roof of thatch and a sprinkling of pretty dormer windows. A raised veranda, covered in creepers, ran the length of the building; lemon trees dotted the front lawn.

They dismounted at the front gate and handed their reins to a young black servant. As they reached the veranda steps, the front door was opened by a tall man with oval spectacles, his wide handsome face framed by a shaggy mane of white hair and a magnificent set of whiskers. He reminded George of an Old Testament prophet, and his black clothes and white linen neckcloth left no doubt as to his identity.

George's uncle spoke first. 'Hello, John. I've brought my nephew, George Hart, to meet you.'

'I didn't know you had a nephew,' said the bishop, shaking hands with George, 'and such a fine-looking one too. Well, do come in.'

They took coffee in the drawing room, the mountain clearly visible through the large bow window. The bishop seemed fascinated by George's life story, and asked a stream of questions. Unused to such directness from a stranger, George tried to change the subject, but the bishop was insistent. 'I find it quite propitious,' he said at last, 'that a British officer with Zulu blood should arrive in Africa at such a time.'

'*Former* officer,' corrected George, coffee cup in hand. 'But why propitious?'

'Because, my dear George,' said the bishop, 'there are many in Natal, the Cape and now the Transvaal who are pushing for war with the Zulus.'

'So I gathered from a particularly obnoxious Natal businessman on the way out. He talked about the need to exploit Zululand's natural resources.'

'There are some who think like that. But the sheer proximity of a powerful black state like Zululand, with its forty thousand disciplined warriors, is enough to make any settler nervous, and senior officials like Sir Bartle Frere and our own Sir Theophilus Shepstone, now Governor of the Transvaal, play on these fears. Their true motives for conquering Zululand are, of course, far more cynical. For Frere it would bring confederation one step closer; for Shepstone, who tends to take a more Natal-centric view, it would solve this colony's overpopulation and security issues – internal and external – at a stroke.'

'Why is Frere so hell-bent on achieving confederation?'

'The oldest motive of all, George, and that's personal gain. If successful, he's been promised the first governor-generalship of South Africa, a peerage and a sharp hike in his salary. Without those incentives he never would have agreed to accept what, for an imperial administrator of his stature, is a minor post. As Governor of Bombay he was master of thirty million souls; here, even in his dual role as Governor of the Cape *and* High Commissioner for Native Affairs in South Africa, his subjects are fewer than two million.'

George shook his head, though he was not in the least surprised by Frere's motives. 'What about Shepstone?'

'He's different. As a local he acts in what he sees as the best interests of the Natal settlers. But the net result will be the same.'

'And if the Zulus are conquered, what will become of them?' asked George.

'They'll be forced on to reservations and their best land given to white settlers, as happened here. For years I believed that Shepstone was acting in the best interests of the local tribes, and that his "Native Policy" would allow both the retention of old tribal structures and, for those who wished to de-tribalize, an easy integration into the white man's way of life. But, as time went on, it became obvious that his only real aim was to ensure that he, as Secretary for Native Affairs, had complete control over the blacks. It is nothing more or less than despotism and will surely be extended to the Zulus.'

'So now you understand, George,' said his uncle, 'why your appearance is propitious. A man with military experience and a foot in both camps, so to speak. You could be very useful to the bishop.'

George turned back to the bishop. 'I don't mean to dampen your hopes, but I can't see how *I* could help. I was only in the army for five minutes, and my knowledge of South Africa in general, and the Zulus in particular, is limited to what I read during the voyage out here.'

'Yes, yes, I know all that,' said the bishop. 'But you're also related to one of King Cetshwayo's chief advisors, and you could prove extremely useful as a go-between.'

'Let me get this straight. You're suggesting I act, to put it bluntly, as your spy?'

'Not so much a spy,' said a female voice from the back of the room, 'more a supporter of Father's humanitarian mission.'

George turned to see a handsome, dark-haired woman in the doorway. She was simply dressed in a long, floor-length skirt and high-necked blouse, its ruffled collar and neck brooch the only slight concessions to fashion. Her hair was pulled back in a chignon, revealing a wide, almost masculine face, with large blue eyes and a sensual mouth. She appeared to George to be in her mid-twenties, but could have been older.

'Forgive my daughter's intrusion,' said the bishop with an indulgent smile. 'She has an unfortunate habit of listening in on other people's conversation. But I'm partly to blame. I've encouraged all my children to support my work, and none has taken to the task with more gusto than Fanny.' He turned to his daughter. 'My dear, come and meet Patrick's nephew, George Hart.'

As the two shook hands, George was struck by the bold, self-assured manner with which Fanny held his gaze.

'I only caught the tail-end of your discussion,' she said to George, 'but I agree with Papa: your connection to Chief Sihayo could prove very useful.'

'Don't think of it as spying,' said the bishop. 'You'll simply be opening up a reliable means of communication between us and Cetshwayo that might, just might, help to avert war.'

'How exactly?'

'Have you heard of the Boundary Commission, which is due to meet presently?'

'My uncle mentioned it but didn't elaborate.'

'Well, it's quite simple, really. The Zulus and the Boers of the Transvaal have long disputed a large wedge of land bisected by the Blood River. The Boers claim that the land was ceded to them by the Zulus; Cetshwayo has always denied this and, until recently, the Natal authorities tended to take his side. But the British annexation of the Transvaal last year has changed everything. The Boers' border dispute has become Britain's, and when negotiations failed towards the end of last year, Sir Theophilus declared his support for the Boer claim. That's when our lieutenant governor, Sir Henry Bulwer, stepped in and suggested a Boundary Commission. Cetshwayo agreed and it's due to meet at Rorke's Drift in a couple of days.'

'I don't see the problem,' said George. 'Surely all parties will abide by the decision of an independent commission?'

'They might, if it was truly independent. But it isn't. It's made up of three nominees of the Natal government, one of whom is Shepstone's brother, John. Fortunately one of the other two commissioners is Colonel Anthony Durnford of the Royal Engineers, a man of high principle and a good friend.' The bishop looked pointedly at his daughter, causing her to blush.

He continued, 'The unknown quantity is the third commissioner, Michael Gallwey, our attorney-general. If he sides with the Shepstones, and it's likely he will, the verdict will go against the Zulus and might well provoke a war. So you understand our eagerness for you to make contact with your cousin, Chief Sihayo. He has Cetshwayo's ear and could prevent an overreaction to the commission's report.'

'Yes, I see what you mean. But you have to understand that, until very recently, I was an officer in the British Army, and this sort of work might be considered by some to be disloyal.'

The bishop's brow furrowed. 'Disloyal to whom, exactly? You, more than any Briton, should sympathize with the Zulus' plight.'

'I do . . . up to a point. But I know next to nothing about my own Zulu kin, let alone the Zulus as a people.'

'Well, here's your chance to find out more. And you wouldn't be doing it for nothing. I'd cover all your expenses and throw in a small salary.'

All along George had been tempted by the offer, despite his conflict of loyalties, because he was keen to meet his Zulu kin and excited by the cloak-and-dagger adventure of it all. He also liked the idea of helping to avert an unjust war. But the clincher was the money. 'In that case,' he said, 'I'd be a fool not to accept. What's the best way to make contact?'

'In person, of course, though you'll need a cover. Any ideas, Patrick?'

'He could go as a trader.'

'Yes, I think that would work admirably,' said the bishop. 'We'll kit you out with a team of oxen and a wagon loaded with goods, and you can tell anyone who asks that you're going to Zululand to trade for cattle and hides. People do it all the time.'

'Does it matter that I've no experience handling oxen?' asked George.

'Not in the slightest. You'll have a driver and a team leader, a *voorloper*, to do that for you. As the proprietor, or transport-rider, as we call him, your job is to ride alongside the wagon and keep an eye on things.'

'I think I could do that. So when do I start?'

'I admire your zeal, George, but you'll have to wait until the Boundary Commission has prepared its report.'

'And how long will that take?'

'A month, maybe two.'

'That long? Well, at least it gives me plenty of time to prepare.'

'Just do your best,' said the bishop, 'that's all we ask.'

'I will – but I can't promise anything.'

'We wouldn't expect you to,' said Fanny, beaming. 'It's just nice to know you're on our side. We don't forget our friends.'

\* \* \*

The ride home passed mainly in silence. George was preoccupied with the rapid turn of events, and strangely excited by the task he had been set, its difficulty notwithstanding. He was much taken with the Colensos, as his uncle had known he would be. After coffee, Mrs Colenso had made a brief appearance, as had her two remaining daughters, Harriette and Agnes, and all three had charmed George with their wit and forthright opinions. But if Fanny took after her mother in looks, she had also inherited her father's charisma and moral certainty. George had never met such an intoxicating combination of vitality and goodness, and, in spite of his feelings for Lucy, was thoroughly smitten. The clincher was when Fanny had blushed at the mention of Durnford as a 'good friend'. George had felt oddly irritated, even jealous, and yet he barely knew Fanny, and next to nothing about Durnford. He decided to rectify the matter as his uncle's homestead came into view.

'Tell me about Colonel Durnford, Uncle. What sort of a man is he?'

'I've only met him a couple of times, at Bishopstowe, and he struck me as a fine, soldierly looking fellow. But he hasn't had the smoothest career. He was in command of the Bushman's River Pass debacle when three men of the Natal Carbineers were killed trying to prevent the Hlubi tribe from crossing the Drakensburg into Basutoland, and many of Natal's leading lights have never forgiven him for implying that some Carbineers performed less than heroically. But the Colensos have never followed the herd, as you may have gathered, and they all think extremely highly of Durnford, particularly Fanny.'

'Yes, I noticed. But is Durnford not old enough to be her father?'

'I suppose he is. He must be nearing fifty, though he could pass for a much younger man.'

'And Fanny?'

'She's twenty-seven, so marriage to a man like Durnford might suit her very well.'

'You talk as if she's almost over the hill,' said George sharply.

His uncle gave a hearty chuckle. 'You know as well as I do, George, that few women who are still unmarried at thirty ever get married. But fret you not because, as things stand, Fanny and Durnford could never wed.'

'Why ever not?'

'Because, my dear George, Durnford is already married. He has a wife and child in England, though he has not seen them for many years.'

'Is that so?' said George, the trace of a smile on his lips.

Over the coming weeks, as George waited impatiently for the Boundary Commission to complete its report, he helped his uncle out on the farm and visited Bishopstowe as often as he could. He spent many hours discussing the internal workings of the colony with Bishop Colenso and, slowly but surely, his sympathy towards the plight of all Africans under white rule grew stronger. According to the bishop, the white settlers were even talking about seizing the land set aside for the locations, hence the popular support for a war against the Zulus that would, if successful, gain more territory. Everyone at Bishopstowe was opposed to such wickedness, and George felt himself in agreement.

The most passionate denunciator of official policy towards the colony's African population was, however, not the bishop but his daughter Fanny. This energy and essential goodness made her even more attractive in George's eyes and he spent as much time with her as he could. She seemed to reciprocate his feelings, and many were the times, as they rode together, or were neighbours at dinner, that her hand strayed on to his forearm. He tried more than once to declare his high regard for her, but she always prevented him, by making a joke or changing the subject. She was fascinated by his mixed-race heritage and asked him endless questions, only some of which he knew the answers to; others he preferred to ignore. 'My mother was – is – an actress; I never knew my father,' he responded to a query about his parents. 'What more is there to say?'

On other subjects he was more forthcoming. When asked by Fanny, during a long afternoon ride in brilliant sunshine, how he felt about his African ancestry, he replied, 'I suppose I'm rather proud. It was shock finding out, of course. But I'd always been the odd one out growing up, on account of my dark skin, and at least now I know the truth. The Zulus sound such a noble, impressive race, and their military exploits speak for themselves. My only worry is that if it does come to war I might be forced to choose sides. It's not a decision I ever want to face.'

George was almost grateful when the deliberations of the Boundary Commission dragged on through autumn and into winter. In late June he learnt that the commission had finally completed its report. But nothing had reached the press by the time George was called to an urgent meeting at Bishopstowe in mid-July.

Fanny was waiting at the front door. 'George, it's so good to see you,' she said, kissing him on the cheek.

'And you,' said a smiling George. 'What news?'

'Come in and all will be revealed. Anthony's here.'

George had yet to meet his rival in love, and could feel his stomach churning as Fanny led him into the drawing room. The bishop was in his favourite arm-chair by the fire; sitting opposite him, on a chintz sofa, was a middle-aged officer in the dark blue patrol jacket of the Royal Engineers and sporting a quite magnificent moustache. It hung down from his chin by a good four inches, and gave him the distinct look of a walrus.

'Ah, George,' said the bishop. 'Come and meet Colonel Durnford. Anthony, this is the young man I was telling you about.'

As Durnford rose, his useless left arm, the legacy of a spear thrust at Bushman's River Pass, hung awkwardly at his side. He was much smaller than George, and slightly built, with thinning sandy hair and a delicate, almost feminine face. He shook hands with a grin. 'So you're the reason why Fanny hasn't had the time – or the inclination I'll be bound – to write more than a couple of letters in the last three months.'

George bristled at this jibe. 'I hardly think—'

'Pay him no heed, George,' said Fanny. 'He's just jealous.'

'I won't deny it,' said Durnford. 'One minute I'm the Bishopstowe favourite; the next I seem to have been supplanted by a youthful Adonis.'

'What nonsense,' said Fanny. 'I've been busy at the mission school, as well you know. And we've *all* enjoyed making George's acquaintance. Isn't that right, Father?'

'It is indeed. He's a kindred spirit, Anthony, and they're in short supply these days.'

Durnford turned to George. 'I gather you're part Zulu and that you've offered to intercede with your kinsman Chief Sihayo?'

'That's right.'

'Well, now might be a good time, because Sir Bartle Frere has our report and it wouldn't do any harm for King Cetshwayo to know its contents. That way he can prepare his response.'

'Can you give me any details?'

'I can. This is highly confidential, mind,' said Durnford, raising a finger. 'We're going to recommend a frontier that follows the line of the Blood River.'

George gasped. 'But that will give virtually the whole of the Disputed Territory to the Zulus.'

'Not quite. The Boers get to keep the land to the west of the Blood River, ceded by Mpande in fifty-four, but that still leaves many Boer farms on Zulu territory.'

'What will become of them?' asked George.

'They'll have to leave.'

'Wonderful news, eh, George?' said the bishop.

'Yes,' said George grudgingly. 'However did you manage it, Colonel?'

'I simply argued that there was no legal basis for the

Boer claim to much of the Disputed Territory, and Attorney-General Gallwey agreed with me. He's a lawyer, of course, and requires a high level of proof. John Shepstone was furious, but he couldn't persuade Gallwey to change his mind.'

'Good for Gallwey,' said George. 'But if, as you say, Bishop, Frere is determined to conquer Zululand, won't he simply find another pretext?'

'That may be his intention,' said the bishop. 'But he won't have the support of the British government. I hear on good authority that Sir Michael Hicks Beach, the colonial secretary, is firmly against a war with the Zulus. So good news all round. I think we should celebrate.'

When champagne had been brought, the bishop proposed a toast. 'To peace!'

'To peace!' echoed George as he glanced at Fanny. To his consternation her eyes were firmly fixed on Durnford.

The bishop beckoned George to one side. 'How soon can you leave for Chief Sihayo's kraal?'

'Um . . .' said George, still distracted by Fanny's obvious preference for Durnford.

'Are you all right?'

'Yes, of course. Sorry. I should be ready in two days. I've already bought the trade goods and arranged for the hire of the wagon and oxen. I just need time to load up and I can be on my way.'

'Good. It should take you about a week to reach the Zulu border at Rorke's Drift. Sihayo's kraal is less than a day's journey beyond that. Once you've given the chief the good news, you must impress upon him the vital importance of the Zulus not doing anything to provoke their white neighbours. Frere and Shepstone will be looking for any excuse to ignore the commission's report, or even amend it, and the Zulus must not give them one. We must, for example, have no repeat of the type of intimidation that caused the mass exodus of missionaries from Zululand in March.'

'I'll tell him.'

'Excellent. Before you go, I'll give you a letter to take to Sihayo, confirming your bona fides. Another glass?'

By now the rest of the family had appeared, and more champagne was opened. But, try as he might, George did not feel like celebrating. He was nervous about his forthcoming trip and felt he had been upstaged, even belittled, by Durnford. He was, moreover, far from convinced the threat of war had passed. Eventually he made his excuses, and Fanny saw him to the door.

He descended the steps, stopped and turned round. 'Can I ask you something?'

'Of course,' said Fanny, framed in the doorway. Her hair was loose about her shoulders, her cheeks flushed pink with champagne. She had never looked lovelier.

'Are you in love with Colonel Durnford?'

'What an extraordinary question.'

'Will you answer it?'

'I have a high regard for the colonel, as you know.'

'Do you love him?'

'I . . . Wait here.' She reappeared wearing her bonnet, shut the door and came down the steps. 'Let's walk a while.'

They took the path to the left of the house, through a pretty avenue of acacia trees, and sat at a bench with a spectacular view of Table Mountain. For some minutes neither of them spoke. George broke the silence. 'The reason I ask,' he said, taking Fanny's right hand between both of his, 'is because I think I'm falling in love with you.'

'But, George, you hardly know me. And you're so *young*.'

'I'm *eighteen*,' blurted George. 'And I've seen enough of you, these last months, to know you're a remarkable woman: intelligent, determined and, above all, a good person.'

'I'm flattered, George, I really am. And I won't deny I've become very fond of *you*. But I'm nine years your senior, for goodness' sake, and there are others to consider.'

'The colonel?' asked George. 'Doesn't he have a wife?'

'He's married, if that's what you mean. But he has no wife. She abandoned him years ago, leaving their daughter to be brought up by the colonel's family in England. She's now twenty – older than you!'

'But what can he offer you while his wife still lives? You can never marry, nor can you be together, even in Natal.'

'That's true, but it doesn't change the way I feel about him.'

George slowly shook his head. 'So there's no hope for me?'

Fanny leant forward, took George's face in both her hands and kissed him on the lips. 'Look after yourself in Zululand. I couldn't bear it if anything happened to you.'

# 9

## *Near Rorke's Drift, Natal, 27 July 1878*

The leather of his saddle creaked as George shifted position for the umpteenth time since leaving his camping ground that morning. His legs ached and the winter sun, though low in the sky, was still hot enough to cause rivulets of sweat to trickle down his back. Up ahead the sandy track rose towards a small saddle, or nek, in the bare rocky hills known as Nostrope Pass. From there, George had been assured, you get your first view not only of the Buffalo River, the border between British Natal and Zululand, but of the Zulu kingdom itself.

He looked back but there was no sign of the loaded wagon and oxen that was providing his cover as a trader. Eager to set eyes on the wedge of territory controlled by his great-uncle, he decided not to wait, and nudged Emperor from a walk to a canter. He had learnt from watching others that no one trots in South Africa; in riding any distance it was best to walk for half an hour, canter for half an hour, and then stop for the same amount of time to let the horse drink and feed off the veldt. That way a horse was never long without sustenance and could cover many miles in a day.

Clouds of dust rose as George breasted the rise and gazed in awe at the spectacle laid out beneath a towering sky. The track fell away sharply, via a number of hairpin bends, to the valley floor, where he could just make out, on a terrace of flat land at the foot of a sizeable hill, two thatched single-storey buildings. Away to the left of the buildings was Rorke's Drift itself, a shallow ford over the Buffalo River, and, a short way downstream, the punts for ferrying heavy traffic. Beyond the silvery ribbon of water, the track wound its way through ten miles of rising, rocky ground to a distinctive, sphinx-like hill the Zulus called Isandlwana, or 'Little Hut', because its peak resembled their traditional beehive dwellings. George knew that somewhere between the river and the hill was located the mountain stronghold of his kinsman Chief Sihayo. They were almost there.

It had been quite a trek since their high-spirited departure from Pietermaritzburg twelve days earlier. George had felt like General Custer himself as, mounted on Emperor, he gave the signal for his single-wagon convoy to roll. His driver, a ragged Boer called Snyman, responded with two pistol-like cracks of his long whip, urging his team of eight pairs of oxen forward. There were no reins, and the direction was set by the *voorloper* – team leader – a young African called Samuel who walked beside the lead pair. Slowly but surely the heavily laden wagon lumbered into life. It was long and narrow, eighteen feet by six, with huge iron-rimmed rear wheels and smaller front wheels that turned on a pivoted axle. And it was covered with double canvas, stretched over wooden hoops fastened to the high sides, which reminded George of those prairie schooners of the North American plains he had seen on countless prints.

In theory a team of sixteen oxen could pull a fully laden wagon for six hours a day at a steady three miles an hour over level ground. At that pace George would have covered the hundred or so miles to Rorke's Drift in just six days. But conditions during the trek were far from ideal. The problems began on day two, when the trek tow snapped and took most of the morning to repair. At the Umroti River, which they reached on day four, the drift was so sandy that they required an extra team, borrowed at great expense, to pull the wagon through. And on day nine, near the tiny settlement of Umsinga, a sudden thunderstorm took just seconds to turn the dry riverbed into a raging torrent, causing them to halt until the water had receded. They had, as a consequence, averaged just eight miles a day, and it had occurred to George more than once during the long trek that a British invasion of Zululand, if it ever came to that, would be no easy matter for reasons of logistics alone.

With so much time on his hands, George's thoughts had turned increasingly to the three women in his life: his mother, Lucy and Fanny. He felt guilty about the first two, having written only once to his mother to tell her he had arrived safely, and not at all to Lucy, the lack of an address providing a convenient excuse for distancing himself from the one person who could implicate him in the shooting of the private detective. And while he thought about Lucy often, fervently hoping she had made something of herself in Cape Town or Kimberley, it was not with the same depth of feeling that he now reserved for Fanny.

He knew his motives for travelling to Zululand were mixed. Yet some nagging questions remained: given his vastly different upbringing, would he have anything in common with his Zulu kin? His first encounter had hardly been propitious. And how would white society in general, with its entrenched views of racial superiority, treat him if it knew he was part African?

Casting such gloomy thoughts to the back of his mind, he spurred Emperor down the switchback track and on towards the tiny settlement near the drift, prettily located in a grove of trees and shrubs. As he approached the building on the right, its chimney and vegetable garden identifying it as the main residence, a short bearded man came out onto the covered veranda. 'Hello,' said the man in a thick accent that George took to be German. 'Can I help you?'

'My name's George Hart. I'm heading into Zululand with a wagon of goods to do a spot of . . . er . . . trading. You wouldn't happen to know the location of Chief Sihayo's kraal, would you?'

'Of course. Everyone on the border knows Sihayo. Come inside and I'll show you on a map. I'm Reverend Otto Witt – of the Swedish Mission Society.'

George dismounted, took off Emperor's saddle and knee-haltered him so he could graze, and followed Witt into the house. It was simply furnished and spotlessly clean, the one concession to domesticity being the handsome floral wallpaper in the parlour. 'Take a seat,' said Witt. 'My wife will bring you some lemonade.'

George sat on the sofa and gazed out of the window in the direction he had come, hoping to catch sight of Snyman and his wagon as they breasted the hill.

'Enjoy the view, Mr Hart. That's one of the few windows in the place. They say the previous owner, Jim Rorke, had an aversion to windows – and internal doors for that matter. This house contains eleven rooms, and six of them can only be accessed from the outside of the building. Strange, but useful if you have small children and want to keep them out of the way. I have three under seven. Do you have children?'

'Not yet. How long have you been here, Reverend Witt?'

'Three years now. It's hard to believe. The Mission Society bought the place after old Rorke died in seventy-five. He used to run a store to which all the local Zulus, on both sides of the border, came for trade goods. I turned the store into a church, as doubtless you noticed, but the Zulus still call the mission kwaJimu, "Jim's Place".'

Witt's wife entered with the lemonade. She was a stern-looking woman, probably in her late thirties, with her dark hair tied in a practical bun.

'Thank you,' said George, taking the drink. She just nodded.

'You must excuse my wife,' said Witt. 'She speaks no English, though her Zulu is tolerable.'

'In that case, *Ngiyabonga*. Thank you.'

Mrs Witt stopped in the doorway and turned. 'You speak the Kaffir language,' she said in Zulu.

'A little. I learnt on the voyage over.'

When Mrs Witt had left the room, George turned back to her husband. 'Tell me, Reverend, what sort of people are the Zulus?'

'That's a hard question to answer. They're godless, of course, and can be ruthless and cruel. The king sets the tone. He rules his people with an iron rod, and he and his chiefs have the power of life and death. The idea of a fair trial before execution is laughable. And many of the laws that are in place would seem draconian to a European. Did you know that adultery is punishable by death?'

'No, I did not.'

'Well, it is, as is disobeying the king's orders. A couple of years ago Cetshwayo gave one of his regiments permission to marry a younger age-grade of girls. When a number of the girls refused, because they already had lovers in a separate regiment, Cetshwayo had them killed. We missionaries object to all of this, of course, and are unpopular as a consequence. I'm safe here, in Natal, but it was getting so dangerous for the missions in Zululand that they upped sticks and left in March. Presumably you heard about that?'

'I did,' said George, putting his glass on a side table. 'But some say that was a deliberate put-up job by Shepstone and the missionaries to make Cetshwayo's regime appear more brutal than it really is.'

Witt snorted. 'What nonsense. I know for a fact that many converts have been murdered out of hand on Cetshwayo's orders, including a member of the Norwegian mission church at Eshowe, Maqamusela Khanyile, who was killed last year; and I myself, on my occasional trips into Zululand, have been manhandled by warriors. Missionaries will not be safe in that benighted country until Europeans are in control.'

'So you'd support a war of conquest?'

'Absolutely. Only then will we be left in peace to save souls.'

'Assuming they want to be saved,' muttered George.

'What's that?'

'Nothing.'

'I can see you have your doubts, Mr Hart, but take it from me: the country will be much better off under the British. The average male is an idle brute. When not on regimental duty or attending council meetings, he spends most of his time working skins, carving wood and sleeping. He's far too superior for manual labour, and leaves the tilling of the fields to the women and young girls, while the young boys tend to the cattle.'

'Makes sense to me,' said George with a straight face.

'I beg your pardon.'

'Never mind, Reverend. Tell me a little about Chief Sihayo. Have you met him?'

'A number of times, most recently when the Boundary Commission met at the drift. He was one of the Zulu delegates, as I'm sure you know.'

'How would you describe him?'

'He's fat, of course, like many of the *amakhosi* – the regional chiefs, I suppose you would call them. But he's extremely handsome and a great talker with a fine sense of humour. Don't be taken in, though. He's a hugely ambitious, utterly ruthless man who will tell you one thing and do the exact opposite. I wouldn't trust him an inch.'

'Has he duped you personally?'

'No, but you hear things. If you do trade with him, fix a price and stick to it.'

'I'll try and remember that,' said George, unconvinced Sihayo was as bad as Witt was making out. All missionaries had a vested interest in overturning the old order, and Sihayo was very much the old order. George was keen to meet him and make up his own mind.

'I hope you don't mind me saying this,' said Witt, an apologetic look on his face. 'I know you said you were a trader, but you have the air of a military man to me. This wouldn't be anything to do with the boundary award, would it?'

Taken off guard, George feigned ignorance. 'I don't know what you mean.'

'Don't take it the wrong way. It's just that we're all waiting on tenterhooks. If the award goes against the Zulus, as we're certain it will, then war is on the cards. Only when the Zulus have been defeated will we be able to sleep easy at night.'

'Do you really believe they'd invade Natal?'

'I do, and so would you if you and your family were sitting defenceless with forty thousand bloodthirsty warriors on your doorstep.'

George caught something out of the corner of his eye: it was his wagon coming slowly down the slope. 'My people at last,' said George, pointing out of the window. 'I'd better be making tracks. You said something about a map?'

'One moment.' Witt came back with a small-scale, poorly detailed map upon which was marked a track that led from the drift to the Zulu capital of Ulundi, a distance of sixty miles. 'Once you're over the drift,' said Witt, tracing the route with his finger, 'follow the track for about a mile until you reach the Bashee River. Cross the river, turn immediately left and you'll come to a huge horseshoe gorge. Sihayo's kraal is directly below the cliff face. You can't miss it, and if you do, his people will show you the way.'

It took the best part of three hours to get the wagon across the drift. First the oxen had to be turned loose to graze, then given a similar amount of time to regurgitate and chew the cud, and finally inspanned to the trek tow and loaded on to the pont, a small ferry that worked the river by means of anchored cables. The water level was so low that George was able to ride across, guiding Emperor between the large flat rocks that jutted above the surface. He was tempted to explore the steep rocky escarpment that lay directly beyond the drift. But he decided to wait for the wagon, and it was not until five in the afternoon, with the sun beginning to set, that they were ready to set off down the dusty, rutted track on the last leg of the journey.

'It'll be dark soon,' said Snyman from the box seat. 'Probably best to camp here for the night if we know what's good for us.'

It was more a statement than a question, and George resented its tone. In truth his temper had been building over the last few days of delay. 'Nonsense,' he replied firmly, from the saddle. 'What have we got to fear? We're not at war with the Zulus, so let's keep going. Another half an hour should do it.'

And it might have done in daylight, but the track was so hard to follow in the failing light, the broken ground so uneven, that George eventually gave up and told a smug-looking Snyman to outspan and set up camp. They followed their usual drill: Samuel turned the oxen loose to graze, while Snyman put up a small two-man tent in the lee of the wagon and George collected wood for a fire. Within twenty minutes they were sitting snug round a blazing campfire, drinking black coffee and eating dried biscuit and boiled ham.

'Any game to be seen hereabouts?' asked George, as he stared nervously into the inky blackness.

'No big game, if that's what you mean,' replied Snyman. 'It was all hunted out years ago. But you still get the odd antelope.'

As if in confirmation, a twig snapped behind them, beyond the wagon. George's raised eyebrows were met with a Boer shrug. 'Probably one of the oxen.'

'Take a look, Samuel,' said George to the young African.

Samuel got up and disappeared into the darkness. There was a scraping sound and what appeared to be a muffled cry. George turned to look and froze. By the light of the fire he could just make out a large group of warriors, armed with shields and assegais, advancing steadily towards them at the crouch. On seeing George, the leader cried, 'Jee!' and dashed forward.

'Zulus!' shouted George, springing to his feet and reaching for the pistol in his waistband. He was too late. As his hand closed on the wooden butt, a Zulu shoulder caught him full in the chest, driving him backwards on to the scrubby ground. A heavy body was pinning him down; the smell of sweat, animal skin and clay was overpowering. George looked up, gasping for breath, and saw two rows of white teeth smiling above him. As his eyes adjusted to the light, he could also see the tip of an assegai poised an inch from his chest. He kept perfectly still.

'Have you secured the other two?' George's assailant asked his men.

'Yes, *Inkhosi*.'

'Good.'

George was hauled to his feet. 'Who are you?' asked the leader, 'and why are you camping on my father's land without permission?'

'You're Sihayo's son?' asked George.

'Answer the question!'

George thought of declaring his kinship, in the hope it would relieve the tension, but the bishop had advised him to reveal neither his identity nor his mission until he was in Sihayo's presence. Instead he said, 'My name's George Hart. I've brought goods to trade for cattle. I mean no harm.'

'Why, then, were you creeping around like thieves in the night?' asked his interrogator, his handsome face cocked to one side, as though he were more amused than angry. He was powerfully built with broad shoulders and muscular arms, and was naked apart from a loin covering and what looked like bunches of white oxtails round his neck, wrists and knees; his hair was set high on his head in two domed ridges, giving him the appearance of being taller than he really was.

'We weren't creeping anywhere,' replied George indignantly. 'We were hoping to reach your father's kraal before dark, but lost our way.'

'I don't believe you, white man. I think you and your accomplices are masquerading as traders; I think your true intention is to survey this territory for the Natal authorities.'

'Why would we do that?'

'To prepare the ground for an invasion. You and I both know the Boundary Commission will rule against the Zulus and that war is likely. You're spies, and the penalty for spying in Zululand is death.'

A chill ran up George's spine. He could not believe what he was hearing. Yes, he wanted to scream, I am a spy but not in the way you think. But would this fiery young warrior, related to him by blood, accept the true version of events? He suspected not, which is why he had to tread very carefully.

'Would it change your mind,' said George, 'if I told you we were related?'

The son roared with laughter. 'How can you, a white man,' he said between chuckles, 'be related to *me*?'

'I'm Ngqumbazi's grandson. You have heard of Ngqumbazi?'

The son's laugh faded to a scowl. 'That dung beetle! We don't speak her name. You say you're her grandson? Then your grandfather must have been the white soldier who seduced her and shamed her in front of her family.'

'I was told her family had forgiven her. That's why she left the baby, my mother, and returned to Zululand.'

'The family *never* forgave her,' said the warrior without pity. 'How could it, and still be respected by its people? She returned, yes, but remained an outcast.'

'What happened to her?' asked George.

'She was banished to a small kraal in the hills, well away from the family. She died there about ten years ago.'

George could feel his anger rising. Cousin or no, he could happily have killed the implacable warrior before him. To think his grandmother had given up her only child to be with her people and they had treated her like this, shunned her like a crazed dog. Try as he might, he was finding it difficult to feel a common bond with this hard, cruel race. 'What is your name?' he asked.

The warrior stood to his full height. 'Mehlokazulu kaSihayo, my father's first-born. It means "Eyes of the Nation".'

'Well, "Eyes of the Nation",' said George with an edge to his voice, 'are going to take me to your father or not?'

'No. I have work to do in Natal, but I will leave two men to guide you in the morning. Your wagon can stay here; it's too big to make the climb.'

He turned, spoke briefly to two warriors, and disappeared into the night, the bulk of his men trotting after him.

George spurred Emperor on, urging him up the steep path that led to Sihayo's eyrie. They had left at first light and, with the two warriors acting as guides, it had not taken them long to reach the magnificent sight of the horseshoe gorge; but the climb was a different prospect, and not for the first time George wondered how an attacking force would fare over ground littered with large rocks and monkey-rope creepers. At last the ground began to level out and there, nestled up against the blood-red cliff face, lay Sihayo's kraal, kwaSoxhege.

Like all Zulu homesteads, it consisted of a circle of thatched beehive-shaped huts built on sloping ground around a central cattle enclosure known as an *isibaya*. Security was provided by an outer perimeter of stakes and thorn trees, with the main entrance at its lowest point. As George entered the kraal on foot, flanked by his escort, he noticed the neighbouring mealie and vegetable fields were full of half-naked women and children, their modesty covered by small rectangles of beadwork and animal skins. So Witt was right again: menial work did not agree with Zulu men.

Inside, George gazed in awe at the sheer size of the place. He put the number of huts, some of them the size of small barns, in excess of sixty: these would house not only Sihayo, his wives and children, but also the families of his younger brothers, married sons and chief retainers. One of these huts, according to the son he had met in the valley, was now empty.

George was led round the brushwood perimeter of the *isibaya* to the hut of the chief's great wife, the *undlunkulu*; it was both the largest dwelling and situated on the highest ground, giving it a commanding view of the entire kraal and its main approach. Outside the hut, he came across a handsome, rotund man of about fifty with salt-and-pepper hair. Reclining on a sheepskin, he was taking snuff and calling on the women and children in the fields to stop chattering and get on with their work. He was scantily clad in a monkey-tail kilt, though his heavily beaded necklace and leopardskin headband denoted a man of substance; and, like all married men, he wore the black head-ring known as the *isicoco*, a fibre circlet about half an inch thick, which was woven into the hair and polished with beeswax, the ultimate recognition of his manhood and adult status. It could only be Sihayo.

'*Inkhosi*,' said one of the warriors in confirmation. 'Your son Mehlokazulu found this white man in the valley below.'

Sihayo looked up and frowned. 'Where is my son? Why did he not escort the white man himself?'

The warrior looked nervous, almost afraid to speak the truth. 'He's hunting, *Inkhosi*.'

'Hunting? Hunting where?'

'In Natal,' interjected George in Zulu.

Sihayo turned his glare upon the stranger. 'Who are you? And what do you know of my son's actions?'

'My name is George Hart. I was sent by Bishop Colenso with news of the Boundary Commission. Last night your son and his men burst into my camp and held my party at spearpoint. When I explained who I was, he told me he was on his way to Natal.'

'The hot-headed fool!' exclaimed Sihayo, the blood draining from his face. 'Didn't I tell him to let the matter lie? Yes, but when has he listened to his father?' He turned to the warrior who had spoken. 'Sithobe, take some mounted men and try and intercept Mehlokazulu and his men before they do something we'll all regret.'

'Yes, *Inkhosi*. But he has a good few hours' start on us and will be in Natal by now.'

'I know that. Do what you can.'

As Sithobe left with the other warrior, Sihayo turned back to George. 'So tell me about the Boundary Commission.'

'Its report will recommend the border follows the line of the Blood River.'

'A generous settlement indeed; Cetshwayo will be pleased. But how do I know you speak the truth?'

George handed Sihayo a letter from Bishop Colenso, which he had kept hidden in the lining of his corduroy jacket. The chief tore open the letter and read the bishop's confirmation that the report would favour the Zulus.

'Aieee,' said Sihayo. 'Durnford is a man of his word, after all. Who would have thought the white man would rule in favour of the Zulu?'

'I know. It came as quite a surprise to the bishop, which is why he sent me in person. He's anxious the Zulus don't commit any aggressive acts that will give Frere an excuse to ignore the report. You must tell Cetshwayo of this as soon as possible.'

'I will, but it may already be too late. Three days ago one of my junior wives, Nandi, went missing; yesterday we received word that she was living just across the Buffalo in the kraal of a Kaffir member of the Natal Border Guard. To think she would leave me, a great chief, for such a traitorous jackal! Anyhow, Mehlokazulu came to me and offered to bring her back by force. I refused. But he seems to have gone anyway.'

'My God!' said George. 'If your son crosses the border into Natal with a war party, all hell will break loose. This might be just the type of provocation Frere needs to justify a war. You must stop him.'

'Sithobe will do his best. In the meantime all we can do is wait. With luck he won't find her and no harm will be done. But if he does return with her, the *isanusi* will decide her fate.'

'The *isanusi*?'

'The diviner of the tribe. It's his job to smell out evil spirits. He will decide if my wife is guilty of adultery.'

'And if she is?'

'She will die.'

'Chief, you can't let that happen. Recovering a Zulu refugee from Natal by force is bad enough, but if you kill her, the people of Natal will be in an uproar.'

Sihayo waved his hand dismissively. 'Why should they care? It's happened before and nothing came of it.'

'Yes,' said George, 'but this time it's different. The high commissioner is looking for any excuse to declare war on the Zulus and you mustn't give him one.'

'I can't interfere with the customs of our people. Let's talk no more of this. We have good news to celebrate. Come.'

George followed the chief into his hut, crouching low through the entrance, and found himself in a dark, windowless room, supported by wooden cross-struts and pillars, with a fireplace at its centre. There was no chimney, and the hut smelt strongly of wood-smoke and cow-dung, a liberal quantity of which had been mixed with clay from white anthills and polished with ash and bullock's blood to produce the smooth mahogany-coloured floor. Sihayo was busy pouring a thick dark liquid from an earthen pot into a smaller clay vessel. This he handed to George, who, unwilling to offend, took a long draught and promptly choked on the heady brew of what tasted like a very strong beer, complete with half-fermented grains. Sihayo laughed and clapped him on the back.

'Sit,' he directed, spreading out a grass sleeping mat. 'Will you share a pipe with me while we wait for my son to return?'

George nodded and Sihayo fetched what looked like a hollowed-out cow's horn, half filled it with water and placed inside it a small bowl containing some dried leaves. A burning coal was put on top of the leaves, and as smoke began to appear, Sihayo clamped the open end of the horn to his mouth and inhaled deeply. Wide-eyed, he handed the horn to George, who followed suit and at once collapsed in a fit of coughing, his eyes streaming tears. 'By Jove,' spluttered George, light-headed. 'That's strong stuff. What is it?'

'*Insangu*,' replied Sihayo. 'It grows wild. Do you like it?'

'I'm sure I could get to like it. But I fear I may need a clear head when your son returns. Are those,' asked George, pointing to a bundle of spears, 'Shaka's famous stabbing assegais?'

'They are.'

'Mind if I take a look?'

'Of course not,' said Sihayo, detaching one from the bundle and handing it to George. 'We call it the *iklwa* because that's the sound it makes as it's withdrawn from human flesh.'

George grimaced, but could not help admiring the workmanship of the fearsome weapon in his hand. Its shaft was made of burnished wood, about thirty inches long and slightly thicker at its base to prevent it from slipping from the user's grasp. The heavy, flat iron blade was a further ten inches long and two wide at the shoulder, tapering to a rounded tip. George tested it with his thumb and immediately drew blood.

'Careful,' said the chief. 'It's very sharp. Let me show you how to use it.'

He took the spear from George and gripped it in his right hand, midway down the shaft. His left arm he held in front of his body, as if he was holding a shield.

'We hook the shield behind that of our enemy and sweep it to the left, so uncovering the exposed flank. Then we move in with the *iklwa*, aiming for the chest.' Sihayo turned his shoulders and demonstrated the underhand stabbing motion. 'Once the enemy is down,' added Sihayo with a smile, 'we slit open his stomach to release his spirit. If we do not, the spirit will haunt us.'

George shivered inwardly. The thought of taking on a Zulu armed with the *iklwa* was not something he wished to contemplate. 'What other weapons do you use?'

'The longer throwing assegai, which is usually released before we close in on the enemy, and the *iwisa,* which white men call a knobkerrie, and is best used as a club but can also be thrown.'

'What about firearms? Do many Zulus own one?'

'Some do, but they're mainly old models bought from Portuguese traders. Most Zulus prefer to fight at close quarters.'

George was quite enjoying the conversation. Then Sihayo replaced the spear in the bundle. 'One thing still troubles me. You say Sobantu sent you. Fair enough. But what's in it for you? Won't the white settlers regard you as a traitor?'

'They might, but they're not *my* people.'

The chief frowned. 'Are you not British like them?'

'I have white blood, it's true. But if you look closer, you might see something else.'

Sihayo stared intently at George's handsome face. There was nothing in his narrow, slightly crooked nose and luxurious black locks, swept back from a side-parting, to suggest African blood. But wait. Were not those lips just a little too full for a white man? Could he not detect a hint of colour in that glossy skin?

'What are you saying?' asked Sihayo.

'I'm saying I have African blood, the same blood that's running through your veins.'

Sihayo's eyes widened to the size of small saucers. 'I don't believe you . . .' He looked again at the face before him and realized it bore more than a passing resemblance to his own. 'It can't be true. It can't be . . .'

'It is. I'm Ngqumbazi's grandson, your great-nephew. I only found out myself a few months ago.'

The chief sat there as if in shock. At last he spoke, tears in his eyes: 'I loved her, you know. She was my favourite sister. But after her disgrace I never saw her again.'

'I just don't understand,' said George, shaking his head. 'She gave up her child, my mother. Wasn't that punishment enough?'

Sihayo's face hardened. 'No. She had been promised to another man, the son of Chief Buthelezi, but of course he wouldn't have her when the truth got out. She was tainted, as was the rest of the family. The only way to make amends was to banish her and pay over a dowry as if the marriage had gone ahead. It cost Father one hundred cattle and almost broke his heart. We couldn't forgive her

177

after that. If you were truly a Zulu, rather than a white man with a few drops of Zulu blood, you'd understand well enough.'

George was loath to admit it, but he suspected the chief was right. He had been brought up to think like a British officer and a gentleman, and he was beginning to realize that the recent knowledge that he had Zulu forebears was not going to overturn years of social conditioning. He might admire the achievements of the Zulus, even sympathize with their political predicament, but he would never be one of them. That was not to say that he had ever felt – or been allowed to feel – entirely comfortable in the role of an English gentleman; the bigots at Harrow, Sandhurst and his regiment had seen to that. But when all was said and done, it was the only role he knew. Perhaps he was destined always to be an outsider, but for all that he would still have to choose sides.

He was about to respond when shouts sounded from outside the hut.

'It must be my son,' said the chief. 'Come!'

From the entrance to the hut they could see Mehloka-zulu and two of his warriors drag a semi-naked woman into the *isibaya* and dump her without ceremony in the small stone enclosure reserved for calves. The warriors stood sentry while Mehlokazulu left the *isibaya* and made his way round to his father's hut.

'Greetings, Father,' he said, ignoring George. 'I've brought back what's rightfully yours.'

'You fool!' exploded Sihayo. 'How dare you take a war party across the Buffalo without my permission. Do you have any idea what you've done? The whites will see this as an act of aggression. It could lead to war.'

His son looked unconcerned. 'I didn't ask your permission because I knew you wouldn't give it. Anyway, all I did was recover a runaway. I even spared her lover. If that leads to war, then so be it. Zululand has been at peace for too long. The army is growing stale and the younger warriors need to prove themselves. Most of my own regiment, the Ngobamakhosi, have reached the age of twenty-four years, and yet none of us has washed his spear in blood. In Shaka's time we would all have been veterans by now.'

'And dead too, no doubt,' interjected George. 'Do you have any idea what you're up against? You can't possibly win a war against the British. If they lose one army, they'll send another, and another, until Zululand lies in ruins. Even your king knows that.'

Mehlokazulu turned to face George. They were about the same height, with the same broad shoulders and narrow waist, but the young Zulu was more physically imposing, his muscular chest glistening with sweat. 'Cetshwayo is not the warrior he was, *cousin*,' he said with a sneer. 'He's getting old and jumps at the slightest shadow. Ever since he allowed himself to be crowned by the British he's been in thrall to you. Only the younger generation can save the country's honour. Take this business with Nandi. If she remains unpunished, other wives will follow her example. The Zulu people will tear apart.'

Sihayo had heard enough and raised his hand as if he meant to strike his son, but Mehlokazulu's unflinching demeanour made him think twice, and he released his anger in a torrent of abuse. 'You faithless, ungrateful viper! Your balls have barely dropped, yet you dare to insult the king, a man who has eaten up countless enemies. Have you washed your spear even once? No, yet you presume to conduct the affairs of the nation.'

His son set his jaw in defiance. 'The white man means to have this country sooner or later. Better to take the fight to him while we're still strong.'

Sihayo turned to George. 'Is he right? Will the white man let us live in peace?'

'I don't know,' replied George. 'Maybe for a while. But one thing is certain: if you provoke war, your country will be destroyed.'

'And if we do nothing, it will die just the same,' said Mehlokazulu. 'I prefer death to dishonour.'

Sihayo looked like a man who knew, deep down, that his son was right. But what good was an honourable death? His responsibility was to his clan, and he would do anything to save it from destruction. He waved his son away. 'Get out of my sight. Before I do something I regret.'

'Gladly, Father, but aren't you forgetting someone?' he said, pointing towards the brushwood fence of the calf enclosure. 'She deserves to die for what she's done.'

'The *isanusi* will decide her fate at dusk. Now go.'

In the few hours left before the 'smelling-out' ceremony, George did his best to persuade Sihayo to intervene and spare his errant wife. But the chief was adamant: tribal tradition could not be overruled, and when George continued to argue he was led away by two burly warriors and confined in a separate hut. There he brooded on the naïve attachment that white humanitarians like the Colensos seemed to have for 'noble savages' like the Zulus. Did they truly understand the Zulus? Did their romantic notions bear any relation to reality? He suspected not.

Shortly after dark, with double-headed drums beating out a steady rhythm, George was escorted into the *isibaya*, where he found the whole community drawn up in a large semi-circle: Sihayo and his brothers at its centre; then their sons, including a grim-looking Mehlokazulu; and finally, at the outer extremities of the crescent, the women and children. Facing them, her hands tied behind her back to a large stake, was the semi-naked Nandi, her beautiful face etched with defiance. The whole eerie scene was lit by flickering torches beneath a star-filled sky.

'Stand by me, nephew,' commanded Sihayo, 'and don't speak until the ceremony is over.'

Hardly had the chief spoken these words than the *isanusi* entered the cattle enclosure, leaping and chanting. He was a ghastly sight, his long hair strewn with the bladders of freshly slaughtered goats and his necklaces and belt hung with animal skulls. In his right hand he carried a wildebeest tail and in his left a short spear with which he lunged at the clearly terrified Nandi in mock attack, leaping in the air and cackling derisively as he did so. Round and round the captive he cavorted, appealing to the spirits for help in proving her guilt.

George looked on wide-eyed. Though he despised Sihayo for putting Nandi through this ordeal, he was entranced by the spectacle and could not take his eyes off the *isanusi*'s wild antics. The dance seemed to go on and on. Until at last, with the crowd thoroughly subdued, the *isanusi* began a low chant that the onlookers emulated, the sound rising steadily in pitch and intensity. In a state of near hysteria, his eyes streaming with tears and his lips flecked with foam, the *isanusi* lurched towards Nandi and collapsed on the ground. He then began to sniff every inch of her statuesque frame, starting with her feet. As he worked his way up her naked torso, the tempo and volume of the chanting increased. Suddenly the *isanusi*'s right hand shot out and flicked the wildebeest's tail in Nandi's face. She screamed as the crowd fell silent.

'What does that mean?' George whispered to Sihayo, though he knew the answer.

'She's guilty.'

'Surely you have the power to—'

'Silence!' Sihayo walked forward and turned to address his people. 'The *isanusi* has spoken. Nandi is guilty of adultery and must die. Mehlokazulu and Mkhumbuka-zulu will carry out the sentence.'

The two brothers – one broad and muscular, the other lean and wiry – walked over to Nandi, who, by this time, was tearfully pleading for her life. Ignoring her entreaties, Mehlokazulu tied a leather thong round her neck and inserted into it a wooden handle about a foot long. He then turned the handle until the thong was taught against her neck.

'Please!' implored Nandi.

Ignoring her, Mehlokazulu turned towards Sihayo for the signal to proceed. The chief nodded.

'No!' shouted George, rushing forward to intervene. But he had barely covered ten yards before he was brought down from behind by one of his two shadows. Though pinned to the ground, he turned his head in time to see his cousin viciously turning the handle so that the leather thong bit into Nandi's neck, slowly throttling her. Nandi struggled for a few seconds, her eyes bulging and her tongue extended, and then slumped forward, her hands still attached to the stake. Just to make sure, the younger brother lifted Nandi's head by her topknot and stabbed her in the throat with his *iklwa*, spraying himself with arterial blood in the process. George closed his eyes, unable to watch any more.

'Cut her down,' instructed Sihayo, 'and bury her in an unmarked grave. As for our squeamish relative, he can spend the night in Nandi's hut. She won't be needing it again.'

# IO

*Bishopstowe, 3 August 1878*

Bishop Colenso stood gazing out of his French windows, shaking his head. The drawing room was silent but for the ticking of the large clock on the mantelpiece. 'Was there nothing you could do to save her?' he said at last.

George shifted uneasily on the sofa. 'No. As I've explained, I tried everything, but they were determined to kill her.'

He had been dreading this moment since his departure from Sihayo's kraal the day after Nandi's execution. A small *impi* – a group of Zulu warriors – had escorted him and his wagon as far as Rorke's Drift, and from there he had ridden ahead, telling Snyman to get the best price he could for the untraded goods. But during the long ride back to Pietermaritzburg, try as he might, he could not expunge the memory of that brutal killing; nor could he escape the nagging realization that, blood ties or no, he had lost all sympathy for the Zulus' predicament. It had helped him make up his mind about his future. He knew that Fanny, in particular, would find it hard to understand his decision, and feared it would give her yet another reason to favour Durnford over him. Yet he felt he had little choice. Certainly he would never again see the Zulus

– his own kin – in the same uncritical light as the Colensos.

The bishop looked at him intently. 'I can see you're upset by your ordeal, George, but you mustn't blame Sihayo and his sons. It's just their way – and has been for generations.'

'Well, it needs to change. How can you, a man of God, justify the execution of a woman for adultery? Such a law in Britain would empty half the drawing rooms of Mayfair.'

'I'm trying to explain their actions, not justify them. I agree that change is necessary, but it will take time. It always does. The Zulus have to be made to see the error of their ways, and only Christ can do that.'

'You're saying missionaries are the solution?'

'Christianity is the solution. Missionaries are merely its agents.'

'But missionaries have been active in Zululand for decades and look what good it's done. Converts are routinely executed and the military system continues as before.'

'As I said, it will take time.'

'You won't thank me for saying this, but I'm beginning to think there might be a case for diplomatic pressure to speed up the process.' George turned to Fanny, who, thus far, had remained silent in an easy chair. 'Surely you, as a woman, would hate to live under the Zulu system?'

'I certainly would. But no country has the right to impose its values on another, particularly not Britain, with its child labour, workhouses and industrial slums. In any case, the colonial authorities only pretend to be interested in better government for Zululand; their real aim is conquest and their motives, as Father has already explained, are far from selfless.'

'I accept that. But if you'd only been in my place, and seen and heard what I did, you might not be so supportive of the "poor, defenceless" Zulus.'

'How can you say that? You're part Zulu yourself.'

'Yes, and I sometimes wish that wasn't the case. I found out what happened to my Zulu grandmother, by the way. She was abandoned by her so-called family and left to die alone. How do you think that makes me feel?'

'We understand your anger, George,' said the bishop. 'But you mustn't let it cloud the overall picture. Frere is determined to fight the Zulus and this Sihayo business might be just the excuse he needs. Thankfully our own lieutenant governor is less of a warmonger and has tried to calm matters down by demanding that Cetshwayo hands over the ringleaders, Mehlokazulu and his brother. Let's hope they come quietly.'

'I wouldn't hold your breath,' said George. 'Mehlokazulu is a firebrand if ever I've met one. He actually welcomes the prospect of war.'

'He's young. Wiser counsels will prevail.'

'I'm not so sure,' said George. He could see his views were not welcome and decided to leave before he said something he regretted. He had, in any case, something he wished to discuss with Fanny in private, so he made his excuses and asked her to accompany him as far as the stables.

On the way he paused and took both her hands in his. 'I did a lot of thinking on the ride back from Zululand.'

'And?'

'Let's just say that things are a little clearer than they were before I went.'

'Go on.'

'Well, I'm certain of one thing, and that's my love for you.'

'George, we've talked about this . . .'

'I know, and I realize I've got a fight on my hands to win you over. But I think you're worth fighting for. To see you arguing just now, Fanny, I admire you so much. I love you.'

'I'm flattered, George. I really am. But you're far too young to be falling in love. You've got your life ahead of you, and I'd hate to think your affection for me might blunt your ambition in any way.'

'Why would it? In any case, I've made a decision about my future. I'm going to join one of the local regiments of irregular horse. It's only part-time soldiering, but the pay's good and I'll still be able to help my uncle out on the farm. More importantly, I'll be near you.'

Fanny released her hands and frowned. 'How can you think of joining the army at a time like this?'

'Because it's all I know. I've been fooling myself that I could make a go of farming, or even prospecting for diamonds without having money for a stake. The only thing I've ever been really good at is soldiering and I want to give it another try.'

'This wouldn't have anything to do with your trip to Zululand?'

'Yes, partly. I've had the scales removed from my eyes. Now that I've seen something of Zulu life I believe that they are not the noble savages that you and your father like to think they are. Their system appears to be oppressive to its own people and is certainly a threat to their neighbours. By joining the irregular horse I'll help to guard against that threat.'

'Do you really believe that?'

'Yes, I do. The younger warriors like Mehlokazulu are itching for a war.'

'So why not give them one, is that what you're saying?'

'Of course not, but something needs to be done. Cetshwayo must be told to introduce reforms.'

'And what if he refuses and it leads to war? Will you fight your own people?'

'The Zulus are not my people. I know that now.'

'You know nothing of the sort,' said Fanny, as she turned on her heel and stalked off.

That evening George walked to the edge of his uncle's pasture and watched the sun set. He felt such a boiling mixture of emotions that he wanted to punch someone or something. How could he tell Fanny that he loved her and that he was joining the army, both in the space of five minutes! Yet what else could he have done? He felt swept along by his passion for Fanny, her beauty, her fine, pugnacious openness. And at the same time, his own integrity would not allow him to deny the things he had said to her. He thought back to the ceremony in the kraal. Yes, he was always going to be an outsider, but if he *was* going to take sides, this was the one he had to choose.

The mystery of his background, the colour of his skin, the very uncertainty of the blood in his veins, these things had brought him turmoil and heartache, but surely there were some things that he *did* know: he was his mother's son, proud and strong, and the army was in his blood somewhere. Beyond any doubt, he knew his father must be a military man of some kind. He had felt at home the minute he first put uniform on. He had lost the opportunity to pursue his career, partly through his own fault. Now he had another chance to make his mother proud and – who knew? – perhaps his father too. There was also the financial incentive. He would not earn much at first, but if he worked hard and gained promotion he would be able to send part of his pay home to his mother. And, as for Fanny, if he could act with honour in all he did, maybe even save the Zulus from themselves, perhaps she would see him in a better light. He prayed that she would. What if the chance to win his father's legacy was not lost after all? It might seem far-fetched, but young officers did win VCs, and Fanny was a gentlewoman.

Returning to the house, George told his uncle of his plans.

'Well, if it's a military career you're after,' said Patrick, 'you could do worse than join the Natal Carbineers. You won't find a smarter, better-disciplined body of horse in southern Africa. It was formed in the fifties to protect the colony from internal rebellion and a Zulu invasion; and it was modelled on the British Yeomanry, so that many of its rank and file come from prominent settler families and consider themselves gentlemen. You should feel right at home.'

George chuckled.

'And best of all,' continued his uncle, 'the regimental headquarters is at Pietermaritzburg.'

'Ideal. I'll ride over there tomorrow. Do you know who the commanding officer is?'

'Offy Shepstone, the son of Sir Theophilus. He's reputed to be a brilliant rider, a first-class shot and an inspiring leader of men. Most people think the Bushman's River Pass debacle would have turned out very differently if he and not Durnford had been in command.'

Next morning found George riding down Longmarket Street past the Dutch-style Church of the Vow, built to commemorate the Boers' victory over the Zulus at Blood River in 1838 and a relic of the town's Voortrekker origins. The Boers, George had discovered, were also responsible for the traditional grid layout of Pietermaritzburg, with an initial eight streets intersected by six more, and all lined with ditches to irrigate the residents' gardens from the Dorpspruit river. But Boer rule had only lasted for five years, and much of the architecture that greeted George on this hot August day was distinctly British in style: red-brick buildings, wrought-iron balconies, tin roofs and white picket fences.

The streets were thronged with buggies and horses, as befitted the capital of the colony, and George lost count of the number of times he felt compelled to raise his hat to passersby. Some of the ladies were exceedingly handsome in their white dresses and bonnets, and if George had not been so preoccupied with Fanny Colenso, he would have considered his prospects set fair. His mind, in any case, was not on women but employment. Spotting a policeman by the roadside, he leant from his saddle and asked directions to the headquarters of the Natal Carbineers.

'That's Fort Napier you'll be wanting,' said the bobby. 'Turn left on Pine Street and head out of town on the Edendale Road. It's on high ground to the southwest. You can't miss it.'

George followed the directions to the letter and soon found himself at the gatehouse to a low red-brick fort, a Union flag hanging limply on its pole.

'Can I help you, sir?' asked a red-coated sentry of the 80th Foot, his red face shiny with perspiration.

'I'm looking for the Carbineers,' said George.

The sentry pointed to a neat brick building to the left of the parade ground. Two sentries were on duty, smartly dressed in white spiked helmets and blue tunics, each with a shouldered carbine. Their brown leathery faces marked them as colonists, and as George entered the office, they snapped to attention.

George was impressed, and said as much to the duty sergeant. 'We like to keep our standards high,' he replied, 'unlike some I could mention.'

'The Eightieth not up to scratch, then?'

'I wouldn't like to say.'

'I rather think you have.' George knew the Carbineer sergeant had a point. The 80th had only been in Natal for a year and, like all regiments recently arrived from Britain, had a high proportion of puny young recruits. 'I've come to see the commandant. Is he available?'

'I'll just check, sir. Who shall I say wants him?'

'Tell him George Hart, formerly of the King's Dragoon Guards, is here to see him.'

The sergeant disappeared into an adjoining room and was gone barely a couple of minutes. 'He'll see you now, sir.'

George entered the room and was met by an officer with a thin, handsome face. 'I'm Captain Shepstone,' he said, his white teeth contrasting with the blackness of his elegantly waxed moustache. 'What can I do for you?'

'I'd like to enlist,' said George.

Shepstone gestured towards a chair as he returned to his own seat behind his desk. 'Military experience is always welcome in the Carbineers, Mr Hart, but I'm afraid we have all the officers we need.'

'That's fine by me. I'd be happy to join as a trooper.'

'Really?' said Shepstone, raising one eyebrow. 'You're not on the run, are you?'

'No.'

'But you *have* held a commission.'

'Yes. In the KDG, as I told your sergeant.'

'And yet here you are, a former officer in a crack British cavalry regiment, happy to join the ranks of a part-time unit of colonial horse. Quite a step-down, is it not?'

'Some might see it like that, but let's just say I found the regular British Army too stuffy. In any event, from all I've heard and seen today, the Carbineers seem as efficient as any British cavalry regiment, and surely more suited to African warfare.'

'Compliment accepted. And you're right. We operate as mounted infantry, and with good reason. The African bush, with its rocky kopjes and dry riverbeds, does not lend itself to sweeping cavalry charges with lance and sabre. But you'll excuse my probing, I'm sure. The regiment is recruited largely from farmers and landowners, men familiar with guns and ponies from childhood, and we're a little wary of outsiders.'

'I can understand that. And I can assure you that there is nothing in my past that would disqualify me from joining your regiment. On the contrary. I know the basic riding drill and can handle a sabre.'

'Only officers use sabres, I'm afraid. Other ranks have to make do with revolvers and carbines.'

'Well, I've got my own revolver, and a horse of course.'

'I saw it from the window. An English hunter, by the look of things.'

'He's Irish, as it happens. Like me.'

'Irish, then. A fine-looking beast. But will he survive the heat of an African summer? I wonder. Most of the men are mounted on Basuto ponies. They're small, but incredibly tough.'

'My horse is also tough. Will you have us, Captain?'

Shepstone smiled. 'I will. The local troop musters here for exercises twice a week, and is liable to be called out at twenty-four hours' notice. A trooper's pay is six shillings for every day on duty. You can draw your uniform and equipment from the quartermaster's stores. Welcome to the Carbineers.'

Just over three weeks later was George's nineteenth birthday, and he and his uncle had been invited to dinner by the Colensos. Although he had parted from Fanny on less than satisfactory terms, he hoped she might have reconciled herself to his point of view a little, and thought the celebration would further help his cause. Before going over to Bishopstowe, George was riding through Pietermaritzburg's market square, on his way back from the Carbineers' bi-weekly muster, when he spotted a familiar figure walking in the street. He was leaner than George remembered, his face tanned a deep brown, but the stooped walk was unmistakeably Gossett's.

'Matthew? Is that you?' hollered George as he reined Emperor to a halt.

Gossett looked up and smiled in recognition. 'George! My dear boy, how good to see you.'

'The feeling's mutual. When did you arrive? I'd heard General Thesiger was in town, but no mention of you.'

'I arrived two days ago. Before that I was in Cape Town tying up all the loose ends from the last campaign.'

'So what brings you all to Natal? Is it connected to the boundary award?'

'Come and join me for a drink and I'll explain all.'

George dismounted, tied Emperor to a hitching post and followed Gossett into the red-brick splendour of the nearby Plough Hotel. Shown to a quiet corner table of the bar, they were served whiskies and soda by an elderly waiter in a white apron.

'Cheers,' said Gossett, clinking glasses. 'You look well.'

'I am. It's my birthday.'

'Is it indeed. Happy birthday! How old?'

'Nineteen.'

Gossett shook his head, marvelling at George's youth. 'I see,' he said, eyeing George's dark blue tunic and leather holster, 'that you couldn't resist the lure of the military.'

George laughed. 'No, it helps to pass the time. And I see,' he added, pointing at the field rank on Gossett's collar, 'that you got your brevet.'

'Yes, I'm a major now, so show me some respect.'

'Did the campaign go well?'

'Eventually it did, George, eventually. We weren't too late, thank God, and spent the first couple of months tramping through the Perie Bush, trying to bring Chief Sandilli's Gaikas to battle. When that failed, the general listened to local advice and divided the area of operations into various districts, each patrolled by a mobile force. That had the desired effect, and within a few weeks we had killed or captured most of the leading rebels. We've just heard the general's to be knighted. And Crealock got his lieutenant colonelcy, of course.'

George's heart began to beat a little faster at the mention of Crealock's name, but he tried not to let Gossett notice. 'What about Wood and Buller?'

'They both performed heroics: Wood as a column commander and Buller with a locally raised cavalry unit known as the Frontier Light Horse. As tough a bunch of border ruffians as you're ever likely to meet, but Buller tamed them and is promoted to lieutenant colonel. He and Wood are en route to the Transvaal as we speak, to protect Boer settlers from the Zulus.'

'Do they *need* protecting?'

'Of course they do,' said a voice behind him.

George looked round. 'Colonel Crealock!'

'Hello, Hart,' said the colonel, clearly enjoying George's discomfort. 'I didn't expect to see you again so soon. I'd have thought, after our last chat, that you'd have made yourself scarce by now. Yet here you are, and in uniform too. Aren't you going to salute a superior officer?'

George scrambled out of his seat and offered a hasty salute, which Crealock returned.

'That's better. Now where was I?' said Crealock, pulling up a chair. 'Oh, yes, your question about the Boers. Surely you know about the recent border violation?'

'Yes,' said George, making no mention of his own involvement.

'Well, it should be obvious even to you that the Zulus' blood is up. There's no knowing how they'll react to the commission's forthcoming boundary award, which is why the general's moved his headquarters here.'

'So you're here purely as a precaution, in case the Zulus attack?'

'Of course, though we'd appreciate a little more assistance from the lieutenant governor. Sir Henry Bulwer is so wary of provoking the Zulus that he's refusing to let us take even the most basic measures of defence, such as bringing more regiments into Natal or raising any more troops, white or black. But he's making a big mistake, because as things stand the colony is absolutely unprepared to meet a sudden raid of Zulus within its borders.'

A month earlier George would have dismissed such talk of a raid as warmongering. Now, having visited Zululand and spoken to the young firebrand Mehlokazulu, he was not so sure. 'It is being said,' he responded cautiously, 'that some of the younger warriors will welcome war.'

'Exactly so, and if Cetshwayo doesn't give them what they want, it's possible he'll be overthrown. Either way, we have to be ready for war.'

George left the hotel, relieved that Crealock had said no more about the Plymouth shooting, and more convinced than ever that the Zulus posed a genuine threat to Natal and that Thesiger was right to prepare for the worst.

He then made the mistake of saying exactly that during the candlelit dinner at the Colensos' to celebrate his birthday. Perhaps it was the champagne he'd been served on top of the whisky he had drunk with Gossett, but no sooner were the words out than he regretted them. What had been a jolly, laughter-filled occasion lapsed into stunned silence. Fanny's jaw fell open as if she could hardly believe what she was hearing.

It was left to the bishop to articulate what everyone round the table was thinking. 'Have you taken leave of your senses, George?' he asked, disappointment etched in his craggy face. 'You sound as if you now support this shameless manoeuvring for war.'

All eyes turned to George to await his response. Guest of honour or no, he knew he was in danger of offending his friends, and so chose his words carefully. 'Given my ties of blood to the Zulus, I would never support the launch of an unprovoked war,' he said, looking directly at Fanny, who was seated opposite him. 'But taking sensible defensive precautions does make sense. The feeling in the Carbineers is that we'll be called out any day now.'

'You still don't understand our government's true aim, do you?' said the bishop. 'This build-up of troops has only one purpose: the invasion of Zululand.'

'I don't agree. I know from my recent trip that the younger warriors are very volatile at the moment. Anything could happen.'

'What utter rot! I don't condone what Sihayo's sons did, but a raid to recover a runaway is very different from a full-scale invasion. And to put the raid into perspective, you should be aware that – until a couple of years ago –

the Natal authorities regarded Zulu refugee wives as chattel goods and routinely returned them. Only last year a party of Zulus crossed the Tugela to kidnap a refugee girl, and we merely informed Cetshwayo of the "crime". Moreover, our police have often crossed into Zululand in pursuit of fleeing Kaffirs. So it's a bit rich to expect Cetshwayo, or Sihayo for that matter, to take our recent demands seriously.'

'All I'm saying,' said George, 'is that it's better to be safe than sorry. Why, all the talk in the regiment—'

'Enough!' said Fanny, rising from her seat. 'I can't listen to any more of this.' She marched from the room, her long silk evening dress brushing on the polished floor as she went.

'I must go after her,' said George apologetically. 'Please excuse me.'

He found her on the front veranda, staring into the inky darkness. 'Fanny, whatever's the matter?'

'I'm surprised you need to ask,' she replied, not looking round. 'Since you returned from Zululand you're a different person, much harder. I don't feel I know you any more.'

'I won't pretend that the sight of that poor girl being strangled hasn't changed the way I feel about the Zulus. It has. But I'm still the same person, just less inclined to take a romantic view of my African cousins.'

Fanny spun round to face him, her eyes flashing. 'Unlike us, you mean?'

'Yes . . . no, not exactly. But you must admit your family has a tendency to look for the good in Africans and ignore the bad.'

'We do. And if more settlers followed our example, the more secure we'd all be.'

'Plenty would disagree.'

'I know, George, but what about you? Would you disagree?'

'I . . . I can't decide.'

'I don't understand you, George. You've only been in the country for a few months. If you'd been here longer, you'd know that Cetshwayo has no intention of invading Natal – and nor, I believe, do younger warriors like Mehlokazulu, despite their bravado. And yet if Frere and General Thesiger have their way, and it comes to war, you'll be expected to fight your kinsmen. How could you even contemplate such an act?'

'Fanny, please try and understand my position. I have no desire to fight for the sake of fighting, but I certainly will if the Zulus attack Natal. When all is said and done I'm British, not Zulu, as are you and your family. I'm quite sure your father would help to defend the colony.'

'Father would fight to protect his family, yes. But never in a war of conquest like the one Frere has in mind. I can see your mind is fixed on this matter, so I will wish you a happy birthday and bid you goodnight.' Fanny opened the front door and was about to go back inside when she added, almost as an afterthought. 'It might be best, under the circumstances, if we don't see each other for a time.'

'Fanny, please!' he implored. 'Let's not allow politics, of all things, to come between us.'

'It's not just about politics, George,' she said, a tear in her eye. 'It's about you, and whether you're the person I thought you were.'

'I haven't changed.'

'I'm not so sure. Goodnight,' she said, closing the door behind her.


After the fiasco of his birthday dinner, George kept away from Bishopstowe and worked long hours on his uncle's farm, helping to move the small herd of cattle from one scrubby piece of pasture to the next. With Natal in the grip of one of the worst droughts in living memory, there had been no rain for months, and the scorched veldt was all yellows and browns – not a hint of green. The spring foliage had come out small and shrivelled, the wild flowers stunted, and grazing was at a premium.

George revelled in the outdoor life, walking beneath the huge canopy of African sky, staring at the vast and beautiful landscape, thinking, Yes, maybe this *is* in my blood somewhere. Maybe I could feel I belong here in a way I never belonged at home. This sense of wellbeing was bolstered by the speed with which George improved his spoken Zulu by spending so much time with Mufungu, his uncle's cowherd.

As the weeks passed, and the cattle grew thinner, he picked up snippets of news from the newspapers and from his fellow Carbineers. Sir Bartle Frere had finally arrived in Pietermaritzburg towards the end of September to supervise the long-awaited award of the Boundary Commission, though an announcement had yet to be made; General Thesiger had become Lord Chelmsford on the death of his father; and two more border incidents had taken place, one involving a surveyor from the Colonial Engineer's Department who had been apprehended and questioned by Zulus as he inspected the Middle Drift across the Tugela River near Fort Buckingham. This incident, in particular, had enraged the settler community, and many Carbineers were describing it as the final straw.

George himself was too upset by Fanny's rejection, too preoccupied with his work, to pay much attention to politics. With not enough grazing for the cattle to survive, every day brought the discovery of another carcass. As a last resort, George rode into Pietermaritzburg to buy fodder with his uncle's last few pounds. He was horrified to discover there was none to be had; it had all been bought by the new Lord Chelmsford's commissariat. There was only one conclusion to be drawn. The Colensos had been right all along: the authorities were preparing to invade.

He returned home with the grim news, and was astonished to hear his uncle not only confirm his suspicions but add to them. 'While you were out,' said Patrick, 'a friend of mine called Will Eary dropped by. He's a member of the Buffalo Border Guard on the stretch of the river that includes Rorke's Drift, which, as you know, is a potential point of invasion for either side. Anyway, Will told me some interesting things about his superior, Henry Fynn, the border agent for the district. Apparently Fynn's been telling his men that war with the Zulus is certain, and that when it comes he will settle his differences with a border chief called Matshana who once refused to sell him some of his best cattle because Fynn was offering below market price. When Fynn lost his temper, Matshana ordered him off his land – and ever since Fynn has vowed one day to get his cattle and not pay a penny.'

'He sounds a nasty bit of work,' said George, shaking his head. 'But, even so, how would *he* know that war was inevitable?'

'I couldn't say for sure. But, according to Will, he's had at least three long meetings with Colonel Crealock, Chelmsford's right-hand man.'

'Crealock?' said George, his heart racing at the mere mention of the name. 'Is your friend certain?'

'Yes. He stood guard at one of the meetings, but has no idea what they discussed.'

'More's the pity. I'd have liked to have been a fly on that wall.'

'Well, it may not be too late to find out.'

'How do you mean?'

'The reason Will is in the area is that he's just escorted Fynn to Pietermaritzburg for a meeting, not just with Crealock but with Chelmsford and Sir Bartle Frere also. It sounds to me very much like a council of war.'

'To me too. When and where does the meeting take place?'

'In the Plough Hotel at two this afternoon.'

George pulled out his watch. 'It's just gone noon. If I leave now, I should have plenty of time to locate the meeting room and find a place to eavesdrop.'

'George, is that wise? If you're discovered, they'll throw you out of the Carbineers, and possibly worse.'

'I know. But I owe it to the Colensos to at least try and find out what the authorities are planning.'

Shortly after one, George strode into the lobby of the red-brick Plough Hotel and almost collided with Major Gossett.

'Hello,' said Gossett, 'what are you doing here?'

George trotted out his cover story. 'Thank goodness I've found you. My uncle's cattle are dying of hunger and I've been told your commissariat has bought all the available fodder. Can you tell me why?'

'It's just a precaution, George, in case the Zulus attack. The general wants to be able to move at a moment's notice, and he can only do that if he has adequate transport.'

'Are you sure that's all there is to it?'

'Whatever do you mean?'

'Well, there are rumours you're planning an invasion.'

'All stuff and nonsense, George, but I won't deny we have to prepare for all eventualities in case it does come to war.'

'So nothing's been decided one way or another?'

'No, absolutely not. The general's meeting Sir Bartle this afternoon to discuss security arrangements for the colony. Nothing more.'

'Will you be present?'

'No, I'm too junior. My job is to see the room's supplied with water, notepaper, that sort of thing.'

'I'll give you a hand. It will give us a chance to catch up properly.'

Gossett nodded his assent, and led George upstairs to a large room on the first floor that was empty but for a long oak table and chairs. George could see at a glance that the only place to hide was in a solid wardrobe in a small ante-chamber off the main room. Crucially the two rooms were not separated by a door.

While he helped Gossett lay out the notepaper, pencils and water glasses, he asked about the award of the

Boundary Commission. 'All I know,' said Gossett, 'is that Sir Bartle is still considering it and will make his announcement in a fortnight at the latest.'

'Why has it taken so long?'

'No idea. Presumably Sir Bartle didn't approve of the commission's recommendation.' Gossett glanced around the room. 'Well, I think that's everything. Like to join me for lunch?'

'No, but thank you. I'd better get back to the farm.'

They parted company with a handshake in the lobby. George left the hotel, and gave Gossett enough time to get settled in the dining room before retracing his steps to the first-floor conference room. He made straight for the wardrobe in the ante-room – a heavy oak affair with a looking-glass on the door – and climbed inside, arranging the hanging overcoats as best he could to cover him. It was stuffy and cramped, with not enough room to stand up straight, but he was unconcerned. Hearing the conversation was all that mattered.

With an hour to wait, George closed his eyes and dozed. He was woken by a deep, authoritative voice he did not recognize. '. . . and so my strategy is this: when the Natal authorities announce the award of the Boundary Commission in early December, they'll also present the Zulus with an ultimatum. And you'll be glad to hear, gentlemen, that Sir Henry Bulwer has at last agreed to drop his objections and sign the ultimatum.' He guessed it was the Cape governor speaking, and soon had confirmation.

'That's wonderful news, Sir Bartle,' said a voice that sounded like the general's. 'However did you manage to persuade the lieutenant governor to change his mind?'

'I simply told him that it was foolish to allow King Cetshwayo to keep up a perpetual army of thirty to forty thousand disciplined warriors, and that we could not simply withdraw our troops from the border without doing irreparable damage to our imperial prestige. All of which is true. I added that the ultimatum did not necessarily mean war, which is also true, but highly unlikely. We're demanding nothing more or less than the total dismantling of the Zulu military system. If Cetshwayo agrees, he will no longer pose a significant military threat and will almost certainly be deposed; if he doesn't, we'll declare war and invade. Either way the Zulus will, in a few months' time, no longer be an obstacle to confederation and – dare I say it, gentlemen? – progress.'

'May I congratulate you, Sir Bartle,' said a third voice, Crealock's, 'on a masterly achievement. The general and I were convinced that Sir Henry would not budge, yet you have him eating out of your hand.'

'Not quite, Colonel. Let's just say that Sir Henry, like most men, knows what's good for him. But enough of that; tell me about your plans if, as he's bound to, Cetshwayo rejects the ultimatum and decides to fight.'

'May I answer, sir?' Crealock asked his chief.

'By all means,' said Chelmsford.

'Thank you. Soon after we arrived in Natal in August, Sir Bartle, I drew up a contingency plan, which I have here. It's called "Invasion of Zululand, or Defence of the Natal and Transvaal Colony from Invasion by the Zulus", but the second part of the title was merely a sop to placate Sir Henry. The plan was always to take the offensive by invading Zululand with five separate columns, each consisting of at least one battalion of British infantry. The intention is for these columns to converge on Ulundi, the Zulu capital, from five different directions. That way we hope to flush the Zulus out into the open, much like driving pheasants. Our chief worry is that they won't fight, and that we'll be forced to withdraw because of supply difficulties.'

'May I take a look?'

'Of course.'

There was a pause while Frere read the document. 'I see that each column will be composed of British infantry, mounted volunteers, artillery and native levies. Will that be enough firepower to stop the Zulus if they concentrate all their force against a single column?'

'Without doubt. Each column will have a minimum of a thousand British rifles, not to mention the supporting troops. They'll be more than a match for anything Cetshwayo can throw at them.'

'How many native levies?'

'None, until yesterday, when Sir Henry finally gave us the go-ahead to train and equip three regiments of native infantry, six troops of native horse and a force of pioneers. We'll have seven thousand in total, split between the columns.'

'Under whose command?'

'Colonel Anthony Durnford of the Royal Engineers.'

'Isn't he a friend of Bishop Colenso?'

'He is, but he's also a soldier and an ambitious one at that. It was his idea to augment each column with native levies, so it made sense to put him in charge. He speaks the lingo, after all, and has some experience commanding black troops. But his real expertise is as a sapper, and he used it to good effect by writing us an extremely helpful memorandum on bridging the Tugela. The surveyor who was apprehended by Zulus at the end of September was actually carrying out Durnford's instructions to inspect the Middle Drift of the Tugela with a view to ferrying troops across.'

Frere chuckled. 'So the Zulus were right to be suspicious.'

'Yes, but he denied everything and they had to let him go.'

George could not believe what he was hearing. Why would Durnford, of all people, help to prepare the invasion? Surely he wanted to prevent war. It did not make sense.

'And we end up turning the incident to our advantage,' said Frere admiringly, 'by expressing outrage that the Zulus have dared to arrest a harmless white surveyor. Now, as you know, my intention is to issue the ultimatum at the same time we announce the boundary award, to sugar the pill, so to speak. What I need to know is when it would make sense to do this from a military point of view.'

'I think,' said Lord Chelmsford, 'that Mr Fynn might best answer that question. He's a local, after all, and has forgotten more than most people know about the Zulus.'

'I'm flattered you have such faith in me, my Lord,' said a voice with a faint colonial accent. 'But could I first ask Sir Bartle how much time the Zulus will be given to comply with the ultimatum?'

'Thirty days.'

'Then early December would be ideal. That way, if the ultimatum is refused, we'll be able to declare war in early January, when the rivers are in spate, so providing Natal with a natural barrier from a counterattack. It's also harvest time and the Zulus won't be able to sustain a long campaign.'

'Excellent,' said Frere. 'Early December it is. Now, are you sure, Lord Chelmsford, you'll have enough men to complete the job?'

'I will if the War Office agrees to send the two extra British battalions I've asked for. I have six already, but would prefer eight: one for each column, one in reserve and two for garrison duty. But it seems that trouble is brewing in Afghanistan and the Cabinet is worried that it won't have enough troops to fight both wars at the same time.'

'Don't worry about that. I've told Hicks Beach at the Colonial Office that it'll be on the government's head if the war goes badly because your request for more troops was ignored. They'll send them, never fear. They can't afford not to.'

'But if the Cabinet's so keen to avoid a war,' said Chelmsford, 'won't it regard your ultimatum as unnecessarily harsh?'

'Sir Henry's ultimatum, if you please. As Lieutenant Governor of Natal it's only right that he should issue it. But you're right about one thing. The government wouldn't thank me if it knew. Which is why I won't send the details until it's far too late. One of the chief benefits of the one-month time-lag between here and

London is that, when the situation demands, we can present policy as a fait accompli. By the time the government learns the truth, we'll have fought and won the war, and no one will be interested in its origins. I'll be well on the way to my peerage and you'll return home heroes.'

'"To the victors the spoils", eh, Sir Bartle?' said Crealock.

'Exactly so, Colonel, exactly so. Well, if there's nothing else, I'll take my leave. I depart for the Transvaal tomorrow and have to be up early.'

'I must go too,' said Chelmsford. 'I need to speak to Colonel Bellairs about the commissariat.'

George heard the door open and close as Frere and Chelmsford departed. He was desperate to be out of the hotel and on his way to Bishopstowe with news of Frere's diabolical plot. But the others seemed in no hurry to leave. George could hear a cork being pulled and the sound of glasses being filled.

'I think congratulations are in order, Colonel,' said Fynn. 'I can't see the Zulus wriggling out of this one. But tell me, how did you win Lord Chelmsford over to our way of thinking? When we last spoke, you said he was hopeful of a peaceful outcome.'

'And so he was, despite Sir Bartle making it perfectly clear to us, when we stayed with him in Cape Town after the frontier war, that he was determined to conquer the Zulus. But I gradually convinced him by arguing that the Zulus posed a considerable security threat to their white neighbours and that it was better to launch first strike than to wait on events.'

'Clever of you. And I take it he knows nothing of our agreement to share the proceeds from the sale of Mat-shana's famous herd of white cattle?'

'Of course not. For all his faults as a field commander, he's the "honourable" type who would never stoop so low as to profit financially from war. More fool him.'

'I'll drink to that. Talking of profit and losses, I take it you've been avoiding the gaming tables since our last meeting.'

'Would that it were so, Mr Fynn. I lost twenty pounds only two nights since. I've sustained considerable losses since I arrived in this blasted country, to say nothing of my debts in London. I have never known a run like it. It's sheer bad luck, but without that cattle money, I'm sunk.'

'Worry not, Colonel. It's as good as ours. Here's to a short, sharp and profitable campaign!'

'I'll second that!' echoed Crealock.

George was aghast at what he had just heard. It was bad enough that Britain's senior political and military representatives in southern Africa were plotting war against the wishes of their government. Far worse was the revelation that two of their subordinates were aiming to make money from the conflict. The only consolation for George was that it gave him a hold over Crealock, the only man who suspected his involvement in Thompson's death. As for Durnford, he was clearly not the pacifist Fanny believed him to be, which could only help George's cause in the battle for her affections.

With these last thoughts uppermost in mind, he waited patiently, if uncomfortably, while the two plotters worked their way through the celebratory bottle of wine. He estimated he had been there for more than two hours and was desperate to massage the circulation back into his cramped limbs. But, fearful of being caught, he was unwilling to do more than shift his position by a fraction of an inch.

Even after the pair finally left the room, he waited a good five minutes before opening the wardrobe door a crack. Both rooms were silent, and obviously empty, so George crept out of the wardrobe, grimacing with pain as the blood began to return to his stiff legs. He hobbled across the conference room as quietly as he could, tried the door and found it unlocked. He was about to leave when he remembered the memorandum that Frere had been given to read. Had they left it in the room? He decided to check, knowing how keen the bishop would be to have it. But as he tiptoed back towards the long, paper-strewn table in the centre of the room, he heard the ominous sound of the door handle turning. With no time to regain the wardrobe, he threw himself to the floor and scrambled under the table.

The door opened and footsteps rang out on the wooden floor, coming to a halt next to where George lay hidden. He could see black boots and, above them, blue trousers with two red stripes down the seam. The only officer he knew with trousers like that was Crealock. George held his breath as Crealock gathered up the documents and turned to leave. But something caused the colonel to pause. He was looking towards the ante-room. George's heart seemed to miss a beat as he realized what Crealock had seen. The wardrobe door was open. He had forgotten to shut it.

Crealock strode over to the wardrobe and looked inside. 'I don't believe it,' he roared. 'A bloody spy!'

George knew he had just seconds to escape. Taking a deep breath, he scuttled out from the table and sprinted for the door, praying that Crealock would not recognize him from behind. His hand closed on the handle as a voice behind yelled, 'Stop, or I'll shoot!'

George spun round to see a pistol aimed at this chest. 'So it was you,' said Crealock. 'You simply can't stay out of trouble, can you?'

George looked defiant. '*Me* in trouble? What about you and your co-conspirators? Your plan to provoke war for your own selfish ambitions is bad enough, but then you and Fynn top it with a base attempt to make money from the fighting. I had no idea you were a gambler, too, Colonel. What, I wonder, would your chief make of that?'

'You dare to threaten me!' roared Crealock. 'I'll have you flogged. May I remind you, Trooper Hart, that as a soldier you're bound by military law, which states that passing intelligence to the enemy is an offence punishable by death.'

'But the Zulus aren't the enemy, are they? May I remind *you*, Colonel, that we're not at war. Not yet, at any rate. And I had no intention of passing any information to the Zulus.'

'So why eavesdrop on our conversation?'

'Because I needed to know.'

'*Needed*? You're a failed officer in your teens, little more than a soldier of fortune. Why would you *need* to know? There's something you're not telling me. What is it?'

George said nothing.

'Why are you so interested in the fate of the Zulus? What are they to you? Come on, out with it!'

George just glared.

'I've heard the rumours, you know,' continued Crealock. 'I just need you to confirm them.'

'What rumours?'

'That the half-breed you're staying with is actually your uncle, which makes you part black too. No wonder you're a pet of the Colensos. I hear the prettiest daughter, Fanny, has quite a penchant for black men.'

The blood rose in George's cheeks; if Crealock had not been holding a gun he would have flown at him. 'How dare you suggest . . . ?'

'Oh, I dare all right. You know, Hart, from the moment I met you I thought there was something not right. You looked so shifty when you first boarded the ship. And then I heard about the murder, saw you with the young girl, and it all became clear.'

'I don't know what you're talking about.'

'No? Well, let's put my suspicions to the test, shall we? Are you prepared to return to Plymouth to help the police with their enquiries?'

'Certainly not. I have no intention of returning to Britain in the foreseeable future.'

'I can well imagine. Let me be frank with you. I know enough about you to send you to the gallows twice over. Your black blood certainly gives you a motive to betray the land of your birth. But I'm prepared to keep quiet about all this if you agree to say nothing about what you've heard today. If your friend Bishop Colenso gets wind of what we're planning, he'll go straight to the press; and if Chelmsford hears about my money-making scheme, he'll sack me on the spot. So not a word. Do we have a deal?'

George knew Crealock had him over a barrel. The spying charge alone would see him court-martialled and end his military career for good. He had to agree. Whether he would stick to that agreement was another matter. 'All right,' he said after a lengthy pause. 'I'll go along with your deal. But just remember it cuts both ways.'

George spent the next week agonizing over what to do. In some ways he welcomed the harder line the authorities were taking against King Cetshwayo; but reasonable demands were one thing, an unacceptable ultimatum quite another, as it made war all but inevitable. More than once he was tempted to ride to Bishopstowe and reveal all. What held him back was the realization that it might not make any difference, that the war would still go ahead and that the loss of his career, and possibly even his life, would be for nothing. He salved his conscience by telling himself he could do more good in uniform than out, by keeping an eye on Crealock and, if it came to war, by trying to prevent the maltreatment of Zulu noncombatants. He was cheered, too, by the belief that Colonel Durnford, his chief rival for Fanny's hand, had made much the same decision to fight rather than resign. And in the end, though he was loath to admit it, he knew that the prospect of war excited him: both the chance to put his training into practice and to prove himself against a redoubtable opponent.

He resolved at least to try and explain some of this to

Fanny, and arranged to meet her in Pietermaritzburg during one of her weekly shopping trips. They had barely sat down to tea in the Queen's Hotel, the only hostelry not full of military men, when Colonel Durnford entered the dining room wearing a Sam Browne belt complete with pistol and hunting knife. He was not dressed for peace, and looked more pugnacious still on seeing that George and Fanny were alone.

'Anthony,' said Fanny, her face lighting up, 'what a pleasant surprise.'

'Please excuse my intrusion,' replied Durnford, trying and failing to disguise his irritation. 'Your father told me I would find you here. I wanted you to be the first to know my news. Lord Chelmsford has offered me the command of one of his defensive columns on the Zulu border.'

Fanny gaped. 'And you *accepted*?'

Durnford's face went red. 'Yes, of course. Why would I not? I'm a soldier, after all. It's my duty.'

'Your *duty*! What about your duty as a Christian? I'm shocked that you, Anthony, of all people, would help to prosecute an unlawful war.'

'I'm sorry you feel that way, Fanny, but it's not for me, or any soldier, to decide whether a war is justified. We must be above politics.'

'Yes, but not above morality. Or else you're nothing more than mercenaries.'

'Please, Fanny,' said Durnford, frowning, 'if I thought for a minute that my resignation would change anything, I would tender it today. But I suspect that war is inevitable, and it will be better for all concerned if it's short and successful.'

'You mean for the British?' asked Fanny.

'And the Zulus too. Everyone suffers in a long war.'

Fanny snorted. 'Why can't you be honest with yourself? I saw the look of triumph in your eye as you told me of your appointment. You welcome this war as an opportunity to prove yourself, and to remove the doubts about your military competence that have persisted since the death of those poor Carbineers at Bushman's River Pass.'

'How can you think that? I wasn't responsible for their death. It was just bad luck.'

'I'm sure it was, but most of the settler community here don't see it like that, do they?'

'I'm sorry you can't be happier for me,' said Durnford bitterly as he replaced his hat. 'I'll leave you to your cosy tête-à-tête. I've got duties to attend to. Do give my regards to your family.'

'I will. But I don't imagine any of them will take pleasure in your news.'

Durnford nodded and left.

'Are you all right, Fanny?' asked George, secretly exulting that his rival had been given such short shrift.

She wiped a tear from under her eye. 'No, I'm not all right. How could he, after all he's said and done to try and prevent war, take such pleasure in his new appointment? If he fights, I don't know how I'll be able to forgive him.'

'So where does that leave me? I joined the Carbineers knowing that war was possible.'

'Yes,' she said sadly, 'don't remind me. But you have at least some excuse. I know you were deeply affected by your trip to Zululand, and that you're convinced change is necessary. But you must know in your heart of hearts that war rarely changes things for the better.'

'I suppose I do. But it needn't come to war if Cetshwayo is prepared to make concessions.'

'What exactly do you mean?'

'I can't say, but all will be revealed in a fortnight.'

# I I

## *Lower Drift of the Tugela, 11 December 1878*

Swollen with the recent rains, the broad river was running fast and strong between the steep green banks of the Lower Drift, just a few miles north of its egress into the Indian Ocean. Shielding his eyes from the glare of the sun, George watched with fascination as, slowly but surely, the small ferry was worked back across the broad stretch of water by bluejackets of the Naval Brigade, their faces red with exertion as they hauled on the ropes attached to the near bank. Squatting nervously in the centre of the boat was a small group of Zulu chiefs and their retainers, members of the delegation that had come to hear the announcement of the long-awaited boundary award. A single white man sat among them.

George was standing with his detachment of Carbineers on a narrow ledge overlooking the drift. Above and behind them, atop the bluff, was the recently constructed earthwork known as Fort Pearson, named after the local British commander; to their left, beneath the sharp shadow of a large awning that had been slung between two fig trees, sat the British deputation that would make the announcement: John Shepstone, Bernard Fynney, the local border magistrate who would translate for the Zulus, and

Colonel Walker of the Scots Guards, Frere's military secretary. George and his troop of Carbineers had escorted Shepstone and Walker down from Pietermaritzburg.

George knew what was coming, and had spent much of the three-day march through the waterlogged terrain of northeastern Natal trying to decide what to say to the Zulu delegates if he had the opportunity. He wanted to emphasize the futility of taking on the might of the British Empire. Whether they, or more importantly Cetshwayo, would listen to him was another matter.

With the pont safely secured on the Natal bank, the Zulu delegates and their white companion disembarked and began to climb the dirt road that led to the meeting place. Minutes later they appeared over the rise to the left of awning, prompting the officer in charge of the naval guard of honour to bellow, 'Attention!'

A double row of boots crashed to the floor as the sailors, in blue tunics and white helmets, stiffened to attention. Behind them stood more sailors, a mixture of black and white, manning two nine-pounder field guns and a single US-made Gatling machine gun. But they were not part of the guard of honour and remained at ease, as did George and the Carbineers, their Martini-Henry carbines cradled in their arms.

'Welcome, welcome,' said John Shepstone, his moustache bristling as he rose to greet the Zulus.

'Hello, John,' responded the white member of the delegation, his handsome, nut-brown face wreathed in a smile as he strode forward to shake Shepstone's hand. 'It's been a long time.'

A fine-looking, powerfully built man, he was wearing a beautifully cut tweed suit and could have been mistaken for an English gentleman on the Yorkshire moors, but for his large wideawake hat and the brace of pistols at his waist.

'Who's that?' whispered George to his neighbour, a young trooper by the name of Walwyn Barker.

'Why that's John Dunn, the White Induna. He's chief of the large district across the river, and a great favourite of Cetshwayo. They say he has forty-nine Zulu wives and yet lives in a European-style house with furniture from London.'

'Extraordinary. How did he end up in Zululand?'

'He began as a border agent and actually fought against Cetshwayo in the fifties. But he later switched sides and has served the king faithfully ever since as an advisor. He's now one of the richest chiefs in—'

'Silence in the ranks!' shouted Sergeant Bullock, their thickset NCO. Barker shrugged his shoulders in resignation.

George turned back to see Dunn and the leading Zulus squatting down in a rough semi-circle in front of the trestle table; behind them, bristling with spears and knobkerries, sat their retainers. Not above fifty men in all, and no match for the firepower the British had assembled.

Shepstone began proceedings by slowly reading the details of the boundary award, pausing after each paragraph so that Fynney could translate. 'The high commissioner,' began Shepstone, 'has graciously confirmed the Zululand–Transvaal border as following the Blood River to its main source in the Magidela Mountains and thence in a direct line to a round hill between the two main sources of the Phongolo river in the Drakensburg.'

As Fynney completed his translation of this crucial first passage, the Zulu chiefs murmured appreciatively. They were less impressed when Shepstone went on to confirm Boer ownership of existing farms in Zululand, while denying Zulu claims to property on the Transvaal side of the line, on the grounds that Boer law did not allow Africans to own land. But the first overt signs of dissatisfaction, in the form of angry muttering, began when Shepstone stated that Cetshwayo was to relinquish all claims to land north of the Phongolo river. On hearing this, Chief Vumandaba, the portly leader of the delegation, sprang up and shouted in Zulu, 'What is this? The British have no right to dictate terms on the Phongolo. It is between us and the Swazi.'

George's grasp of the Zulu language had come on in leaps and bounds, thanks to long conversations with Mufungu, his uncle's cowherd, and he understood the gist of the chief's angry words. He was surprised, therefore, when Shepstone's noncommittal response – that any Trans-Phongolo claim would have to be submitted to the British government – seemed to smooth the chief's ruffled feathers.

Shepstone further mollified the Zulus by announcing a break in proceedings so that a freshly slaughtered ox could be cooked and eaten. The Zulus were delighted, and used their assegais to carve strips of meat from the carcass, which they washed down with liberal quantities of maize beer. The mood of the delegation seemed relaxed and jovial, and George took the opportunity to speak to a young induna who was squatting on the fringes of the main group. '*Sakubona!*' said George, raising his hand in greeting.

The young chief looked up at George with a quizzical expression on his broad, handsome face. He was naked but for a genet loincloth, and powerfully built with broad shoulders and muscular arms. His assegais and large rawhide shield, black with white spots, lay close to hand.

George introduced himself as a cousin of Chief Sihayo. The Zulu raised his eyebrows. 'How can you be Sihayo's kin? You're a white horse soldier.'

'A soldier, yes, but not entirely white. My grandmother was Sihayo's sister.'

'How can that be?'

George tried to explain but the chief looked unconvinced. At last, a smile spreading across his face, he rose to clap George on the shoulder. 'It's so unlikely it must be true. I'm Kumbeka, son of Chief Vumandaba, good friend of Sihayo's son Mehlokazulu. We're both junior indunas of the Ngobamakhosi Regiment.'

'A ringless regiment, I see,' said George with a grin, gesturing towards the absence of an *isicoco* in Kumbeka's hair.'

'Sadly, yes. But we're still young, and live in hope that our king will permit us to marry once we've proved ourselves in battle.'

'Fighting anyone in particular?'

'Who knows? We have many enemies: the Boers, the Swazi and soon, depending upon the outcome of these talks, maybe even the British.'

'That's what I wanted to—'

'Trooper Hart!' barked a voice behind George, who turned to see his red-faced troop officer, Lieutenant Scott, striding towards him. 'What do you think you're doing?'

George frowned. He had never heard Scott, a quiet man with a droopy moustache and a penchant for amateur dramatics, raise his voice in anger before. 'I was just trying out my Zulu, sir. May I present Kumbeka, son of Chief Vumandaba.'

'No, you may not. You weren't given permission to fraternize with the Zulu delegation. Kindly return to the ranks.'

George was about to respond but the cold, angry look on Scott's fine-boned face deterred him. Instead he raised his hand in farewell to Kumbeka and strode back to the other Carbineers. It had to be a bad sign, thought George, when the mild-mannered Scott began to treat the Zulus as if they were already the enemy.

With lunch over, the Zulus returned to their places in front of the trestle table so that Shepstone could read out Frere's ultimatum. This was the moment that George had been dreading. 'The Zulu king,' intoned a grim-looking John Shepstone, 'has not kept the promise he made at his coronation in 1873 to introduce laws for the better government of the Zulu people. The military system, moreover, is destroying the country by not allowing men to labour for themselves and to live in quiet and in peace, with their families and relatives. And the army was not for self-defence but an instrument for the oppression of the people.'

This was too much for Kumbeka to take, and he growled, 'Have the Zulus complained?'

Ignoring him, Shepstone continued in his deep baritone voice, 'While Cetshwayo keeps such a huge standing army, it is impossible for his neighbours to feel secure. The British government has been forced to keep large numbers of imperial troops in Natal and the Transvaal to guard against possible aggression by the Zulu king, and this is a state of affairs that cannot be allowed to continue.'

Shepstone paused before reading out Frere's demands. He knew there would be no turning back and the Zulu delegates seemed to sense it too. Their angry murmurs had died away and they sat there stony-faced, expecting the worst. George could hardly bear to listen.

'Her Majesty's high commissioner,' resumed Shepstone, 'has now, therefore, to require that the Zulu king will forthwith send in to the Natal government, for trial under the laws of the colony, for the offence committed by them in the colony, the persons of Mehlokazulu and Mkhumbukazulu, the sons of Sihayo. They must be sent in and delivered over to the Natal authorities within twenty days of the date that this demand is made. A fine of five hundred cattle must also be paid by that date.'

But worse, far worse, was to come. 'It is necessary,' said Shepstone, 'that the military system which is at present kept up by the king should be done away with, as a bad and hurtful one; and that the king should, instead, adopt such military regulations as may be decided on after consultation with the Great Council of the Zulus and with representatives of the British government.'

No sooner had this general clause been translated by Fynney than the Zulu delegation erupted in a storm of protest. Shepstone raised his hand to still the cries and, when they had subsided, continued with the specifics: the Zulu army to be disbanded and the men returned to their homes; all able-bodied men would still be liable for military service in the defence of their country, but until then to be allowed to live quietly at home; no man to be called up without the sanction of the Council of Chiefs and British officials; every man to be free to marry 'when he pleases'; no Zulu to be punished for a crime unless convicted by a court of 'properly appointed indunas'; no one to be executed without a fair and open trial and the right of appeal to the king; a British resident to reside in or near Zululand to enforce the terms of the ultimatum; and missionaries and Christian converts to be allowed to return to Zululand. The deadline for meeting these demands was thirty days.

The Zulu delegation listened in shock as, one by one, the harsh terms were translated. Taken together they amounted to nothing less than the total emasculation of the Zulu state, and were clearly unacceptable. George glanced across at Kumbeka. He was shaking his head, his face a mask of proud defiance. His portly father, wearing a splendid headdress of blue crane feathers with leopardskin earflaps, was the first to speak. Rising to his feet, his face quivering with emotion, he denied the coronation laws had been broken. 'Nor can I understand,' he added, 'the need to disband an institution as ancient and necessary as the army.'

'Because,' replied Shepstone, as though he was talking to a child, 'it poses a serious threat to the subjects of Natal, whereas Cetshwayo knows the British government presents no threat to the Zulus.'

'What about them?' asked Vumandaba, pointing towards George and the armed escort.

'They are for defence, and are only here because of Cetshwayo's actions.'

Vumandaba snorted in derision. Shepstone, he realized, would not be swayed by argument and further discussion was pointless. After conferring briefly with Dunn and the leading indunas, he asked Shepstone for an extension to the deadline. 'Thirty days,' he implored, 'is far too little time for the Royal Council to discuss and respond to these demands. On matters as important as these, no time limit should be set. We ask, too, that a British representative is present when these demands are presented to the king so that he can verify their accuracy.'

Shepstone was unmoved by what he saw as a feeble attempt to deflect Cetshwayo's anger by allowing a Briton to deliver the bad news. 'I have no authority to agree to such a request,' he said coldly, 'or to alter any of the terms of the ultimatum.'

Declaring the meeting over, he strode forward and handed copies of the boundary award and the ultimatum to John Dunn, who was squatting next to Vumandaba. 'Can you make sure Cetshwayo gets these?' said Shepstone. 'And can you tell him that the thirty-day limit is final. There will be no extension.'

'I will tell him, John. But you do know he can't comply. If he does, he's finished in Zululand.'

'Which is exactly what he'll be if he doesn't. Make sure he knows that.'

Dunn nodded, made a sign to Vumandaba and, as one, the Zulu delegation rose to its feet and began to depart down the track to the drift.

George knew it was now or never. 'Sir,' he said to Lieutenant Scott, 'permission to fall out and relieve my-self.'

'Yes, go on, then. The fun's over.'

George ducked behind a nearby thicket, found a path that seemed to be heading down to the drift and followed it. He was just in time. As he emerged from the scrub on to the flat ground that led to the river bank, the first of the Zulu delegates were climbing aboard the pont. Fortunately Kumbeka, the man he had come to talk to, was at the rear of the group. As George ran towards him, still clutching his carbine, one of the Zulu escort misread his intention and sprang forward, assegai in hand, to bar his path. He was young and fit, the muscles of his chest tensed in anticipa-tion, and clearly determined that George would not pass. In his left hand he clutched the distinctive black shield with white spots of the Ngobamakhosi Regiment; in his right a stabbing assegai. With George just yards away and the warrior poised to strike, Kumbeka glanced round and shouted at the warrior to lower his weapon. He did so, leaving George to sprint past and come to a breathless halt in front of Kumbeka, the other Zulus eyeing him warily.

'I must speak with you,' said George, bending forward to ease the pain in his stomach from running.

'What is there to say?' replied Kumbeka. 'Your chiefs are determined on war, and war they shall have. Cetsh-wayo cannot agree to their demands. If he does, he shames not only himself but the nation. The army is his strength, the only thing keeping the more powerful chiefs in order. If he disbands it, he might as well kill himself, because others surely will.'

'I understand that, but the alternative is far worse for the Zulus. If you take on the British, you will lose. Many warriors will die and the country will be eaten up by the white man. Cetshwayo must put his people first. If he doesn't agree to at least some of the demands, Zululand will not survive.'

'There is much sense in what you say, and I will try, through my father, to make Cetshwayo understand. But it won't be easy. The more hot-headed of his advisors and warriors will demand he stands firm.'

'Of course, but he must ignore them.' George leant forward and grasped Kumbeka's hand. 'Tell my cousin Mehlokazulu that if he and his brother give themselves up to the British, Sobantu will do everything he can to secure their early release.'

'I will tell him. *Sala kahle*, brother, and thank you,' said Kumbeka, as he waved the last of the Zulu delegates into the pont.

'*Hamba kahle!*' replied George, unconvinced he had done anything more than delay the inevitable.

# 12

It was a baking hot day and George and Bishop Colenso were sitting in easy chairs on the front veranda, drinking glasses of lemonade. The air was heavy with the scent of lemons and tropical flowers. It was an idyllic scene, but George had little time for his surroundings. 'I'm sorry to be the bearer of bad news, John,' he said, after the black maid had left them, 'but I've just heard from my friend Major Gossett that war is imminent.'

'But when you called a week ago,' said the bishop, 'you said that your advice to Kumbeka might have done some good, and that Cetshwayo had offered to surrender Sihayo's sons, pay the cattle fine and submit the other ultimatum demands to his advisors.'

'It's true, he did make that offer in a letter to Frere. But he also said he needed more time and Frere has refused to give him any. He's warned Cetshwayo that if the men and cattle aren't handed over by the first deadline tomorrow he'll order Chelmsford to invade, but not take any hostile action until the expiry of the thirty-day deadline. He's not leaving anything to chance. He knows the recent rains have made it almost impossible for Cetshwayo to hand over the cattle in time. He also knows that early January is the best time to invade because the rivers are at their height and it's harvest time.'

'The whole thing's monstrous,' said the bishop, his mutton-chop whiskers quivering with indignation. 'Frere planned this from the start, I'm sure of it.'

'So it would appear,' said George, though he knew only too well the truth of the bishop's words. 'I'm sorry, I truly am.'

'Don't apologize. You did what you could, and for that I'm grateful. I just hope it's over soon, with as few casualties as possible on either side.'

'I hope so too. And if I can do anything to prevent unnecessary suffering, I will.'

'Thank you, George. You have a good heart.'

'Well, I must be leaving,' said George, rising. 'I'm on duty at first light and have a long ride ahead of me.'

The bishop stood and embraced George. 'God bless you,' he said, 'and keep you safe. Wouldn't you like to say your farewells to Fanny? She should be back from town about now.'

'I . . . don't think that's a good idea, under the circumstances. I'm sure she'll understand. Goodbye, John.'

'Goodbye.'

George had barely reached the bottom of the veranda steps when a lady trotted into view riding sidesaddle. It was Fanny, causing George's heart to skip a beat, as it always did when he saw her.

He walked over to hold the horse while she dismounted.

'Thank you, George,' she said, smiling. 'It's good to see you.'

'And you. I wasn't expecting to see you before . . .'

'Before?'

'. . . I leave for the front.'

'What front?' said Fanny, her pretty face screwed in consternation. 'Father told me that Cetshwayo was trying to negotiate.'

'He is, but Frere won't give him any more time. He means for us to invade on or soon after New Year's Day.'

Fanny buried her face in her hands. 'That monster,' she sobbed. 'We had such hopes the boundary award would bring peace. But now it seems Frere only allowed the commission to distract the Zulus while he gathered his forces.'

That's not the half of it, thought George as he tried to comfort her by placing his arm round her shoulder. 'Please don't,' said Fanny, pushing him away. 'You've got your war. Just go.'

'That's not fair. I didn't want this war, and tried hard to prevent it. But if some some good comes out of it – like the destruction of Cetshwayo's brutal system of rule – then it won't have been entirely in vain.'

'You're so naïve, George. When has good *ever* come out of war?'

'It does occasionally, Fanny. Some wars *have* to be fought.'

'I don't believe in "just wars", George. And even if I did, this certainly isn't one.'

'No. I'm not denying the cynicism behind it, but the outcome might just be positive for the Zulus in the long term.'

'Do you really believe that?'

'Yes I do. It may not be obvious to you, but I feel a strange affinity to this land, and genuinely care what happens to its people.'

'Then why fight against your own kind?'

'Because they're not my own kind. Do I look or sound like a Zulu to you? No, because I'm not. I may have a little Zulu blood in my veins, but all my instincts and prejudices are those of a British soldier.'

'Who are you trying to convince, George? You say you feel an affinity to Africa, and that's because part of you *is* African.'

'Maybe you're right. But I'm also a British soldier and my duty now is to fight.'

Fanny shook her head slowly. 'Anthony said the same thing, but at least he's got the excuse of a long career.'

'Fanny, please! I don't want to part on bad terms. It may be . . .' His voice tailed off.

Fanny snorted contemptuously. 'What? The last time we see each other? It might well be. And whose fault is that? Why can't you admit you're excited by the prospect of war? All men are.'

George knew there was some truth in what she said, but he was loath to admit it. 'I know you don't want me to fight. But please believe me when I say I'll try to do the right thing.'

'The right thing is not to go.'

'I can't resign again. Soldiering is in my blood, and it's the only way I know how to make a living. And, though I haven't told you this, I desperately need money to support my mother.'

'There are other ways to earn money.'

'Not for me.'

'I'll say no more, George. You know my feelings.'

George nodded. 'Fanny, I appreciate this isn't a good time to ask, but I may not see you again for a while and I have to know.'

'Know what?'

'Whether there's any hope for *us*.'

Fanny stared intently at George's face, as if consigning it to memory. His clean-shaven complexion was much darker now, his hair longer, but the colour of his eyes was as she remembered: light brown with flecks of green and amber, much like a ripe hazelnut.

'I prefer you without a moustache,' she said quietly.

'You haven't answered my question.'

'There's always hope, George, but it's fading fast.'

The rain fell steadily as George walked Emperor towards the Central Column's huge tented camp at Rorke's Drift on the Zulu border. It had moved there from Helpmekaar two days earlier, on 8 January, and was situated on the flat, thorny scrub that lay between the river and Witt's mission station, which, with the invasion imminent, had been taken over by the military, the church reverting to a store and the house converted into a makeshift hospital. Witt had elected to stay on to guard his property, though he had sent his wife and children to stay with friends at Umsinga, twenty miles to the south.

As he rode, George mulled over events since the expiry of the first deadline on 31 December. Lord Chelmsford had been forced by a lack of transport to modify his original plan to invade with five columns, and would now use just three: the Northern, Central and Southern Columns under Colonels Wood, Glyn and Pearson respectively. He would accompany Glyn's – the largest of the three, to which George was attached – but it, along with Pearson's, was not scheduled to invade until after the expiry of the second deadline that evening. Wood's column was already in Zululand, having crossed the border on 6 January. The plan was still for all three columns to converge on the Zulu capital of Ulundi, hoping to bring the main Zulu army to battle in the process. This much George had learnt from his good friend Major Gossett, who had arrived in camp with the rest of the headquarters staff a week earlier.

George had been out since dawn, scouting the river bank to the south for any sign of a Zulu ambush, but had seen only civilians gathering wood. With luck the crossing of the river, scheduled for the following morning, would be unopposed.

'Who goes there?' barked a voice in the murky drizzle.

'Trooper George Hart of the Carbineers, back from patrol.'

'Password?'

'Aldershot.'

'Pass, friend.'

George rode on, nodding to the bedraggled redcoat sentry as he passed the outer picket. The Carbineer lines were at the far end of the camp, and to reach them he had to pass the tents and wagons of the various corps that made up the invasion force: two incomplete battalions of imperial infantry, the 1st and 2nd/24th, in red tunics with green facings; N/5 Battery of the Royal Artillery in blue with red piping; a squadron each of Imperial Mounted Infantry and Natal Mounted Police in red and black respectively; a small detachment of the Army Hospital Corps in dark blue with lighter blue velvet collars and cuffs; a company of NNC Pioneers in redcoats and white trousers, the uniform Durnford had intended for the rest of the contingent; two battalions of Lonsdale's 3rd Natal Native Contingent in traditional costume; and, lastly, the Natal Carbineers in blue. It was a veritable kaleidoscope of colour. Staff officers and civilian wagon-drivers – most of whom were of Dutch descent and spoke Afrikaans – brought the total to more than 4,700 men, with Africans making up more than half the total.

As George walked Emperor between the immaculately spaced bell-tents of the 2nd/24th Regiment, a Welsh voice cried out, 'George! Can it be you?'

George turned and could just make out an officer in the red tunic and dark forage cap of the 24th. What gave him away was his toothy grin.

'Jake!' said George, leaping from his horse and engulfing the shorter and lighter man in a hearty bear hug. 'My God, I didn't expect to see you here. I was told your company was being held in reserve at Helpmekaar.'

'It was, but we finally got the order to march here yesterday and only arrived an hour ago. I didn't think I'd see you either. I imagined you in Kimberley, awash with diamonds and surrounded by lovelies. And yet here you are,' said Jake, gesturing towards George's dark blue uniform and standing back to look at him, 'a lowly trooper with the mounted volunteers. Couldn't keep away, eh?'

'Something like that. I'll fill you in over a drink, but first let me tether Emperor and make my report.'

Two hours and half a bottle of whisky later, George was nearing the end of his extraordinary tale. 'And so here I am: an Irish Zulu of unknown paternity about to fight against his grandmother's people in a war that's been cynically engineered by our superiors. I knew what they were up to, but thanks to that rogue Crealock, there was nothing I could do about it.'

'I need another drink,' said Jake, reaching for his cup of whisky and almost knocking over the flickering candle in the process. They were sitting on campbeds in the tent that Jake shared with his fellow subalterns, both of whom were still carousing in the nearby mess-tent. 'I can't believe you're still sane after all you've been through. First Harris, now Crealock. You don't have a lot of luck in your dealings with superior officers, do you? But I still think you did the right thing by joining the Carbineers. I'm not convinced you'd have made a success of diamond prospecting, whereas you and I both know you're a natural at soldiering.'

'Maybe so, but it doesn't lessen the unease I feel about taking part in *this* war. The Zulus are far from innocent, and as a people they'd undoubtedly be better off without Cetshwayo, but what right do we have to make that decision for them? Because one thing's for certain: Frere and the others did not plan this war for the benefit of the Zulus.'

'No, but you have to see the wider picture, George. We now have – for good or ill – the greatest empire the world has known, and yet most of it was acquired not by design but by accident or, to quote a well-known historian, "in a fit of absence of mind". Every year hundreds of British soldiers like us lay down their lives to win or defend some godforsaken, disease-ridden territory. Why do we do it? Not for money, not for ten shillings a day. We do it for our mates, our country and our queen. And who benefits from our sacrifice? Not many. Oh, I won't deny there's a profit to be turned by a few trading companies, arms manufacturers and, occasionally, in the case of India, the British exchequer. But let's not fool ourselves. Most colonies are expensive to run and maintain, which is why our government doesn't want any more. No, the real beneficiaries of empire are the poor benighted natives who, in return for a little kow-towing, get all the benefits of our civilization: better roads and railways, improved trade and education, and law and order. And Zululand won't be any different.'

'I take your point, Jake. But ask yourself this: if you'd been born and bred a Zulu, would you bow down to men of a different race and colour, whatever the ancillary benefits?'

'No, I don't suppose I would.'

'Quite. And don't forget I've seen Zulus at first hand. They're a proud, cruel warrior race and won't change their ways without a fight.'

'Well then, you can comfort yourself with the thought that war with Natal was bound to happen sooner or later.'

As Jake spoke, George looked for signs that his old friend – his only true friend – had changed, that his brief time in the army and on active service had made him a different person. He certainly appeared older and wearier, his eyes sandwiched between dark smudges and horizontal frown lines, but maybe that was to be expected after three months under canvas in the Perie Bush. He seemed fit and healthy enough, and his bright blue eyes, so unusual for a redhead, had lost none of their sparkle.

'So how do you think they'll react to our invasion?' continued Jake. 'The general feeling in our mess is that they'll harry our slow-moving columns but won't make a stand. It could take months to flush them out of their forests and mountain strongholds.'

George shook his head and laughed. 'Jake, I'm surprised at you. Have you forgotten everything they taught us at Sandhurst? Remember the phrase "the Horns of the Buffalo"?'

Jake shook his head. 'You know I preferred the practical stuff, building fortifications and blowing up bridges. I never paid much attention in the history classes.'

'Well, a Zulu army, or *impi*, is divided into the three distinct parts of a buffalo: the "chest", made up of the most experienced warriors, to close with the enemy and hold it fast; two "horns" of the youngest and fittest warriors to encircle the enemy and, having met, to fight their way back to the "chest"; and the "loins", or reserve, which is placed behind the "chest" and deployed when necessary. It's almost as if they've studied the campaigns of Hannibal and are trying to replicate Cannae. And bear in mind that their weapon of choice is the short stabbing assegai, which can only be used at close quarters. The point is, they can only fight one way: aggressively.'

'So not like the Kaffirs on the frontier, then?' said Jake, grinning. 'We spent months trudging through wild forests, trying to entice them to fight, but it was like chasing shadows.'

'This war's going to be very different; and if Lord Chelmsford thinks otherwise, which I suspect he does, he's in for a shock. The hilltop kraal of my great-uncle Chief Sihayo is just a few miles the other side of the river. If he decides to defend it we're going to lose a lot of troops. It looks a fiendishly difficult place to assault.'

'Are you not dreading the prospect of fighting your kin?'

'A little, but I have much less sympathy for them since they executed Sihayo's wife. But tell me about your battalion. What are the officers like?'

Jake sucked air through his teeth. 'They're not a bad bunch. But apart from the colonel, Degacher, and one or two of the senior officers who've served in the Crimea and the Mutiny, hardly any of them have seen action. The Second Battalion was only raised in fifty-eight and the war we've just fought is its first.'

'What about your company commander?'

'He's a duffer called Lieutenant Gonville Bromhead, a nice fellow but deaf as a post and unconquerably idle. The colonel knows his faults, of course, which is why he's ordered the company to remain behind here to guard the supply depot at the mission station. I can't believe we're going to miss the start of the campaign because of him.'

'Poor you, but I'm sure you'll be called into action before too long. Something tells me Chelmsford will need every man he can get.'

'That's as may be, but someone has to guard the supply lines and I can't help feeling that, on account of Gonny's failings, B Company will be here for some time.'

'What about the men? Can they be relied on?'

'Well, many of them are young recruits and pretty green, but their experience on the frontier has toughened them up nicely and they shouldn't let anyone down. We do have a few old hands in the company and one young soldier of outstanding promise, a Private Owen Thomas from Raglan. I gather you know each other?'

'We do indeed. We met on the voyage over. He struck me as a clever, self-confident fellow, if a little lacking in judgement. You heard about his flogging?' Jake nodded. 'A bad business all round,' continued George. 'But I'm glad to hear he's over it and doing well.'

'He is. He's already been appointed the company clerk, and when we were in the bush he displayed real gallantry by rescuing a wounded corporal under fire. He was commended by the colonel and is sure to receive early promotion.'

'I'm glad to hear it,' said George, glancing at his pocket-watch. 'It's getting late and we've got an early start. I'd better turn in.'

Jake rose to his feet and embraced his friend. 'It's great to see you again, old fellow. And don't worry too much about Colonel Crealock. The advantage of being an irregular is that you can keep well away from the staff at headquarters.'

'I'm not sure I want to keep well away. What's that old saying by Sun Tzu? "Keep your friends close, and your enemies closer." It certainly applies to Crealock. I know all about his money-making scheme with Fynn, and, to be honest, I'd feel much better if I was in a position to do something about it.'

# 13

'Wake up, damn you!'

George opened his eyes. He could feel an arm tugging on his shoulder and quickly twisted round to see Major Gossett holding a lantern.

'At last! Now get dressed, George. The general wants to see you immediately.'

'Why? What's the matter?'

'The general will explain.'

George threw on his uniform, grabbed his helmet and holster belt, and joined Gossett outside the tent. It was still pitch-black and the camp was still. As they walked, the lantern threw ghostly shadows on the rows of tents. At last they came to the huge marquee, divided into compartments, which served as Lord Chelmsford's headquarters. Gossett paused at the entrance. 'Just remember, George, that what you hear inside is not to be repeated.' George nodded his assent.

They entered and found Chelmsford leaning over a trestle table, studying a map of Zululand with Colonel Crealock and a civilian George did not recognize but suspected was Fynn. He was clad in an ill-fitting bush jacket and corduroy breeches and, with his huge shaggy beard, looked every inch the frontiersman.

Chelmsford looked up. 'Ah, Hart, we meet again. Crealock said you'd seen sense and joined the Carbineers. The reason I've woken you a little early is because I need a personal galloper I can rely on and you fit the bill. I'm told you're a good rider, speak Zulu like a native and, as a former officer, you'll be able to use your initiative if the occasion demands it. It will be dangerous work, of course, but that shouldn't deter you. And as an added inducement you'll be promoted to the local rank of second lieutenant. It's only a temporary commission, of course, but if you carry out your duties to my satisfaction, I'll see it's made permanent. What do you say?'

Surprised by the offer, George took a moment to consider the pros and cons. As Chelmsford's galloper he would carry his orders and be privy to all his decisions, and as such would be in a better position to influence the course of the campaign and ensure that as little harm as possible came to any Zulu women and children. He would also be ideally placed to keep an eye on the hated Crealock and, with luck, foil his and Fynn's plan to steal and sell Chief Matshana's cattle. The promotion was welcome, too, in that it put his military career back on course and made his father's legacy just that little bit more attainable. The only downside was that he would have to leave his friends in the Carbineers and become a regular soldier again, with rates of pay that even for a junior officer did not quite compare. With this in mind he decided to negotiate.

'I'd be delighted to serve as your galloper, my Lord,' said George. 'But may I continue to draw my pay as a

Carbineer? The reason I ask is because I'm a little strapped for cash at the moment and, as you may be aware, a Carbineer on active service receives slightly more than even a British Army second lieutenant.'

Chelmsford turned to Crealock. 'Is that true?'

'It is, my Lord. The daily rate for a Carbineer is six shillings, that of a junior subaltern slightly less. But I really don't see why we should make an exception in Hart's case.'

'Well, I do. You've got yourself a deal, Hart. And as you'll continue to be paid by the Carbineers, there's no need for you to replace your tunic. Just get the regimental tailor to add some braid.'

'I will, sir.'

'Good. You know Crealock and Gossett, of course, and this is Henry Fynn, the local border agent,' said Chelmsford, gesturing towards the civilian. 'He grew up among the Zulus and knows the terrain on both sides of the Buffalo like the back of his hand.'

I bet he does, thought George, taking Fynn's hand and finding the grip surprisingly strong for a man of such slender frame. He looked in Fynn's eyes for a sign that he knew about the eavesdropping episode, but could see none.

'Fynn's received intelligence,' continued Chelmsford, 'that Chief Sihayo is still at his kraal, a couple of miles northeast of the drift, with up to eight thousand men. I very much doubt he'll wait for us to attack, because if he does there'll be no means of escape once our troops are in position. But either way I intend to burn his kraal and collect his cattle.'

'I'm sure Mr Fynn's right, my Lord,' said George, 'though I didn't see any sign of such a large force on my reconnaissance yesterday. But if Sihayo does withdraw, is it necessary to destroy his homestead? Won't that deprive his womenfolk of shelter?'

Fynn snorted. 'Admirable sentiments, I'm sure, Mr Hart. But remember this is war, not a picnic. And you might also bear in mind that it was Sihayo's family that was responsible for the abduction and murder of those women last July.'

'I'm well aware of that, but you can hardly blame his wives and children.'

'This is not about blame; it's about punishing a wrong. Force is the only thing these natives understand.'

'But surely the principle of crime and punishment is that it's practised on offenders, not the innocent.'

Chelmsford raised his hand. 'Enough, Hart! Fynn's right. This is war and we must prosecute it as vigorously as we can. The kraal will be destroyed, *pour encourager les autres*. I've made my decision and it's not negotiable. Now, gentlemen, we cross the Buffalo at dawn, three hours from now. Colonel Wood's column is already ensconced in Zululand at Bemba's Kop to the north, and I've arranged to meet him halfway, at Nkonjane Hill, ten miles above the drift, at nine o'clock, which gives us plenty of time to get there. As Pearson won't cross the Tugela with his column until tomorrow, it's vital Wood and I coordinate our movements and don't give the Zulus any opportunity to slip between us. Gossett, can you inform Major Russell that the Mounted Infantry will act as my escort?'

'Of course, my Lord.'

'Well, that's it, gentlemen,' said Chelmsford. 'There's no going back, and with luck we'll be in Ulundi by the end of the month.'

As Crealock left the tent, George followed him. 'Excuse me, Colonel. I'd like to have a word.'

'About what?' said Crealock, barely concealing his dislike.

'I'd like to know why you recommended me for the staff.'

'I would have thought that was obvious. Partly as a reward for keeping your mouth shut, but it also enables me to keep an eye on you and make sure you don't step out of line. You're a dangerous man, Hart, and dangerous men need to be watched. You'll be glad to hear I haven't mentioned your eavesdropping escapade to anyone, even Fynn. But if I so much as suspect you of interfering with my plans, I'll come down on you hard. Do you understand?'

George nodded.

'Good. Is that all?'

'Yes.'

'Well, get some sleep, then,' said Crealock, striding off into the darkness.

The far bank was obscured by drizzle and mist as a lone horseman urged his mount into the Buffalo's cold, fast-flowing current. Halfway across, with the water over the top of his boots, he paused. Was it too deep? What horrors were waiting for him on the other side? Casting all doubts aside, he spurred his mount forward. As his horse scrambled up the bank, he tensed his short, squat body, half expecting the cold, exquisite pain of an assegai thrust.

But none came; the bank was empty. He raised his white sun helmet with its red scarf in relief.

Waiting on the Natal bank with Chelmsford and the rest of his staff, George tried hard to suppress a chuckle, but failed.

'Something funny, Hart?' asked Crealock.

'Oh, nothing, Colonel. But it's ironic, is it not, that the honour of being the first man into Zululand has gone not to a soldier but to a newspaper correspondent?'

'What? Is that Norris-Newman of the *Standard*?'

'The very same, Colonel. He's attached himself to the headquarters of the Native Contingent.'

'Bloody correspondents,' interjected Chelmsford, 'always getting in the way. I told Frere it was a mistake to let him accompany the column, but he was insistent. Good for public awareness of the campaign, he told me. Not if Norris-Newman gets himself killed, it won't be. All right, Gossett, give Russell the signal to advance.'

Gossett raised his hand and the red-coated Mounted Infantry began to splash across the shallow river ford known as the old drift in open column, four abreast, followed by the various contingents of volunteer cavalry, including George's comrades in the Carbineers, with the Natal Mounted Police bringing up the rear. A couple of horses were washed off their feet by the current, but they managed to swim the rest of the way with their riders clinging to their saddles.

Chelmsford nodded with satisfaction as the mounted volunteers spurred towards the high ground to establish a chain of outposts that would prevent the column from being surprised as it crossed. 'So far, so good,' said Chelmsford, 'Where's Colonel Glyn?'

'Here, my Lord,' replied a short, stocky officer with a bushy beard and a red face.

'Very good. Now I expect you, as column commander, to issue the necessary orders for setting up camp on the Zulu bank. Get the infantry across first, and once you've secured the camp perimeter, you can bring the guns, wagons, oxen and supplies over. It will take most of the day so you'd better get on with it.'

'Yes, my Lord,' said Glyn. 'Shall I bring all the infantry over the new drift in the ponts?'

'No. Just the white troops. Commandant Lonsdale's Kaffirs can wade across. And use both drifts: it will save time.'

'Is that wise, my Lord? The new drift is much deeper, and with the current as strong as it is, we might lose a few.'

'Just do it, Glyn. The sooner we have the fighting troops across, the better.'

'Yes, my Lord. And do you want me to circle the wagons into a defensive laager?'

'No. There's no need.'

'Begging your pardon, my Lord, but your own instructions advise laagering every night in Zululand.'

'Yes, Colonel, I know what my instructions say. I wrote them. But they only apply if there's an imminent threat of attack from the main Zulu army. At the moment that couldn't be further from the case. Anything else?'

'No, my Lord.'

'Good. Gentlemen,' said Chelmsford, turning to his staff, 'shall we?'

\*     \*     \*

The ride to Nkonjane Hill was over broken, hilly terrain and took a good three hours. Only one Zulu was sighted, and he quickly scuttled into cover as Chelmsford's mounted escort spurred forward to relieve him of his small herd of cattle. The staff hollered their approval, but George stayed silent, aware the cattle almost certainly belonged to his kinsman, Sihayo. Shortly before nine, the horsemen crested Nkonjane's flat summit to be met by Colonel Wood and a small party of Frontier Horse, off-saddled among a pile of loose rocks.

'Good morning, my Lord,' said Wood, touching the brim of his wideawake hat. 'I trust your crossing of the Buffalo is going to plan?'

'Like clockwork,' replied Chelmsford. 'I've left Glyn in charge. How are you, Wood? It's good to see you.'

'And you, my Lord. I'm well.'

The general and his staff dismounted and sat on boulders next to Wood. 'Buller not here?' asked Chelmsford.

'He's rounding up cattle, as per your instructions.'

'Excellent. And thank you for marching south so speedily to cover my flank. Fynn's spies were convinced that Sihayo would contest the crossing and your movement might have dissuaded him.'

'It might have, my Lord. But all the intelligence I've received still points to the first serious Zulu attack falling on the Central Column. As far as I'm aware, the main Zulu army is still at Ulundi, and has been since it gathered for the First Fruits Ceremony on the ninth. But when it moves, it will strike the Central Column first. You must be on your guard because Cetshwayo's warriors can cover forty miles in a day and could be up with you in three.

Apparently Cetshwayo's strategy is to win a crushing victory that will force us to negotiate.'

Chelmsford tugged at his beard. 'I wish that were true, Wood, because I have every confidence in the Central Column's ability to repulse any number of Zulus. But I very much doubt they'll risk an attack. What do you say, Mr Fynn?' he enquired of the civilian advisor sitting alongside him.

'I don't wish to contradict the colonel, my Lord, but my spies paint a very different picture. They say the main Zulu army will aim to slip between our two columns and try to cut our lines of communication.'

George's ears pricked up. Was this the start of Fynn and Crealock's plan to point Chelmsford in the direction of Chief Matshana? It sounded like it.

'Hear that, Wood?' said Chelmsford. 'And that's from a man who knows the Zulus and has contacts close to the king himself. If he's right, and we have to assume he is, our main priority is to prevent the Zulu army from sidestepping our columns and attacking us from the rear. That is why a careful coordination of all three columns is vital, and to that end I would ask you not to continue your advance for a further three days, to give Colonel Pearson the chance to catch up. He doesn't cross the Lower Drift with the Southern Column until tomorrow and, as you know, has the furthest distance to cover.'

'I quite understand, my Lord. I'll hold fast at Bemba's Kop until the fifteenth. But do take care. I have a number of Boers with me who've fought the Zulu, and they all warn against a sudden attack.'

'Well, let's hope they're right, Wood,' said Chelmsford,

smiling, 'because the Central Column only has supplies for two weeks. How long can you stay in the field?'

'Seven weeks, my Lord. Mr Hughes, my commissariat officer, has performed miracles.'

'He's to be congratulated. But I'd hope to be back in Pietermaritzburg long before the spring. Well, I must be off,' said Chelmsford, rising. 'Glyn was wittering on about defensive arrangements and has probably built a fort in my absence. Keep in regular contact and don't forget: hold your ground until the fifteenth at the earliest.'

'I will, my Lord. By the way, is that young Hart I recognize among your staff?'

'It is. He saw fit to join the Carbineers and is now my galloper.'

'I'm glad to hear it,' said Wood. 'Buller took quite a liking to him on the boat and thinks he will make a fine soldier.'

'We'll see.'

'Good luck, my Lord.'

'Luck don't come into it, Wood. It all comes down to careful planning, and making sure these damn Zulus don't slip through the net. See you in Ulundi.'


As the lone bugle sounded Reveille, George looked at his pocket-watch and groaned. It was 3 a.m, and in just three hours a portion of the column would leave its camp on the Zulu bank of the Buffalo and assault Sihayo's kraal. There was every possibility that George's kin – Sihayo himself, or at least some of his sons – were in residence, and the very thought made George uncomfortable. Not that he felt, since his trip to Zululand, any particular ties of loyalty to them – far from it – but nor did he wish to take part in the destruction of their home.

He rose and made his way in darkness to the head-quarters marquee, his boots sinking deep into the sodden turf. All around, the camp was stirring, with men lighting fires for coffee and cattle lowing. Two redcoats snapped to attention as George entered the marquee. Inside, grouped around the map table, he found the general and his senior officers and staff.

'Good of you to join us, Hart. Now pay attention. Our objective this morning is to capture Sihayo's kraal. It's a natural stronghold, situated in a huge horseshoe-shaped gorge on the far bank of the Bashee River, about two miles from here. We'll follow an old traders' track as far as the river, but from there on the going is extremely tough. Thick bush, ravines and rocky ground will bar our path. And that's even before we've reached the gorge, which, if defended, will have to be scaled and taken in hand-to-hand fighting. The First Third NNC will lead the frontal attack, with four companies of the First Twenty-Fourth in support. I will be present, but Colonel Glyn will command. Any questions?'

'If I may be so bold, my Lord,' said Fynn.

'Yes?'

'Have you considered sending mounted troops to out-flank the position, my Lord? That way you'd prevent any defenders from getting away.'

'It's a good idea, but is there a way up?'

'Yes, sir. Horsemen could ascend by a track I know to the right of the gorge.'

'Well, that's what we'll do. Any *other* questions?'

'Just one, my Lord,' said George. 'Could I ask whether any instructions have been issued on the subject of non-combatants? There are bound to be women and children in Sihayo's kraal.'

Chelmsford raised his eyes to heaven. 'Gentlemen, we have a humanitarian in our midst; never a good thing in war. But the answer to your question, Hart, is yes, I have issued instructions. I expressly told both battalions of NNC, when I spoke to them two days ago, that no women or children were to be injured in any way. I also told them that no prisoners were to be harmed. I hope that's satisfactory?'

George ignored the sarcasm. 'Very much so, my Lord, in so far as the native troops are concerned, but have our white troops been told?'

Chelmsford snorted. 'You forget yourself, Second Lieutenant Hart. A British soldier doesn't need to be told how to behave on the battlefield. He knows.'

'Sir,' interrupted Crealock, 'might I make a suggestion?'

'Please do.'

'If young Hart is so keen to make sure our troops don't get out of hand, why don't we let him accompany the lead battalion of the Native Contingent? Then he can relay back to us any vital information.'

'Good idea. All right with you, Hart?'

'Yes, sir,' said George. From the look of satisfaction on Crealock's face he suspected he was being deliberately put in harm's way, but there was not a lot he could do about it.

'Good. Now if there are no further questions, would you all return to your units and make your final preparations? Happy hunting, gentlemen.'

\*   \*   \*

The advance began as the first streaks of dawn appeared from the direction of Sihayo's kraal, away to the north-east. Captain Shepstone and his Carbineers led the way in open skirmishing order, followed by Chelmsford and his staff, the rest of the mounted volunteers, the Natal Native Contingent and the four companies of redcoats. The flanks and rear of the column were protected by Mounted Infantry.

The old traders' track had been reduced to a quagmire by days of heavy rain, and even the horses had difficulty lifting their hooves clear of the sticky mud.

'Damn it,' said Chelmsford, peering down at the ground as he rode. 'This track's going to need a lot of work before the guns and wagons can pass over it. Crealock, what's your opinion?'

Crealock nudged his horse forward until he was level with his leader. 'I'll get the sappers on to it, my Lord, but it could take up to a week.'

'A week! I can't spare a week. We're barely into Zululand and already the problems mount. My God, if we carry on at this rate we'll be lucky to reach Ulundi by Easter.'

Two lengths behind Chelmsford, George caught the gist of the conversation, but his mind was distracted by other matters, not least the imminent prospect of combat. He had killed before, of course, but that was in the heat of the moment. This was different: a planned assault on a natural fortress that was bound to cost many lives on both sides, possibly even his.

An hour into the trek and a Carbineer cantered back from the head of the column. 'A message from Captain

Shepstone, my Lord. The Zulus are driving their cattle back towards Sihayo's stronghold.'

'I must see for myself. Gentlemen, follow me.'

Chelmsford spurred his horse forward, George and the others trailing in his wake, and came to a halt next to Offy Shepstone and a knot of troopers on the crest of the next rise. Below them the track fell away to a shallow stream, and beyond that, to the left of the track, rose the towering red cliffs of a huge gorge. A large herd of cattle, several hundred strong, had just forded the stream and was being driven by a handful of frantic Zulus towards the gorge's entrance.

'My Lord,' said Shepstone, his eyes flashing with excitement, 'there is still time to intercept them before they reach the gorge. May I advance with my squadron?'

'No, you may not, Captain,' said Chelmsford. 'There's no knowing how many Zulus are hiding in the gorge. It might be a trap.'

Shepstone looked towards Glyn, silently imploring the column commander to intervene. Glyn averted his eyes.

'Colonel Glyn will carry out the attack as planned,' continued Chelmsford. 'Carry on.'

George kept his head down as he stumbled across the familiar broken ground that lay between the Bashee River and the mouth of the gorge. Bullets were flying in all directions, and already a warrior of the Native Contingent had gone down with his thigh streaming blood. Up ahead, the short figure of Major Black turned and shouted in his broad Scotch accent, 'C'mon, men, stay together.'

George urged those warriors around him to keep moving, but the gunfire was so intense that many had already gone to ground. As he tried to drag one to his feet, a bullet whizzed uncomfortably close to George's ear, causing him to duck. He let go of the warrior, fell to one knee and fired his carbine in the direction of the enemy muzzle flashes. The heavy foliage and mass of creepers made it impossible to see individual targets, but the mere act of firing made him feel better.

The sound of running feet caused him to look behind. Heading towards him at full pelt, and looking alarmingly like Zulus, was the support battalion of the 2nd/3rd NNC, led by a young officer in a blue patrol jacket. Clean-shaven and tanned, he was wearing the type of light-coloured slouch-hat favoured by colonials.

'Am I glad to see you,' said George. 'We can't advance without covering fire. Where the devil are the four companies of the Twenty-Fourth?'

'They're scaling the high ground to the left, which is why we've been sent up in support. I'm Lieutenant Henry Harford, by the way, staff officer to Commandant Lonsdale, the commander of the Third NNC.'

George introduced himself and asked if he had heard Harford speaking Zulu.

'You did. I was brought up in Natal before joining the Ninety-Ninth Regiment. I'd like to chat more but you may have noticed there's a battle on. Where's Major Black?'

'Up ahead.'

'Good. Let's go.'

The two of them set off at a run and found Black crouching behind a large boulder. Next to him was a huge white-faced corporal, wrapping a field dressing round his foot.

'Hot work, sir,' said Harford.

'I've been in worse fights, Lieutenant,' replied a smiling Black.

Typical Scottish soldier, thought George; never happier than in a battle.

'Do you know where they're firing from, sir?' asked Harford.

Black pointed ahead to a mass of rocks, caves and crevices that lay at the foot of the sheer wall of the ravine. 'They're in there. You're welcome to try and flush them out.'

'Thank you, sir. I will.' Harford had barely finished his sentence when he fell to his hands and knees as if hit. George rushed forward but found Harford busy putting an insect into a small tin box.

'What on earth are you doing?'

'Oh, just collecting this beetle,' said Harford, grinning. 'It's very rare.'

'I'm sure it is. But this is hardly the place.'

'We entymologists have to take every opportunity we can get. Right, that's him safely stowed. Let's see about these Zulus.'

By now the bulk of Harford's warriors had come up and they were sent by Black to work their way round to the left of the caves. Harford preferred to climb the cliff to the right of the caves, and George offered to go with him. Ten minutes later, halfway up the cliff, they reached the base of a horseshoe-shaped ledge of rocks that curved away round the gorge. Directly opposite them on the far side of the ledge was the mouth of a large cave, below which were suspended several dead Zulus caught in monkey-rope creepers and thick undergrowth. Muzzle flashes indicated the presence of more Zulus in the cave.

Harford was inclined to hold his position until the rifles of the 1st/24th were in a position to provide covering fire, but George wanted to press on, knowing the destruction of the main kraal would take place as soon as the defenders had been overcome. He began to climb round the ledge towards the cave, signalling for Harford to follow. It was tough going as they clambered over a jumble of huge rocks, and at least twice George almost lost his footing and tumbled into the valley below. Then, barely thirty yards from the mouth of the cave, a Zulu popped up from behind a rock, put the muzzle of his musket to George's head and pulled the trigger. Time froze. *Snap!* went the cap, but no explosion followed. The musket had misfired.

George raised his carbine but already the Zulu had dropped his faulty weapon and was scampering back towards the cave. He yelled an oath and set off in pursuit, firing at the Zulu's back.

'Did you get him?' shouted Harford, as he followed George over the jumble of rocks.

'I think I might have winged him. Come on. He can't have got far.'

They came upon the wounded Zulu at the entrance to the cave. He was clutching his side and in obvious pain. 'Lay down your spear,' said George in Zulu. 'If you surrender quietly, I'll see no harm comes to you.'

The Zulu did as he was told, and then squatted down in an act of submission.

'Is there anyone else in the cave?' asked Harford.

The reply was negative.

'I'd better check,' said Harford to George.

'Be careful,' said George, his carbine trained on the wounded Zulu, the narrowness of his own extraordinary escape from death only now beginning to dawn on him.

'I will.'

As Harford crept slowly into the cave, appealing to any Zulus inside to give themselves up, George expected at any moment to hear the sound of gunfire or a cry of pain. But it never came, and after an anxious wait of a couple of minutes, he was relieved to see Harford reappear with three uninjured prisoners in tow. 'There's another one inside,' declared Harford. 'But he's too badly wounded to move. We'd best get back. Was that your first time in action, Hart?'

'Yes, sir.'

'Good for you.'

Having retraced their steps to the valley floor, George and Harford were met by Chelmsford, Glyn and their respective staffs. 'Well done, you two,' said the general from his horse. 'We've been watching your gallant efforts for some time.'

'Thank you, my Lord,' replied Harford. 'But I can't take credit for the climb round the cliff. That was Hart's idea and he led the way.'

'You've both done well. Now, what have we got here?' said Chelmsford, gesturing towards the four Zulus.

'Prisoners, my Lord, as per your instructions.'

'I'm perfectly aware of their status. What I'm querying is their condition. The youngest looks forty if he's a day. Hardly in their prime, are they?'

'Well, no, sir,' interjected Harford. 'But they fought bravely all the same.'

'That's as may be, Lieutenant,' said Colonel Crealock, leaning from his saddle. 'But the absence of younger warriors confirms my theory that the cream of the Zulu army will not stand and fight. Why, there can't have been more than three hundred warriors in opposition to us today. And as soon as the Twenty-Fourth flanked them, they scuttled off as fast as their legs could carry them.'

'Crealock's right,' said Chelmsford. 'It's not a good sign. If we can't force these blighters to stand and fight we'll never end this war.'

The conversation was interrupted by the sound of approaching horsemen. Offy Shepstone and the Natal Carbineers were the first to appear, one trooper with a Zulu corpse across the front of his saddle.

'What happened?' asked Chelmsford as Shepstone reined in next to him.

'It was heavy going, my Lord, and when we did finally reach the high ground, most of the Zulus had already gone. We could see a number of them away in the distance, most on foot and even a few on horseback. About thirty of the bolder spirits stood their ground and we managed to kill ten of them. One's dressed like a chief, which is why we brought his body back.'

'Show me,' said Chelmsford.

The trooper tipped the corpse on to the ground. He was of medium build, about twenty years old, with the tall headdress of an induna. He had a bullet hole in his temple, from which ran two small rivulets of blood, but his face was unmarked and still recognizable.

'Does anyone know this man?' asked the general.

'I do,' said George. The last time he had seen those features was the night Sihayo's wife had perished in the *isibaya*. It was the face of his cousin, one of the two murderers. 'It's Mkhumbukazulu, the son of Chief Sihayo.'

Chelmsford turned to his civilian advisor. 'Is he right?'

'Yes,' said Fynn. 'I know him well.'

George stared down at the sightless corpse. He had hated Mkhumbukazulu that night of the murder, as he had hated his brother and father, but his death was still a shock.

'Excellent. Sir Bartle will be pleased. Now you're sure, Fynn, it's not the elder brother, Mehlokazulu?'

'Quite sure, sir. Mehlokazulu is much more heavily built. He's also a junior induna of the Ngobamakhosi Regiment and, as such, will have been with the rest of the army at Ulundi for the First Fruits Ceremony.'

'Yes, of course. Well, no matter, his time will come. A good day's work, gentlemen; all that remains is to destroy Sihayo's kraal. Colonel,' said Chelmsford to Glyn, 'have you given the necessary orders?'

'Yes, my Lord. The four companies of the Second Twenty-Fourth that you ordered up during the skirmish are carrying out the task as we speak.'

'Good. Crealock, see that Harford's wounded Zulu is taken to the hospital at Rorke's Drift. We can't have it getting about that we've maltreated prisoners.' Chelmsford turned back to George. 'And, Hart, given your concern for noncombatants, I thought you might like to accompany the troops to Sihayo's kraal. That way you can assure any Zulus you meet that no harm will come to those who surrender.'

'I'll do that, my Lord. Thank you.'

George retrieved Emperor from Major Gossett's keeping and, ignoring the possibility that stray Zulus might be hiding in the undergrowth, rode hard up the familiar steep track that led to Sihayo's kraal. As he neared the entrance, the first of the huts burst into flame.

'Where's the officer in charge?' he demanded of the nearest redcoat, who was busy filling his haversack with onions from the vegetable patch.

'That's Lieutenant Pope, sir. He's burning the bigger huts at the top of the hill.'

All around, huts were catching fire as soldiers touched lighted torches to their dry thatch. George dug in his spurs, but the intense heat, and the crackle and hiss, were too much for the frightened gelding and he refused to budge. George realized he would have to leave his horse. He dismounted and set off on foot.

At the top of the hill he found a monocled officer he recognized as Lieutenant Charles Pope of G Company, 2nd/24th. 'Yes, Second Lieutenant,' drawled Pope. 'How may I be of service?'

'Lord Chelmsford sent me to ensure that no civilians are harmed.'

'Did he, indeed? Well, you can report to the general that the kraal is deserted.'

'Have the men searched all the huts, sir?' asked George.

'They have, and not a soul to be seen. As for booty, apart from a few shields and spears, there isn't any. What a country. I can't wait till this bloody war's over and we can all get back to civilization.'

'Would you mind, sir, if I double-checked the great wife's hut?'

'Which one's that?'

'The big one over there.'

'Be my guest. It's got nothing in it worth having, I can assure you of that.'

George reached the hut as a tall redcoat was about to set light to its thatch. 'Hold on, Private, I'd like to take another look.'

'Yes, sir,' said the soldier, staying his hand.

George ducked inside. It was as he remembered, with the back of the hut wreathed in shadows. 'Anyone here?' he shouted in Zulu as he looked behind the few sticks of furniture. 'It's your last chance to show yourself before we burn the place.'

No response. George repeated the warning, but nothing. He was about to leave when he saw, out of the corner of his eye, a piece of the dirt floor begin to move sideways until a large hole was revealed. It was the cleverly concealed entrance to a grain pit, and out of it climbed three old women and a small girl. All were shaking with fear.

'You're safe now. Follow me.'

Lieutenant Pope saw them emerging from the hut and ran over. 'I'll be damned. Lucky for them you happened by, Hart, but I'll take over now.'

'I'm sure they'll be less trouble with me, sir. I speak their language.'

'Do you? Excellent. You can ask them a few questions.'

'Can't it wait, sir? They're obviously frightened out of their wits.'

'All the better. That way they're more likely to tell the truth. Ask them who they are.'

George did so and was answered briefly by one of the women, a toothless old crone in a knee-length skirt. 'She says they're all relations of Sihayo's, even the child.'

'Well, that makes sense,' said Pope. 'Do they know where Sihayo and the rest of his men are?'

George translated the woman's response. 'She says they left yesterday for the king's kraal at Ulundi.'

'Just as we suspected: it's going to be a long war. All right, Hart, take them away.'

As George led the women down the hill from the kraal, the girl clinging grimly to Emperor's saddle, the crone piped up, 'I remember you. You tried to save that faithless bitch Nandi.'

George stopped to face the crone. 'You're right, I did. Are you saying she deserved to die?'

The crone had a look of pure scorn. 'Of course. Marriage is sacred to Zulus. She broke that trust.'

'And what about my grandmother Ngqumbazi?' said George, his voice shrill. 'Was her fate justified?'

'Your *grandmother*? So you're a half-breed. I weep for people like you, a foot in both camps but not truly part of either.'

'That's not true,' said George. 'I'm British. I know that now. And you haven't answered my question.'

'Ngqumbazi survived. In Shaka's time she would not have been so lucky.'

# 14

## Central Column's camp, Zulu bank of Rorke's Drift, 13 January 1879

George could barely keep his eyes open as the conference in Lord Chelmsford's headquarters tent entered its second hour. Images of faceless, spear-wielding Zulus had disturbed his night's rest, and he was finding it hard to concentrate through Glyn's report of the battle and Fynn's assessment of the latest intelligence. Now it was Chelmsford's turn, and as he spoke George could feel a bead of sweat trickling down his back. It had poured with rain the day before, soaking the troops and their prisoners as they retraced their steps from Sihayo's kraal, but the air was still heavy with moisture and very hot.

'It's just possible,' said Chelmsford, 'that the storming of Sihayo's stronghold and the capture of so many of his cattle may have a salutary effect in Zululand, and either bring down a large force to attack us or else spark a revolution to overthrow Cetshwayo and bring the war to an end. After all, Sihayo is one of Cetshwayo's chief lieutenants and the destruction of his homestead will cause quite a stir. But in the short term we must press ahead with our original plan to advance on Ulundi. To that end a large working party of natives, protected by four companies of the Second

Twenty-Fourth, will today begin digging ditches on both sides of the track that passes through the Bashee valley, near Sihayo's kraal, in the hope of draining enough water to make the track passable. That should take a week, by which time we'll have stockpiled enough supplies at Rorke's Drift to enable the advance to continue. We need at least a month's supply there, over and above the fifteen days' regimental supply with the column. Crealock, what news from Durnford's Reserve Column?'

'None yet, my Lord. I sent an order four days ago for him to move his two strongest Native Contingent battalions north to Sandspruit to protect the Masinga District from a Zulu counter-invasion. But we still haven't had confirmation.'

'Well, let me know as soon as we do. The colonel has a headstrong reputation and it wouldn't do for him to be taking matters into his own hands. His job is to remain strictly on the defensive unless he hears to the contrary. What news of the other columns?'

'Wood is still at Bemba's Kop, as you know, and Pearson is due to begin his advance from the Lower Drift on the eighteenth. He anticipates reaching the Nyezane river four days later.'

'Good. Anything else?'

'Yes, sir,' said Crealock. 'It concerns reinforcements. Given that a sizeable proportion of the column will be busy roadbuilding over the next week, might I suggest we bring forward the company of the Second Twenty-Fourth at Rorke's Drift and replace it with one from Helpmekaar.'

'That's for Colonel Degacher to decide. Well, Colonel?' said Chelmsford, turning to a grizzled veteran of the

Crimea with a salt-and-pepper moustache. 'Do you want B Company to rejoin your battalion?'

'Frankly no, sir,' said Degacher. 'The original company commander was wounded on the Cape frontier and his successor, Bromhead, is simply not up to the task of leading a company on active service.'

'What are you saying?'

'I'm saying, sir, that he's a great favourite in the regiment and a capital fellow at everything but soldiering.'

'Then why's he in the army?'

'I don't imagine he had much choice. His father's a baronet and a general who fought at Waterloo.'

'Heaven help us!' said Chelmsford. 'But I accept your point. B Company remains at Rorke's Drift, and one of the companies at Helpmekaar will move up to support the column.'

Outraged that Jake would not see active service because of the incompetence of his company commander, George felt compelled to interrupt. 'My Lord, might I speak?'

'Go ahead.'

'I wonder if Colonel Degacher would consider making an exception of Bromhead's second-in-command, a young officer called Morgan. I know him from Sandhurst. He's an active, highly capable fellow and is itching to do something useful.'

'Well, Degacher?'

'Yes, I'd be more than happy to have Morgan with the rest of the battalion. He did well in the bush and is wasted guarding stores. He can move to Pope's G Company – it has a vacancy for a subaltern.'

'That's settled, then. All right, gentlemen, let's get to work.'

That evening, as he was about to turn in, George was called to Chelmford's tent. He arrived at the entrance to find him deep in conversation with Crealock. 'That bloody man. You warned me it was a mistake to give him an independent command, and once again you were right. How dare he disobey a direct order from me on the basis of a damned *rumour*. If I listened to every rumour that reached this headquarters, we'd never have crossed into Zululand! Well, this is his last chance. One more slip and he's out.'

The general noticed George hovering at the tent flap. 'Ah, Hart, do come in. I apologize for the lateness of the hour, but I need you to deliver an urgent message. Crealock will explain.'

Crealock handed George a sealed envelope. 'You're to deliver this to Colonel Durnford at Kranskop. We've just received word from him that, in direct contravention of a previous order, he still hasn't moved his two strongest NNC battalions to Sandspruit. He gives as his excuse the rumour of a possible Zulu counter-invasion and says he intends to guard against this by moving his entire force down from his camp at Kranskop to the Middle Drift. It's all nonsense, of course. The river's too high and, according to Fynn, there's no sizeable Zulu force in the vicinity. We suspect it's a ruse by Durnford to prevent the break-up of his command. But it won't work. Your job is to get to him before he moves and set him straight. It's a ride of several hours so you'd better get started.'

'You want me to go tonight?' asked George.

'Yes, tonight. I take it you have no objections to riding in the dark?'

George knew he was being taunted and his temper flared anew. He imagined his fist driving into Crealock's face, and for a brief moment considered that the pleasure it would bring him might be worth the disciplinary consequences. But sanity prevailed. 'No, Colonel,' he replied. 'I have no objections.'

Within a quarter of an hour, George had crossed the drift and was on the road south to Kranskop. Despite being back in the relative safety of Natal, he had heard enough rumours of hostile Zulus on both sides of the border to be kept permanently on edge as he rode by the light of the moon. Only as he neared his destination did he relax and allow his mind to wander. He was thinking back to the good times he had spent with his mother at their cottage in the Wicklow Mountains, to laughter-filled summer picnics and cosy evenings in front of a peat fire, when Emperor shied at something in his path. George at once drew his pistol and strained his eyes to see.

Directly ahead, he could just make out a large dark shadow, bigger than a man but not tall enough to be a horse and rider. He reined in and waited for the shadow to move, and when it did not, he nudged Emperor with his spurs. The horse refused to budge. George was about to dismount and and lead Emperor forward when the shadow began to lumber down the track towards him. He could just make out a pair of horns and realized it was a lone bull, separated from its herd and disorientated in the dark. Its huge bulk began to gather pace and George knew, with a thousand pounds of muscle and bone bearing down on him, that he and Emperor were seconds from disaster.

With a yell and a vicious jab of his spurs, he forced Emperor off the track and into the scrub, the bull following close behind. Thorns tore at his legs, but on George rode, praying Emperor would not stumble. The bull seemed to be closing in on them and, in desperation, George yanked the reins sharply to the right. As Emperor turned, the bull crashed blindly on over the edge of a steep krans that George had not seen but must have sensed. The bull's brief roar was followed by a sickening thud. George reined in, his heart hammering and his shirt drenched with sweat. Relieved to be alive, he dismounted and led Emperor back to the track, cursing Crealock all the while and vowing to get the better of him.

It was two in the morning when Durnford's camp finally came into view on the hill ahead. Finding the camp deserted, George rode on and discovered Durnford's troops lined up in orderly columns on the edge of the bluff, ready to descend to the drift below. Durnford was on horseback, conferring with his staff officer, Captain George Shepstone, the brother of Offy, when George rode up. 'Colonel, I have an urgent message from Lord Chelmsford.'

'George,' said Durnford, squinting in the gloom, 'is that you? It is. How good to see you. But what could be so urgent that you're required to ride through the night?'

George handed the message over. As Durnford read, his face drained of all colour. 'I can't believe it,' said the colonel. 'He's actually threatening to replace me.'

George remained silent.

'He says I've disobeyed orders by not carrying out his previous instructions to move two battalions to Sandspruit. But if I had, and the Zulus had attacked across the Middle Drift, what then? They still might.'

'According to Fynn, that's not likely.'

'How can he be certain?' said Durnford angrily.

George paused before answering. He knew that Durnford's command was hanging by a thread and was tempted to let him stew in his own juice, secure in the knowledge that it would end any hopes he had of becoming a hero and impressing Fanny. But then he realized that this was not about romantic point-scoring, but winning a war, and he chided his selfishness.

'He can't be certain,' replied George, 'but he has Chelmsford's ear. Colonel, can I be frank with you?'

'Please.'

'Chelmsford suspects you're exaggerating the threat down here as a means of keeping your command together.'

Durnford's eyes flashed with anger. 'That's nonsense. But I won't deny it's been frustrating watching from the sidelines while your column and the others have crossed into Zululand. Next I'm told that I'm subordinate to Colonel Pearson's Southern Column and mustn't move until he's cleared the ground opposite the Middle Drift. And then the final insult: I'm to split up my command and send part of it north to Sandspruit. All I want, George, is an opportunity to show what I can do.'

'I understand, Colonel, but if you don't obey orders, you won't even have a diminished command.'

'I suppose you're right, and it's not all bad news. In his note, Chelmsford also promises that I can use my initiative once we're over the border. He writes,' said Durnford, reading from the note, ' "When a column is acting *separately* in an *enemy's country*, I am quite ready to give its commander every latitude, and would certainly expect him to disobey any orders he might receive from me, if information which he obtained showed that it would be injurious to the interests of the column under his command." '

'Exactly so, Colonel, and all the more reason to toe the line until you're in Zululand.'

'Sound advice. Captain Shepstone?'

'Yes, Colonel.'

'Be so good as to order the men to return to camp.'

'Right away, sir.'

Durnford turned back to George. 'Tell me, have you heard from Fanny since the war began?'

'No.'

'Nor me. Do you think she'll ever forgive us for fighting her beloved Zulus?'

'I don't know,' said George. 'She can be very stubborn.'

'Yes. But if she only knew the threat the Zulus posed to civilians along the Natal border, she might not be so precious.'

'Is a Zulu counter-invasion likely?'

'I'd go further than that and say it's inevitable. And when it happens, Fanny and her family will be singing a different tune, mark my words.'

Four days later, George was back at Chelmsford's headquarters on the Zulu bank of the Buffalo, attending yet another conference with the staff and senior officers, when Henry Fynn entered the tent.

'Mr Fynn!' said Chelmsford, looking up from a map of Zululand. 'What a pleasant surprise. When you were recalled to your duties at Umsinga, I feared we'd seen the last of you.'

'And I too,' replied Fynn, smiling, 'but it seems Sir Bartle changed his mind. I can't help thinking Your Lordship must have put in a good word.'

'I wrote to Frere on the subject, it's true, but I didn't expect such prompt action. Yet here you are, and not a moment too soon. We were just discussing the progress the troops have made in repairing the road. A few more days should do it. But it's vital we know the movements of the Zulu army. What news from your spies?'

'I've just heard on good authority that Sihayo and the bulk of his warriors are bivouacked near Ibanbanango Mountain, which, as you know, is about halfway between here and Ulundi, and not far from the site you've chosen for your advanced depot at Siphezi Hill. The bulk of the main Zulu army is still at Ulundi but will leave tomorrow. Its plan is to link up with Chief Matshana's tribe and shelter in the Mangeni Gorge, to the right of our line of advance, and wait until we've marched past so that it can sever our lines of communication and attack us from the rear.'

George's ears pricked up at this first mention of Chief Matshana. Clearly Fynn and Crealock's plan was to fake intelligence so that Chelmsford felt compelled to attack the chief before continuing on to Ulundi.

'You're certain of this, Fynn?' asked Chelmsford.

'I am, my Lord. I'd trust these spies with my life.'

'In that case we must proceed cautiously. In two days, as planned, we'll establish an intermediary camp in the shadow of the Isandlwana Hill, ten miles from here,' he said, pointing to the map, 'from where we can clear the border region to the southeast, including the Mangeni Gorge. Only then will we move to Siphezi Hill in preparation for the final advance on Ulundi. For the moment, Wood can remain on the defensive, but Pearson and Durnford's columns must stay in close contact until we've secured the country behind the Tugela and Buffalo Rivers. Crealock, do we know how Pearson's column is getting on?'

'It's still en route for the Eshowe Mission.'

'Good. When it gets there, he's to leave part of his force and take the rest to the Entumeni Mission. What about Durnford?'

'I don't think we'll have any more trouble from him. Your order for him to march on Rorke's Drift with one battalion, the mounted troops and the rocket battery should have reached him on the sixteenth. I estimate he'll arrive at Rorke's Drift tomorrow.'

'Excellent. His mounted Kaffirs will be extremely useful when we clear Chief Matshana out of Qudeni Forest, and, to be honest, I'd prefer him close so that I can keep an eye on him.'

'A wise precaution, my Lord,' said Crealock. 'It might even make sense to put him under Colonel Glyn's orders.'

'I don't think that's necessary – not yet, at any rate. So that's our strategy, gentlemen, to coordinate our movements so that Cetshwayo has no hope of slipping through the net. We shall oblige him to keep his force together, when it will suffer from want of food and become thoroughly discontented; or else he'll attack, which will save us going to find him.'

George stepped out of the humidity of the tent into the sunshine. All around him the camp was humming with industry, like a well-oiled machine that could not fail. Or could it? Because Chelmsford, thanks to Fynn and Crealock's machinations, was basing his whole campaign strategy on intelligence reports that were impossible to verify. What if they were wrong? What if the Zulu army was planning to attack the Central Column at the earliest opportunity, as was its habit? As he looked up towards the distant hills, he had a sudden premonition that they would all be fighting again sooner than the general thought.

The mood was festive as the huge Central Column, after days of inactivity, rumbled to life during the morning of 20 January. The ten-mile journey from the Buffalo River to the intermediary camp near Isandlwana Hill would take the slow-moving ox-wagons – 110 of them in all – almost the whole day, but few of the column's 4,700 soldiers were minded to complain. After so many months of preparation and waiting, they were just glad to be on the move.

Even George was infected by the high spirits, chatting amiably with Gossett as they and the rest of the staff followed the mounted troops at the head of the column. Once through the Bashee valley, the track made a slight ascent over a low saddle and on to a plateau, which was intersected here and there by small streams, before dropping down to a valley bounded on the right by steep ravines and rocky kranses, and on the left by a fresh range of hills. At the base of the valley was the one remaining obstacle for wagons if not horsemen, a rocky stream known as the Manzimnyama, and beyond that it was a short uphill ride through bush and rocks to the broad saddle of land – or nek, as such a feature was known to the colonists – that lay between the peak of Isandlwana and a much lower, rock-strewn hill that the soldiers had already christened the Stony Koppie.

As the horsemen drew rein on the gently sloping grassland beyond the nek, to the left of which the site of the camp had already been marked out with whitewashed posts by Major Clery, Glyn's principal staff officer, George was struck by the rugged beauty of the terrain. The track continued on towards Siphezi Hill across an undulating plain, five miles wide and twice as long, strewn with rocks and crisscrossed with narrow watercourses and deep, dry riverbeds known as dongas. To the south of the plain lay the broken country where Chelmsford hoped to find the main Zulu army: the Malakatha Hills, the Mangeni Gorge and, beyond it, Qudeni Forest which led down to the Buffalo. To the north was a steep escarpment known as the Nyoni Ridge, which led up to the Nqutu Plateau. This plateau, George noted, could be reached by way of several steep ravines, the biggest of which began just beyond a distinctive conical hill that rose from the plain a mile or so from where he sat on horseback.

But dominating all was the steep, stocky eminence of Isandlwana itself. No more than 700 feet high, it rose boldly from the surrounding country to a rocky peak that reminded George of a crouching lion. Gossett disagreed. 'It's much more like the Sphinx at Cairo, which is quite a coincidence when you consider the Twenty-Fourth wear a sphinx on their collars for good service during the Egyptian campaign of eighteen hundred.'

'So they do,' said George, picturing the badge on Jake's uniform. 'Do you think it's auspicious?'

'I bloody hope so.'

'Gentlemen,' interrupted Chelmsford, looking at his pocket-watch, 'It's twelve o'clock and time for a spot of early lunch. In an hour we leave with the mounted troops to scout Chief Matshana's stronghold in the Mangeni Gorge. We've got a hard ride ahead of us if we're to be back before dark, so be ready to leave at one o'clock precisely.'

The route to the gorge took Chelmsford, Glyn and their staffs over a hard rolling plain, intersected at intervals by yet more dongas. With scouts out in front and on either flank, they headed in a southeasterly direction, keeping the Malakatha Hills to their right, and took more than two hours to cover the ten miles to the dramatic waterfall at the head of the gorge. It was a hot day and the thirsty horses drank greedily from the swift waters of the Mangeni as their riders gazed down into the precipitous gorge below, its steep rocky sides riddled with caves.

'So that's Matshana's stronghold, is it, Fynn?'

'It is, my Lord,' replied Fynn, mopping his brow with a handkerchief.

'And you're convinced the main Zulu *impi* is due here any day now?'

'According to my spies, it left Ulundi on the eighteenth and will be here tomorrow or the next day.'

'To link up with Matshana?'

'Yes, my Lord.'

'And yet we haven't seen a single Zulu today, nor any of their livestock. Are you sure they haven't all scarpered?'

'They're here, you can be certain of that. You can't see them because they're probably hiding in those caves below.'

With Chelmsford seemingly unconvinced, Colonel Crealock chipped in, 'I'm sure Fynn knows what he's talking about. After all, he's the local expert.'

'I'm well aware of that, Colonel, but we have to be careful not to put all our eggs into one basket. And even if Matshana's men are in the caves below, it will be a devil of a job to flush them out.'

'For white troops maybe, my Lord,' said Fynn, 'which is why I'd use Lonsdale's Kaffirs. They're used to fighting in caves and, let's be honest, are more expendable.'

'I agree with Fynn, sir,' said Crealock. 'And just to make sure the Kaffirs stay out of trouble, we can send the mounted troops along too. Between them they'll discover if there are any hostile Zulus between our camp and here.'

Chelmsford scratched his beard. 'I suppose it wouldn't do any harm to send Lonsdale's men and the cavalry down here tomorrow. But not the imperial infantry, mind. We'll keep them in camp until the picture is a little clearer. Now, if that's all, we'd better be getting back. We'll go across the Malakatha Hills this time, if you please Mr Fynn, and see what we find.'

In the event they found nothing but a few deserted kraals, from one of which they saw women running away with bundles on their heads. George volunteered to search the kraal and was accompanied by Glyn's orderly officer, a dapper young lieutenant with a neat beard called Nevill Coghill, who was keen to find food for the colonel's pot. George, on the other hand, was on the lookout for any information that might challenge Fynn's assertion that the Zulus were not about to attack the column. As he entered the first of the huts, revolver in hand, he heard a squawk, a shout and then a cry of pain. Running outside, he found Coghill on the ground, clutching his knee. 'What happened?'

'I was trying to catch that bloody bird,' said Coghill, nodding towards a scrawny chicken at the far side of the kraal, 'when I fell and twisted my knee.'

George knelt down and felt Coghill's knee. 'There's a lot of swelling. Do you think you can walk?'

'I can try.'

George helped the grimacing Coghill to his feet. 'Damn it to hell! It hurts like fury.'

'Best sit down while I finish off here.'

Coghill did as he was told, waiting patiently while George checked the remaining huts. In one there was a pot of Zulu porridge still warming on a fire, but no sign of life. He was about to leave when he sensed someone behind him. He spun round to see an old man, his face wizened with age, rushing him with an assegai. Loath to shoot him and lose a possible source of valuable information, George dodged the feeble blow and struck the Zulu full in the face with the barrel of his revolver. The old man's nose gushed with blood as he fell to his knees.

'Drop the assegai or I'll shoot,' said George in Zulu, pointing his revolver.

The spear clattered to the floor.

'Here,' said George, handing the old man his handkerchief to stem the flow of blood. 'Now tell me your name.'

The old Zulu was shaking with fear, but said nothing.

'Answer me! Or I'll personally see to it that every one of those women we saw running away a short time ago is hunted down and shot.'

It was, of course, an idle threat – one George was neither able nor willing to carry out – but the Zulu was taken in.

'My name is Mpatshana.'

'Good. That's a start. So tell me, Mpatshana, what you know about Cetshwayo's *impi*. Will it come soon?'

'All I've heard is that it will camp near Siphezi tonight.'

'Tonight? Are you sure?'

'That's what my nephew told me. He left today to join the Uve Regiment.'

'And what then? Will the *impi* join forces with Matshana?'

'I don't know. But it will fight, you can be sure of that.'

Yes, thought George, nodding, I'm sure it will. 'Thank you, Mpatshana. I'll leave you in peace. But stay inside until we've gone; if my colleagues see you, they'll want to take you prisoner.'

George left the hut and made his way over to where Coghill was sitting on the ground.

'I've just had a very interesting chat with an old Zulu.'

'What did he say?'

'That the Zulu army is heading in this direction.'

Coghill punched his fist into an open palm. 'Just my confounded luck: a battle in the offing and I'll be confined to my campbed. Hopefully it won't be the last. Help me on to my horse, would you, Hart? We mustn't keep the general waiting.'

Dusk was beginning to fall as the mounted column passed through the outer infantry picket and rode the remaining mile to the camp. Pitched in the shadow of the mountain, it had appeared as if by magic: row upon immaculate row of eight-man bell-tents, grouped in order of regimental importance: to the right of the track, in pride of place, the tents of the 1st/24th, then the mounted troops, the artillery, the 2nd/24th and lastly the two native contingent battalions on the extreme left. Most of the wagons had been placed on the nek, the broad saddle of land to the rear of the camp, while the headquarters and hospital tents were pitched behind the centre of the camp, under the scarped face of the mountain. No attempt had been made either to entrench the camp or to laager the wagons in accordance with Chelmsford's own field regulations. When Sub-Inspector Mansel of the Natal Mounted Police presumed to ask why, at the council of war held later that evening, Lord Chelmsford was brusquely dismissive. 'Because, my dear Sub-Inspector, this is not a permanent camp. We shall remain here a couple of days at most. In any case, the ground is far too stony to dig and the wagons are needed to ferry up supplies from Rorke's Drift.'

'But, sir,' persisted Mansel, 'we know from the intelligence gleaned by Second Lieutenant Hart that the main Zulu *impi* is on its way. What if it decides to attack the camp?'

'It won't.'

'But it could, my Lord. So would it not make sense to post a chain of pickets to the rear of the camp?'

'No, it would not,' said Chelmsford firmly. 'You seem to forget that it is my troops that will do all the attacking. And even if the enemy does venture to attack, the mountain will serve to protect our rear.'

'Might I make a suggestion, my Lord?' offered Colonel Crealock.

'Do.'

'If the police are nervous, we could always place a picket of native pioneers behind the camp.'

'We could,' said Chelmsford with a smile. 'Will that do, Sub-Inspector?'

The policeman reddened, but said nothing.

'Good. Now let's move on to more pressing matters. Fynn, have you learnt anything today to alter your conviction that the Zulu army will make for the Mangeni Gorge?'

'No, nor do I expect to,' said Fynn smugly. 'I have heard, however, that Chief Sihayo's brother Gamdana is willing to lay down his arms. His kraal is on the edge of the Malakatha Hills, on the way to the gorge, and I intend to go there tomorrow morning to speak to him. He may well know the whereabouts of his brother.'

'Good. I'll come with you. So that's settled. First thing tomorrow, Commandant Lonsdale will search the Malakatha Hills with his two battalions of Kaffirs, less four companies that will remain behind to guard the camp, while Major Dartnell takes the mounted police and volunteers along the old track that we used today. They are to link up in the vicinity of the Mangeni Gorge, and between them should determine whether any large parties of Zulus are occupying the ground to our southeast. Major Gossett will accompany the mounted troops. Any questions?'

'Yes, my Lord,' said Gossett, raising his hand. 'How many days' rations will the troops require?'

'You'll be back by nightfall, so one will suffice.'

'And what if we encounter the enemy, my Lord?' asked Lonsdale, a short rotund man with a waxed moustache who had distinguished himself on the Cape frontier.

'You're to use your initiative of course, Commandant, but if in doubt, report back to me for further orders. Nothing else? Good. Get some sleep, gentlemen. Some of you have an early start.'

George left the headquarters tent convinced that Chelmsford was courting disaster. So great was the general's contempt for his foe, so over-reliant was he on Fynn's suspect intelligence, that he seemed happy to ignore every basic military precaution, including his own field regulations for column commanders to fortify *every* camp. And to top it all he was about to split his command, sending the weakest part of his force, the native contingent, on a wild-goose chase through some of the most difficult terrain in southeast Africa. None of it made any sense. If by some miracle Fynn had not invented his intelligence, and the main Zulu army *was* heading towards the Mangeni Gorge, what was the point of sending Lonsdale's warriors in the same direction with only a portion of the mounted troops in support? But if Fynn was misleading Chelmsford for his own selfish ends, and the camp became the target as a result, it was in no way prepared to meet an attack.

# 15

George watched the dawn departure of Dartnell's horsemen and Lonsdale's foot battalions with a sense of
foreboding. Yet the black troops seemed cheery enough,
laughing and joking, and many carrying pots full of
steaming-hot porridge which, given the uncertainty of their
next meal, they were loath to abandon. They surged
forward in an unruly mass, making little attempt to keep
military formation, and looking for all the world like a
swarm of bees as they advanced across the plain. Even on
ponies, Lonsdale and his officers had trouble keeping up.

George looked up and could see, hovering directly
above the plain, a dark, low-lying cloud that resembled
the trail of smoke from a steamship. At first the cloud was
tinted blood-red, but as the sky lightened it became ash-
brown with golden edges, a glowering presence that
seemed to augur ill. George shivered, though the temperature was far from cold, and returned to his tent to
snatch a last hour or two of sleep before his morning
reconnaissance with Lord Chelmsford.

Shortly before nine o'clock, after a hearty breakfast of
boiled ham and eggs in the headquarters' mess-tent,

Chelmsford and his staff rode out of camp and took less than an hour to reach the kraal of Chief Gamdana, Sihayo's brother, on the edge of the Malakatha Hills. There was no sign of life and, fearing a trap, Chelmsford sent Fynn ahead to investigate. He confirmed that the kraal was empty, though some of the fireplaces contained ashes that were still warm, a sign that the departure was recent.

'Has Gamdana been playing us false, do you think?' Chelmsford asked Fynn.

'It's possible, my Lord, though it's also possible he panicked at the sight of Lonsdale's warriors. They would have passed close to here.'

'I suspect the former. He's probably gone to join Chief Matshana. Either way, there's nothing more to be done here, so back to camp, gentlemen; I hear the cook's got beefsteak for lunch.'

George could bear Chelmsford's insouciance no longer. 'My Lord,' he said as Chelmsford was about to move off, 'I know Mr Fynn's intelligence suggests the main Zulu army is heading for the Mangeni Gorge, but would it not make sense, to be on the safe side so to speak, to send another reconnaissance patrol up the Ulundi road as far as Siphezi Hill? I'd be happy to go along as an interpreter.'

Chelmsford reined in. 'That's very selfless of you, Hart, but I need you with me. Your suggestion, however, is a good one. Colonel Crealock, have Russell send a patrol to Siphezi Hill.'

'Very good, sir,' replied Crealock, his frown betraying his distaste for a general acting on the advice of a second lieutenant. 'But with most of the mounted troops absent today, I suggest we keep the patrol as small as possible. An officer and four riders should suffice.'

'Very well, and inform Russell his men are to take no risks. If they see Zulus they are to report back immediately. To camp, gentlemen,' added Chelmsford, spurring his horse on. 'Lunch awaits.'

So beautifully laid was the table in the headquarters mess-tent, with its crisp white linen and sparkling silver cutlery, that the setting could have been mistaken for a Pall Mall club. Chelmsford saw no sense in roughing it on campaign unless it was absolutely necessary, and though he never touched a drop of alcohol himself he was happy for his staff to partake. The meal, as a result, was a jovial affair, with the imminence of battle encouraging one or two to drink more than was advisable in the middle of the day. Chelmsford was all bonhomie, regaling his staff with tales of the famous Abyssinian Campaign, which he had accompanied as Sir Robert Napier's adjutant-general. 'If you think Zululand poses supply difficulties,' he said, leaning back in his chair, 'you should have been in Abyssinia in sixty-eight. We had to move an army of ten thousand men across three hundred miles of road-less mountain and desert, with not a drop of water to be had. And yet we managed it, thanks to British ingenuity, scrupulous staff work and first-rate intelligence. Any of you heard of a chap called Speedy?'

'Wasn't he Napier's political,' remarked Crealock, 'who went native and used to dress in lion skins?'

'He was indeed, Colonel. Knew the country like the back of his hand, and ran a first-class network of spies. A bit like our own Mr Fynn.'

Fynn raised his glass of claret. 'You're too kind, my Lord.'

George inwardly seethed. He was now more convinced than ever that Fynn had faked the intelligence for his own ends, and that Crealock knew this. George could bear the company no longer, but as he tried to think of a reason to excuse himself, the steward hurried up to Chelmsford and whispered in his ear.

'Gentlemen,' announced Chelmsford, 'we have an unexpected guest. Chief Gamdana has chosen to grace us with his presence after all.'

All eyes swivelled to the tent flap through which walked the younger brother of Chief Sihayo, a man George had last seen on that fateful night at kwaSoxhege. Leaner than his elder brother, and with far less natural authority, Gamdana looked ill at ease, his eyes darting from side to side. He was dressed like a chief, with a profusion of necklaces and an impressive headdress of otter skin and widow-bird feathers, but something about his shifty demeanour suggested a man disgruntled with his lot.

'Do come in, Chief,' said Chelmsford, making no attempt to rise from his seat. 'We missed you earlier, but no matter, you're here now. I take it you've come to submit.'

'I have,' said Gamdana in Zulu, causing Chelmsford to turn to Fynn for the English translation.

'Ask him where his weapons are,' said Chelmsford. 'He knows he can't submit without them.'

Fynn did so. 'He says they're outside.'

'Well, have them brought in. No need to break up the party early.'

Fynn went outside and returned with four of Gamdana's warriors, each clutching an armful of spears and firearms. They dumped them on the ground next to Chelmsford's seat.

'Is that it?' asked the general.

Gamdana nodded.

Chelmsford leant down to inspect a couple of the firearms. Some were muskets, some rifles, but all were muzzle-loaders. 'They're all obsolete,' said Chelmsford, shaking his head. 'Ask him what he's done with his best weapons.'

The Zulu looked indignant. 'These are my best weapons, and I don't surrender them lightly. Cetshwayo has sent an *impi* to eat me up, but it has not yet arrived. It is said to be camped to the right of Siphezi Hill.'

Fynn translated, but omitted to mention the last important detail, causing George to intervene. 'He also confirms, my Lord, what the old Zulu told me yesterday: that the main *impi* spent last night at Siphezi, which is barely twenty miles distant.'

'I wouldn't believe a word he says,' said Fynn. 'How could Cetshwayo know of his plans to surrender? I suspect he's feeding us false intelligence so we'll look in the wrong place.'

'My Lord,' persisted George, 'might it be possible the chief is telling the truth? He is, after all, a younger brother of Chief Sihayo and could be hoping to take his place as the head of the tribe.'

'Nonsense,' said Fynn. 'He's obviously a plant. You've only got to look at the quality of the weapons he's brought in to deduce that. They can't be the best he has.'

Ill feeling crackled across the tent between George and Fynn. George felt himself almost bursting with the frustration of his knowledge.

'Crealock,' said Chelmsford, 'what do you think?'

'I agree with Fynn. All our previous intelligence indicates that Cetshwayo's *impi* is intending to link up with Chief Matshana in the Mangeni Gorge. This mention of Siphezi Hill could be a deliberate attempt to lure us away from there.'

'I believe you're right,' nodded the general. 'If Gamdana really was prepared to betray his brother and his king, his life would be forfeit. Get the blackguard out of my sight.'

'Is he to be held prisoner, my Lord?' asked Fynn.

'No, I can't spare the men to guard him. Just tell him to leave.'

'Is that wise, my Lord?' asked Crealock. 'He's seen the layout of the camp. If he means to play us false he could pass this information to the Zulu commanders.'

'I hope he does, but I doubt it will make a difference. Their strategy is to avoid a pitched battle; ours is to bring one on. And to do that we've got to winkle them out of their hiding places. Talking of which, is there any word from Major Gossett?'

'Not yet, my Lord,' said Crealock.

'Damn. I want to scout the Nqutu Plateau to the north of the plain this afternoon, so leave word in camp of our whereabouts. And get rid of them,' said Chelmsford, nodding towards the waiting Zulus.

George rose from his seat and led Gamdana and his men out of the tent.

'You look familiar,' said the chief, studying George's face.

'I came to kwaSoxhege last year.'

'You're the white Zulu who tried to save Nandi?'

George nodded.

'Is that why you've come with the white soldiers now, for revenge?'

'Maybe. But tell me, cousin, why you're here rather than with your people.'

'Because I don't wish to see my kraals destroyed. We can't win this war. Our only hope is to submit before it's too late.'

'I apologize for the way you were treated in there. My chief doesn't believe you've come in good faith. He thinks you're out to mislead us.'

'Then he's a fool. Cetshwayo's *impi* is near. Tomorrow it will fight.'

'Where?'

'I don't know. It will strike anywhere it sees a weakness. Now I must go. Without British protection I'm a dead man.'

It was gone three o'clock, much later than intended, by the time Chelmsford and his staff reached the Nqutu Plateau, having ascended the broad spur that connected it to the north end of Isandlwana Hill. They rode east, across a broken, difficult terrain strewn with rocks and boulders, and had covered about two miles when a frantically waving rider was seen to their left. It was Major Gossett. He cantered over to Chelmsford, drew rein and saluted.

'My Lord, I've just come from Major Dartnell. About an hour ago his scouts made contact with a large force of Zulus, about fifteen hundred, on the neck of a hill close to the Mangeni Gorge. He doesn't think he's strong enough to attack them on his own, so has asked Commandant Lonsdale to join him. He requests permission to stay out overnight so he can keep an eye on the Zulus.'

Chelmsford smiled broadly. 'Do you hear that, gentlemen? It seems Dartnell has made contact with Matshana's men, and possibly even the vanguard of Cetshwayo's army, just as Fynn predicted. Of course he must stay out. Crealock, arrange for rations to be sent out on pack horses, and send Dartnell a written order to attack as and when he thinks fit.'

'Shall I send Hart, sir?' asked Crealock.

'No, send a mounted infantryman. I need Hart with me.'

The patrol continued for a further mile along the plateau until it reached the furthest cavalry outpost, consisting of two Carbineers from George's regiment, on the crest of a hill known as iThusi. Asked by Chelmsford if they had anything to report, they pointed to some high ground a further three miles to the northeast where, clearly outlined against the horizon, could be seen a number of Zulu horsemen. George counted fourteen.

'How long have they been there?' asked Chelmsford.

'About an hour, this time,' answered the senior of the two Carbineers, a freckle-faced corporal called Pearce. 'They keep coming and going.'

'Have you reported this?'

'We have, sir, more than once.'

Chelmsford turned to his civilian advisor. 'What do you make of it, Fynn?'

'Oh, I wouldn't worry about it, my Lord. It's probably just Sihayo's men trying to work their way round to his kraal to assess the damage. They're among the few Zulus who ride horses.'

'I see. Could they be acting as scouts for the main Zulu *impi*?'

'They could be,' said Fynn, 'but then they wouldn't be heading in that direction. All my intelligence indicates that the main *impi* is heading southeast towards the Mangeni Gorge, and if we take Dartnell's report at face value, it might already be there.'

'Yes, well, just to be on the safe side I'll send out a patrol to the northeast first thing in the morning. It wouldn't do to be caught on the hop.'

Back at camp an hour later, Chelmsford received further hints that the Zulu army was near. The first was a message from the commandant of one of Lonsdale's battalions, timed at one o'clock that afternoon. It read:

> *Sir,*
> *While skirmishing along the southern edge of the Malakatha range, my men captured two Zulus who, under interrogation, claimed to have left the main Zulu army in the vicinity of Siphezi Hill earlier today to visit their mother. I thought you should know. I'm sending this message back with forty cattle that we've also managed to capture.*
> *I am, etc.,*
> *George Hamilton Browne, Comdt, 1st/3rd NNC*

The second was a verbal report from the young lieutenant of the Imperial Mounted Infantry who had led that day's patrol to Siphezi. 'We saw no Zulus until the ride back to camp, my Lord,' stated the officer as he stood rigidly to attention in Chelmsford's headquarters tent, his white sun helmet under his arm.

'How many were there?' asked the general.

'I'd say about thirty on foot, and eight on horseback. They tried to cut us off, but we galloped round them, shooting a couple in the process.'

'Any casualties?'

'No, sir.'

'Well done, Lieutenant. That'll be all.'

Chelmsford stood up from his canvas chair and began to pace round the tent. Silently watching him were the senior members of his staff, Crealock and Gossett, as well as Fynn and George. At last Chelmsford spoke. 'A number of reports suggest the main Zulu army *was* in the vicinity of Siphezi Hill, and probably camped near there last night. The hill is, of course, on the direct route from the Zulu capital to here and is an obvious stopping-off point for the *impi* as it advances. The question is, where is the *impi* now?'

Fynn spoke first. 'I've heard nothing to change my original assessment. The Zulu *impi* plans to hide in the broken ground to our southeast, and is either there already or en route. It makes complete sense for it to camp at Siphezi before heading south towards the Mangeni Gorge.'

'Crealock?'

'I agree, sir. The force discovered by Dartnell is probably part of that army. Certainly we've had no sighting of any significant body of warriors to the north of Siphezi.'

'Gossett?'

'I'm largely in agreement, sir. My only qualm is the presence of those mounted Zulus to the north of Siphezi. Given King Shaka's reputation as a master of deception and surprise, is it not possible that the current generation of Zulu commanders are trying to emulate him by splitting their forces and appearing where least expected?'

'What exactly are you trying to say, Gossett?' asked Chelmsford.

'That the Zulu army was indeed at Siphezi last night, but since then it has divided into two wings, one moving to the north, hence the mounted scouts, and one to the south.'

'Why would it weaken itself by choice?'

'I don't know, sir; possibly because it would then be in a position to attack us from two directions at the same time, a favoured Zulu tactic.'

I couldn't have put it better myself, thought George. But would Chelmsford be swayed?

The answer was no. 'I'm afraid, Gossett, you misunderstand these natives. Put them up against another tribe and they'll show dash and aggression, but not against white troops. They know they can't withstand our firepower. It was the same on the Cape frontier.'

George wanted to scream, *We're not on the Cape frontier; the Zulus are different*. But Crealock was fixing him with a hard stare, and so complete was the hold that he and Fynn had over the general that George doubted any outburst or accusation from a second lieutenant would make a difference.

Chelmsford, meanwhile, seemed satisfied that he had

everything in hand, and was about to bring the meeting to a close when a man entered the tent in the black uniform and white spiked helmet of the Natal Mounted Police. 'A message from Major Dartnell, sir.'

Having read it, Chelmsford smiled broadly. 'Gossett, you can put your mind at rest because it seems Fynn was right all along. The major has reported an increase in the size of the Zulu force opposite him to several thousand. It can only be the main Zulu army, and Dartnell wants to know if I think it prudent for him to attack the following morning.'

'I think he should, sir,' said Crealock, 'before the Zulus have a chance to melt into the hills.'

'But if it is the main Zulu army,' said Gossett, 'shouldn't we send some of the imperial infantry to support him?'

'No,' said Crealock, 'it's too far and too late in the day.'

'I agree,' said Chelmsford. 'Put in the reply, Crealock, that Dartnell is to judge for himself if and when he should attack. We'll wait and see what transpires and, if necessary, we'll move out with the infantry first thing.'

George left headquarters in a fury and headed straight for the camp of the 2nd/24th Regiment. He needed to speak to Jake, to warn him that a Zulu attack was imminent, but he could find no sign of him or any other G Company officer.

'They've just taken over picket duty from us on the camp perimeter,' explained a young subaltern called Mainwaring at the entrance to the officers' mess-tent. 'And very welcome they were too. We didn't expect to be relieved until the morning.'

'Where exactly are they?'

'They're about half a mile to the camp's right front, due southeast. You can't miss them.'

It was a chill, clear evening, and as George picked his way across the dark, rock-strewn plain he felt heartily sorry for Jake, cold and exposed on the camp's outer perimeter while his fellow officers were safe and warm in their mess. He looked back at the huge tented camp, undefended but for a thin string of outposts, and wondered again at Chelmsford's folly. Behind it rose the dark menace of the leonine mountain, like a beast waiting to pounce.

He found Jake and two privates huddled round a small fire. 'Hello, George,' said Jake, looking up as he approached. 'What are you doing here?'

'I need to speak to you in private.'

'All right. I won't be long,' said Jake to his men. 'Keep your eyes peeled.'

Jake led George out of earshot, taking care to avoid the thorn bushes that ringed his position. 'I can't be away from my post long. What is it?'

'You remember I told you about Fynn and Crealock's plan to destroy Chief Matshana and sell his cattle?'

Jake nodded.

'Well, it's about to come to fruition. They've convinced Chelmsford to ignore all intelligence to the contrary and focus on Matshana's stronghold in the Mangeni Gorge. While he's been doing that, the Zulu army has been creeping ever closer and may well attack tomorrow.'

'Attack where? Here?'

'I don't know. Either the camp or the detachment in the hills, maybe both at the same time.'

'What have you heard?'

'Reports have been coming in all day that the main Zulu army camped last night near Siphezi Hill. That's under a day's march from here. We've also received word from Dartnell that he's located a sizeable Zulu force near the Mangeni Gorge. About an hour ago he sent a second message, saying the hostile force had grown to several thousand. If it is the vanguard of Cetshwayo's *impi*, then I don't give him and Lonsdale much hope of survival.'

'This doesn't make any sense. If Chelmsford knows the detachment has come up against strong opposition, why hasn't he either recalled him or sent out infantry reinforcements?'

'Good question. Gossett suggested sending either yours or the First Battalion, but Crealock persuaded Chelmsford it was too late in the day. My feeling is that Crealock and Fynn want Dartnell to take some casualties so that Chelmsford has no option but to march to the Mangeni Gorge and destroy Matshana's force. If the imperial infantry arrives too soon, the Zulus might not give battle.'

'Yes, I see that. But what makes you think the Zulus might attack the camp?'

'Only that this afternoon, from iThusi Hill, I saw mounted Zulus on high ground to the northeast. It might be nothing. But if they're scouts from the main Zulu army it could indicate that at least part of Ceshwayo's *impi* marched north from Siphezi and not south.'

'What was Chelmsford's reaction?'

'He ignored it, because Fynn has managed to convince him that the Zulus will hide in the hills to the southeast.

Dartnell's messages have simply confirmed for him that Fynn was right.'

Jake sighed. 'So what can we *do*?'

'I don't know. If I try to speak to Chelmsford I'll be cutting my own throat.'

'I could try.'

'You could, but even if you *do* manage to get past Crealock and speak to Chelmsford in private, he'd never believe you. Let's just hope I'm wrong about all this. In the meantime, stay vigilant and make sure your men do the same. The Zulus could attack at any time, though you're probably safe at night.'

Jake smiled, his white teeth just visible in the gloom. 'That's good to hear. Sleep well.'

'I don't think there's much chance of that.'

# 16

George woke to the sound of muffled voices in Chelmsford's tent next door. He listened hard and could just make out Crealock's voice. 'Is Major Clery to issue orders to Colonel Durnford?'

'No,' replied Lord Chelmsford, 'you do it.'

George sat up and lit a candle. Something serious must have happened for orders to be issued in the middle of the night – but what? George pulled on his trousers and boots and went outside. It was a pitch-black moonless night, the only light coming from his tent and that of the general. He reached the entrance to Chelmsford's tent as Crealock was leaving, lamp in hand.

'Ah, Hart,' said Crealock with a smile. 'I was about to rouse you.'

'Sir?' asked George guardedly.

'We've just received a message from Dartnell saying that the enemy is gathering in increasing numbers and he didn't feel strong enough to attack them in the morning without white troops. His Lordship is convinced it's Cetshwayo's *impi* and has given orders for the Second Twenty-Fourth Regiment, four of the six guns and all the remaining mounted troops to be ready to march at day-break. He also wants Durnford to move up from the supply depot at Rorke's Drift to reinforce the camp. I need you to carry the order.'

I bet you do, thought George; with me out of the way there'll be no one to interfere with your plans. But Chelmsford had other ideas: 'No, not Hart,' came a cry from inside the tent. 'I need him with me tomorrow and he'll never get back from Rorke's Drift in time. Send that transport officer – Smith-Dorrien I think he's called. He's been up and down that track countless times and should know it like the back of his hand. '

'Very good, sir.'

'A lucky escape for you, Hart,' said Crealock, contemptuously. 'I can't imagine you'd have enjoyed a night ride to Rorke's Drift with the Zulus so near. You can at least deliver the message to Lieutenant Smith-Dorrien. He's sharing with Lieutenant Coghill, beyond the column office. Tell him,' said Crealock, handing over a folded piece of paper, 'he's to hand this to Colonel Durnford in person.'

Even with a lamp, George had trouble finding the tent. By the time he did manage to locate it, curiosity had got the better of him and he paused to read the message:

*You are to march to this camp at once with all the force you have with you of No. 2 Column. 2nd/24th, Artillery and mounted men with the general and Colonel Glyn to move off at once to attack a Zulu force about ten miles distant.*

George thought it odd that there was no specific mention that Durnford was to reinforce the camp, much less to take command, but knew it was too late to do anything about.

Having delivered the message to a bleary-eyed Smith-Dorrien, George returned to his tent and lay on his campbed fully clothed. He found it impossible to sleep, and was still working through the various scenarios for the following day, from a full-scale battle in the hills to no action at all, when a lone bugle sounded Reveille. It was 3 a.m., and as he got up it suddenly occurred to George that Jake's was the only company from the 2nd/24th on outpost duty and, as such, would probably be left behind with Colonel Pulleine's five companies of the 1st Battalion and the four companies of the NNC – barely 1,300 men in all – to defend the camp. He prayed to God that they were not attacked.

The relief column left at sun-up and quickly split into two parts: George riding ahead with Chelmsford, his staff and a small escort of mounted infantrymen; Glyn remaining behind with his staff and the slower-moving redcoats as they plodded, four abreast, towards the hazy purple of the high ground that led to the Mangeni Gorge. A heavy mist hung over the hills, but it was beginning to clear by the time Chelmsford and his horsemen reached Dartnell's bivouac on a grassy ridge, a couple of miles short of the gorge, at a little after 6.30. The group dismounted and, with barely a word of greeting, Chelmsford asked an exhausted-looking Dartnell, his eyes hollow and his moustache unkempt, where the enemy was.

Dartnell looked apologetic as he pointed to the hill opposite, where a few Zulus and some smouldering campfires were all that were visible.

'That's what's left of the huge *impi* you reported?' asked Chelmsford, his tone incredulous.

'They must have moved off under the cover of darkness, my Lord.'

'That's stating the obvious, Major. So where are they now?'

'I don't know, sir.'

'You don't know! Why haven't you dispatched mounted patrols to find out?'

'We didn't get much sleep, sir. Lonsdale's Kaffirs thought we were being attacked and stampeded off the hill, waking the whole bivouac.'

Chelmsford turned to Lonsdale, who also looked the worse for wear after a night sleeping rough. 'Is this true, Rupert?'

'It is, my Lord. The officers did their best, but the men were in a panic and wouldn't listen. It took about an hour to round them up.'

Chelmsford rubbed his forehead. 'That's all very well, Major Dartnell, but it doesn't excuse your failure to keep in contact with the enemy. He can't have just disappeared. Send out patrols immediately and find him.'

'My Lord,' interrupted Fynn, who was standing a little apart from the main group, 'I think I've found what you're looking for. Over there.'

All eyes followed the direction of Fynn's gesture beyond the hill with the campfires to some high ground at least two miles further on, where hundreds of tiny figures were moving ant-like across a plateau towards a spur that ran down into the Mangeni Gorge. 'Do you think it's the main *impi*, Fynn?' asked Chelmsford.

'I'm certain of it, my Lord.'

'In that case we'll attack at once. Rupert, send your two battalions to occupy the spur they're heading towards. If the Zulus get there first, drive them off it. Dartnell, your men will cover Lonsdale's right flank.' He then turned to George. 'Ride back to Glyn and tell him to direct the guns and the infantry up the valley to the left of the spur. With a bit of luck we'll catch them in a pincer attack and crush them. The Mounted Infantry are to cover Glyn's left flank.'

George saluted, mounted Emperor and picked his way back down the hill. He was far from convinced that the force they had seen was the main Zulu *impi*. It was not big enough, for a start, though how many warriors lurked behind the high ground was impossible to tell. That, though, was surely the point. Chelmsford thought he had located the main *impi*, but he could not know for certain. What if, as George feared, it *had* split into two halves at Siphezi, one marching north, the other south? That would still leave at least 10,000 warriors in a position to threaten the unsuspecting camp. It did not bear thinking about.

Fifteen minutes of hard riding brought him up to the head of the column. Having delivered Chelmsford's message to Glyn, he returned to the bivouac site and arrived just as the Zulus were retiring in the face of Lonsdale's advancing battalions, off the spur and back towards Siphezi Hill. 'You see, my Lord,' said Fynn to Chelmsford, 'I told you they wouldn't stand.'

'Yes, it's just like the frontier war. Ah, Hart, there you are. How soon will Glyn's men be in position?'

'Not for another thirty minutes at least, sir.'

'Damn. With the Zulus in full retreat they'll arrive far too late to spring our trap. Oh well, we'll just have to follow them up and hope for the best.'

For the next two hours the Zulus continued their withdrawal from the spur above the Mangeni Gorge in scattered bodies of men, ranging in size from ten to 500, disappearing from one hilltop and reappearing on the next. It was like chasing shadows and, with the sun now high in the sky, the infantrymen were soon red-faced and sweating as they toiled up the valley in their heavy serge tunics. The only fighting took place on the left of the advance, close to Matshana's stronghold in the gorge, where Offy Shepstone and the Natal Carbineers managed to cut off about 300 warriors who took refuge in some caves. The task of flushing them out was given to the Natal Contingent, and while this operation was underway, Chelmsford, Glyn and their respective staffs dismounted on a knoll to watch the main body of Zulus being pursued towards Siphezi Hill by the Mounted Infantry.

'Bloody cowards,' muttered Chelmsford as he peered through a telescope at the retreating Zulus. 'All this effort for nothing.'

'I wouldn't say that, my Lord,' said Crealock, a look of quiet satisfaction on his face. 'We're giving Matshana a good thrashing and, in the process, we've prevented Cetshwayo's army from joining him and hiding in the hills.'

'He's right, sir,' added Fynn. 'Once we've polished off the rest of Matshana's men and collected his cattle, we can get on with the rest of the campaign. We'll be in Ulundi in no time.'

'I hope you're right,' said Chelmsford.

Behind him, George shook his head at the sheer audacity of Crealock and Fynn in shaping a campaign for their own benefit. What the cost would be to the column, only time would tell. At that moment he spotted a lone rider approaching at speed from the valley below. As the rider crested the knoll, George recognized him as Trooper Will Devine of the Carbineers. His horse was on its last legs, its flanks coated with lather. George rushed forward to hold the trooper's horse. 'What is it, Will?'

'A message from Colonel Pulleine,' said Devine, as he slid off the horse. 'Scouts have sighted Zulus advancing on the camp.'

'How many?'

'I don't know. Hundreds, maybe thousands.'

'Let me see the message.'

Devine handed over a slip of light blue paper. It read:

> *Staff Officer,*
> *Report just come in that the Zulus are advancing in force from the left front of the camp (8.05 a.m.).*
>  *H.B. Pulleine, Lt Col*

George wrote on it the time of receipt, 9.30 a.m., and handed it to Clery, who at once showed it to Chelmsford. The general briefly scanned the note, returned it to Clery and resumed his scan of the horizon.

His brow furrowed, Clery waited for a response, and when there was none he asked, 'What is to be done on this subject?'

'There is nothing to be done on that.'

Clery shrugged his shoulders in resignation and handed the note to Glyn, who also read it without comment.

George looked on aghast. The camp was clearly in danger from a sizeable, if unknown number of Zulus, and Chelmsford was behaving as if nothing had happened. He had to say something. 'My Lord,' he said, 'the camp may be under attack as we speak. Should we not return at once?'

'Certainly not. The note shows no sign of panic, nor does it request our presence. If our experience this morning is anything to go by, the Zulus will make a show of advancing and then retire. I hope they do attack the camp, but I doubt they will.'

'But, sir, what if Pulleine's scouts have sighted the main *impi*?'

'Impossible, my Lord,' intervened Fynn. 'We've been chasing it for most of the morning.'

'I agree, sir,' said Crealock. 'If we return to the camp now, we'll have to break off our attack on Matshana's stronghold. Pulleine can look after himself.'

'Exactly so. But there's no harm in being certain, Crealock, so I want you to send two officers with telescopes up that tall hill opposite. They should be able to see the camp from there, and can report any enemy activity. In the meantime, let's halt the troops for breakfast.'

'An excellent notion, my Lord,' said Crealock. 'May I also suggest that we camp tonight in the Mangeni Gorge so that we're well placed to finish off Matshana in the morning?'

'Good idea. Send a galloper with instructions for Pulleine to send on tents and supplies.'

'Yes, sir. Shall I send Hart? That way he can verify the security of the camp for himself.'

'All right, then. But no dawdling, Hart. You're to return as soon as you've delivered the message.'

'Yes, sir,' said George, keen to get away. If the camp *was* being attacked, every second counted. With the message in his pocket, George swung into the saddle, dug in his spurs and was over the lip of the knoll and gone. It had taken Trooper Devine an hour and twenty minutes of hard riding to reach Chelmsford and deliver his message. George did the return journey in just over an hour, driving Emperor harder than he had hitherto dared in African conditions. As he passed the conical hill, two miles from the camp, he could see to his right large numbers of Zulus on the eastern end of the Nqutu Plateau, their shields and spears silhouetted against the clear blue sky. A chill of fear seemed to run up his spine as he realized he had been right all along: the Zulus *were* advancing on the camp.

He pressed on and, seeing the picket of G Company covering the track up ahead, George considered making a quick detour to his left to speak to Jake. But he knew that time was precious and so continued on through the picket towards the camp, where he could see a large body of black horsemen, obviously Durnford's men, drawn up in front of the tents of the NNC. To their left, on the parade ground ahead of the main camp, stood the rest of the fighting troops, their uniforms a blur of dark blue, black and red.

In the camp itself, George felt no air of urgency. Large number of noncombatants – farriers, bandsmen, cooks, clerks, wagon-drivers and *voorlopers* – were going about their business as if the threat from the Zulus was neglible. There was no sign of a defensive laager, though a number of wagons on the nek beyond the camp were harnessed to their oxen, and no attempt had been made to lower the tents, standard procedure with a battle in the offing.

'Where can I find Colonel Pulleine?' shouted George to a cook of the 1st/24th, stirring a dixie of food.

'At the column office.'

George rode on, heading for the huge Union flag hanging limply from its pole, which marked the head-quarters tents at the back of the camp. A handful of soldiers in various uniforms were loafing outside the white bell-tent that served as the column office. George dismounted, handed one his reins and hurried inside.

The tent was full of officers George knew – among them Lieutenant Melvill, the officer who had presided over Thomas's flogging on the boat – but no one noticed his arrival. All eyes were fixed on the heated exchange between the two senior men, Lieutenant Colonel Pulleine and Colonel Durnford. The former was a thickset man of medium height, wearing the scarlet tunic and blue trousers of the 1st/24th Regiment, and sporting impressive mutton-chop whiskers. Durnford was in his usual frontier garb of blue serge patrol jacket, scarlet waistcoat, dark cord breeches, boots and spurs. He wore a broad leather belt over his right shoulder and one round his waist, support-ing a revolver holster and a hunting knife. In his left hand he was carrying a soft felt wideawake hat with one side of its broad brim turned up and a crimson turban tied round its middle. His magnificent moustache was, if anything, even droopier than George remembered.

'I'm sorry, Colonel Durnford,' Pulleine was saying, his jaw set, 'I cannot agree to lend you two companies of infantry. My orders are to defend the camp.'

'But damn it, man,' replied Durnford, 'you heard the latest message from the scouts on Isandlwana Hill. The Zulus are retreating, and it's my duty to follow them up and prevent them from threatening Lord Chelmsford's rear.'

'We've been getting many reports, Colonel Durnford, and they don't all concur. One minute we hear the enemy are advancing up the Nqutu Plateau in three columns, the next they're retiring.'

'All the more reason to go out and see for ourselves.'

'Excuse the interruption, gentlemen,' said George, pushing his way through the crowd. 'I've just come from the general and as I passed the conical hill I didn't see any sign that the Zulus on the plateau were threatening him. On the contrary, they seemed to be moving in this direction.'

Pulleine turned to face George. 'Is Lord Chelmsford on his way back, Hart?'

'No, sir. He intends to camp tonight near the Mangeni and asks if you'll send on the tents and supplies for the troops in the field.'

'Didn't he get my earlier message about the Zulus advancing in force?'

'He did, but he didn't consider it sufficiently urgent to warrant a retrograde movement. He thinks you've got enough men to look after yourself.'

'Has he been in action himself?'

'Yes, but it's hard to tell whether they were Matshana's men or part of the main Zulu *impi*. Most of them refused to give battle and retired on Siphezi Hill.'

'So we can't be sure we're safe from attack?'

'No.'

'All the more reason, then,' said Pulleine to Durnford, 'not to send away any of my infantry on a wild-goose chase.'

'Very well,' said Durnford, 'perhaps I had better not take them. I will go with my own men. Where's Captain Barton?'

'Here, sir,' said a thin-faced officer with sandy hair.

'Right, Barton, here's the plan. I want you to take your two troops of horsemen up on to the Nqutu Plateau to our left front and drive any Zulus you find back down it and on to the plain. Meanwhile I'll advance up the Ulundi track with the rest of the mounted men and rocket battery, and try to intercept the Zulus as they come down off the plateau. But you've got furthest to go, so you'd best set off now.'

Barton saluted and left.

Durnford looked at his pocket-watch. 'It's now eleven fifteen. Major Russell should be here soon with the rocket battery. We might as well have a spot of lunch while we're waiting. All right with you, Pulleine?'

'Of course. I'll ask the cook to prepare some bread and cold meat.'

George looked around at the smiling faces with mounting apprehension. He seemed to be the only one present who regarded Durnford's plan as more than a little foolhardy. Pulleine appeared happy enough now that his command had been left intact, while Melvill and Coghill were laughing at some private joke. Durnford himself was all affability as he briefed his junior officers between mouthfuls of sandwich and gulps of beer. George knew he had to say something before it was too late. 'Excuse me, Colonel, may I have a word in private?'

'I suppose so, Hart, but you'll have to make it quick.'

They found a quiet spot outside. 'Colonel,' said George, 'may I speak frankly?'

'You may.'

'I know we haven't always seen eye to eye, for obvious reasons, but I hope you'll listen to what I have to say.'

'Go on.'

'I'm convinced the Zulus are about to attack the camp in force. If they do, your plan to intercept the Zulus on the plateau will leave the camp hopelessly exposed.'

'And what makes you so convinced? You're nineteen, for God's sake, with barely a year's military experience and – your Zulu blood notwithstanding – you know even less about Africa and its natives. I, on the other hand, have been in the army for thirty years and in southern Africa since seventy-two. I think I'm slightly better qualified to second-guess Zulu tactics.'

'Maybe, Colonel, but this is not about second-guessing; it's about protecting the camp. I spoke to Colonel Crealock, shortly after Lord Chelmsford issued the order for you to move here, and he was very specific about your task being to reinforce the camp.'

'The order says nothing about me reinforcing the camp. I have it here,' said Durnford, reaching for his top pocket.

'I know what the order says, Colonel, and I'm telling you that Chelmsford's intention was for you to supplement the camp's garrison, and not go chasing after Zulu *impis* whose size and location you cannot be certain of. Pulleine's orders are to act strictly on the defensive. As the senior officer you inherit those orders.'

'What rot. My command is independent of Pulleine's. Why, only a couple of days ago Lord Chelmsford said he wanted to use my column against Chief Matshana, which is what I intend to do now.'

George grabbed Durnford by the shoulders. 'Listen to me: Chief Matshana is a red herring. The only reason Lord Chelmsford is blundering around the Mangeni Gorge is because Fynn has a personal score to settle with the chief. Those Zulus on the heights are not Matshana's men, they're Cetshwayo's, and heaven knows how many are yet to show themselves.'

'So you say,' said Durnford, removing George's hands, 'but I don't agree. This is my opportunity to influence this campaign, and I won't throw it away by kicking my heels in camp. Why, the general himself said he was prepared to give a column commander *every latitude* when he was operating in an enemy's country, even to the extent of disobeying orders.'

'Well, that's what you'll be doing.'

'Nonsense. Show me,' said Durnford, taking the order from his pocket and offering it to George, 'where it says I'm to take command.'

'It's implied.'

'Well, that's not good enough.'

'At least wait until the situation is a little clearer, until you hear back from Captain Barton.'

'No. If I'm to take the Zulus in the flank, I must leave now.'

'This is not just about you!' yelled George, his temper snapping.

Durnford fixed him with an icy stare. 'What did you *say*?'

'I *said* this is not just about you and your need to redeem your battered military reputation.'

'How dare you talk about things you don't understand. I did my duty at Bushman's River Pass and have nothing to make amends for.'

'Then why are you being so reckless? Do you need to prove something to Fanny?'

Durnford looked as if he could commit murder, but he made no move to strike George. Instead he said coldly, 'I see no point in continuing this conversation. I'm riding out to engage the Zulus, and if your fluttering heart will permit, you're welcome to accompany me.'

George ignored the insult. 'My orders are to return directly to the general.'

'Well, that's where I'm heading.'

George hesitated. He had done his best, but Durnford would not be dissuaded. And maybe he was right; maybe the Zulus had thought better of attacking the camp. They would soon find out.

'I'll come with you as far as iThusi. If the route is clear, I'll carry on to the general.'

'Please yourself,' said Durnford, turning away.

Back at the column office, Durnford was met by a grave-looking officer with a moustache and side-whiskers, wearing a dark blue patrol jacket and the blue trousers with the scarlet stripe of the Royal Artillery.

'Ah, Russell, you've arrived. Grab a quick bite to eat and then take your battery and escort along the track that leads to Ulundi. I'll ride ahead with two troops of horse. The Zulus are retiring along the Nqutu Plateau to the left of the track and we must make haste to outflank them.'

Durnford then sought out Pulleine. 'We're setting off, Colonel. But if you see us in difficulties you must send out troops to support us.'

'I will,' replied Pulleine. 'God speed.'

As George was leaving the tent, he overheard Pulleine say to his adjutant, Lieutenant Melvill, 'Send Cavaye's company up the Tahelane Spur so they can support the horsemen on the Nqutu Plateau. The rest of the fighting troops can return to their messes for lunch. But they're to keep on their accoutrements, eat as quickly as possible and be ready to turn out at a moment's notice. We're not out of the woods yet.'

# 17

## Near the Central Column's camp, Isandlwana, 22 January 1879, 11.45 a.m.

The steady beat of 400 hooves on the hard earth of the sun-baked plain reminded George of field days in the 1st Dragoon Guards. Then the enemy had been imaginary; now he was all too real.

They had left the camp by the Ulundi track at 11.30 a.m., George trotting just behind Colonel Durnford at the head of a hundred black troopers in slouch-hats and khaki tunics, with bandoliers slung across their chests, and riding hardy ponies without stirrups. Half of them were Christian converts from the Edendale Mission, the other half Basutos, and all fiercely loyal to their leader, Durnford.

It had not taken the horsemen long to overtake Russell and his rocket battery, its V-shaped iron troughs and thin seventeen-inch rockets strapped to the back of a string of mules. But as they thundered on up the plain, George kept glancing nervously to his left where the ground rose sharply to the Nqutu Plateau, and where it appeared the Zulus, in scattered groups, were indeed withdrawing in the face of Barton's advance.

'You see, Hart,' shouted Durnford above the din, 'I was right all along. And if they're going towards the general, we must stop them at any cost.'

They had been riding for a good fifteen minutes, and were almost level with the end of the Nqutu Plateau, four miles from the camp, when they were overtaken by a scout from the Carbineers who signalled for them to stop. Durnford raised his hand in the air and the column reined in as one. 'Hello, Tommy,' said George, recognizing the freckle-faced youngster as the teenage son of the Pietermaritzburg mayor. 'What's the hurry?'

'You're riding into a trap. Two of our men have just discovered a huge Zulu *impi* squatting in the valley beyond the plateau.'

'How big?' asked Durnford.

'They didn't count. But many thousands.'

The blood drained from Durnford's face. He knew he had been outwitted, and was looking for someone to blame. 'Sergeant Major,' he shouted to the nearest native rider, a huge man with a broad face, 'where the hell are those scouts you sent out earlier?'

The man was about to reply when a burst of gunfire broke out on the plateau above them.

'Captain Barton must have found the *impi*,' said George. 'We'd better get back to the camp.'

'Colonel,' shouted the sergeant major in alarm, 'Up ahead!'

George looked and his blood froze. A solid wall of Zulus was racing up the plain towards them, their shields held high and their plumed headdresses nodding as they effortlessly ate up the ground. Hundreds more were debouching on to the plain from the valley beyond the plateau and coming on in their turn.

'Draw your weapons,' roared Durnford. 'We'll conduct a staggered withdrawal. One troop firing while the other takes up a position four hundred yards to the rear, and so on. Take the Edendale Contingent back first, Lieutenant Davies. Henderson's Basutos can hold here. Volley-fire at six hundred yards, if you please, Lieutenant Henderson.'

'Yes, sir,' replied a baby-faced officer with a droopy moustache. 'Troop dismount.'

George followed the troopers' lead, sliding off Emperor and handing his reins to one of the men in charge of the ponies. Drawing his Martini-Henry carbine from the bucket in front of his saddle, he joined the firing line. His heart was going like a steam-hammer as he fell on one knee, loaded the carbine with a cartridge from his pouch and adjusted the sight.

'On my command,' shouted Durnford, pistol in hand.

George raised the carbine to his shoulder. The Zulus were barely half a mile away now, with one fleeter-footed warrior, possibly an induna, a good ten yards ahead of the main body, his headdress bobbing as he sped across the turf. George drew a bead on the leading warrior. There was something about his lean physique, the way he moved, that seemed familiar. But he pushed all thoughts to the back of his head, held his breath and waited for the order.

'Fire!'

The volley from fifty carbines was deafening. George peered through the smoke, half expecting the Zulus to have halted, or at least slowed. But they were still coming on as before, with the odd gap in their ranks as evidence of the damage the carbines had wrought. Of the leading warrior there was no sign.

'Reload and adjust your sights to three hundred yards.'

George ejected the cartridge by depressing the lever behind the trigger, but his hand was shaking so much he had trouble placing the next bullet in the breech.

'Come on, Hart,' said Durnford with a frown, 'we haven't got all day.'

George took a deep breath to calm himself and pushed the bullet home.

'Fire!'

The Zulu front rank seemed to shiver as the bullets slammed into flesh and bone, but those who fell were simply hurdled by the warriors behind, their pace never slacking.

'Mount up,' instructed Durnford. 'We'll pass through Davies's Zikalis and form a new line behind.'

George was no sooner in the saddle than he heard, from back down the plain, a hideous shrieking noise as one of Russell's rockets arced towards the plateau in a trail of white smoke and yellow sparks, exploding with a loud boom. 'Russell must have seen Zulus on the plateau above him,' said Durnford. 'We'd best make straight for the camp or they might cut us off. Follow me.'

They passed through Davies's men, shouting for them to mount up and follow, and as the plain narrowed between the conical hill and the edge of the plateau they came upon the remnants of Russell's battery. Four bodies lay beside a single iron trough, the one that must have been used to fire the rocket. There was no sign of the escort, the mules and the remaining gunners.

'Leave them,' said Durnford from his horse.

'What about the others?'

'There isn't time. We've got to get to the camp before the Zulus.'

George looked back the way they had come. The pursuing Zulus were less than half a mile away and closing fast. Up on the plateau the crack of carbine and rifle shots was growing louder and more persistent. So much for Zulu caution, thought George, as he pursued Durnford and his men along the plain.

As they approached the Nyokana Donga – a dry watercourse with steep sides that bisected the plain a mile from the camp – Durnford raised his hand to slow the column. He could see from the presence of helmets and carbines that the donga was partially occupied by a mixed force of around fifty men from various mounted regiments. They had left their horses in the cover of the donga and were manning the lip of its steep, east-facing bank. Durnford at once ordered his men to do likewise, extending the defensive line towards the heights, with Davies's Zikalis on the extreme left.

George followed Durnford as he sought out the officer in command, Captain Bradstreet of the Newcastle Mounted Rifles. 'Who placed you here, Captain?' asked Durnford.

'Colonel Pulleine, sir,' replied the officer, his walrus moustache only a shade smaller than Durnford's. 'He'd just received news from one of your officers, Captain Barton, that a huge Zulu *impi* was advancing on the camp.'

'What other defensive arrangements has he made?'

'He's sent two companies of British infantry up on to the plateau to support your troopers, and placed the remaining four companies and the guns along the front of the parade ground.'

That meant, George knew, the main defensive position was at least half a mile from the camp, and protected by just 600 British soldiers. It was a line, moreover, that had no defence against an attack from the rear, and one that was far from unbroken, with dangerous gaps between its three strongpoints: the troops on the plateau, those in front of the camp and the horsemen with George in the donga, who were themselves 500 yards to the right front of the main position.

'What about the native contingent?' asked Durnford.

'They're supporting the British infantry in both positions.'

George looked over his left shoulder and could just make out a thin line of redcoats, some kneeling, others lying down, almost certainly the men of Jake's G Company. Then there was a gap before more redcoats, some NNC and what looked, at a distance, like the two seven-pounder guns, which were firing at an unseen target on the heights.

Durnford turned to Bradstreet. 'Tell me, Captain, has Pulleine informed Chelmsford of our predicament?'

'He has, sir. He sent a message informing the general of heavy firing to our left front.'

'Nothing else? I think he could have been a bit more specific.'

'Here they come!' shouted a Carbineer to their left.

The same warriors who had pursued Durnford from iThusi were making straight for the donga. Most were carrying black shields, the sign of a young regiment.

'Fire!' ordered Durnford, and 150 carbines obeyed. Down went Zulus in heaps, but others kept coming.

George reloaded as fast as his fumbling fingers would allow, just in time to join the second volley. Again, the donga was momentarily wreathed in a thick bank of white smoke, which hid the defenders from their onrushing foe and seemed to take an age to clear. *Boom* went the carbines on Durnford's command and more warriors fell. And so it went on, until the advance of the Zulu left 'horn' slowed, faltered and then came to a stop, the warriors lying down behind bushes, folds in the ground and the corpses of their comrades. Some fired their rifles from this prone position; others rose up between volleys to gain forty or fifty yards before taking cover.

Once the attack had stalled, Durnford ordered independent fire and remounted. With his withered left arm thrust into the pocket he had had sewn on the front of his tunic, and his body exposed above the top of the donga, he rode up and down the line, encouraging his men with jokes and praise. 'Well done, my boys,' he urged, 'keep it up. It's too hot for them.'

But as the Zulu counter-fire began to find its range, with bullets pinging off the lip of the donga, the big African sergeant major became concerned for Durnford's safety and pleaded with him to keep down. 'Please, *Inkhosi*, it's too dangerous.'

'Nonsense,' replied a smiling Durnford. 'These Zulus couldn't hit a house at fifty paces.'

With the firing incessant, more and more carbines jammed, their brass shells refusing to eject. Each time Durnford calmly dismounted, held the gun between his knees and winkled out the cartridge with his knife. But there was soon a far more serious threat to the defenders' rate of fire than the odd jammed cartridge. Each man had ridden out of camp that day with seventy rounds of ammunition, but after thirty minutes of constant firing, very few had more than ten rounds left.

George brought the problem to Durnford's attention. 'Colonel, we need more ammunition.'

'Do you think I don't know that? I've already sent a messenger back but he hasn't returned.'

'He might have been killed. I'll go. Where are your supply wagons?'

'They were en route and should have reached the camp by now. If not, try and scrounge some rounds from another regiment. But hurry. We can't hold out for long.'

George untied Emperor's knee-halter, mounted and rode hard up the track for the camp, his body hunched forward to produce the smallest possible target for a stray bullet. About a third of the way there, he came upon the right edge of Jake's G Company, arrayed in two staggered lines roughly ten yards apart, with ten yards between each prone soldier, providing a rifle for every five yards of front.

'Where's Second Lieutenant Morgan?' George shouted to the nearest redcoat.

'Over to the left,' replied the soldier, barely pausing in his repetitive task of loading, aiming and firing. George found him in the centre of line, near Pope, directing the fire.

'George!' said Jake, looking up. 'What are you doing here? Is Chelmsford on his way?'

'No. He was convinced the Zulus wouldn't attack and sent me back with orders for Pulleine to send on supplies.'

'The bloody fool. So where are you headed?'

'Back to the camp to fetch ammunition for Durnford, who's holding the donga up ahead. How are you for bullets?'

'We're running through them fast. We've sent runners back but they haven't returned.'

'I'll see what I can do. I won't be long.'

George dug in his heels and Emperor cantered on down the track towards the camp. The mood was very different from when he had ridden in an hour and a half earlier: then it had been calm and unconcerned; now it was like a disturbed wasps' nest with civilians and soldiers, black and white, running in all directions, some leading mules with boxes of ammunition strapped to their back, others carrying weapons and heading for the firing line. One or two, with furtive looks over their shoulders, were edging towards the nek at the back of the camp where the track dropped away towards Rorke's Drift, unconvinced that the British had enough troops to hold the camp.

'You,' shouted George at one such young *voorloper*, 'where are you going?'

The man ignored him and hurried on.

With no sign of Durnford's supplies, George made straight for the ammunition wagon at the back of the Carbineers' tents. It was occupied by the quartermaster, a strapping fellow called London, who was busy handing out packets of bullets to a long line of waiting soldiers. George rode to the head of the queue and shouted,

'Quartermaster, I need ammunition now. Colonel Durnford's mounted troops are almost out.'

'Officer or no, Hart, you'll wait in line like everyone else.'

'You don't understand. The situation's critical.'

'It's critical everywhere. You'll wait your turn.'

George looked beyond London to the huge pile of mahogany ammunition boxes, each one containing sixty ten-round packets. One of London's assistants was going from box to box with a screwdriver, removing the two-inch brass screw that secured the box's sliding lid. 'Let me help that fellow, Quartermaster. We'll be here all day.'

'There's no point. We've only got one screwdriver.'

'Ye gods!' roared George, looking right and left for an alternative supply.

'Try the Second Twenty-Fourth next door,' suggested London. 'They've only got one company in the firing line and should have plenty of bullets to spare.'

'*You've* got plenty of bullets,' roared George in frustration.

'We're doing our best.'

George galloped along the back of the 2nd/24th's tents, sneaking a glance to the front of the camp where the firing seemed, to him at least, to be dropping in intensity. The scene that greeted him at the 2nd/24th's ammunition wagon was, if anything, even more chaotic. A crowd of men were clamouring for bullets, but the florid-faced Quartermaster Bloomfield, wearing shirtsleeves and braces, was having none of it. 'I've signed for this ammo,' he said in his Geordie accent, 'and it's only going to the

Second Battalion. All the other units have got their own supplies.'

'I'm from G Company of the Second Battalion, sir,' piped up one young drummer boy who could not have been more than sixteen.

'Give that boy some packets,' said the quartermaster to his assistant. 'The rest of you can scarper.'

'Are you insane?' barked George. 'The Zulus are about to break through and you're worrying about which units you're supplying.'

'I've got to account for every bullet, and if you think . . .'

George stopped listening. He needed bullets and nothing was going to stop him from getting them. He dismounted, tied Emperor to the front wheel of the ammunition wagon and walked round to its back flap, which he began to untie.

'What are you doing?' asked a voice.

George swung round to see Lieutenant Smith-Dorrien, the long-chinned officer who had delivered Chelmsford's message to Durnford. 'What does it look like I'm doing, Lieutenant? That fool Bloomfield will only supply his battalion, so I'm taking matters into my own hands.'

Smith-Dorrien nodded. 'Good thinking. Let me help.'

Together they untied the flap and removed the wagon's back board. Then they grabbed the nearest ammunition box by its rope handles and threw it to the ground.

'Christ, that's heavy,' said George, gazing down at the solid two-foot-long mahogany container.

'Stop complaining,' said a grinning Smith-Dorrien as he reached for the next box. 'It only weighs eighty pounds.'

When they had a dozen on the ground, they set about breaking them open, George with the butt of his carbine, Smith-Dorrien with a rock. The noise of splintering wood brought Bloomfield round from the front of the wagon. 'For heaven's sake,' he said to Smith-Dorrien, 'don't take that, man. It belongs to our battalion.'

'Hang it all,' replied Smith-Dorrien. 'You don't want a requisition slip now, do you?'

'Yes, I do. You're not entitled to those bullets.'

'Well, we're taking them anyway,' said George, 'and if you try to stop us I'll put a bullet between your eyes.'

Bloomfield was about to respond, but the look on George's face made him think twice and, muttering to himself, he retreated back round the wagon.

'Right,' said George. 'I think we've got enough bullets. Now we must get them to Durnford.'

'Where is he?'

'Holding a donga about a mile from the camp.'

'You'll need a cart. Wait here.'

Smith-Dorrien reappeared a couple of minutes later with a mule harnessed to a small cart, and together they threw the contents of six boxes – 3,600 rounds in all – into the back.

'I'll get going,' said George, as he hitched Emperor to the rear of the wagon. 'You organize some more for the infantry and let's pray we meet later. Good luck with the rest.'

'Thanks. I'll need it.'

George climbed into the box seat and whipped up. But with the mule refusing to go faster than a jog-trot, George was still moving along the back of the camp when he was overtaken by Lieutenant Melvill on a tall black charger. 'Hart! Where are you going?'

'I'm taking ammunition to Colonel Durnford in the donga.'

'Good, you'll save me the journey. Can you ask Durnford to pull back his men closer to the camp? Colonel Pulleine wants to tighten the defensive perimeter.'

'To where?'

'To a line a couple of hundred yards in front of the tents. He's already withdrawn the two companies on the plateau; they're now holding the far end of the camp.'

'I'll tell him, but it's going to be very difficult for the men in the firing line to disengage. Look what we're up against . . .' George swept his hand along the thick mass of Zulus pressing towards the camp, from the spur above the camp to the plain in front of the donga, where more and more warriors were edging to their left in an effort to outflank Durnford's position. They were making a low, musical murmuring noise, like a swarm of bees getting closer and closer. 'If the men fall back, the Zulus will charge. We need a redoubt. Why hasn't Pulleine laagered the wagons?'

'Have you any idea how long it takes to do that? There isn't time. Just deliver the order, there's a good fellow.'

George whipped up, shaking his head in disgust, and had just turned on to the wagon track when he sighted Durnford and his men galloping back from the donga, the dust rising behind them in a thick cloud. They came to a juddering halt next to George's cart. 'We couldn't hold out any longer,' explained Durnford, his dusty face streaked with little runnels of sweat. 'We're almost out of bullets and they were getting round our flank. I see you got some more.'

'Yes, but only about twenty per man.'

Durnford turned to the officers behind him. 'Lieutenant Henderson, give your men thirty rounds each and then try and locate our supply. Davies, you do the same. The volunteers and mounted police can seek out their own supplies. We'll rendezvous on the nek in five minutes. No longer. If we can't keep the horns apart the camp is doomed.'

'Sir,' said the officers, almost in unison. Bradstreet and Lieutenant Scott of the Carbineers led their men away, while Henderson and Davies transmitted the orders to their NCOs and the resupply began, each trooper riding forward in turn and being handed two packets of bullets.

George, meanwhile, had informed Durnford of Pulleine's intention to pull his troops back closer to the camp. 'Much good it will do him,' commented Durnford, pulling on his moustache. 'There are too many of them, George. They've hoodwinked us good and proper this time.'

'You should have listened to me, Colonel.' George couldn't help saying it.

'I know, and I'm sorry. I've always been a headstrong fellow. Do you think they'll blame me for this too?'

'Let's forget about blame while there are lives to save!'

'You're right. Our only hope is to collect all the troops for a last stand. Do you know where Pulleine is?'

'I imagine he's still at the column office.'

'Good. Come with me.'

George nodded, dashed to the back of the cart and untied Emperor. Seconds later he and Durnford were clattering between the tents of the 1st/24th and the mounted volunteers, dodging the camp casuals who were making their way on foot, on wagons and on mules towards the top of the camp where the wagon track crossed the nek – the broad saddle of land between the hill of Isandlwana and the Stony Koppie – before dropping steeply towards the Manzimnyama stream on the first leg of its circuitous ten-mile route to Rorke's Drift. 'Like rats leaving a sinking ship,' remarked Durnford sourly.

Just before the nek they turned right and rode along the base of the mountain until they reached the tent that served as the column office. A corporal was burning papers on a campfire, a bad sign. 'Where's Colonel Pulleine?' demanded Durnford.

The soldier looked up, a sheaf of papers in hand. 'He and Lieutenant Melvill left a few minutes ago for the First Twenty-Fourth's tents to the right of the track.'

'Why?'

Before the soldier could reply, a limping Lieutenant Coghill appeared at the entrance to the tent. 'He's gone to save the battalion's colours. We lost both to the Sikhs at Chillianwala in the Second Sikh War and Pulleine doesn't want that to happen again.'

For a brief moment, as he tried to take in the full absurdity of Coghill's explanation, Durnford was too stunned to speak. 'Is he *insane*?' he shouted, his face mottled with fury. 'The Zulus are about to overwhelm the camp and he's worried about the damn colours! If we don't shore up the right of our line, and prevent the Zulus from outflanking us, we're all dead men, every one of us.

We need to get troops over to the nek, and I mean now. I don't care who they are, as long as they can hold a gun. Do you think you can manage that, *Lieutenant*?'

'I'll try.'

'Good, and you can start with him,' said Durnford, pointing towards the corporal. 'George, come with me. We'd better get over to the nek and see what needs to be done.'

On the way they passed the hospital tent, so full of casualties that Surgeon-Major Shepherd was treating the overflow of wounded on the ground outside. Durnford drew rein to warn him that time was running out. 'Surgeon-Major! We're trying to organize a last stand on the nek. You must make your way there *now*.'

Shepherd looked up from his patient, a redcoat with a jagged abdominal wound. 'What about the wounded?'

'They'll have to stay where they are. There's no time to move them.'

'In that case, Colonel,' said Shepherd, wiping his bloody hands on his apron, 'I'm staying with them.'

'Don't be a fool, Surgeon-Major,' interjected George. 'You can still save yourself. All the noncombatants are leaving for Rorke's Drift.'

Shepherd shook his head.

'All right,' said Durnford. 'We'll keep the Zulu horns apart for as long as possible. If you change your mind . . .'

'I won't.'

Durnford nodded and dug in his spurs, George following. They found the nek choked with wagons, their panic-stricken drivers yelling at their cattle and each other, desperate to get on to the Rorke's Drift track and away.

Civilians on foot dodged round, and even over, the lumbering wagons, all heading in the same direction. 'This is hopeless,' shouted Durnford above the din as he urged his pony, Chieftain, through the traffic. 'We'd best make for the Stony Koppie beyond the saddle and rally there.'

From the rock-strewn lower slopes of the koppie, they had a panoramic view of the camp and the battlefield beyond. George could see a dense mass of Zulus pressing ever closer to the thin red and black line, not even continuous, which was defending the front of the camp. Already the Zulus had worked beyond the right of the line, Jake's G Company, which had been left exposed by Durnford's withdrawal from the donga. It was only a matter of time, thought George, before G Company itself fell back. He wondered what was going through Jake's mind. Was he frightened by the prospect of death, or just too preoccupied with loading and firing to dwell on the matter?

'Where the hell have Henderson and Davies got to?' asked Durnford, interrupting George's morbid thoughts. 'They've been gone for more than ten minutes.'

There was no sign of any black troopers on the nek. But other horsemen were forcing their way through the traffic, led by Bradstreet and Scott. Durnford waved furiously until the horsemen spotted him and made their way over. 'I hope you got some bullets,' said Durnford.

'We did, sir,' replied Scott. 'Fifty a man. Quartermaster London was killed by a stray bullet as he served us.'

'Poor bastard. Tell your men to dismount and form a line facing the plain. Pope's company can't hold on much longer, and when it breaks we need to give it covering fire.'

The two officers did as they were told, detailing a handful of troopers to hold the horses while the rest knelt in two lines on the edge of the koppie. No sooner were they in position than George noticed the sound of firing from the centre of the battlefield begin to lessen in intensity until it ceased altogether.

'Christ, Colonel,' said George to Durnford, 'they must have run out of ammunition.'

'Or received Pulleine's order to withdraw.'

The latter seemed the more likely scenario as first one company of troops, then another turned its back on the enemy and began to flee towards the camp. The Zulu regiments were quick to get over their surprise, rising from the ground and rushing towards the gaps in the line, causing the remaining companies to break before they were outflanked. George watched with horror as the lightly encumbered Zulus rapidly overhauled the lumbering British soldiers, weighed down by their rifles, heavy boots and a multitude of straps and pouches. Some turned and fought with fixed bayonets, selling their lives dearly, but most were stabbed and clubbed to death as they ran.

Cutting a swathe through the mass of running men were the two horsedrawn guns of N/7 Battery, bouncing and crashing their way over the uneven terrain as soldiers clung desperately to their limbers; two officers, Major Stuart and Lieutenant Curling, rode alongside. With no time to mount the guns, most of the gunners were following on foot, easy prey for their eager pursuers. Once in the camp, the progress of the guns was slowed by the congestion at the saddle, giving Lieutenant Coghill, who had appeared from the direction of the column office on a roan charger, the opportunity to speak to Curling. But instead of sending the guns towards the Stony Koppie, where Durnford was organizing a last stand, Coghill sent them over the saddle and himself followed soon after.

'What does he mean by sending the guns away?' roared Durnford. 'If we don't stand together we're all doomed.'

Suddenly reminded of Jake's predicament, George swung round and squinted towards the right front of the camp, where G Company had been holding the extreme right of the rapidly disintegrating defensive line. Shielding his eyes from the glare of the early afternoon sun, he could see a body of redcoats, led by their two officers, Pope and Jake, struggling up the track towards the camp, closely pursued by cheering Zulus.

'Colonel!' yelled George. 'G Company have broken. We must give them covering fire.'

Durnford took one look and concurred. 'Independent covering fire for G Company!' he bellowed. 'And mind our men.'

George squinted down the sight of his carbine. Some of the rearmost redcoats were already mixed up with Zulus. He could feel his heart hammering against his chest. Rivulets of sweat trickled down his back. He wanted to fire but could not for fear of hitting Jake. Others, less particular, were firing into the oncoming mass of red and black as quickly as they could load. It was the right decision because it caused the Zulu chase to slacken momentarily, allowing about fifty redcoats to reach the bottom of the camp just seconds ahead of their pursuers.

There, on the orders of their officers, they turned and fired a volley as the young men of the ringless Umbonambi Regiment, with their black shields and bunched white cow-tail necklaces, gained the honour of becoming the first Zulus to enter the camp.

As some redcoats fought the Umbonambi hand to hand, the rest of G Company fled up the track and made a second stand at the top of the camp, not far from Durnford's position on the Stony Koppie. George could just make out Lieutenant Pope in the centre of his men, the sun glinting off his monocle as he fired his pistol into the approaching Zulu hordes. Next to him, also firing his pistol, was Jake. He had lost his helmet and his distinctive red hair shone through the drifting gunsmoke. George felt a brief moment of elation that Jake was still alive, quickly replaced by a knot of fear that his friend's options were running out.

By now about seventy British soldiers, remnants from the companies holding the far side of the camp, had taken up a position on the lower slopes of Isandlwana, opposite the Stony Koppie, and the fire from all three strongpoints held the Zulus back long enough for most of the remaining fugitives – a chaotic crowd of men, horses, mules, sheep and oxen yoked to wagons – to cross the saddle in a cloud of dust and gunsmoke that made it difficult to distinguish friend from foe. Among the last of the horsemen to pass by George was the red-coated Lieutenant Melvill, carrying across his saddle the eight-foot wooden staff and leather case containing his battalion's Queen's Colour, a large gold-fringed Union flag with a royal cipher in its centre.

'Bring it here, Melvill!' shouted George, assuming the lieutenant's intention was to use the colour to rally the troops. But if Melvill heard George's cry, he ignored it and he carried on over the saddle, the only officer of the 24th Regiment to abandon his men. Seconds later warriors from the *impi*'s right horn swarmed on to the saddle, having passed round the back of the mountain, and drove into the exposed rear of Jake's position, slashing and stabbing as they went.

The encirclement was almost complete. George knew it, and Durnford knew it too. 'Get your horse, George,' said the colonel as he scribbled in his notebook. 'I want you to take this message to Rorke's Drift. The officer in charge is to fortify the mission and hold it at all costs.'

'The Zulus are behind us. I'll never get through.'

'You can at least try. If you stay here, you'll perish.'

George looked at the scene of horror before him. Apart from the three enclaves of resistance, the camp was in the possession of thousands of Zulus who were slashing and clubbing every living thing they encountered. He could not avert his eyes as one warrior dragged a young blond-haired drummer boy from his hiding place in the back of a wagon and slit his throat. He did not want to die like that. But he did not want to leave Jake either.

'Can I take Second Lieutenant Morgan with me, Colonel? Two will have more chance of getting through than one.'

'All right, but you must leave now.'

George took the note and tucked it into his tunic. Durnford offered his good hand and George clasped it. It was surprisingly delicate, like a girl's. 'Do you have any

334

personal messages you want me to deliver?' asked George, ducking his head as a bullet zipped overhead. 'If I get through, that is.'

'Tell Fanny I love her and always will. And tell her she was right and I was wrong. I shouldn't have fought in a war I didn't believe in. But I had to try to exorcize my demons.'

'And have you?'

'I think so. Now go.'

George ran over to Emperor, untied his knee-halter and vaulted into the saddle. 'Don't let me down now,' he whispered to the horse.

The Zulus were close now and had all but overwhelmed G Company below the nek. One officer was still standing, and it looked like Jake. As George spurred towards him, the officer shot two of his assailants in quick succession.

'Jake!' bellowed George as Emperor burst between a knot of Zulus, clipping one warrior and sending him flying.

Jake heard his friend's cry. He turned and waved, a look of hope on his face, but as he did so, his features seemed to freeze. He staggered a few paces forward, dropped his revolver and fell to the ground, a throwing spear protruding from his back.

'No!' bellowed George, just thirty yards away and closing fast.

A warrior tried to grab George's reins but he shot him with his carbine, the bullet blowing off the top of the man's skull in a red and grey spray of blood and brains. He looked back to where Jake had fallen and could only see a Zulu squatting on the ground, hacking at something with his *iklwa*. That something, he realized, was Jake. It was too late to save him.

He fired at Jake's killer and missed, but the bullet was close enough to cause the warrior to turn his head. The broad, handsome face was unmistakeable. It was his cousin Mehlokazulu. As the pair locked eyes, the Zulu seemed to nod. George had never felt such hatred towards another human being. But with more warriors closing in, the chance of avenging Jake's death had gone and, with a final cry of anguish, George turned Emperor and galloped towards the lower slopes of the Stony Koppie, hoping to cross the top of the nek before the Zulus completed their encirclement.

Some Zulus on the low part of the nek saw his intention and raced uphill to cut him off, the tough soles of their feet seemingly impervious to the thorny ground. But Emperor was quickly into his stride and, realizing the horseman would win the race, one warrior stopped to hurl a throwing assegai, which would have caught George in the shoulder if he had not twisted his body at the last moment, allowing the spear to pass harmlessly by and clatter into the rocks beyond.

Thrown momentarily off balance, George grabbed Emperor's mane to right himself, and would have done so if the panicked horse had not slipped on a rock. Horse and rider went down, George hitting the ground with a sickening thud that loosened his grip on the carbine. Nursing a badly bruised shoulder, he staggered to his feet. Emperor had also risen from the fall and was standing barely ten yards away, his flanks still quivering with shock.

'Please don't let him be injured,' muttered George, as he stumbled towards the horse.

With just a couple of yards to go, he could hear someone behind him with a footfall so soft it could only be a Zulu. He reached for his holster and was fumbling with the flap, not helped by his injured shoulder, when a voice spoke in Zulu. 'We meet again, cousin.'

George spun round to see, not ten yards off, the grinning face of Mehlokazulu. His powerful, nearly naked body was streaked with dust, sweat and gobbets of blood; not his own, but that of his victims. In his left hand he clutched his shield, in his right an *iklwa*, its blade red with Jake's blood.

'That soldier you just killed was my friend,' said George.

Mehlokazulu scowled. 'That soldier invaded my country and deserved to die, as do you for betraying your people.'

George wondered if he had time to draw his revolver before Mehlokazulu closed with him. Probably not, he decided, and the shot would just bring other Zulus. 'I may share your blood,' he said, inching back a little closer to Emperor, 'but the Zulus are not my people. Your father said as much, and he's right.'

'But why fight against us?'

'I'm a soldier. I was ordered to.'

'You lie. You seek revenge, for your grandmother, and for Nandi, and it will cost you your life.'

'Haven't you killed enough, cousin?' asked George, desperately stalling for time.

'No, and I'll go on killing until every white invader is dead.'

George glanced over Mehlokazulu's shoulder as if someone was approaching. As his cousin turned to look, he attempted to mount Emperor, but was hampered by his injury and had barely got his foot in the stirrup when the razor-sharp blade of an *iklwa* was placed against his throat.

'Prepare to die, cousin,' said Mehlokazulu.

George closed his eyes, waiting for the cold searing pain as the blade sliced through his neck. It never came because a second voice shouted, 'Stop, brother! Let him go.'

'Why?' protested Mehlokazulu.

'You have the same blood. And he's not like other white men. Remember the Lower Drift. He tried to prevent this war.'

It must be Kumbeka, thought George, the junior induna he had met while the ultimatum was being delivered. But would Mehlokazulu listen to him?

'But he failed, didn't he, and now he must die.' George could feel the blade starting to bite into his throat.

'No!' shouted Kumbeka. 'There are many white men still fighting in the camp. Let us wash our spears in their blood, and not in the blood of a good man such as this.'

Mehlokazulu seemed torn. 'If I let him go now I will live to regret it. I killed his friend in the camp and he hates me for it. I could see it in his eyes.'

'You fear his vengeance? You surprise me, brother. But if you need reassurance, I'm sure your kinsman will provide it.'

George could just make out Kumbeka to his right. 'If he lets you go, white man, will you swear never to set foot in Zululand again?'

'Yes,' came the instant reply.

'Then go!' said his cousin at last, lowering his spear. 'And don't come back.'

George scrambled on to Emperor's back, nodded his thanks to Kumbeka and urged Emperor down the hill without looking back. One day, he vowed, he would have his revenge; but first he had to survive. The world had seemed to stand still during their conversation. Now it started again in a maelstrom of dust and din.

The valley ahead was a vision from hell, its downslope littered with corpses, dead livestock and stationary wagons, their contents scattered all around. The track to Rorke's Drift was completely blocked by a dense crowd of Zulus, and most of the fugitives had veered off to the left down a rock-covered slope. George followed and at the bottom of the slope came to a deep donga in which the two guns had come to grief, held fast in dense scrub. Zulus were milling about the guns and, anxious not to attract their attention, George pressed on, following the twisting course of the donga for a mile or so until it opened into the marshy bed of a tiny tributary of the Buffalo River.

Gunshots rang out from the far bank. George peered across and could just make out, through thorn bushes and scrubby trees, a small and ever-dwindling band of redcoats, assailed on all sides by scores of Zulus. He knew he could do little to help and carried on along the stream, drawing his pistol with his uninjured left hand. The route was littered with the detritus of flight: blankets, hats, clothing of all description, guns, ammunition belts, saddles, revolvers, and even shields and assegais, which the Zulus must have discarded in their haste to kill the invaders. And everywhere lay the mutilated bodies of the fugitives: white and black, young and old.

George paused next to a trooper he had served with in the Carbineers, a twin by the name of Tarboton. He was lying on his back, his chubby face unmarked; but his tunic had been torn open and his stomach opened up from breastbone to waistband by a single assegai cut, the red of the wound contrasting starkly with the white of his skin. The ground beside him was slick with blood and guts, and black with flies.

George gagged and, with Jake also in mind, felt a murderous urge to strike back and kill the first Zulu he came across. The wait was short. Over the next rise, as the stream began to fall away to a final ridge that led down to the wooded banks of the Buffalo, he saw a warrior crouched over his victim, so engrossed in his mutilation that he did not hear the horse approaching. From fifteen yards, George drew a bead on his back and fired, the bullet entering between the Zulu's shoulders and tumbling him across his foe. George's satisfaction was brief because, seconds later, alerted by the gunshot, four more warriors came hurtling through the bush, bloody spears to the fore. '*Usuthu!*' they chanted as they spied their prey.

George fired one shot, which missed, and urged Emperor down the rocky slope, the Zulus in pursuit. Fifty yards ahead he could see a sergeant of the 24th, near to exhaustion as he stumbled and tottered down the hill. Spotting George and the Zulus behind, the sergeant implored, 'For God's sake give us a lift.'

There was no time to stop, so George offered his left hand and managed to pull the sergeant up behind him. But a throwing assegai whistled through the air and thudded into the sergeant's back, causing him to grunt with pain and tumble from the horse. George urged Emperor on, down the hill towards the ridge that overlooked the Buffalo, all the time expecting his own back to explode in pain.

At the ridge a bottleneck had been formed by a small crowd of fugitives, all anxiously glancing back up the hill as they waited their turn to descend the precipitous path that led down to the river. George recognized a number of officers, including Major Stuart of the Artillery, Lieutenants Coghill and Melvill, with the latter still clutching the colour, and Lieutenant Smith-Dorrien, who was helping to bind with a handkerchief the badly wounded arm of a mounted infantryman.

'Move!' screamed George. 'The Zulus are right behind me.'

The crowd surged forward in panic, as a couple of the cooler hands fired beyond George at the Zulus charging down the hill. There were at least fifty Zulu pursuers now, and it was obvious to George that if he joined the mêlée he was doomed. So he yanked Emperor to the right, desperately searching for an alternative route down the cliff, and was rewarded by the sight of a blue patrol jacket leading a horse through some scrub. He followed suit, dismounting at the entrance to the scrub, and was about to ask the officer if he knew where he was going when shouts and screams to his left heralded the arrival of the Zulus. The officer glanced back in alarm.

'Don't stop!' hissed George. 'They'll be here any moment.'

The officer turned and plunged down the slope, his horse slipping and sliding behind him. George followed, his shoulder screaming with pain every time Emperor dug his hooves into the loose surface of stones and slippery rock. With about a hundred yards to go to the river, and the rocky path getting steeper by the step, a warrior burst out of the undergrowth and on to the path between the two men.

'*Usuthu!*' he roared, as he ran downhill and, before the officer could react, drove his assegai into the flank of his mount, the startled horse shrieking with pain before collapsing to the ground, its legs twitching. The officer ran, but not before loosing off a single hurried shot that came closer to hitting George than the Zulu, who, by now, had turned and was heading back towards him. George fell on one knee, aimed his revolver and pulled the trigger. There was no discharge, just a metallic click. The gun was empty. George gripped its barrel, ready to use it as a club.

The Zulu came on at the run, his large rawhide shield covering his body and his spear ready to strike. Anticipating a stab on his left side, George sidestepped at the last moment to his right, driving his shoulder into the Zulu's shield and knocking him off balance. For a second the two were locked together, the Zulu trying vainly to stab George round his shield. But George managed to grab the edge of the shield and pull it to his left, exposing the side of the Zulu's head, which he struck as hard as he could with the gun butt, the loud crack more like a shot than a blow. The Zulu slumped to the ground.

George grabbed Emperor's reins and plunged on down the slope, almost losing his footing as the path stopped abruptly on the edge of a precipice. Thirty feet below, down a sheer rock face, lay the Buffalo River, swollen by recent rains into a broad, fast-moving torrent. The only way down was to jump, a desperate course of action that the officer must already have taken. As George weighed up his own chances of avoiding the jagged rocks poking above the foam, the sound of running feet made up his mind. Hauling the terrified horse behind him, he jumped, hitting the water hard, but fortunately not the rocks. The cold, racing current closed above his head, spinning him round as he fought desperately to regain the surface. He could not tell up from down, and was close to drowning when his hand touched and then gripped Emperor's tail.

George was towed through the water and deposited, coughing and heaving, and utterly exhausted, on the shingle of the Natal bank. Bullets pinging off the rocks close to his head brought him to his senses. The Zulus had reached the far bank and, unwilling to brave the rough water, were taking pot shots at those who had been lucky enough to escape. George crawled behind a large boulder and found his hiding place already occupied by the officer from the path, sodden and not a little shamefaced.

'You might have helped me with that Zulu,' said George. 'I was out of bullets.'

'Me too,' said the officer with a grimace, clutching his lower leg.

'Are you hurt?'

'I twisted my ankle as I hit the water. It's swollen like an orange.'

'Well, we can't stay here. The Zulus are probably crossing as we speak. If I help you up on to Emperor, will you promise to wait for me at the top of the hill yonder?'

The officer nodded, and George broke cover to find Emperor grazing behind a thorn bush, oblivious of the gunfire. He led him back and helped the officer into the saddle. 'What's your name, by the way?' asked George.

'James Hamer. I'm Durnford's commissariat officer.'

'Why weren't you with him earlier?'

'I went with the two mounted troops on to the plateau. We found the Zulu army sitting in a valley, in perfect order, quiet as mice and stretched across in an even line. When they saw us they charged.'

'Any survivors from the two troops?'

'I don't think so.'

'All right, you'd better be off. But top of the hill, mind,' said George, wagging his index finger, 'and no further.'

Hamer spurred up the rocky slope, dodging between cacti and thorn bushes, as George followed on foot, his waterlogged boots squeaking at every step. He had barely covered thirty yards when a voice cried out, 'Help me, please!'

He looked back and could just make out the red-coated figure of Lieutenant Melvill in the water, still clutching the Queen's Colour. He had lost his mount and was being swept towards a large rock in the centre of the river, atop which clung an officer of the Native Contingent in a blue tunic. As Melvill was swept past, he threw the colour to the officer. But in catching it the officer lost his hold on the rock and was also taken by the current.

George ran towards the bank and was joined there by Lieutenant Coghill, still mounted on his tall roan charger.

Meanwhile Melvill and the officer had been washed into a stretch of still water, though neither had the strength to reach the bank. George at once waded in to help, with Coghill following on horseback. A fusillade of shots rang out from the far bank, most striking the water but one hitting the biggest target, Coghill's horse. It staggered and fell, pinning the lame Coghill beneath it in the shallow water. George freed the spluttering officer and pulled him to safety, shouting at the others to leave the colour and save themselves. They did so and both, in turn, were helped the last few yards to the bank by George.

'Thank you, Hart,' said Melvill, his stomach heaving with exertion. 'I just wish I could've kept hold of the colour for Colonel Pulleine's sake.'

'Did he tell you to save it?'

'No, he was killed in his tent soon after the Zulus entered the camp. But it's what he would have wanted.'

George knew the loss of a colour was the biggest disgrace that could befall a British regiment. Was that the real reason Melvill took it, he wondered, or just a convenient excuse for saving his own skin? 'Never mind the colour,' he said with a dismissive wave, 'we won't escape with our lives if we don't get up that hill. Do you think you can manage that?'

Melvill nodded, as did the other officer, a Lieutenant Higginson of the Native Contingent.

'What about you, Coghill? How's your knee?'

'Not good. But if someone assists me I should be all right.'

'He's all yours, gentlemen,' George said to the two able-bodied officers. 'I would help but I've got an urgent message to deliver to Rorke's Drift. My horse should be waiting for me at the top of the hill. Good luck.'

George set off at a gentle trot, stopping every few hundred yards to catch his breath. He was tired and thirsty, and felt strangely light-headed as the sun bore down on his uncovered head. About halfway up he heard two pistol shots from lower down the slope, but the intervening scrub obscured his view. Then, shortly after reaching the summit, as he searched in vain for Hamer and Emperor, Higginson rode over the lip on a sweat-streaked horse.

'Whoa!' shouted George. 'What happened to Melvill and Coghill?'

Higginson looked uncomfortable, unwilling to meet George's eye. 'They said they couldn't go another step, and that I was to carry on without them.'

'They *told* you to leave them?' asked George disbelievingly.

'Yes.'

'What about the shots?'

'We were being followed by two Zulus. Coghill killed them.'

'And the horse?'

'I found him by chance. He must have thrown his rider.'

Higginson's nervous manner told George he was lying. 'Why didn't you offer the horse to Coghill? He can barely walk.'

'I was going to, but as I got near I could see they were surrounded by Zulus. They're both dead.'

'Are you certain?'

'Yes. Now, I must be going.'

'Hold up! I've got to get that message through to Rorke's Drift, and I can't do that without a horse. There's no sign of mine, so will you lend me yours? Either that or take the message yourself.'

'Sorry,' said Higginson, digging his heels into the exhausted horse's flanks. 'I've done enough for one day.'

George tried to bar his way, but was booted roughly aside. 'You'll pay for this,' he shouted after the departing horse.

George sat on the ground, head in hands. He knew that Rorke's Drift was upriver, and that to reach it he needed to keep the Buffalo valley on his right. He knew he must make the attempt, not least because Jake's old B Company was defending the drift and, for all he knew, they were about to be attacked by the whole Zulu army, fresh from its victory at Isandlwana. Having failed to avenge Jake's death, he could at least try to save his men, Thomas included.

Yet many doubts gnawed at his resolve. What were the chances of him reaching Rorke's Drift on foot, unarmed and with a damaged shoulder? And even if he did make it, would he arrive in time to make a difference? Was there any point in throwing his life away unnecessarily? He felt certain someone else would pass on news of the defeat. He had done his bit. His duty now – to his mother, to Fanny, to Lucy – was to survive. At least, that was what he started to tell himself. But the more he tried to justify not going to Rorke's Drift, the guiltier he felt.

At last he made up his mind. He would go because it was the right thing to do, and hang the consequences. He got awkwardly to his feet and was about to set off when, from the direction of Helpmekaar, the sound of hoof beats heralded an approaching rider. Had Hamer had second thoughts? A riderless Emperor provided the answer as he cantered round a bend in the track, his ears pricked and his saddle askew.

George was delighted. 'Whoa!' he shouted, hands raised. 'Easy, boy.' He caught Emperor's reins and took a moment to calm him. 'So you threw Hamer, did you?' he said to the horse, as he adjusted his saddle. 'Well done. I hope the selfish bastard broke his neck.'

George looked at his watch. It was 2 p.m., which gave him at least three hours of daylight to deliver Durnford's message. 'Please, God, let me be in time,' he muttered to himself, as he hauled his tired and battered frame into the saddle and pointed Emperor in the direction of Rorke's Drift.

# 18

*Near Rorke's Drift, 22 January 1879, 2.30 p.m.*

George was barely awake as he guided Emperor round the track that skirted the west side of the Oskarberg, the steep rocky hill that lay between him and the supply depot at Rorke's Drift. Up since 1.30 a.m., he had ridden more than thirty miles and fought in a desperate and shocking defeat, barely escaping with his life. He was physically and mentally exhausted, and wanted nothing more than to slide off his horse and sleep. Yet something kept him going. Not military duty as such; he had done his bit and more. Rather a determination to do the right thing by Durnford, who had given him a viable excuse to leave the battlefield, and who himself had paid the ultimate price for his rash miscalculations. But he was also fiercely determined that Jake's death would not be for nothing, and that he, a survivor from Isandlwana, would help to save the men of his friend's former company.

He half expected word of the defeat to have reached Rorke's Drift already, and that he would find the supply depot at Witt's Mission a hive of activity, but as he rounded the Oskarberg, nudging his weary horse from a walk into a half-hearted canter, he could see no sign of defensive precautions. The garrison's tents, situated to the right front of the former mission station, were still standing, and those soldiers not on picket duty were carrying on with their normal routine, cooking rations, making tea and cleaning weapons.

'Who goes there?' challenged the sentry at the entrance to the camp.

'Second Lieutenant Hart,' replied George wearily. 'Where's the officer in charge?'

'That's Major Spalding, sir, but he left for Helpmekaar a short while ago. You'd better have a word with our company commander, Lieutenant Bromhead. He's having a nap,' said the sentry, pointing to a lone tent at the rear of the camp.

George rode over and called out Bromhead's name. No response. He dismounted and, inside the tent, found Bromhead lying on his back on his campbed, fully dressed but for his tunic, and snoring gently. He had a pleasant oval face, an aquiline nose and fair curly hair, parted in the centre, with matching moustache and mutton-chop whiskers. George shook him roughly.

'What the devil!' muttered Bromhead, trying to focus. 'Who are you and what do you want?'

'I'm Second Lieutenant Hart of Chelmsford's staff. I've just come from the fight at the camp with a message from Colonel Durnford.'

'Message, you say,' said Bromhead, sitting up. 'What is it?'

George took the piece of folded paper from his tunic pocket and handed it over.

Bromhead read it aloud: ' "To the officer commanding at Rorke's Drift. The camp at Isandlwana has been attacked and taken by thousands of Zulus. You are to fortify the post and hold it at all costs."' He looked at George, open-mouthed. 'This can't be true?'

'It is.'

'My God! If the camp couldn't hold out, what chance have we got?'

'A very good chance if you act now and turn the post into a fortress. That was what they failed to do at Isandlwana. How many men have you got, Lieutenant?'

'About a hundred fit for duty, and a further thirty-five sick and wounded in the hospital. We've also got a company of NNC under a Captain Stephenson, which amounts to another hundred or so.'

'Good. The Africans can help build the barricade. Your sentry says the senior officer, Major Spalding, left a short while ago for Helpmekaar. Why?'

'To hurry up the infantry company that was due here today. We knew a battle was in the offing and Spalding feared an attack here.'

George frowned. 'If you expected an attack, why didn't you put the post into a state of defence?'

Bromhead shrugged. 'Don't ask me. Spalding left Lieutenant Chard of the Engineers in charge. He got his lieutenancy before me.'

'Where is this Lieutenant Chard?'

'Down at the drift, supervising the ponts.'

'Well, you'd better get him over here. If he's a sapper he'll know a thing or two about fortification. In the meantime, it might be an idea to strike the tents and make a start on the barricade.'

'Shouldn't we wait until Chard arrives?'

'No, every second is vital, Lieutenant Bromhead. We must act now.'

'Very well. Colour Sergeant!' he called loudly.

By the time Chard and another officer arrived from the ponts ten minutes later, the tents were lying flat on the ground and Bromhead and Stephenson's men were busy converting the two brick and stone buildings of Witt's Mission – now used as a hospital and a storehouse – into a fortress. Some soldiers were knocking small loopholes in the walls of the buildings at chest level, through which rifles could be fired, while others built a defensive perimeter from bags of mealie corn, the staple African cereal, two huge pyramids of which stood in front of the former chapel. Witt himself was nowhere to be seen, having an hour or so earlier elected to climb the Oskarberg with the surgeon and the padre to verify reports of a battle at Isandlwana.

Chard dismounted and strode up to George and Bromhead, who, assisted by a commissary officer named Dalton, were directing the construction of the redoubt from the open space between the two buildings. Chard was shorter and stouter than Bromhead, his florid West Country face partially obscured by a large walrus moustache, and, unlike Bromhead, who was now clad in his scarlet officer's tunic, he was wearing the ubiquitous blue patrol jacket.

'John, thanks for coming over so promptly,' said Bromhead. 'I know it's hard to believe, but Second Lieutenant Hart here has just brought word that the camp at Isandlwana has fallen to the Zulus. '

'I know.'

'How do you know?'

'That officer over there,' said Chard, pointing to the blue-coated figure still on his horse, 'is Lieutenant Adendorff of the Natal Contingent. He's just come from the camp. He says that scarcely anyone escaped, that Lord Chelmsford and the rest of the column have probably shared the same fate, and that part of the Zulu *impi* is on its way here as we speak.'

Bromhead turned to George. 'Is that true, Hart, the bit about Chelmsford, I mean?'

'I doubt it. He was a good ten miles away when the battle was taking place, though the loss of the camp means he's marooned in hostile territory without supplies and will have to fight his way through to safety, which is why it's imperative we hold this position.'

'Will the Zulus attack us, do you think, Hart?' asked Chard.

'They chased us as far as the Buffalo downstream. They're bound to come here next.'

Chard rubbed his forehead. 'We haven't a hope of holding out here with so few men.'

'My thoughts exactly,' said Bromhead.

'And we need to consider the welfare of the men in hospital. They can't defend themselves: they'll be sitting ducks. I propose we evacuate the post to Helpmekaar and make our stand there. What do you think, Gonny?'

'I agree.'

'Hart?'

'I'm sorry, sir, I can't agree. If we abandon this post we'll be sealing Chelmsford's fate, because he'll never get out of Zululand with Rorke's Drift in enemy hands.'

'*If* he's still alive,' said Chard, 'which Adendorff doesn't think is likely.'

'Either way, I don't think we should leave until we know for sure. I'm certain we can hold out here. We would have held the camp at Isandlwana if we'd been concentrated within a fortified position. And even in the open, while our ammunition lasted, we were able to hold the Zulus at bay and must have inflicted fearful casualties. We can do the same here if we don't run out of bullets.'

'I admire your optimism, Hart,' said Chard, 'but the realist in me says we can't possibly hold this post if thousands of Zulus attack; far better to live to fight another day.'

'If you leave, Lieutenant,' said George, stony-faced, 'you'll be disobeying a direct order.'

'What order?'

Bromhead handed Chard the note from Durnford. 'It says we're to hold on at all costs.'

Chard read the note. 'So it does,' he said, crumpling the note in his hands and tossing it away. 'But Durnford is no longer with us, is he? My responsibility is to the men under my command, and I won't throw their lives away on the off chance that Lord Chelmsford and the rest of the column are still alive. I've made my decision and it's final. We'll load up the invalids in the two wagons and withdraw at once to Helpmekaar. Bromhead, give the necessary orders.'

Bromhead saluted and went to speak to his senior NCO, Colour Sergeant Bourne. Within minutes all work on the half-finished defences had ceased and the two wagons were being harnessed with their teams of oxen.

George suspected that Chard was genuinely thinking more of his men than himself, and tried hard to get him to change his mind. But nothing he said made any difference, not even his dire warning that Chelmsford, if he survived, would never forgive him for abandoning his post. He was still arguing with Chard when the short, bearded figure of Assistant Commissary Dalton stepped forward.

'Begging your pardon, sir,' he addressed Chard, 'but Second Lieutenant Hart is right to say we should stay put. Zulus can move much faster than wagons, and if we leave, we'll all be overtaken and killed.'

Chard turned to Bromhead, a worried frown creasing his brow. 'Is he right, do you think, Gonny?'

'The Zulus are known for rapid marching. It's said they can cover sixty miles in a single day with barely a halt.'

'Well, I wouldn't know,' said Chard, 'having only been in this godforsaken country a couple of weeks, but I'll take your word for it. This puts a slightly different complexion on the matter, I must say.'

'So you'll stay?' asked George.

'Yes. I think that would be for the best. My priority is to protect the invalids.'

'Of course,' said George, aware that the inexperienced Chard would need as much encouragement as possible, not to mention practical assistance, if the post was to hold out. 'Might I make a further suggestion?'

'Please do.'

'Now we no longer need the two wagons for transport, would it not be sensible to incorporate them into the unfinished south wall, facing the mountain?'

'Good idea,' said Chard, nodding. 'And the mealie-bag

walls will need to be at least four feet high to do any good, so we'd better get on with it. All hands to the pump, gentlemen.'

In a race against time, the 200 able-bodied men at the post, white and black, strained every muscle to complete the defences. With a burning African sun overhead, most had removed their tunics and were sweating freely as they struggled in pairs to carry the heavy 200-pound bags of corn from the pyramids in front of the storehouse to the unfinished sections of wall. As they did so, many cast anxious glances towards the river.

Slowly but surely the mini-fortress took shape. The front wall extended from the veranda of the storehouse, the former chapel, to a solid stone kraal, a little to its right front, and from there followed the line of the natural rock ledge that ran along the front of the post, eventually linking up with the left front of Witt's farmhouse, now the hospital, where George had discussed Chief Sihayo and the Zulus with the reverend all those months ago.

The back wall continued from the right rear of the hospital to the front left of the storehouse, leaving the rear part of each building open to attack. As such, the doors and windows of these vulnerable sections were barricaded with mealie bags. In total, the defensive perimeter extended for almost 800 feet, and contained an area of roughly an acre.

To defend the perimeter Chard had roughly one man every four feet, though half of them were untrained and poorly armed blacks of the Native Contingent. A small additional source of defenders was the steady trickle of pale and breathless fugitives from Isandlwana who rode past the post. Every time one appeared, work on the defences was disrupted as men clustered round the fugitive to hear the news. Each was asked if he would stay and fight, but apart from George and Lieutenant Adendorff, none would agree to do so. A trooper of the Natal Mounted Police stopped briefly to speak to a colleague who was being treated in the hospital for rheumatism. 'Is it true the camp's been taken and everyone killed?' asked the patient.

'Yes, it's true,' replied the glassy-eyed trooper, still on horseback. 'And if you stay here, you'll die too.'

Soon afterwards, however, George was helping a straight-talking Geordie corporal called Allen to carry a mealie bag to the back wall, when the baby-faced Lieutenant Henderson and eighty of Durnford's native horse swept down the track. George hastened over to welcome him.

'Hart!' said Henderson, as if he had seen a ghost. 'You got out, then?'

'Yes. What happened to you?'

Henderson looked uncomfortable. 'We found our wagons below the nek, but by the time we'd replenished our ammunition, the Zulus had got between us and the camp. The men refused to run the gauntlet, so Davies and I rode back into the camp alone. Unfortunately we couldn't find Durnford and were lucky to escape. Davies followed the majority of the fugitives to the right; I carried on along the track and met up with the rest of the men. We waited for a time on a neighbouring rise to provide covering fire for anyone else who came that way, but no one did, and after we'd watched the Zulus dragging two captured artillery

357

pieces into the camp, we came here. Did Colonel Durnford get away, do you know?'

George shook his head.

'You're sure?'

'Well, I didn't see his dead body, if that's what you mean. But when I left him he was with about thirty Carbineers and police on the Stony Koppie and the Zulus were all around.'

Henderson hung his head for a moment, then turned to his sergeant major and announced that their chief was probably dead. As the news passed down the ranks, a wail of grief rose from the column of black horsemen, their nervous hand movements and hollow stares testament to the horrors they had witnessed.

At this very moment Lieutenant Chard reappeared on horseback from the drift where he and the small guard had secured the ponts in midstream to prevent the Zulus from using them.

'Sir,' said George, 'this is Lieutenant Henderson of the Natal Native Horse. He and his men narrowly escaped the Zulu encirclement.'

'Are we glad to see you,' said Chard to Henderson. 'You'll stay and help us out?'

Henderson nodded.

'Thank you. I just need to decide how best to use you.'

'Should they not form outposts to give us warning of any Zulu attack,' suggested George, 'and to slow it down, before retiring into the fort?'

'Well, I'm no cavalryman,' said Chard, 'but that sounds a sensible tactic. Lieutenant?'

'Yes, of course,' said Henderson.

'Good. In that case would you place one detachment down at the drift, and another beyond the Oskarberg. If the Zulus do come, your men are to hold them up for as long as possible. Understood?'

'Understood,' replied Henderson, before issuing the necessary orders. As rapidly as the horsemen had arrived, they dispersed.

'What a stroke of luck,' commented Chard. But George was not so sure. He could tell from the nervous sidelong glances of the black horsemen that they had little appetite for further combat. The fact that they had refused to ride to Durnford's rescue was a bad sign, as was their over-emotional response to the news of his death. He could see them opposing the Zulus' advance for a time, but leaving their horses and throwing in their lot with the post's defenders was quite a different matter. Only time would tell.

With the construction of the two mealie-bag walls almost complete, George went over to inspect the defences in the hospital. He knew from his conversation with Witt that many of the building's nine rooms did not have interconnecting doors and could only be accessed from the outside. All these doors and windows had now been barricaded with mealie bags, effectively trapping the occupants like fish in a barrel; if the Zulus broke in there would be no escape.

George strolled along the back of the hospital and peeked through a loophole into the room on the left rear corner. 'Anybody in there?'

Up popped a redcoat with a long, thin nose and a bushy moustache. 'Who's asking?'

'Second Lieutenant Hart. And you are?'

'Private Henry Hook, sir, the hospital cook.'

'Is that so? Well, how do you feel about fighting rather than cooking?'

'I don't mind, sir. It'll make a change.'

George marvelled again at the stoicism of the average British private. No wonder they made the best soldiers in the world. 'Who have you got in there with you, Hook?'

'Private Thomas, sir, and a Kaffir with a broken leg.'

'Owen Thomas?' said George, suddenly remembering the articulate young private who got himself flogged for stealing alcohol on the voyage.

'Yes, sir.'

'Can I speak to him?'

Hook's craggy face disappeared from the hole in the wall and was replaced, a few seconds later, by Thomas's familiar features. 'Well, I'll be,' he said, recognizing George. 'It's Mr Hart, isn't it, from the ship?'

'It is indeed, though I'm now Second Lieutenant Hart. It's good to see you looking so well.'

'Thank you, sir. The African climate seems to agree with me. Not that our fellows in G Company would agree. Is it true they're all dead?'

'I'm afraid it is, Thomas. I was there and witnessed their last stand. But they sold their lives dearly, I can assure you of that.'

'Including your friend Lieutenant Morgan?'

'Yes, including him.'

'I'm sorry, sir.'

George could feel his eyes pricking with tears. 'So am I, Thomas. But we've got our own problems to think about.

I bet you didn't bargain for this fix when you signed up to see the world.'

'No, not exactly, sir. But it's what we're paid to do.'

'Quite right. Tell me, is the African in there with you one of ours?'

'No, he's a prisoner. He was taken at Sihayo's kraal.'

'Well, keep a close eye on him. He might try to help his people if the Zulus attack.'

'I don't think he's in any condition to do that, sir. But I'll keep an eye on him, never fear.'

'Good luck, then.'

On returning to the front of the redoubt, where a small gap had been left in the wall, George spied three men approaching on foot from the direction of the Oskarberg. One of them was Witt. 'We meet again, Reverend Witt,' said George, as the exhausted trio came up the path.

'Mr Hart,' said Witt, breathing heavily, 'and in uniform too. So I was right: you *were* on military business when you visited in August.'

'Not exactly . . .'

'Well, you shouldn't have come back. The Zulus are coming.'

'How many?' asked George.

'A huge column is approaching as we speak,' blurted out one of the others, an eccentric-looking fellow with a long red beard, and wearing a frayed alpaca frock coat that was turning green with age. 'We thought they were Natal Contingent at first, fugitives from the battle. But as they got closer we realized our mistake. They'll be here in minutes. We must leave while we've still got the chance.'

'Too late for that, Padre Smith,' said Chard, appearing

through the gap in the wall. 'In any case, our orders are to defend the post.'

George smiled at Chard's change of tune. He was not a bad sort; just inexperienced and in need of a little moral encouragement.

'You stay if you want, Chard,' interjected Witt, 'but none of you will leave here alive.'

'But it's your home, Reverend Witt. Are you not staying to defend it?' asked Chard.

'No. My priority is to my wife and children at Umsinga, and from the look of the damage your soldiers are doing to my home,' he added, gesturing towards the loopholes in the side of the hospital, 'there won't be much left to come back to.'

Chard was about to reply when a gunshot sounded from beyond the hill to the rear of the post, followed by another, and finally a fusillade.

'Zulus,' said Smith nervously. 'We'd better go inside.'

Chard led the way, telling the soldiers on either side of the entrance to wait until the horsemen had returned before they closed it up. George was about to follow when he spotted the black hood of Witt's buggy disappearing up the track to Helpmekaar. He paused to watch its progress, wondering if he would have done the same thing in Witt's position if Fanny and their children were waiting for him, and only tore his eyes away when he heard horses approaching from the back of the hospital. Henderson's men rode into view, but instead of taking the fork to the post, they carried on up the hill after Witt.

Some of the defenders manning the front wall realized what was happening and gave off a howl of disapproval, catcalling and shouting. But only a single rider detached himself from the mass. It was Lieutenant Henderson, and by the time he had reached the front of the post, George and Chard had been joined there by Bromhead.

'Where the devil are your men going?' shouted Chard, his calm resolve shattered.

'I'm sorry,' said Henderson, 'but they won't obey orders. They saw the Zulus coming and bolted for Help-mekaar. I'll do my best to rally some, but I can't promise anything.'

'You're leaving too?'

'I must follow my men.'

'At least tell us how many Zulus we're up against and how long we've got.'

'Several thousand, and they'll be here in under ten minutes.'

'Christ,' said Chard, the blood draining from his face.

As Henderson cantered off after his men, the three officers re-entered the fort to be met by a sea of anxious looks. 'Why are they leaving, sir?' asked Colour Sergeant Bourne, a short young man who looked scarcely old enough for his rank.

'Because they're bloody cowards,' responded Chard. 'But no matter. We can hold out just as well without them.'

No sooner had Chard spoken than a commotion broke out near the rear wall of the redoubt where Captain Stephenson's hundred black warriors were gathered in little clumps, chatting nervously and gesticulating in the direction of the retreating troopers. Suddenly one warrior, evidently the chief, vaulted on to the wall and urged the others to follow, which they did without hesitating.

George and the other officers ran over, but by the time they reached the wall most of Stephenson's men had melted into the surrounding countryside.

'Why didn't you stop them?' Chard demanded of their startled captain, a rotund, red-faced colonial who did not look cut out for war.

'It all happened so quickly. But let me go after them. I'm sure I can persuade a few to return.' And with a nimbleness that belied his rotund physique, the captain scaled the wall and made off after his men, closely followed by his two white NCOs.

'Wait!' shouted Chard, but the trio kept running.

'Shall I fire a warning shot?' asked George.

But before Chard could answer, a shot rang out from further down the wall, hitting one of the corporals in the back and sending him sprawling to the ground.

Bromhead ran over to discover the culprit. 'Who fired that shot? I gave no permission to fire.'

The soldiers defending that part of the wall looked sullenly defiant, but said nothing.

'I'm not going to ask you again. Who fired that shot?'

'I did,' said a bearded sergeant. 'The cowardly bastard deserved to die.'

'That's as may be, Sergeant,' responded Bromhead. 'But it wasn't your decision to make. I'll deal with you later.'

George was more worried about Chard and the effect this latest desertion had had on his fragile confidence. 'Sir,' he said, 'we've got about ten minutes before the Zulus get here. Don't you think we should use that time to reduce the size of the perimeter? We'll never be able to defend the existing area with the men we've got left.'

Chard was staring out over the wall, in the direction Stephenson's men had gone, and seemed not to hear. Then he replied, 'There's no time.'

'What about an inner redoubt?' persisted George. 'We could use the heavy wooden biscuit boxes to build an inner wall from the edge of the storehouse to the mealie-bag wall to its front. That way we'll have a smaller area we can withdraw into if we can't hold the original perimeter.'

'Yes,' said Chard enthusiastically, as if suddenly rejuvenated by George's suggestion. 'Good idea. Half the garrison can get on with that, while the other half man the walls.'

'And the patients?'

'What about the patients?'

'We can't leave them in the hospital or they'll be cut off when we move behind the biscuit boxes.'

'I'm sorry, Hart, but that's a risk we'll have to take. There's no time to move them now. We've got enough on our hands building this new wall.'

Events proved Chard right, because it was still just two boxes high, and far from complete, when a lookout on the thatched roof of the storehouse reported the approach of a huge Zulu column from behind the Oskarberg.

Bromhead put down the box he was carrying. 'How many are there?' he shouted to the lookout, an anxious quaver in his voice.

'Four to six thousand, sir,' came the reply.

'Is that all?' muttered a wag close to George. 'We can manage that lot very well for a few seconds.'

'Stand to,' bellowed Chard, drawing his revolver and

making for the rear wall closest to the Oskarberg. 'Volley-fire at five hundred yards. Wait for the order to fire.'

George grabbed his carbine and took his place on the south wall between a private and the sergeant who had shot the fleeing white NCO. He could feel his heart racing as he waited, not for the first time that day, for the Zulus to come within range. He had been lucky so far, very lucky, he told himself; but would his luck hold?

He was about to find out. From round the west side of the Oskarberg trotted the Zulu vanguard, a dense mass of warriors from the veteran Utulwana Regiment with white shields and otter-skin headbands, and bristling with spears and knobkerries. At a signal from a mounted induna, they made straight for the centre of the south wall, between the hospital and the storeroom, where George was standing with his carbine propped on a mealie bag.

'Here they come!' shouted the sergeant in a thick Irish accent. 'As thick as grass and as black as thunder!'

George drew a bead on the lead warrior, a magnificent-looking six-footer whose long stride was eating up the ground, and held his breath.

'Fire!' commanded Chard.

The south wall erupted in a wreath of flame and smoke, bringing down Zulus in heaps. George's bullet passed through the lead warrior's soft rawhide shield and thudded into the left side of his chest, lifting him in the air and depositing him on his back, his outstretched right arm still clutching his *iklwa*.

'Reload and adjust to two hundred. Steady. Steady. Fire!'

More gaps were torn in the Zulu line, but on they came now in small rushes, using the cover provided by the trees, banks and brick cookhouses at the back of the post to approach within fifty yards of the mealie-bag wall. Chard had ordered independent firing by now, and George scanned the undergrowth, looking for a target. Suddenly a warrior leapt up from the grass barely twenty yards away and loosed his throwing spear. George saw it late, but swayed just in time, the spear passing harmlessly over his shoulder and thudding into the red earth behind. He snapped off a shot in retaliation and saw the warrior fall.

By now the assault on the south wall had stalled, caught in the crossfire from the two buildings, but a burst of firing from the end of the hospital suggested a switch in the focus of attack.

'Every second man to the north wall. Go!' shouted Chard.

George joined the sprint across the compound and made it to the wall in front of the hospital at the same time as the Zulu attackers. A fierce hand-to-hand fight developed, with the defenders shooting and bayoneting every Zulu who tried to cross the wall. With no time to reload his carbine, George drew his revolver and was blazing away when the man next to him, a tall, fair-haired young soldier, had his rifle pulled from his grasp by a huge warrior. Defenceless, the private was seconds from being speared when George shot his assailant in the face, the bullet leaving a tiny entry hole but carrying away the back of the warrior's head in a shower of blood and skull fragments.

More Zulus joined the struggle, and their weight forced the defenders back towards the hospital veranda, enabling a handful of warriors to leap over the wall. George could see to his left a Zulu trying to wrestle the rifle off a white-faced corporal of the Army Hospital Corps. But the corporal refused to panic and, clinging to his weapon with one hand, managed to grab a bullet from his pouch, reload his weapon and fire. The Zulu shuddered and fell, only releasing his grip as he lay twitching on the floor.

Supporting fire from the hospital now drove the Zulus from the space in front of the veranda, enabling the defenders to return to their post at the wall. A couple of soldiers went round the Zulu casualties, ruthlessly dispatching those who displayed any signs of life with shots and bayonet thrusts.

'Is that necessary?' George asked one.

''Fraid so,' intervened Bromhead, who, like George, had shot a number of warriors with his revolver. 'Better to be safe than sorry.'

In his heart, George realized now that both sides would fight to the death, the defenders because they had to.

He flinched as a bullet smacked into the mealie bag he was leaning on. More shots struck the ground behind him. He turned round and could see little puffs of white smoke coming from the ledge of rocks and caves that ran along the centre of Oskarberg Hill to their rear. Having failed with their initial assault, the Zulus had surrounded the post and were firing from behind every scrap of cover, including the five-foot wall in front of the hospital and the rough stone kraal to the right of the storehouse. With the advantage of height, the Zulu gunmen on the Oskarberg had a clear field of fire into the unprotected backs of those, like George, who were manning the north perimeter. Yet, thankfully, most were poor marksmen, with a tendency to fire high, and proved as dangerous to their own side as to the British.

For much of the remaining hour of daylight, the Zulus launched a series of piecemeal attacks against the hospital and the north wall from the orchard and some brush to its front. After each attack the Zulus would melt back into the thick undergrowth while their comrades provided covering fire. Then, after a brief pause, they would rise as one and rush the wall, the bolder spirits trying to grab the eighteen-inch lunger bayonets that barred their passage. But a burst of gunfire and a flurry of bayonet thrusts were enough to clear the wall and send the warriors scuttling for cover.

With darkness falling, George was crouched behind the wall, checking his pockets for more ammunition, when he noticed a slight figure crawling along to his right. As the figure got nearer, he could see it was Padre Smith, dragging beside him a helmet full of rifle bullets, handfuls of which he was doling out to each defender.

'Don't suppose you've got any for this?' George asked, waving his revolver.

'Sadly no,' replied a grim-faced Smith, seemingly recovered from his earlier loss of nerve. 'You could ask Bromhead. But before you do, could I ask you to caution the men about their swearing? I've never heard the like.'

George chuckled. It was not unusual for soldiers, in the heat of battle, to let off steam by swearing. 'Let them be, Padre,' he replied. 'If it makes them fight harder, then so much the better.'

A hand tapped George on the shoulder. It was Bromhead. 'Good work, Hart. I saw you save Private Hitch's life earlier. He's one of my best young soldiers, and I wouldn't want to lose him.'

'It was a lucky shot,' said George, grinning. 'Talking of which, I don't suppose you have any spare revolver bullets?'

Bromhead frowned. 'I'm running out myself. I can give you half a dozen.'

'Six rounds!'

'Take them or leave them.'

'I'll take them.'

Bromhead handed over the bullets and left. As George loaded his revolver, mindful that each bullet would have to count, a voice shouted, 'Here they come again!'

'Stand to! Stand to!' roared Chard from the direction of the storehouse. 'They're attacking from both sides.'

George peeked over the wall and saw to his dismay a solid line of warriors bearing down on the north wall; a quick look over his shoulder confirmed that the south wall was also under attack.

'Oh Christ!' muttered a Welsh private close by. 'We're for it now.'

'Fire!' shouted Chard, and more than a hundred Martini-Henrys complied, bringing down scores of Zulus. But there were many more to take their place, and barely had a second volley been fired before the front rank of warriors had reached the walls on both sides, stabbing, clubbing and hacking at the defenders. George ducked to avoid a flying knobkerrie, and as he rose to his feet a head-ringed warrior clambered on to the wall, stabbing spear in hand. Before he could bring his pistol to bear, the Zulu was springing through the air towards him. George avoided the spear, but not the man, and the pair went down in a sprawling tangle of limbs. The Zulu lifted his assegai for the killing blow, but as his arm came down, George caught it by the wrist and held the fearsome blade inches from his chest. Grunting with exertion, the Zulu was using both hands to drive the spear home; George fought fiercely to prevent him, but fraction by fraction the tip was getting closer.

In desperation, George called out in Zulu, 'Don't kill me, brother.'

For a brief moment the Zulu relaxed his pressure and looked at George quizzically. He was about to say something when his body jerked and the tip of a bayonet emerged from the centre of his chest, and was just as quickly withdrawn. He looked down at the wound in surprise and then collapsed. A large hand pulled the Zulu corpse aside and helped George to his feet. It was Corporal Allen.

There was scarcely time for thanks before George and his rescuer had resumed their places on the wall, George using a discarded rifle and bayonet to save his remaining bullets. For a time they kept the Zulus at bay, inspired by the example of Commissary Dalton, who was coolly moving up and down the barricades, fearlessly exposing himself and using his rifle to deadly effect. But as more Zulus joined the assault, it became obvious to George that they could not hold out indefinitely, and that the time to withdraw to the inner redoubt was almost upon them.

Crouching low, he ran across the open ground to where Chard was directing the defence from an eight-yard gap in the centre of the biscuit-box wall. 'Sir,' said George, ducking as a bullet passed close, 'I think it's time.'

Chard nodded. 'Yes, I think you're right. Private,' he said to the nearest soldier, 'tell Lieutenant Bromhead and everyone in the vicinity of the hospital to fall back on the second line. Quick now.'

'Sir,' saluted the private, before setting off at the run.

Chard turned to George. 'That should reduce the area we need to defend by at least two-thirds.'

'Yes, but what about those *in* the hospital?'

'As I said before, they'll have to take their chances. We'll give them what covering fire we can.'

By now the word had spread and the withdrawal to the gap in the biscuit-box wall had become a stampede, with Bromhead, in true officer fashion, bringing up the rear. 'Not a moment too soon, John,' he said, gasping for breath. 'I don't think we could have held them for much longer.'

George scanned the dark compound they had just vacated, expecting at any moment to see warriors pour over its now undefended perimeter. But, as yet, the Zulus seemed unaware of the withdrawal and only the occasional shot from the hospital gave an indication of their continuing presence outside. Then, through the gloom, George saw a small flame flickering on the edge of the hospital roof. 'My God,' he shouted, 'they've set fire to the thatch. We must *do* something.'

'What can we do?' said Chard, helplessly.

George looked across at the hospital. On the left side of its end wall he could just make out a single high window. It was the only possible escape route, but would the defenders use it? And what about those unfortunates like Hook and Thomas in sealed rooms on the far side of the hospital? How would they get out unless someone showed them the way? Someone had to take the initiative or all the hospital's occupants would die. He thought of Jake and how he had been powerless to save him. Well, he was not powerless now and, suicide mission or no, he would never forgive himself for not trying.

He pointed up at the window. 'That's the only way out. If I can get through it I can guide them out.'

'Don't be a fool, man,' scoffed Chard. 'You'll never get them across the open ground.'

George knew that Chard was right, that his chances of success were slim. He thought of the heartbreak he would cause his mother if he didn't make it; of his passion for Fanny and respect for Lucy; of the father he had never known – the man who, indirectly, had brought him to this; and of the things he had not yet achieved. Was he prepared to throw away even the slim chance he now had of surviving for them? he asked himself. And he realized that the answer was yes. 'I'll stand a better chance if someone volunteers to help me. Any takers?'

George looked eagerly at the soldiers clustered behind the biscuit boxes. Most avoided eye contact, including Chard and Bromhead, but one man stepped forward.

'I'll help, sir,' said Private Hitch. 'I owe you that.'

'And you can count me in,' said Corporal Allen in his gruff Geordie accent. 'Hook's a mate.'

'Good. Once I'm in, you'd best return here and wait until the patients are ready to come out. All right?'

'Sir,' they said in unison.

'And I'd appreciate it if you'd provide covering fire, Lieutenant Chard.'

'Of course.'

'Right, let's go.'

With George in the lead, they sprinted across the open ground to the hospital, the light from the burning thatch casting long shadows as they ran. One or two shots were fired at them, but the majority of the Zulus who had made it to the far side of the mealie-bag walls were keeping their heads down as they waited for the next assault. 'Help me up!' said George.

Hitch linked his hands and hoisted George up to the window while Allen covered them with his rifle. George looked inside and could see six patients lying on makeshift beds raised a few inches off the hard dirt floor by bricks. Two soldiers were firing through loopholes in the back wall. He tried the window but it was secured from the inside, so he used the butt of his revolver to smash the pane. One of the startled soldiers pointed his rifle.

'Don't shoot!' urged George. 'It's Second Lieutenant Hart. You've got to get out. The roof's on fire.'

'Some of the patients are too badly wounded to move, sir,' said the soldier, a tall young Welshman with a bushy moustache.

'They must try. If they stay, they'll die.' George climbed through the window and dropped to the floor. The room was long and thin with no interconnecting doors. George counted four injured men sitting huddled in the far corner. 'What's through that wall at the end?'

The other soldier, much older than the first, replied, 'Another sealed room.'

'Any patients?'

'No, but I think there are some in the room next to that. I don't know how many.'

'What are your names?'

'We're both Private Jones, sir,' said the older soldier. 'I'm Bill; he's Bob.'

'Right, Bill, you keep a lookout for Zulus, and Bob and I will try and break through to the room next door. Once we've got everyone gathered in here, we'll start passing the wounded through the window. No point in alerting the Zulus until we're all ready to go. Any tools about?'

'There's a pickaxe, sir,' said Bob.

'Good. Pass it here.'

George set to work with the pickaxe, while Bob assisted with his bayonet; it only took a few minutes to knock a hole through the plaster and thin course of mud bricks. George poked his head through. 'Anyone there?'

There was no reply. George wriggled through, and as he did so he could hear banging from the opposite wall. Someone was trying to break through. 'Who's there?' shouted George.

'Private Williams,' said yet another Welsh voice. 'With Hook and Thomas and eleven patients. The smoke is getting worse. For God's sake help us!'

'Hold on.' George retrieved the pickaxe and began widening the small gap that Williams had made from the far side. Above he could hear the hiss and crackle of flames as they inched along the rain-dampened thatch; black smoke was beginning to seep through the ceiling. He knew it would not be long before the roof collapsed.

As soon as the hole was big enough, George peeked through. The room was filling with smoke, and at the far end he could just make out Hook and Thomas standing in front of a narrow doorway, a small pile of Zulu corpses at their feet, men they had shot and bayoneted as, one by one, they tried to break in. A spear came whizzing past Hook's head and clattered into the wall above George's head.

'Hurry!' shouted Hook. 'We can't hold them for much longer.'

Williams started manhandling the patients through the hole, with George assisting. Some were walking wounded; others were just sick and were able to get through on their own. After the tenth patient came Williams himself.

'Is that it?' asked George.

'There's one more, a Private Connolly, with a bad knee. He's refusing to move.'

George shouted through the hole, 'Leave him! Save yourself.'

Thomas came first, grinning at George as he pulled himself out of the hole. But when it came to Hook's turn he ignored George's advice and grabbed hold of Connolly's collar to drag him through as well. Roaring with the pain from his injured knee, Connolly was bundled through the hole, swiftly followed by Hook himself. Zulu shouts filled the room they had vacated.

'Well done, Hook,' said George. 'Now I need you and Thomas to guard this hole while we get the patients through to the next room. What happened to the wounded Zulu, by the way?'

'They killed him too.'

'Is there anyone else left alive?'

'I don't think so.'

'All right. Williams, start passing them through.'

Every so often a Zulu would try and squeeze through the hole that Hook and the others had used. But each time one emerged, Hook or Thomas would skewer him in the back, forcing the Zulus following behind to drag the corpse out of the way before trying again. Five had been killed by the time George called for Hook and Thomas to follow him through the hole into the end room, where Williams, the two Joneses and fifteen patients were waiting. With everyone assembled, and the two Joneses now guarding the hole with their bayonets, George climbed up to the window and signalled for Hitch and Allen to recross the space and help with the wounded.

The roof was burning fiercely now, and the flames had lit up the forty yards of no-man's land that separated the hospital from the new defensive perimeter. But neither man hesitated, and both made it across safely, covered by fire from the storehouse and the line of biscuit boxes.

One by one the patients were helped by George through the window and into the waiting arms below; those who could walk were left to run the gauntlet alone. One of the last was the rheumatic trooper of the Natal Mounted Police. Moving at a painfully slow pace, the trooper had covered barely half the distance to the biscuit boxes when a figure moved out of the shadows to his right. Allen shouted a warning but it was too late. The warrior knocked him to the ground and stabbed him repeatedly before he, in turn, was killed by a bullet from Allen's rifle.

By now the room was rapidly filling with black, acrid smoke. With a rag across his mouth, and barely able to see, George asked if there were any more patients left inside. 'Only Sergeant Maxfield,' replied Thomas. 'But he's delirious with the fever and won't move.'

'Where is he?'

'Over there,' said Thomas, pointing to the far end of the room where the two Joneses, coughing and spluttering, were still guarding the hole.

'I'll get him. The rest of you, leave now!'

As Thomas and the remaining four redcoats scrambled, one after the other, through the window, George crawled on his hands and knees through the gloom, revolver in one hand and feeling with the other for a prone body. 'Sergeant Maxfield, can you hear me?'

No reply.

'Sergeant Maxfield?'

George could feel a hand. It was still warm. He tugged it but there was no response. Putting his hand on the man's chest, he felt the warm, unmistakeable stickiness of blood and hastily snatched his hand away. The sergeant was dead, which could only mean one thing.

A sound to his left caused George to swing round, but not quickly enough, because the next sensation he felt was a searing pain in his left upper arm, as if his bicep was on fire. He fired wildly, missing his assailant, but the flash from the muzzle provided enough light for him to see a warrior, crouched low, ready to strike again with his *iklwa*. George fired again as the spear arced towards him, hitting the warrior in the jaw and blowing off the back of his head. The spear clattered to the floor.

The noise had attracted more Zulus. George could hear them crawling through the hole.

George's left arm had gone numb, and he knew he could never reach the high window with his damaged right shoulder. He looked desperately around the room for a place to hide, but could see nothing large enough to cover him apart from a straw-filled mattress against the far wall. He scuttled over to it, his left arm hanging limply by his side, as more Zulus crawled into the room, their cries of anger signalling the discovery of their dead comrade.

George lifted the mattress as soundlessly as he could, thanking his lucky stars the room was murky, and crept under it. There was a good chance, he thought, that the smoke would soon drive the Zulus from the room, allowing him to escape through the barricaded door.

George held his breath as footsteps approached. He had two bullets left. If they discovered him and there were more than two of them, he knew he was done for.

The side of the mattress began to lift. He was about to fire when a huge section of the roof above fell in with a whoosh of flames and sparks, crushing the Zulus. The smell of burning flesh was overpowering, as was the heat, and George knew he had to get out fast or he would share the Zulus' fate. Pushing the now flaming mattress aside, he stood and paused for a moment to get his bearings and then stumbled through the burning room towards the blocked doorway. Part of the barricade had been demolished by the falling roof, and it was a simple task for him to push over the remaining mealie bags and step outside into the cool night air, great lungfuls of which he greedily drank.

He crouched down and looked from side to side. There were no Zulus in sight, but he could hear them all around, noisily celebrating the destruction of the hospital. A volley of shots came from the far side of the post as the jubilant warriors made yet another attempt to overwhelm the reduced perimeter. To reach it George knew he would have to cross at least sixty yards of open ground, scale the original south wall and then gain entry through the gap in the biscuit boxes without being mistaken for a Zulu. To defend himself he had just two bullets. He weighed up the odds and decided that, with the battle still raging, it would be suicidal to try; far better to lie low until one of the periodic lulls in the fighting, then make his move. But where could he hide? Suddenly he remembered a small drainage ditch he had seen earlier, about thirty yards from the hospital in the direction of the Oskarberg. He began to crawl towards it.

After a few yards he bumped into a body and, fearing the worst, lay still. Fortunately it was lifeless and he crawled on. Using his last reserves of strength, he managed to locate and roll into the shallow depression, covering himself as best he could with his cloak. He lay listening to the sounds of battle, preparing himself for the terrifying journey he must make, but he was losing blood all the time and soon his head began to swim and he lost consciousness – only to be revived by the full weight of a warrior stepping on his wounded arm.

'Aaagh!' he cried in shocking pain before remembering his predicament.

'Sorry, brother!' said a voice in Zulu. 'I didn't see you. Are you badly hurt?'

The warrior was so close that George could smell his stale sweat. He knew that if he shot the Zulu the noise would bring others.

'Help me, brother,' said George, raising a filthy hand. As the Zulu bent to grasp it, George pulled him off balance down to the ground. Using the last of his strength, and with excruciating pain shooting through his arm, he grappled for the warrior's spear and, with a force he would never be able to explain, wrenched it from his grasp and plunged it into his throat. Blood gushed warm across them both as George blacked out.

# 19

*Rorke's Drift, 23 January 1879, 6.30 a.m.*

George's sleep was fitful and fevered. He dreamt he was back in the hospital, trapped in a smoke-filled room as the flames crept nearer; next he was running in the dark, pursued by an unseen foe; and finally he lay shivering in a ditch, hands clamped to his ears, as Zulus all around chanted songs of praise.

Someone was tugging at his right hand, threatening to pull his damaged shoulder out of its socket. This time he knew he did not have the strength to fight. This was the end. This was death. He thought he should open his eyes to face it.

He blinked and saw not a Zulu but a redcoat with a determined expression, doing his damnedest to relieve George of his grandfather's signet ring. It was Private Hook, one of the last men to escape from the burning hospital.

'Unhand me, you thieving rascal!' croaked George.

Hook's eyes widened. 'I'm sorry, sir,' he said, dropping George's hand like a hot coal. 'You were lying so still, like, I reckoned you were dead.'

'And so you thought to rob me?'

'A ring's no good to a dead man, sir.'

'But I'm not dead, am I?'

'No, sir. My mistake. I'm glad to see you made it out safely.'

George nodded and sat up. He was confronted with the sightless stare and sickening, metallic smell of his blood-soaked Zulu victim, lying barely two feet away. Beyond the corpse were many more, a veritable carpet of tangled limbs and torsos that stretched all the way to the post.

George had half expected to see the storehouse in ruins, the defenders all slain, but, lining the ramparts, as they had done all night, were the gallant survivors of B Company, 2nd/24th. They had done it, exulted George; the post was safe and Chelmsford's line of retreat secure.

George rose unsteadily to his feet. He felt faint from loss of blood, and it was as much as he could do to stagger a couple of steps towards the post, trying to avoid the bodies of dead Zulus as he did so.

'Looks like a nasty scratch you've got there, sir,' said Hook, noticing the blood soaking George's left sleeve. 'Let me give you a hand.' Placing George's right arm on his shoulder, he helped him towards the post. 'Keep a keen eye out, sir,' observed Hook as they walked. 'I almost had my rifle taken from me by a Zulu who was shamming. I shot him in the end, but it was a close shave.'

'Tell me about the fighting last night. What happened after the hospital was burnt?'

'It was touch and go, sir. They drove us out of the stone kraal next to the storehouse, and Lieutenant Chard ordered us to make a last redoubt to put the wounded in. I thought it was all over then; we all did. But everyone fought like tigers, especially Lieutenant Bromhead, and the Zulus eventually lost heart.'

'When was that?'

'Well, the last full-scale rush was made at around nine thirty, though they kept firing from all sides until midnight. After that, the firing gradually died down, and by daybreak had stopped completely. Most left then, except for a few still gathered on a hill to the southwest. Before they left, though, they sang songs, like they were literally singing our praises. Sent a shiver down your spine, it did, sir.'

Well, that explains the singing in my dream, thought George.

'Did Private Thomas make it?'

Hook shook his head and sighed. 'I'm sorry to say he was killed during the final attack. He was trying to save a mate. It's a crying shame after his heroics in the hospital. He was a fine young lad and deserved better. Did you know him well?'

'Well enough,' said George quietly. The news of Thomas's death had suddenly drained him of what little energy he had left, and if Hook had not been supporting him, he would have fallen.

'You all right, sir?' asked Hook, tightening his grip.

'Not really,' said George, after a pause, 'but I'm alive.'

'And so, you'll be pleased to hear, sir, is your horse.'

'Is he? That's wonderful. Where is he now?'

'In the stone kraal. We found him grazing in the vegetable garden, without a care in the world.'

George smiled ruefully. 'I wish I felt the same.'

Hook helped George through a gap in the mealie-bag wall and into the inner redoubt. It was a shambles. Cartridges, shells, spears, bayonets and discarded helmets littered the floor. Everywhere lay sleeping soldiers, their faces blackened by gunpowder and soot from the hospital. Some were sitting next to the redoubt that Hook had mentioned, a tall circular structure a good twelve feet in diameter and at least twenty high. It was empty, the wounded having been removed to the storehouse veranda, where they lay in one long row, their bodies swathed in bloody bandages. Among them George recognized Dalton, Allen and Hitch, the last of whom was being tended to by Dr Reynolds.

'One more for you, Doctor,' said Hook cheerily.

Reynolds looked round. 'Hart, you're alive!'

'So it seems.'

'Come over here, old fellow, and I'll take a look at that arm.'

Reynolds inspected the wound. There were two neat gashes on either side of the bicep, both still seeping a little blood. 'The good news is that it's just a flesh wound, though it's going to be a while before you can use the arm again. I'll get it properly dressed and then you can rest.'

As the doctor worked, George began to take in the atmosphere of stunned relief in the camp, but all he could think was that it had been the most ghastly twenty-four hours of his life. His best friend was dead, as was the young soldier he had met on the ship, not to mention countless others, British and Zulu. And why? Because a handful of greedy and ambitious men had deliberately engineered a war for their own ends, and because a weak-willed general had allowed his strategy to be manipulated by subordinates with their own selfish agenda.

George's melancholic thoughts were interrupted by Lieutenant Chard. 'Hello, Hart. So you're alive. But where on earth have you been?'

George blinked his eyes open. Chard was standing there, hands on hips, an enquiring look on his face. 'Where have I been?'

'Yes. We all thought you'd been killed in the hospital.'

'No, sir, just wounded,' said George wearily. 'I managed to get out after the roof collapsed, but then must have blacked out through loss of blood. I spent the night lying amongst the enemy dead.'

'I see. So you never had the opportunity to return to your post before you collapsed . . . ?'

'No!' said George indignantly. 'In any case I was surrounded by hundreds of Zulus who would happily have dispatched me if they had known of my presence.'

'All right, all right. I need to get some details for my report, but I can see you're tired so we'll talk about this later.'

'Lieutenant Chard!' shouted a lookout from the roof above.

Chard stepped off the veranda and looked up. 'What is it, Private?'

'There's a large column approaching the drift.'

'Is it friendly?'

'It's hard to tell.'

'Can you see any redcoats?'

'A few, sir, but most are natives.'

'Oh God,' muttered Chard. 'Please don't let them be Zulus.'

Bromhead walked over, sipping from a bottle of Indian pale ale. 'Something amiss, John?'

'I don't know. Your lookout's reported a large column of natives heading for the drift. Some are wearing redcoats, but they could have got them from Isandlwana, or even from Chelmsford's column. Better order your men to stand to.'

'Stand to!' roared Bromhead.

All around, the fatigued soldiers were rousing themselves, grabbing their rifles and taking their places on the reduced perimeter. George picked up a discarded rifle with his good hand and joined them. The men looked shattered but determined, and George knew they would fight tooth and nail if the column did prove to be hostile.

As the seconds ticked by, and no word came from the lookout, few spoke and the air was thick with tension.

'What can you see?' demanded Chard.

'I can see a flag,' called the lookout.

'What kind of a flag?' asked Bromhead.

'Does it matter?' said Chard. 'The Zulus don't carry flags. It must be Lord Chelmsford.'

The lookout provided confirmation. 'It is, sir. I can see horsemen, and white faces. They're ours all right.'

'Thank God,' said Chard, bowing his head in relief. 'Now, where's that beer, Gonny? I'd kill for a swig.'

The first riders across the drift were the redcoats of Major Russell's Mounted Infantry, followed a few minutes later by Lord Chelmsford, Colonel Crealock, Henry Fynn and the rest of the staff. Their arrival at the battered post was met with wild celebration as the able-bodied defenders danced jigs, threw their hats in the air and cheered themselves hoarse. Chard and Bromhead confined themselves to broad grins as they waited to greet the general in front of the smoking ruin that had once been the hospital.

Chelmsford dismounted and clasped both officers warmly by the hand. His eyes were red-rimmed from lack of sleep, his uniform crumpled, yet his expression was that of a condemned man granted a last-minute reprieve. 'Gentlemen,' he said, with tears in his eyes, 'we owe you our lives. We feared the worst when we saw the flames last night. I can't tell you what a relief it was to hear your cheers and know the post was still in your hands. You have saved Natal. However did you manage it?'

Chard spoke first. 'I don't rightly know, my Lord. There were so many of them we never thought we could hold on. We shot them down in the hundreds but they just kept coming. It went on for hours, long into the night.'

'How many did you lose?'

'Fifteen dead, my Lord, and about the same number wounded, two seriously. We were down to our last box and a half of ammunition when they gave up.'

'Remarkable,' said Chelmsford, shaking his head in admiration. 'I wouldn't have believed it possible.' For a moment he seemed lost in wonder; then, as if suddenly realizing that the occasion demanded more of him, he said, 'You have performed one of the most courageous feats of resistance in the history of the army, and you and your men deserve every accolade. Were there any particular acts of gallantry?'

'My Lord,' said Bromhead, 'every man was a hero. I lost count of the times that I thought the perimeter was gone for good, only to see someone put himself bodily in the breach and beat them back with a bayonet. With the hospital gone . . .'

'The hospital, you say?' pressed Chelmsford, when Bromhead paused.

'Some of my men were stationed in the hospital, my Lord. They helped to rescue the patients after we'd been forced to abandon that part of the perimeter in the evening. The Zulus set fire to it. And the rooms in the hospital have very few connecting doors. The soldiers were forced to knock holes in the walls as they moved from room to room.'

'How many patients did they save?'

'Thirteen, my Lord. Only four perished.'

'Incredible. Who was the last man out?'

'I think it was Second Lieutenant . . . No, in fact it was Private Hook.'

'Fetch him, will you, Bromhead? I should like to congratulate him.'

A sergeant was dispatched to fetch Hook, who was making tea for the wounded and sick in front of the storehouse. He appeared a minute or so later, an unlikely looking hero in his shirtsleeves, with his braces hanging down.

'Lieutenant Bromhead tells me,' said Chelmsford in a fatherly tone, 'that you were the last one out of the hospital and that – thanks to you and four others – the patients were saved.'

'Not the last one out, my Lord,' said Hook, a sheepish expression on his face. 'That was Lieutenant Hart, who was organizing the rescue, like.'

'Did you say Lieutenant *Hart*? Second Lieutenant George Hart?'

'Yes, sir, though I never heard his Christian name.'

Chelmsford turned to Bromhead. 'You never mentioned Hart. I thought he'd perished at Isandlwana.'

'No, my Lord. He escaped before the end and brought us an order from Colonel Durnford to fortify the post and hold on at all costs.'

'Did he indeed? And he was also involved in the hospital rescue, Hook?'

'Yes, sir. Second Lieutenant Hart helped me and Privates Thomas and Williams get the patients through a hole we'd made in the wall and into the end room, where we met up with Bob and Bill Jones and the patients they was guarding, fifteen in all. The two Joneses guarded the hole while we got the patients out through a small window, assisted on the outside by Corporal Allen and Private Hitch. One patient was killed crossing the yard, but the rest escaped.'

'What happened next?'

'Lieutenant Hart told the five of us to get out, and Thomas was the last.'

'And Hart?'

'He went back to get Sergeant Maxfield: he was delirious and refusing to leave. That was the last we saw of the second lieutenant. We thought he was dead. That is, until this morning, when I found him unconscious in a ditch outside the post, with a badly wounded arm. He was the real hero of the rescue, sir. We couldn't have got out without him.'

At this point Colonel Crealock leant forward and whispered in the general's ear. Chelmsford nodded and asked, 'Where is he now?'

'On the veranda of the storehouse with the rest of the wounded, my Lord.'

'Thank you, Hook. The gallant deeds you and your comrades performed last night will not be overlooked. But now I should like to speak to Second Lieutenant Hart in private. Can that be arranged, Chard?'

'Of course, sir. I'll have him moved to a room in the storehouse.'

'Good, and then I would like to speak to you again.'

George had demanded to know why he was being separated from the rest of the wounded, but the soldiers who assisted him would only say it was at the general's request. So none the wiser, still angry with Chard for his grudging attitude and discomforted by the nagging pain in his arm, he was in exceedingly low spirits by the time Chelmsford and his scheming military secretary made their appearance, shutting the door behind them. George had been put in the main storeroom off the veranda, a large space with a single high window that was packed with boxes of tinned meat and biscuits. George's campbed occupied most of the remaining floor space, leaving just enough room for two rough wooden chairs, which Chelmsford and Crealock now occupied.

'I'm glad to see you made it, Hart,' said Chelmsford. 'You've got quite a story to tell your grandchildren.'

'I have indeed, my Lord,' said George coldly, 'and not all of it reflects credit on those involved.' He glared at Crealock.

'No, indeed, which is why I choose to speak to you in confidence. Lieutenant Chard has informed me of your services yesterday. Very creditable, I must say, up until the point you went missing.'

'*Missing?* I was—'

'Trying to avoid capture? Lying low for a while? I understand. You'd had a long, traumatic day. Anyone would have done the same thing.' George was furious at

Chelmsford's imputation, but the general raised his hand for silence and continued. 'But I'm not interested in that so much as the sequence of events at the camp yesterday. You were present, I take it, during the battle?'

'I was.'

'And you spoke to Colonel Durnford?'

'I did. I accompanied him on his reconnaissance out of the camp with the intention of carrying on back to the Mangeni, in line with your orders. But the Zulus attacked and I never got the opportunity.'

'So you say, but can you explain why, in contravention of a direct order to take command of the camp and act on the defensive, Durnford took part of his force away from the camp and thereby enabled the Zulus to overwhelm it? If he had concentrated his force, and utilized the material at hand for a hasty entrenchment, I feel sure the Zulus would never have been able to dislodge him.'

'You may be right, my Lord. I said the same to Colonel Durnford at the time. But he had received a report that the Zulus were retreating, and wanted to intercept them before they could attack *you*. He did not, however, disobey orders, because he was never told to take command of the camp. The order he received, written by Colonel Crealock here, simply instructed him to march at once to the camp with all his force. I know because I read it.'

Chelmsford turned to Crealock. 'Is that true?'

'No, sir,' said Crealock, his face betraying no hint of his mendacity. 'I distinctly wrote he was to "take command" of the camp. And on arriving at the camp he should have inherited the orders that Clery left for Pulleine, namely that he was to act strictly on the defensive.'

George listened in disbelief. He knew that Crealock was lying, but with Durnford dead it would be difficult to prove. What George could not decide was whether Crealock was acting on his own initiative or with Chelmsford's encouragement. He suspected the former, because the motive was obvious: to exonerate Chelmsford for the disaster at Isandlwana and put the blame on the dead Durnford, a convenient scapegoat; only that way could Crealock hope to obscure the real reason that he and Fynn had encouraged Chelmsford to split his force and attack Matshana.

'That's not how I remember it, my Lord,' said George, 'but there's one way to settle this. I assume Colonel Crealock made a copy of the order?'

'Of course,' said Crealock, 'but I left the order book in the camp and it's probably been destroyed.'

'Very convenient. I can see what you're trying to do, Colonel, but it won't wash. I know what I read.'

'What you *think* you read,' said Chelmsford, rising to his feet in annoyance. 'Do you doubt the colonel's word? It's your word against his. Who do you think is going to be believed? But let's not bicker. I'm going to be honest with you, Hart. I made mistakes during the campaign, I know that now. I relied too heavily on Fynn's intelligence, and missed the signals that the Zulus were planning to attack the camp. But I still maintain that if the troops had been properly handled, the camp could have been saved. They weren't, and Durnford must take the blame.'

George shook his head. 'I can't accept that. There's no doubt his conduct was a little rash, but he had his reasons and he made up for it at the end. After the defensive perimeter had collapsed, he organized a last stand near the nek so that others could get away. A good few hundred soldiers owe him their lives, me included.'

'That's as may be, but Durnford got you into that fix in the first place!'

George looked Chelmsford in the eye. 'Did he, General . . . or did you and your advisors?'

There was silence as Chelmsford measured his response. At last he spoke. 'I'd choose my words a bit more carefully if I were you, Hart. Your own conduct yesterday is hardly beyond reproach. First you disobey my instructions to return to headquarters as soon as you've delivered the message to Pulleine, preferring to accompany Durnford on his ill-fated reconnaissance; and later, having joined the garrison here, you go missing after the hospital rescue. But I'm not here to cast aspersions, merely to point out that none of us has come through this ghastly episode whiter than white. So it might be better for all of us if certain finer details do not see the light of day.'

'I'm sorry, sir,' said George defiantly. 'But I've done nothing to be ashamed of.'

'I'm not sure the court of inquiry will see it that way.'

'What court of inquiry?'

'The one I'm bound to convene to investigate the loss of the camp. But I'll leave you now to discuss this further with Colonel Crealock. I trust you'll do what's right.'

As the door closed behind the departing general, George looked at Crealock with disdain. 'This is all your doing, isn't it, Colonel? You're desperate to keep your own base motives for attacking Matshana a secret, and so hope to exonerate Lord Chelmsford and yourself from any responsibility for the defeat yesterday by blaming Colonel

Durnford. I take it that his Lordship knows nothing of the diabolical plot that you and Fynn hatched to destroy Matshana, and simply wishes to save his military reputation?'

Crealock said nothing; he did not need to.

'As I thought,' continued George. 'But there's just one fly in the ointment, isn't there?'

Still Crealock remained silent, his eyes locked on George's.

'And that's me. You must have got quite a shock when you heard I'd survived not one battle but two. My death would have been very convenient for you, wouldn't it? After all, other than Fynn, I'm the only man alive who knows of your greedy machinations.'

Crealock smiled. 'That's true, but you're in no position to speak your mind, are you? So let's forget about all that and return to the matter in hand. What his Lordship was trying to say is that one good turn deserves another. If you keep quiet about the order to Durnford, and any other matter that casts his Lordship in a bad light, we'll turn a blind eye to your own lapses in judgement.'

'*What* lapses in judgement? The attack came in at Isandlwana before I had a chance to rejoin the headquarters staff, and Lieutenant Chard will vouch for my conduct during the defence here.'

'I think not.'

'What do you mean?'

'He'll say you showed courage and resource up to the fall of the hospital. But he will also feel that your subsequent failure to rejoin your hard-pressed comrades must leave a slight question mark as to your dedication to duty.'

'*What?*' said George loudly. 'How do you know he'll say that?'

Crealock merely smiled.

'I don't believe you. If anyone has reason to thank me for my actions yesterday it's him. Why, if it hadn't been for me and Commissary Dalton, he and Bromhead would have packed up and . . .'

'And what?'

George lay there open-mouthed, unable to finish the sentence. All, suddenly, had become clear. My God, he thought, what a fool I am! Chard can't afford to share the limelight with me in case the truth about his own defeatism ever gets out. And Crealock, no doubt, was already encouraging his fears and insinuations.

'You're rambling,' said Crealock. 'So let me finish what I have to say. As an added incentive for your cooperation, the general is prepared to recommend you for a Victoria Cross for your gallantry in rescuing the patients from the hospital, along with Hook and the others.'

George put his hand in the air. 'Stop right there. One moment the general is accusing me of dereliction of duty, the next he's recommending me for a VC. I can't be a villain *and* a hero – so which is it?'

'That's for you to decide. Think over what I've said, and I'll be back for an answer within the hour. Take it from me,' said Crealock, wagging his finger, 'Lord Chelmsford won't make the same mistakes a second time, and is determined to win this war and make the Zulus pay for their barbarity to our troops. Don't stand in his way.'

George watched Crealock's departing back with a mixture of anger and scorn. What a contemptible man he was, prepared to lie and scheme to save his reputation and that of his master. And yet he and Fynn, more than anyone, were responsible for the catastrophe that had claimed Jake's life, along with so many others. Chelmsford's only failing, it seemed to George, was that he was weak-willed and easily led.

George pondered on what to do. He was determined not to be cowed by their carrot-and-stick approach, partly because he knew they would never dare haul him before a court of inquiry, or a court martial for that matter, for fear of what he might say that would harm them; but chiefly because he owed it to Jake, Durnford, Owen Thomas, and all the others who had died, to tell the truth.

The door creaked open and in stepped Major Gossett, his face drawn and his blue trousers covered in specks of blood. 'George, old fellow, you're alive!' he said, a thin smile on his face. 'When you didn't return I feared the worst and was sure you'd been killed at the camp. But, no, and not content with one fight, you join another one here. Incredible.'

'It's good to see you too, Matthew,' said George, tightly clenching Gossett's proffered hand. 'How I survived I'll never know. Many better men than me did not.'

'Don't say such things. From what I hear you performed heroics last night.'

'Not according to Chard. But tell me, did you pass through the camp on your way here?'

Gossett looked grave. 'Far worse than that, George. We returned as night was falling and were forced to bivouac on the nek, amidst the bodies. It was terrible, George, simply terrible. The ground was literally wet with blood and the smell indescribable. I couldn't sleep – no one could – so I passed the time looking for people I knew. I found Charlie Pope, with his monocle still in place.'

'Did you see Jake Morgan's body?'

'Yes, he was close to Pope. Both had multiple stab wounds. They and the others were all clustered together, as if they'd made a last stand.'

'They did. I saw them.'

'You *saw* them? Then how did you escape?'

'Durnford gave me a message to carry here. I was lucky. I'll tell you about it another time. What I need to know from you, Matthew, is why Chelmsford didn't return to the camp sooner. Surely he received Pulleine's message that we were under attack.'

'He did. It mentioned heavy firing to the left of the camp, if I recall, but because it made no request for assistance, he agreed with Colonel Crealock that we should ignore it.'

'What then?'

'Well, about the same time, he received word that the guns and two companies of infantry were returning to the camp on the orders of Colonel Harness of the Artillery, who, apparently, had heard from one of the NNC battalions that the camp was in danger. His response, again on the advice of Crealock, was to countermand the order. I remember Crealock accusing Harness of disobeying his orders to march to the Mangeni, and utterly ridiculing the idea of any assistance being necessary at Isandlwana. It was only later, at about two thirty p.m., that Chelmsford finally accepted that something might be amiss and set off with an escort to see for himself. He met Lonsdale en route and was told that the Zulus had taken the camp.'

'My God, what a catalogue of deceit and incompetence. But something tells me none of this will come out in the court of inquiry. Chelmsford and Crealock are trying to pin the sole blame for the disaster on Durnford, Matthew, and they want me to help them.'

'How?'

'By keeping quiet about Chelmsford's errors and by going along with the lie that Durnford was ordered to take command at Isandlwana and act on the defensive.'

'Was he not?'

'No. I saw the order, and it said nothing about taking command.'

'I'm not doubting your word, George, but I find it hard to believe that Lord Chelmsford would deliberately lie about something like this.'

'I agree with you. I don't think he would. The man I hold responsible for the lie, and much more besides, is Crealock.'

'Crealock? Are you sure? It's true he exerts great influence over Lord Chelmsford, but I'm not convinced even he is capable of a bold-faced lie.'

'He is. Take it from me.'

Gossett frowned, as if uncertain what to think. After a long pause he said, 'I hope you'll forgive my bluntness, George, but all this sounds a little far-fetched.'

'I appreciate that.'

'So what do you intend to do?'

George thought for a moment. 'I can't decide. But what I won't do is lie about the Durnford order.'

'I admire your integrity, George, but is that wise? Chelmsford is a powerful, well-connected man and could make things extremely difficult for you. You're still under military authority, after all.'

'I know, Matthew, and Crealock even had the nerve to say Chelmsford would recommend me for a VC if I went along with their version of events. But I couldn't live with myself if I let Chelmsford and Crealock off the hook by allowing Durnford to take the blame.'

'Well, if you ask me you *deserve* a VC twice over for what you did yesterday. But you won't get one unless you cooperate, is that what they're saying?'

'Yes.'

'And still you're determined to speak out?'

'I am.'

'In the full knowledge that a VC would provide your career with an immeasurable boost?'

Not to mention a good deal of money, thought George. But Gossett knew nothing of his father's bequest, so George simply nodded.

Gossett slowly shook his head. 'I can see you're determined to do it your way. Just promise me one thing.'

'What?'

'That you'll return to Britain before you spill the beans about Durnford's order. If you do that here, you'll be at Chelmsford and Crealock's mercy. They might even try to court-martial you.'

It irked George to think that he would have to hold his tongue until he was beyond Chelmsford's reach, but Gossett had a point. 'You might be right,' he said at last. 'He's already hinted as much . . . All right. I promise. But in return you can do something for me.'

'What's that?'

'See that a Native Contingent officer called Lieutenant James Hamer is reduced to the ranks. I lent him my horse on the retreat from Isandlwana on condition that he waited at the top of the next hill. He rode on, and if Emperor hadn't thrown him I never would have made it to Rorke's Drift.'

Gossett smiled. 'It'll be a pleasure.'

# 20

*Military Hospital, Pietermaritzburg,
6 February 1879*

A pretty blonde nurse with freckles poked her head round the door of George's whitewashed hospital room. 'You've a visitor, Lieutenant Hart. Shall I show her in?'

'Yes, please,' said George, putting down his copy of the *Natal Witness*. Since his transfer from Helpmekaar four days earlier he had devoured every newspaper he could get his hands on. Most were fiercely critical of Chelmsford's conduct of the campaign thus far, and wondered at the unseemly haste with which he and his staff had abandoned the remnants of Glyn's demoralized column on 24 January to return to Pietermaritzburg to confer with Frere. At the same time they were full of praise for Colonel Pearson, whose Southern Column had repulsed a heavy Zulu attack on the same day as Isandlwana, and positively lionized the heroic defenders of Rorke's Drift who, they were quick to assert, had saved Natal from a Zulu invasion. As for apportioning blame for Isandlwana, they were only too happy to point the finger at Durnford, a man for whom few Natalians had had any sympathy since the disaster at Bushman's River Pass. That day's paper was typical, containing as it did a memorandum by Colonel Bellairs, deputy adjutant-general, on the recent court of inquiry that had sat at Helpmekaar. It read:

> From the statements made before the court of inquiry it may be clearly gathered that the cause of the reverse sustained at Isandlwana was that Lt Col Durnford, as senior officer, overruled the orders which Lt Col Pulleine had received to defend the camp and directed that the troops should be moved into the open, in support of a portion of the Native Contingent which he had brought up and which was engaging with the enemy. Had Lt Col Pulleine not been interfered with and been allowed to carry out his distinct orders given him to defend the camp, it cannot be doubted that a different result would have been obtained.

The paper also contained transcripts of the evidence given to the court of inquiry by various officers who had fought at Isandlwana and lived to tell the tale, including Lieutenant Smith-Dorrien and others who had been with Chelmsford, like Colonels Crealock and Glyn, and Major Clery. It made George's blood boil to read Crealock's falsehood that he had ordered Durnford to 'take command' of the camp on 22 January. But he had been expecting nothing less, and it came as no surprise to discover that Chelmsford, to protect himself from criticism, had limited the scope of the inquiry to the 'loss of the camp'; nor that Chelmsford had silenced Colonel Harness, the man he had prevented from returning to the camp during the battle, by making him one of the three members of the court, none of whom were allowed to give evidence.

George, of course, had not been asked to testify; but then nor had he been singled out as one of the heroes of Rorke's Drift in any of the early reports. He would, he knew, receive no official recognition of the part he had played in either battle. That was his punishment for not going along with Chelmsford and Crealock's cover-up, and he was happy to accept it. For now.

The door opened and in stepped a vision of loveliness in a green satin day dress with matching hat and shoes. Her chestnut hair was piled high on her head, the pale beauty of her face offset by a little rouge. She looked so elegant and poised, every inch the lady, that it took George some time to recognize her. When he did, his jaw fell.

'Lucy? Can it really be you?'

She nodded, tears in her eyes. 'Yes, it's me. I saw your name in the casualty lists and came as quickly as I could. Tell me you're not badly hurt!'

'I'm fine,' he said, patting his bandaged arm. 'It's just a scratch.'

'It looks more than a scratch. But it seems you'll live. It's *so* good to see you.'

'And you.'

Lucy bent forward over the bed, put her arms round George's neck and kissed him on the lips. 'I missed you,' she whispered.

'And I you,' said George, with genuine conviction. The sight of Lucy, the taste of her lips, had roused feelings of desire he had not expected. They were accentuated by the smell of her perfume, so sensuous in the austere confines of the hospital. 'Sit down and tell me what you've been up to. You've obviously done well for yourself.'

'I get by,' she said, settling on the side of the bed. 'I used the last of the money you gave me to get to Kimberley, where I found work in a saloon owned by a former actor called Barney Barnato. He and his brother have some of the most valuable claims in the Kimberley diamond mine. Anyway, he must have thought I had potential because it wasn't long before he put me in charge. It's the best saloon in town, with the highest prices, and Barney says he'll give it to me one day.'

'Does he now?' said George, feeling more than a little jealous. 'And what exactly does this Barney expect in return?'

Lucy blushed. 'He's not like that, George, and nor am I. But you haven't told me about *your* adventures. You joined up, then, like I said you would.'

'Yes,' said George, looking out through the window at the hills beyond, 'though there were times when I wish I hadn't. War's a cynical business.'

'I'm just glad you're out of it, George. Was it as bad as the papers say?'

'Worse. My best friend, Jake Morgan, was killed at Isandlwana.'

'I'm so sorry,' said Lucy, taking his hand. 'But you survived; that's all that matters to me. What will you do next?'

'Go back to London. There's something I have to do.'

'But you can't go back!' said Lucy, her face all concern. 'They'll still be looking for Thompson's killer.'

'I'll take my chances. I have to.'

Tears began to roll down Lucy's cheeks. 'Please come back to Kimberley with me. At least until you're better.'

'That's a tempting offer, Lucy, and very generous considering the way I left you to fend for yourself. But I can't take you up on it. Not yet, at any rate. I plan to leave Durban by mail packet as soon as I'm well enough to travel.'

'Well, come for a short stay. I live in a spacious house and you won't want for attention. I'll nurse you myself.'

'I can't. It wouldn't be fair to you.'

'Why ever not? I love you, George, I always have.'

'And I'm very fond of you. But I must tell you this: I'm in love with someone else.'

Lucy released George's hand. 'Who?'

'Her name is Fanny Colenso.'

'Does she love *you*?'

'I think so.'

'You *think*? You're not sure?'

'No. It's complicated.'

'Where is she now?'

'At her father's home, I imagine, not far from here.'

'Has she been to visit you?'

'No, not yet.'

'Why not?'

'I don't know. I've written asking her to come, but she hasn't yet.'

'Forgive me for saying this, George, but it doesn't sound like love to me.'

'No, not when you put it like that. It's hard to explain.'

'Try.'

George closed his eyes. After a pause he said, 'I wasn't the only one vying for her affections. I think she was in love with both of us.'

'*Was?*'

'He was killed at Isandlwana.'

'Leaving the way clear for you. How very convenient,' said Lucy, attempting sarcasm but sounding bereft.

'Yes. No. It's not like that.'

'Isn't it?'

George was silent. What could he say? After a long pause, Lucy stood up. 'I'm staying at the Plough Hotel and leave for Kimberley at eight tomorrow morning. If you change your mind . . .'

'I'm sorry. I won't.'

'Goodbye, then.'

'Goodbye.'

For a long time after Lucy's departure, George reproached himself for being so heartless. She had, after all, travelled hundreds of miles to see him. Surely he could have found a way to let her down more gently? Possibly, but anything less than brutal honesty would have encouraged false hopes. No, he decided at last, what he had done was for the best. And with that moral certainty clear in his head, he fell asleep.

It was almost dark when George woke from his nap. He was lying on his back, facing the ceiling, and could just make out a shadowy figure seated to his right. 'Who's there?' he demanded.

There was no reply, but as George's eyes became accustomed to the gloom, he could see it was a woman in dark clothes, wearing a veil. 'Lucy, is that you again?'

'No, it's me.'

'Fanny! You've come at last!' said George, his voice cracking with emotion. 'I can't tell you how much I've been longing for this moment.'

Fanny's response was cool, almost distant. 'There's something I need to ask you.'

'Ask away.'

'Is it true what everyone's saying, that Anthony's to blame for the disaster?'

George sat up and turned towards her. 'No, it's not true, Fanny. His decision to leave the camp was an error, but he did it because he genuinely believed the Zulus were retreating and might threaten Lord Chelmsford. He still thought of his command as independent of Glyn's.'

'But Colonel Crealock has testified under oath that he ordered Anthony to take command of the camp.'

'He's lying to save Chelmsford's skin, and his own of course. I saw the order. It simply instructed Colonel Durnford to move his column to Isandlwana.'

'So if he wasn't ordered to take command, he wouldn't have inherited Pulleine's orders to act defensively?'

'Exactly. At that stage nobody but me had any suspicions the camp might be in danger.'

'Why were *you* suspicious?'

'Because we'd received various bits of intelligence the previous day that suggested the main Zulu *impi* was approaching the camp. But Chelmsford ignored all of this. He had been convinced by certain members of his staff, namely Fynn and Crealock, that the Zulus wouldn't risk a frontal attack and were instead planning to hide in the broken ground to the southeast.'

'And he was wrong on both counts?'

'Yes.'

'Which is why he's blaming Anthony?'

'Yes. Dead men can't defend themselves.'

'No, but you can defend him. If you know all this, why haven't you said something?'

'I intend to, but not in Natal. While Chelmsford is still in command, my voice would quickly be drowned out in a chorus of denial. I might even meet with a convenient accident.'

'Aren't you being a bit dramatic?'

'No, I don't think I am. Chelmsford and Crealock are fighting to save their reputations, as is Frere. Such men are extremely dangerous. But in Britain I'll be beyond their reach.'

'When will you go?'

'By the next mail.'

'Meanwhile Anthony's reputation is being dragged through the mud. It was bad enough hearing about his death. But this is worse. I feel so helpless.'

George leant forward and took Fanny's hand. 'He asked me to tell you something, in case he didn't survive.'

'*What?*' she said eagerly.

'That he loved you, and would always love you. And that you were right: he should never have fought in a war he didn't believe in.'

Even before George had finished the first sentence, Fanny began to sob, great heart-rending cries that told him what he did not want to hear: that Fanny loved Durnford and not him. When she had calmed down a little, she asked George why Durnford had not tried to escape.

'I don't know. I think he felt partly responsible for the disaster and wanted to make amends by saving as many of the men as possible.'

'And did he? Make amends, I mean.'

'I think so. I know I owe him *my* life, which is why I will move heaven and earth to clear his name.'

'Thank you, George,' she said, leaning forward and kissing him on the cheek. 'That means a lot to me. I know I won't be able to rest until Chelmsford admits his responsibility.'

'I will strive for that too, Fanny, but you must accept it might never happen.'

'Why must I?'

'Because Chelmsford is a powerful man with many friends to protect him, here and also in Britain.'

'I don't care. If he refuses to take his share of the blame I will hound him until my dying day.'

'That's madness, Fanny. You're grieving, and angry, but you can't let this bitterness destroy your life.'

'Why should it matter to you?'

'You know perfectly well. Because I love you,' he said, his voice quavering with emotion, 'and hope one day to marry you.'

Fanny seemed genuinely shocked. 'How can you say such a thing, when you know I'm grieving for Anthony? I love you too, George, but not in the way I loved Anthony. From now on all my energies will be devoted to restoring his reputation. I simply won't have the time, or the inclination, for romance.'

'You say that now, but—'

'No,' she said firmly. 'Believe me when I tell you my mind is fixed.'

The night passed agonizingly slowly as George drifted in and out of consciousness, his dreams a surreal echo of the past few weeks. In one it was Durnford and not he who rode away from Isandlwana as the Zulus closed in. But the worst, by far, took him back to the hospital at Rorke's Drift. This time he was not saved by the falling roof; instead he was dragged from under the mattress, pinned to the ground and disembowelled while still alive, his screams continuing long after he woke, his pyjamas bathed in sweat. After that he lay for some time listening to the quiet moans of the other patients, and only as it got light did he allow himself to sleep.

He was woken at 9.30 by the pretty nurse. 'This was left for you,' she said, handing over a small white envelope.

He struggled to open it with one hand, so the nurse helped him. She pulled out a folded note, and as she did so something fell from it on to the bed. George looked down and gasped. There, nestling in a fold of the bedclothes, was a cut diamond the size of the nail on his little finger. He picked it up and turned it, its many faces sparkling like a star.

'Oh, Lieutenant Hart,' said the nurse, her eyes wide, 'it's huge.'

George nodded. 'Isn't it just.'

He knew the identity of the donor at once, and the note provided confirmation:

*The Lucky Strike*
*Long Street*
*Kimberley*
*Cape Colony*

*7 February 1879*

   *My darling George,*
   *By the time you receive this I'll have left for Kimberley. Please accept the diamond as a small token of my gratitude for your help in saving me from Sir Jocelyn and paying my passage to South Africa. I am for ever in your debt. If you require any assistance in the future, you need only write to the above address. I wish you luck with your career, and every happiness with Miss Colenso.*
   *Your loving friend,*
   *Lucy*

# 21

## London, 29 March 1879

'Get on there!' shouted the driver as the cab jolted forward, rocking George in his seat. It was a beautiful spring day, crisp and clear, and Piccadilly was so thronged with pedestrians, horses and wheeled traffic that George began to worry he would be late for his appointment. As he stared out of the window in frustration, his mind wandered back to the last time he had crossed London in a cab: then he had been on his way to see his father's lawyer and hear the terms of his outrageous legacy; now he had an interview with one of the most important men in the land, HRH the Duke of Cambridge, commander-in-chief of the British Army and first cousin to Queen Victoria.

Since reaching London by train from Southampton two days earlier, George had written two letters: one to his mother, informing her that he was alive and well, and enclosing a money order for £500, half the balance from the sale of Lucy's diamond; and the second to Major General Sir Arthur Horsford, the military secretary at the Horse Guards, offering to give a blow-by-blow account of events leading up to and during the battles of Isandlwana and Rorke's Drift, signed by a member of Chelmsford's staff who had fought in both. The response from General Horsford was short and to the point:

*The Horse Guards*
*Pall Mall*

*28 March 1879*

> *My dear Acting Second Lieutenant Hart,*
> *I thank you for your interesting letter of the 27th instant. I have been instructed by HRH the Commander-in-Chief to inform you that he will receive you at ten o'clock tomorrow morning.*
> *I am, etc.,*
> *Maj. Gen. Sir A. Horsford*

George was taken aback by the speedy reply. Ever since word of the defeat at Isandlwana had reached Britain in early February, and more particularly since the publication of Lord Chelmsford's unconvincing official dispatch a month later, both press and politicians had become increasingly critical of the civil and military authorities in South Africa. 'When any general suffers such a defeat as was suffered by General Lord Chelmsford at Isandlwana,' declared one Liberal MP, 'there is a *prima facie* case of incompetency against him.'

And yet all this time, in their official statements at least, the queen, the government and the Horse Guards had been strongly supportive of Sir Bartle Frere and Lord Chelmsford. Only two days earlier, the very day George's ship had docked at Southampton, the government had comfortably defeated a motion of no confidence in Frere in the House of Commons by sixty votes. It was looking increasingly likely that Chelmsford, too, would survive the demands for his sacking.

The cab turned down St James's Street and, finally free of Piccadilly, began to pick up speed. At the bottom of the street it turned left into Pall Mall and, soon after, pulled up outside Schomberg House, a handsome four-storey, red-brick mansion on the south side of the road that, for the previous eighteen years, had been home to the War Office. In 1871, as part of his unwelcome subordination to Secretary of State for War, the Duke of Cambridge had been forced to move his office from the old Horse Guards building in Whitehall to the War Office in Pall Mall, yet he had continued to head his letters 'The Horse Guards', much to the government's irritation. He had even insisted upon a separate entrance to the building, and it was through this side door that George was ushered.

The ante-room was crowded with officers from every branch of the army, in a variety of different coloured uniforms, all waiting for a personal interview with the commander-in-chief that might gain them a promotion or a plum posting. As George squeezed on to a long wooden bench, he overheard one major bemoaning the fact that he had already been there for two hours. But George, who was by far the most junior officer present, had barely sat down when he was called for his appointment. He followed the frock-coated clerk through long corridors, and up countless flights of stairs, before arriving at a nondescript door marked 'Commander-in-Chief'. The clerk knocked, opened the door and announced, 'Acting Second Lieutenant Hart to see you, Your Royal Highness.'

'Show him in.'

George entered a large, handsomely furnished room, its walls adorned with oils of famous battles, including the Alma and Inkerman. At the far end of the room, behind a magnificent walnut, leather-topped oval desk, and with his back to a large bay window that looked out over Carlton Gardens and St James's Park beyond, sat the Duke of Cambridge. Almost sixty, his bald head and white whiskers in stark contrast to his red field marshal's tunic, the duke remained oddly expressionless as George strode up to the desk and saluted. He responded with the briefest nod, his blue eyes scanning George's smart civilian rig and the white sling supporting his injured arm, and then bade him sit.

'I trust your wound is healing tolerably, Second Lieutenant Hart?' enquired the duke.

'It is, Your Royal Highness, thank you.'

'Good.' After a pause, the duke continued, 'I was intrigued by your letter. But before we talk about the campaign itself, I would like to hear more about your unorthodox military career. I see from your records that you passed first out of Sandhurst and then served just five months as a cornet in the First King's Dragoon Guards before resigning your commission. And yet barely twelve months later you resurface in South Africa as a trooper with the Natal Carbineers, whoever they may be, before receiving a temporary commission on Lord Chelmsford's staff at the outset of the war against the Zulus. You're clearly an officer of great promise, so why did you resign your regular commission?'

George had not been expecting this line of questioning and, unsure whether Harris was a friend of the duke's, felt he had to tread carefully. 'I'm ashamed to admit it, Your

Royal Highness, but I have no private income and found it difficult to live on my pay.'

The duke nodded, his jowly face showing little trace of his youthful good looks. 'A not uncommon problem in a smart cavalry regiment, it's true. But why resign? Why not exchange to a less fashionable regiment, even the infantry?'

George sensed the duke knew he was lying, and decided to come clean. 'If truth be told, Your Royal Highness, I didn't get the chance. Money *was* a factor, but it was more to do with a clash of personalities. My former commanding officer took against me from the start and constantly found fault with me for imaginary offences; and when that didn't succeed in driving me from the regiment, he accused me of cheating at gambling and . . . um . . . another serious impropriety.'

'Which was?'

'Trying to force myself upon one of his lady houseguests.'

'And were you guilty of these charges?'

'Absolutely not. It was a set-up and I fell for it. Colonel Harris, my CO, gave me the option of resigning or being reported to the Horse Guards for behaviour unbecoming. I resigned.'

'And why, pray,' said the duke, frowning, 'would Harris go to such unscrupulous lengths to see the back of you?'

'He'd heard rumours about my background and didn't think I was worthy of his regiment.'

'What rumours?'

'That I was illegitimate.'

'Anything else?'

'Yes, he made constant disparaging references to my dark complexion.' For a brief moment George thought of going the whole hog and mentioning the attempted rape of Lucy and the death of the private detective. But something made him stop; he had said enough.

The duke, meanwhile, had closed his eyes and was squeezing the bridge of his nose between thumb and forefinger as if lost in painful thought. At last he spoke. 'You have made a serious charge against a superior officer which, if untrue, would disqualify you from ever again holding your queen's commission. But I'm minded to believe you, and the reason is this: barely a day goes by without an officer of the King's Dragoon Guards – my old corps, I might add – sending in a complaint against Harris. I would happily have removed him from his command before now if it had been possible to prove just one of these charges of unwarranted victimization. But it has not, and I suspect your own charge would be equally difficult to validate before a court martial. In any case, Harris and his regiment are on their way to South Africa as part of the reinforcement that Chelmsford has requested, and the government has seen fit to authorize. So there the matter must lie for now. But I can assure you of one thing: Harris will receive no further preferment while I remain at the head of the army.'

George breathed a sigh of relief, delighted that the duke had believed him and, more importantly, that Harris's career was as good as over, even if he was at last getting his wish to see some action. It only remained for him to convince the duke that Lord Chelmsford and his staff, and not Colonel Durnford, were chiefly responsible for the disaster at Isandlwana. And that, he suspected, would not be so easy if he did not mention – as he could not for fear of retaliation – Fynn and Crealock's plan to destroy Matshana.

'Now we've cleared that matter up,' said the duke, looking up from scribbling a quick *aide-mémoire*, 'I'd like to hear your account of the recent disaster. Was it, in your opinion, avoidable? And if so, what mistakes were made and by whom? The evidence given to the court of inquiry points the finger of blame squarely at Colonel Durnford. I gather from your letter you don't agree?'

'No, sir. The disaster was certainly avoidable, and the chief culprits were Lord Chelmsford and his senior advisors, Henry Fynn and Colonel Crealock.'

'Go on.'

And so George did as he was bidden, recounting the events of the eleven-day campaign in such detail that he spoke non-stop, bar the odd query from the duke, for more than an hour. Durnford was not absolved of all blame for the defeat – his decision to leave the camp and pursue the 'retreating' Zulus was, George admitted, 'a rash and ultimately fatal error of judgement' – but his harshest criticism was reserved for Lord Chelmsford and his advisors. 'From the word go,' George concluded, 'they belittled the fighting capacity of the Zulus, failed properly to reconnoitre the ground ahead of the Central Column or to fortify the camp at Isandlwana, ignored intelligence that indicated the main *impi* was in the vicinity, and then, as if all that was not enough, Lord Chelmsford divided his forces not once but twice, thus leaving his base camp and all his supplies to be captured by an overwhelming force of Zulus. When all was over, Colonel Crealock tried to shift the blame on to Colonel Durnford by falsely stating the latter had been ordered to take command of the camp at Isandlwana, when no such order was ever sent. They knew I knew the truth, and so tried to buy my silence by offering to recommend me for a Victoria Cross for my actions on the twenty-second. I, of course, refused to cooperate.'

The duke sat there shaking his head, as if unconvinced by what George had told him. His face was immobile, his expression fixed. George feared the worst.

After a considerable pause the duke spoke. 'Your actions in coming here and speaking so plainly must have taken a lot of courage. And I don't mean physical courage, but moral. Nothing could have been easier than for you to hold your tongue and return home a hero, the recipient of a Victoria Cross. But you chose instead to tell, as you saw it, the truth. I won't ask your reasons. I only know that you must have appreciated the risk you were running: a junior officer informing on his superiors. I doubt you even thought, in your heart of hearts, that your tale would be believed. But I do believe it, and I'll tell you why. When I first read the Reuters telegram giving news of the defeat, on the eleventh of February, I naturally assumed that Chelmsford had failed to take adequate defensive precautions. Yet I was prepared to withhold judgement until I had read his official dispatch. Her Majesty the Queen, on the other hand, was easily convinced that Durnford and not Chelmsford was to blame, and had the War Secretary send a note to the latter expressing her entire confidence in him. The other members of Cabinet were furious, of course, because it seemed as if my cousin had pre-empted any government move to recall Chelmsford before the true cause of the disaster was known.'

The duke paused before continuing. 'In any event, when the dispatch did finally arrive on the first of this month, I found it neither good nor clear, and the whole thing inexplicable. Even the queen thought the dispatch was a poor one and did not give the reasons for what had occurred. So I instructed General Ellice, the adjutant-general, to write and ask Chelmsford to explain certain points he had omitted or left in doubt, such as the steps that were taken on the twentieth and twenty-first of January to reconnoitre the country on his flank, and why he failed to put the camp at Isandlwana into a state of defence prior to his departure on the twenty-second of January.

'We still await his response, but you have provided credible answers to many of these queries. It would appear, from what you say, that Chelmsford never did put Colonel Durnford in command of the camp. Doubtless finding himself senior officer on the spot when the action had already commenced, Durnford, according to the custom of the service, took command, but this was too late in the day to remedy the errors that had already been made. Do you agree?'

'I do, Your Royal Highness.'

'Your candour is much appreciated, Lieutenant Hart, and I will do all I can to effect the removal of both Chelmsford and Crealock. I should warn you, however, that I may face considerable obstacles in the form of Her Majesty the Queen, who is a warm supporter of Lord Chelmsford, and even our esteemed prime minister, who agrees with Abraham Lincoln that it is unwise to swap horses while crossing a stream.'

'I quite understand.'

'Good. Now, there is one other matter I would like to discuss with you. A total of eight men – two officers and six other ranks – *have* been recommended for Victoria Crosses for their valour at Rorke's Drift. Six were cited by Lieutenant Bromhead. They are,' said the duke, reading from a typed note on his desk, 'Corporal Allen and Privates Hook, Hitch, Williams, Jones, W., and Jones, R., Lieutenants Bromhead and Chard were added to the list by Chelmsford himself. My question to you is this: are these awards deserved?'

'All the men deserve the cross,' said George, 'particularly Hook, Williams and the two Joneses, who helped to get the patients out of the burning hospital. Another man was also involved in this feat of gallantry, Private Owen Thomas, but he was killed later in the action.'

'I'm sorry to hear that. But as you know, the Victoria Cross cannot be awarded posthumously. There is a device known as the Memorandum Procedure, whereby a soldier is mentioned in the *London Gazette* as deserving of the VC had he lived, but it could only be activated in Thomas's case with the relevant recommendation from his commanding officer. That, sadly, was not forthcoming. What about Bromhead and Chard? Do they deserve the cross?'

George paused before answering. He was tempted to mention their initial instinct to abandon the post, and the fact that he had had to bolster Chard's confidence at every opportunity. Chard, moreover, had infuriated George after the battle with his petty insinuations, inspired no doubt by the knowledge that George and not he had shown the greater fortitude and leadership. Yet George could not deny that both officers had performed well enough during the battle, particularly Bromhead, and felt it would be churlish to lessen their chances of a VC when he, George, had not been present for much of the fighting.

'On balance I think they probably do. But a commissary officer called James Dalton did as much, if not more, to organize and inspire the defence. If they get the cross, then so should he.'

The duke nodded. 'What about you? You fought at both battles, did you not? And I gather you were part of the hospital rescue, though Chard barely mentions you in his dispatch.'

George could feel his heart hammering with excitement. For almost the first time he took seriously the prospect of winning the Victoria Cross *and* gaining £10,000 of his father's money. 'That's all true,' he said hurriedly, 'and I suspect the reason is that Chard doesn't want me, or Dalton for that matter, to steal his thunder.'

'Mmm,' said the duke as he digested George's words. 'I'll look into the other cases and see what I can do. But I must tell you that without the recommendation of at least one officer witness I can't advise Her Majesty to award the cross.'

Hearing these words, George's spirits sank as quickly as they had risen because he knew, in his heart of hearts, that Chard would never recommend him.

'Nevertheless,' continued the duke, 'you have performed a vital service for your country, both during the campaign and since, and deserve some form of recompense.'

The duke paused while he weighed up the options. 'I propose,' he said at last, 'to offer you a commission in a regiment of your choice, and an immediate promotion to the rank of captain. What do you say?'

'I–I–' George stammered, so taken aback was he by this new turn on the wheel of fortune.

'You *do* intend to pursue a military career?'

'Certainly, sir. I'm just overwhelmed by your offer. I had no expectations. I just wanted to set the record straight.'

'And you have. So you'll accept my offer?'

'Gladly, sir,' said George, a broad grin on his face.

'Good. It only remains for you to choose a regiment, but there's time enough for that while you recover from your wound.'

'I don't know how to thank you enough, Your Royal Highness.'

The duke waved away his thanks. 'Just don't waste this second opportunity to make something of yourself. Well, goodbye, Captain Hart,' said the duke, rising from his chair.

'Goodbye, sir,' said George, saluting.

It was only as he left the building that the full enormity of what had just taken place was brought home to him. The commander-in-chief, a prince of the royal blood no less, had believed his account of the Zulu War and, as a result, had promised to replace Lord Chelmsford and his staff, exonerate Colonel Durnford and investigate those overlooked for their heroism at Rorke's Drift. He, George, would not be among their number, but he had been given a second chance in the army and a double jump in promotion. This meant at least a chance of reaching the rank of lieutenant colonel before the age of twenty-eight, an achievement that would net him £5,000 of his father's money after all.

He sat on the steps, shaking his head, trying to take it all in. On returning to his hotel, he would write to his mother and give her the good news; then he would do the same for Fanny and Lucy. But first there was one more person he had to meet.

He looked at his pocket-watch. It was 11.46, which gave him fourteen minutes to make his assignation at London's newest landmark, the Albert Memorial. He hailed the first cab he saw, and as he climbed inside, he noticed a man watching him from across the street. The man was tall and lean, and wearing a long double-breasted overcoat and a small top hat known as the 'Muller cut-down'. It was this unusual hat – named after the murderer whose headgear led to his identification – that brought him to George's attention. But he did not recognize the face and quickly dispelled him from his thoughts.

The traffic was even heavier on Piccadilly for the journey west, but George still had a couple of minutes to spare as the cab came to a stop in Kensington Gardens. He looked across the road and there, shimmering in the midday sun, was Queen Victoria's extraordinary memorial to her beloved husband who had died, aged just forty-two, in 1861. The centrepiece was a beautiful golden statue of Albert, seated in the robes of the Garter and surmounted by an elaborate marble canopy and tower designed by the great Sir George Gilbert Scott in the Gothic-revival style. At the outer corners of this central area stood four sculpture groups representing the continents of Europe, Asia, the

Americas and Africa. George had chosen the Africa group as his meeting place.

Finished just four years earlier, the memorial was still enough of a novelty to draw large crowds, and today was no exception. Several people were peering at the African sculptures, a seated camel and several Arabic figures, and George scanned the faces of the sightseers without finding the person he was looking for. He sat on some nearby steps to wait and did not notice the tall man approaching from the direction of Hyde Park Road.

'Excuse me, sir,' said the man, 'are you Second Lieutenant George Hart?'

George looked up and saw the man in the 'Muller cutdown' who had been watching him in St James's Street. He had small intense eyes and seemed edgy, as if unsure of George's next move. 'I was a second lieutenant,' replied George. 'I've just been promoted to captain. Have you been following me?'

'Yes. I'm Inspector Willis of the Plymouth CID. I'd like to ask you a few questions about the suspicious death of a private detective called Henry Thompson on the thirty-first of January last year.'

George's instinct was to run, and the inspector must have read his mind because his right hand moved towards his overcoat pocket, where, George surmised, he had doubtless concealed his gun. 'I wouldn't do that if I were you.'

'I don't know anyone called Thompson,' said George, rising from the step.

'So you say, but we have reason to believe that you do, and that you shot and killed him during a fight.'

'What reason?'

'We received a tip-off from Thompson's employer, a Colonel Sir Jocelyn Harris. Apparently you were with a young woman called Lucy Hawkins, one of the colonel's maids, and Thompson was sent to recover her. When Thompson tried to do his job, you shot him. Do you deny it?'

'Of course I deny it. I had nothing to do with his death.'

'Yet you *were* in Plymouth that morning, and embarked on the SS *American* shortly after the shooting. We know that much from the shipping records. We also know you spent the previous night in the Angel Inn with a young lady, and that a young couple was seen running from the scene of the crime. More than a coincidence, wouldn't you say?'

George's mind raced. They could prove he was in Plymouth that morning, but he doubted a jury would convict without the murder weapon or a witness to the actual shooting. Admit nothing, he told himself, and stay calm. 'No, I would not, Inspector,' he replied with as much sangfroid as he could muster. 'I *was* in Plymouth that morning, but I know nothing about the death of a private detective.'

'I think you do,' said Willis, pulling a pair of handcuffs from his coat pocket, 'which is why I'm arresting you on suspicion of murder. Now, if you'll just put your hands out.'

George could not believe this was happening: that, after all he'd been through in Africa, he was about to lose his liberty on a safe London street bathed in sunshine. He knew he was innocent of murder, but would a jury believe his version of events? As he imagined the noose closing round his neck, he could hear blood pounding in his ears. He was close to losing control when a female voice interrupted. 'What on earth is going on here?'

It was Mrs Bradbury, wearing a Norfolk jacket with matching hat and parasol, and looking every bit as ravishing as she had when George first met her at Westbury Park.

'Madam,' replied Willis, 'I'm an inspector of police on official business. This is not your concern.'

'But I know this man, Inspector,' she said, holding her ground. 'He arranged to meet me here and I want to know why you're arresting him.'

Willis sighed. 'I'm arresting him on suspicion of the murder of a private detective in Plymouth last year. Now, will you please let me get on with my job?'

'I heard about that murder, but George involved? I've never heard anything so ludicrous.'

'I can assure you, madam, this is a serious matter, and Captain Hart is the prime suspect.'

She glanced at George, who was shaking his head. 'When exactly did this murder take place, Inspector?'

Willis looked puzzled. 'The thirty-first of January. Why do you ask?'

'And the time?'

'Around seven thirty in the morning.'

'In Plymouth, you said?'

'Yes.'

'It was the day I left for Africa,' said George. 'They're saying I spent the previous night in an inn with a young lady called Lucy Hawkins, and that I shot the private detective as we made our way to the docks.'

She gave George a reassuring smile. 'Well, if that's the case, then he *can't* be guilty.'

'How could you possibly know that?' asked Willis.

'Because, Inspector, I was with him at that time.'

George's mouth fell open, then quickly closed as he tried not to let Willis see his surprise.

'Go on,' urged the inspector.

'George and I have been – how can I put it? – intimate friends for some time now. On the thirtieth of January last year I travelled down to Plymouth to say goodbye to him before he sailed for South Africa. We spent the night together in an inn and next morning, after breakfast, I accompanied him to the docks and saw him on to the ship. He could not have killed that man because at the time of the murder he was . . .'

'Yes?'

'. . . still with me.'

She cast her eyes downwards, as if embarrassed. George could not believe what he was hearing. Willis was nonplussed. 'You say you spent the night with Captain Hart and never left his side? Are you certain, madam? And, more importantly, are you prepared to say as much in an open court of law?'

'I am,' said Mrs Bradbury. 'Though I hope it won't come to that. You must appreciate the delicacy of my position, Inspector. If the circumstances of my relationship with Captain Hart ever became known, it would destroy my standing in society.'

'Mmm,' said the inspector, as if unsure Mrs Bradbury had any standing left to destroy. 'Thankfully that's not my concern. But I can't deny this evidence casts a new light on the case. It would certainly help Captain Hart's defence if you were willing to repeat your claims in a written statement. Are you?'

'Of course, Inspector.'

'In that case, I'll ask you – and not Captain Hart – to accompany me to Scotland Yard. And I won't be needing these,' he added, pocketing his handcuffs.

'Before you go, Inspector,' said George, 'I'd like to speak with Mrs Bradbury.'

'Of course, but don't take too long,' said the inspector, gruffly.

Once Willis had moved off a few yards, George turned back to Mrs Bradbury. 'Don't think for a minute I'm not grateful, but why would you perjure yourself for me?'

'Because I owe you that. When I received your letter yesterday, suggesting a meeting, I knew I had to come and explain my shameful part in Sir Jocelyn's conspiracy. Giving you an alibi for the shooting of that hateful man is my way of making amends.'

'But have you thought this through? First off, you don't look anything like Lucy, who *did* spend the previous night with me; and there are bound to be witnesses from the inn who will testify that we left *before* the killing took place.'

'Don't you worry about that. My current protector is a man with great estates and much influence in the West Country. If necessary, the witnesses will be bribed. There will be no court case. Trust me.'

'All right, so your alibi might stand up. But answer me this: why, if you're so contrite now, did you get involved in the first place? How is it possible for any woman to betray a man she's just made love to? I thought you liked me.'

'I'm sorry but I did it for Sir Jocelyn. Us. I thought he was in love with me, and that we would marry. I was under his spell. Now I know him for what he is.'

'So what opened your eyes?' asked George, though he knew the answer already.

'It was the night he tried to assault Lucy. And he would have succeeded, too, if I hadn't intervened.'

'Lucy told me. It seems you've already paid part of your debt.'

'Yes,' smiled Mrs Bradbury. 'And your alibi is another down-payment. But I don't think I'll ever truly forgive myself for what I've done.'

'Well, I already have,' said George, taking her hand and kissing it.

'Thank you, George. That means a lot to me.'

Out of the corner of his eye, George could see Willis pacing impatiently. 'You haven't asked me if I did it or not.'

'No, I haven't.'

'Why not?'

'Because I don't want to know. And even if you did pull the trigger, I'm sure you had good reason. I must go, but a word of advice before I do.'

'Yes?'

'Stay away from Harris.'

He smiled. 'I assure you, I have no intention—'

'I'm serious, George,' she said, grim-faced. 'He's a powerful man who never forgets a slight.'

George nodded. And neither do I, he thought, neither do I.

# Author's Note

This book came out of a meeting I had with George MacDonald Fraser, the creator of the Harry Flashman novels, two years before his death in 2008. I asked Fraser whether he planned to make good on hints in previous books that he would depict Flashman in the Zulu War of 1879. He said no. Six months later I pitched the idea of a novel set in that war to Hodder and *Zulu Hart* is the result.

I knew my central character had to be very different from Fraser's scurrilous anti-hero. Thus I created George Hart, the son of an English VIP and brought up a gentleman, but of mixed Irish-African descent on his mother's side and therefore a man with a foot in both camps, capable of seeing the British Empire from the perspective of both ruler and ruled. He is, I hope, a character that modern readers can empathize with.

As a historian of Victorian warfare, I was determined to make this book as authentic as possible. George's VIP father, for example, is a real historical figure who had 'a penchant for actresses', secretly (and illegally) marrying one and having two illegitimate sons by her. Both were gamblers and spendthrifts who went on to have moderately successful military careers. Their father fought in the Crimea, but did not cover himself with glory at the hard-fought battles of Alma and Inkerman, where he failed to cope under pressure.

George's nemesis Sir Jocelyn Harris is a fictional creation but very loosely modelled on that arch-snob and martinet Lord Cardigan, who quarrelled with most of his officers, wounding one in a duel and secretly recording the conversation of another (for which he was condemned and sacked from the command of the 15th Hussars). Cardigan had earlier abused the 'purchase system' to rise from cornet to lieutenant colonel in just six years. He would go on to command the infamous Charge of the Light Brigade, and return from the Crimea a hero, but questions about his conduct that day would contrive to dog him.

The brief time George spends with the 1st (King's) Dragoon Guards in 1877 is a faithful record of that regiment's activities when it was, as I state, stationed in Manchester. Among its troop officers was a Captain Marter, who later gained fame as the captor of King Cetshwayo in Zululand in August 1879. Its second-in-command, Major Winfield, had a few years earlier invented the game of 'Sphairistike', an early form of lawn tennis.

Many of the details of George's trip out to Africa are based on the diary of a Lieutenant Molyneux, aide-de-camp to Lord Chelmsford, who travelled out with his chief on board the steamer SS *American* in January 1878. Also on board were Lieutenant Colonel Wood, VC, Major Buller, Major (later Lieutenant Colonel) Crealock, Captain (later Major) Gossett and Lieutenant Melvill. The flogging of Private Thomas (another fictional creation) is based on an actual punishment parade that took place a year later on board a troopship bound for Durban.

Most of the main events in Africa prior to and during the Zulu War were as I describe: the long deliberation of the Boundary Commission (one of whose members was Lieutenant Colonel Anthony Durnford); the pro-Zulu stance of the Colenso family; the recapture and execution of two (I only mention one) of Chief Sihayo's wives by his sons and one of his brothers; the gradual build-up of troops on the Zulu border; Sir Bartle Frere's cynical delivery of an ultimatum that he knew the British government did not support and King Cetshwayo could not accept; and, finally, the invasion of Zululand and the blunders that resulted in the catastrophic defeat at Isandlwana and, just a few hours later, the heroic defence of Rorke's Drift.

For the purposes of plot I have taken one or two minor liberties with the historical record. There is, for example, no evidence that Bishop Colenso ever tried to give King Cetshwayo an early warning of the Boundary Commission's favourable decision, nor that Henry Fynn had a grudge against Chief Matshana and plotted with Colonel Crealock to destroy him. On the other hand it *was* Fynn who convinced Lord Chelmsford that the main Zulu army intended to link up with Matshana in the vicinity of the Mangeni Gorge, thus prompting the general to fatally divide his column on the morning of 22 January 1879. Colonel Crealock, meanwhile, *was* the man who orchestrated the cover-up for the defeat by lying on oath to the court of inquiry that he had ordered Durnford to 'take command' of the camp at Isandlwana in Chelmsford's absence. The actual order – recovered from the battlefield and suppressed for a number of years – had simply instructed Durnford to 'march to this camp at once with all the force you have with you'. Only when the truth about the battle became known later that year did HRH the Duke of Cambridge, the commander-in-chief, exonerate Durnford in a secret memorandum that did not come to light until the 1960s.

At our meeting in 2006, George MacDonald Fraser told me the trick to writing about real people was to 'stay true to the spirit of the person'. I have tried to heed that advice, particularly in the case of Colonel Crealock. There is, for example, no doubt that Crealock was hugely influential in all of the bad decisions that Lord Chelmsford made during the Zulu War. Sir Garnet Wolseley, Chelmsford's replacement, acknowledged this when he described his predecessor in his journal as a 'weak tool in the hands of Crealock, whom everyone execrates as neither a soldier nor a gentleman'. Such a man was certainly capable, if not guilty, of the misdeeds that I attribute to him.

For any readers who would like to delve further into the history of the period, I recommend the following books:

Daphne Child (ed.), *The Zulu War Journal of Colonel Henry Harford, C.B.* (1978)

Richard Cope, *Ploughshare of War: The Origins of the Anglo-Zulu War of 1879* (1999)

Saul David, *Zulu: The Heroism and Tragedy of the Zulu War of 1879* (2004)

R.W.F. Droogleever, *The Road to Isandhlwana: Colonel Anthony Durnford in Natal and Zululand 1873–1879* (1992)

John Laband (ed.), *Lord Chelmsford's Zululand Campaign 1878–1879* (1994)

Major-General W.C.F. Molyneux, *Campaigning in South Africa and Egypt* (1896)

Donald Morris, *The Washing of the Spears: The Rise and Fall of the Great Zulu Nation* (1966)

C.L. Norris-Newman, *In Zululand with the British* (1880)

Wyn Rees (ed.), *Colenso Letters from Natal* (1958)

Sir Evelyn Wood, *From Midshipman to Field Marshal* (1906)

Writing a novel, I discovered, is very much a collaborative effort. The most telling contributions were made by my editor Nick Sayers and his assistant Anne Clarke who together helped to transform my pig's ear of an early manuscript into something approaching a silk purse. And to everyone else at Hodder who has worked so hard on the book – Kerry, Susan, Mark, as well as Kelly, Lucy, Diana, Jason and their teams, in particular Aslan and Laura – I'm extremely grateful.

A big thank-you, also, to my publicist Richard Foreman who suggested I try my hand at writing a historical novel and who set up my initial meeting with Nick; to my good friend Matt Jackson, who helped me with plot and character while we were sailing off Turkey; to the novelist Aminatta Forna for much invaluable advice; to my agent Peter Robinson who never voiced any doubts that I could make the difficult transition from non-fiction to fiction; and to my wife Louise who did voice one or two doubts, but who read the manuscript chapter by chapter and provided invaluable advice regardless.

# Glossary

*amakhosi* – regional chiefs (sing. *inkhosi*)

assegai – slender iron-tipped spear of hardwood, with variations for throwing and stabbing (see *iklwa*)

donga – ravine or dry watercourse with steep sides

drift – river ford

head-ringed – indicative of manhood and adult status (see *isicoco*)

*iklwa* – short stabbing assegai with a broad, flat blade

*impi* – Zulu army

induna – minor Zulu chief

*inkhosi* – regional chief or great man (pl. *amakhosi*)

*insangu* – wild hemp, a popular narcotic for Zulu men and older boys

inspan – harness cattle to a wagon

*isanusi* – tribal diviner or medicine man

*isibaya* – cattle enclosure

*isicoco* – black head-ring worn by married men

*iwisa* – Zulu name for a knobkerrie

knobkerrie (see *iwisa*) – hardwood club with a thick handle and bulbous head

kopje – small hill

kraal – village of huts enclosed by a stockade and containing a central enclosure for cattle (see *isibaya*)

krans – sheer rock face, precipice

laager – circle of wagons to protect a camp

loophole – a small gap or hole in a wall for firing through

nek – broad saddle of land between two hills

off-saddle – unsaddle a horse to give it a rest

outspan – unharness cattle from a wagon

*undlunkulu* – a chief's great (or principal) wife

*Usuthu!* – Zulu war cry, derived from the Usuthu faction that supported Cetshwayo's claim to the throne in the 1850s

veldt – open grassland

*voorloper* – leader of a team of cattle

wideawake – broad-brimmed hat

Don't miss

# HART OF EMPIRE

the next thrilling instalment in the George Hart series.

### GEORGE HART

is asked by Prime Minister Disraeli to undertake a secret
mission to Afghanistan.

### EXPENDABLE

Hart's mixed race makes it easy for him to go undercover, and with
his past catching up on him in England, he accepts the job.

### THIEF

Hart must journey through a strange and violent land to steal
the iconic Prophet's Cloak, a potent symbol of rebellion for
religious extremists.

### PATRIOT OR TRAITOR?

But, on the run with a dangerously alluring Afghan princess,
Hart finds himself questioning his mission. Loyalty to his
Conscience or his country – Hart must decide.

'As precocious as ever, our daredevil hero is once again
in the thick of things as he takes on anyone and everyone
who dares to cross his path. Great stuff.' *Daily Mail*

Out now in paperback and as an eBook.

Turn the page to read the first two chapters now.

HODDER

# I

'Thirty-three black!' announced the croupier. George shook his head, scarcely able to believe his luck.

He preferred gambling at cards, but neither baccarat nor chemin de fer had been kind to him today and he had switched in desperation to roulette, placing his last £15 on black. It had won, and for want of a better strategy, he had bet on the same colour for five more spins, each time doubling his money, so that with this latest success, he now had the considerable sum of £960. One more win would give him the £2,000 or so that he desperately needed. He took another gulp of whisky and decided to let the money ride. All or nothing.

But something in his drink-befuddled brain told him it couldn't be black again, not seven times in a row, though he knew the odds on each new bet were same for either colour. At the last moment, as the croupier was about to spin the wheel, he leant forward and moved all his chips to red. Then he closed his eyes and prayed.

As the ball was released, George glanced nervously round the dingy gambling hell, its candelabras casting ghostly shadows over the few remaining players. He was alone at his table but for the croupier, a small wiry man with greasy hair and a lopsided bow-tie, who was staring at the wheel as if his life depended upon it. Maybe it did, because his brow glistened with beads of sweat and his hands were gripping the table so hard the knuckles were white.

George looked back at the wheel, and didn't see the croupier move his right thumb below the level of the table, feel for a small button and press it. Seconds later the ball ran out of momentum and fell into the bed of the wheel, rattling along the numbers before finally coming to rest.

'Zero green,' announced the croupier, with as straight a face as he could muster, before raking George's neat pile of chips from the red diamond at the side of the baize.

Oh my God, thought George, it's fallen into the only number I didn't consider, the one that gives the house its advantage. But even as his racing heart and clammy hands registered the consequences, he noticed the visibly-relieved croupier grinning at someone behind him. He swung round to see the rotund proprietor, Mr Milton Samuels, advancing towards him.

'So sorry for your loss, Captain Hart,' said Samuels, thumbs crooked in his bright checked waistcoat. 'You win some . . .'

George's eyes narrowed. He had lost money before, of course, but Samuels had never felt the need to console him. Something was wrong. He looked from boss to employee, and back again, and felt sure he had been cheated. 'Don't give me all that flannel, Samuels,' he said, a hard edge to his voice. 'You're not sorry at all. And why would you be when you've just fleeced me of everything I own.'

'Now, now, Captain Hart, there's no need for that.'

'Isn't there?' said George, his voice rising. 'So you keep your temper when you've been rooked, do you?'

The room had fallen silent, all eyes on the altercation. Samuels glanced beyond George to the stairs. 'I assure you that nothing untoward—'

'I don't believe you. I saw your croupier gripping the side of the table, and wouldn't be surprised if you had some mechanical device to ensure the ball landed on green. If you're so sure of yourself, you won't mind me taking a look.'

George strode towards the croupier's end of the table but Samuels intercepted him, his arms outstretched. 'I don't want any trouble, Captain Hart, so if you leave quietly we'll say no more about it.'

'I'm not going anywhere without my money.'

'That right, Cap'n?' said a new voice behind him. Before George could turn he felt an iron-like grip on his throat as an arm pinned him from behind. The more he struggled, the more the pressure increased. He could feel blood pounding in his ears and knew he was close to blacking out. But then the pressure on his throat eased a little and, coughing and spluttering, he regained his senses. 'Like I was saying,' snarled Samuels, 'I don't want any trouble, but you would insist. All right, Paddy, throw him out.'

George felt as helpless as a rag doll as he was dragged backwards up the stairs, through the entrance, and propelled onto the pavement, the boisterous Haymarket crowd parting for yet another drunk. Furious, George scrambled to his feet and advanced towards O'Reilly, the huge doorman, who had thrown him out and was now standing coolly on the steps, his arms crossed. 'Don't be a fool, Cap'n. I'll make mincemeat of you, so I will, and it'd be a shame to damage that handsome figurehead of yours.'

George knew he was no match for this former prize-fighter, and was likely to receive a thrashing, but he was so angry and drunk he didn't care. He swung a right hook that missed as the battle-scarred Irishman swayed out of range, moving his large frame with the speed and grace of a cat; overbalanced, George stumbled forward and into a hammer of a counter-punch, O'Reilly's right fist slamming into his solar plexus, driving the air from his lungs and dropping him to his knees. He had never been hit so hard.

'You won't get away with this,' said George, gasping for breath. But he knew that they would, for he could hardly complain to the police about an illegal gambling hell.

'Go home and sober up, Cap'n, though I'll wager home for you is far from these shores.'

Normally such an insulting reference to his dark skin, which made him look more southern Mediterranean than British, would have provoked a violent response. But the blow George had already received had knocked much of the fight out of him, and as he crouched on the pavement, he realized he had only himself to blame for his humiliation. He rose to his feet, dusted himself down, and with a last scornful look at O'Reilly, set off in the direction of his hotel in Knightsbridge. It was a fair distance and he would normally have hailed a cab. But he decided to walk: to save money and to clear his head.

Half way down Piccadilly – oblivious to the fashionable swells in their frock coats, checked waistcoats and tight blue trousers, and the ladies in dolman-style cloaks and narrow-brimmed bonnets – he pulled out his mother's letter and read it a second time.

*17 Connaught Square*
*Dublin*

*Darling George,*
*It was wonderful to have you to myself again for those few short weeks of your convalescence, and to hear all your news. I'm so proud that your gallantry in South Africa has been rewarded with a regular commission, and that you now have a second chance to make something of your military career.*
*I'm so grateful for the £500 you sent on your return to England. I've never been good with money, and since your father stopped paying your allowance it's been a constant struggle to keep my creditors at bay. In truth the £500 was quickly eaten up by debts and I've been forced to resort to moneylenders. But their interest is exorbitant and they've warned me that if I don't come up with the £2,000 I owe by the end of the year they'll force me to sell the house! I hate to burden you with this, my darling, particularly after your recent generosity, but I don't know where else to turn.*
*Your loving mother,*
*Emma*

George closed the letter and groaned. He knew he had been a fool to try and raise the money his mother needed by gambling, but what was the alternative? Since kitting himself out in his new regimental uniform he had been left with barely £200. Now, thanks to his idiocy, that money was gone, and tomorrow he would return to South Africa to join his new regiment. It was almost a relief.

He set off at an unsteady walk and, twenty minutes later, was in sight of his hotel on Queen's Gate when he registered footsteps behind him. They gradually got louder, and as the pedestrian caught up, George moved aside to let him pass. Instead he felt a tap on the shoulder.

'What do you—' said George, as he turned, freezing in mid-sentence. There, standing before him in a top hat and cape, was a ghost. The ghost of a man he had killed in a fight the year before: the same huge frame, clothes and blotchy red face; it couldn't be, yet he seemed real enough in the flickering light from a nearby gas-lamp.

'It can't be . . .' whispered George. 'You're dead.'

'Not me,' snarled the man, 'my brother, John. I'm Bob Thompson.'

'Your *brother*?' asked George, aghast.

'Yes. And I'm here to see you pay.'

George looked down at the man's hands, expecting to see a weapon. They were bunched into fists. 'Now just hold on a minute, Mr Thompson. I can understand your anger, but your brother drew a sword on me. I had to defend myself.'

'That's not what you told the police. They said they were about to arrest you when a lady gave you an alibi. And yet you've just admitted to me that you did kill my brother, and that it was self-defence.'

A voice in George's head was screaming at him to stop incriminating himself and say no more, but perhaps because of the drink, perhaps the shock, perhaps because in truth he was haunted every day by his distress at having killed a man and run from the fact, he spoke:

'It was self-defence, I swear.'

'Then why not swear to the police, and let a jury decide.'

'Because I don't believe I'll receive a fair trial. I fought your brother because he was trying to apprehend a young girl I was travelling with. She'd just left the employment of my former commanding officer, Colonel Harris, who wanted her back.'

A shadow passed over the big man's face. 'So my brother was acting on Harris's orders?'

'Exactly.'

'And you say he drew a sword on you?'

'Yes, a sword-stick to be exact.'

Thompson swore. 'John always were a bully, quick to use his fists. But he never killed no one, not to my knowledge.'

'Well he almost killed me. As I say, he left me no alternative.'

'I don't believe you,' said Thompson, shaking his head. 'I reckon you were taking a beating and you pulled a pistol.'

'That's not how it was.'

'So you keep saying, but old Bob can't speak for himself, can he?'

'No.'

'Which is why I'm asking you nicely, *Captain* Hart, to

hand yourself in. Our poor old mum won't rest until she knows justice has been done.'

'I'm sorry for her; I truly am. But no jury influenced by Harris is going to believe I was justified in using a pistol against a sword-stick, though I know I was. If I admit to killing your brother I'll swing, and I don't deserve that.'

'And that's your final answer?'

'Yes.'

'You bloody coward,' spat Thompson as he lurched forward, swinging a left-handed haymaker at the side of George's head.

But George, though drunk, was the nimbler of the two, easily slipping the punch and countering with one of his own, a straight right that caught Thompson flush on the jaw with a crack that echoed down the empty street. It was a blow made all the more potent by the humiliation George had already suffered at the gambling hell, and Thompson reaped the consequences. He staggered and fell backwards into a sitting position, his eyes glazed.

'Like your brother, you left me no choice,' said George, 'I had no choice.' Suddenly sober, he walked briskly away.

# 2

George's heart was still pounding as he entered the lobby of his small, discreet hotel at the bottom of Queen's Gate. It had been an evening to forget and he wished he could be on the ship to South Africa this very minute.

'Room thirty-two. Any messages?' he asked, more out of habit than expectation.

'Yes, sir,' said the tail-coated concierge, handing over his key and a thick white envelope. 'This came for you an hour ago.'

Recognizing at once the crest of the Commander-in-Chief, George tore open the letter and read it:

*The Horse Guards*
*Pall Mall*

   *My dear Captain Hart*
   *There is a matter of some urgency I would like to discuss with you this evening at my private residence, 6 Queen's Street, Mayfair. Would you be so good as to arrive no later than half past nine. I look forward to renewing our acquaintance then.*
   *I am, etc.*
   *George Cambridge, Field Marshal*

George pulled out his pocket-watch and cursed. It was ten minutes past nine, which gave him just twenty minutes to clear his head, change his clothes, hail a cab and get himself over to the Commander-in-Chief's house in Mayfair. He grabbed his room key and ran for the stairs, taking two at a time.

A quarter of an hour later found George's cab snarled in traffic on Piccadilly, as a swearing, tangled mass of horse-riders, private carriages and hansoms jostled for position. The evening seemed to be going from bad to worse. 'How much longer?' he asked the driver perched high above him.

'Don't worry, sir,' shouted the cabbie as he steered his horse left off Piccadilly into Half Moon Street. 'Almost there.'

A couple of minutes later the cab drew up in front of No. 6 Queen Street, a substantial but far from palatial Georgian townhouse, the home of HRH the Duke of Cambridge and his morganatic wife, the former stage actress Mrs Fitzgeorge. George had not heard from the duke since their interview two months earlier, and could only assume there were some last minute instructions or messages the War Office wanted him to convey to South Africa. But why not summon him to Pall Mall, as before? Why ask a lowly captain to his private residence? It did not make sense, yet George was intrigued nonetheless, and not a little flattered. He was also hoping to meet Mrs Fitzgeorge, like his mother a famous beauty of the stage, who was said to have secretly – and illegally – married the duke *after* she had had two illegitimate sons by him. They had since had another and all three were serving officers and known by the royal suffix 'Fitz' or bastard son of

George. Yet because of her humble origins as the daughter of a Bow Street printer, Mrs Fitzgeorge had neither been accepted by society, nor acknowledged by the Queen, the duke's first-cousin. George also occupied an ambivalent position in the British class system – dark-skinned and illegitimate, he had been sent to Harrow and Sandhurst and almost felt he was now masquerading as an officer and a gentleman – and assumed they would have much in common.

The door was opened by a florid-faced butler who, having taken George's hat and coat, led him upstairs to the first-floor drawing room. 'Captain George Hart,' he announced.

'At last,' said a voice George recognized as the duke's, 'Show him in.'

George saw immediately that he would not be meeting the duke's wife, for the room contained just three men in evening dress: the duke himself was standing by the empty fireplace, a portly figure with his familiar bald pate and white mutton-chop whiskers; seated on a sofa to his left was a younger man George did not recognize, also bald but with a full beard and a pince nez hanging from his neck; and opposite him on a second sofa was the un-mistakeable figure of Lord Beaconsfield, the Prime Min-ister, with his thin pinched face, prominent nose and trimmed beard. George stood open-mouthed, trying to fathom out why this legendary politician would want to meet him.

'You look as if you've seen a ghost, Captain Hart,' said the duke, with a chuckle. 'I can assure you Lord Beacons-field is flesh and blood. As is Lord Salisbury,' he added, gesturing towards the second man. 'Come over and all will be explained.'

George was even more taken aback – the Prime Minister *and* the Foreign Secretary – but he did as he was bidden, bowing slightly as he shook the duke's hand. Salisbury rose to greet him, but not Beaconsfield, who remained sitting. 'Forgive my *impolitesse*, Captain Hart,' said the premier, 'but I've been unwell and my doctor advises rest – as if that were possible in these troubled times.'

'I quite understand, Prime Minister.'

'Now, before we start,' said the duke, 'would you like a drink?'

George knew it was unwise to accept, but needed to calm his nerves. 'Yes, please. A whisky.'

While the butler poured George's drink, the duke apologized for not being able to explain in his note the purpose of their meeting. 'But what you are about to hear,' he added, 'is a matter of national security and must not be repeated without our authorisation. Secrecy is paramount. Do you understand?'

George nodded as he took his drink from the butler, who then left the room, closing the double doors behind him.

'First, may I congratulate you, Captain Hart,' began Beaconsfield, 'on surviving the catastrophe at Isandlwana. I don't mind telling you that receiving the news of that defeat was one of the darkest moments of my life, and that the government might have fallen there and then without the glimmer of sunshine provided by the heroic defence of Rorke's Drift. I gather you fought there too?'

Unwelcome memories of the vicious fighting, particularly the death of his best friend Jake, swirled into George's head. 'I did, your Lordship,' said George, as if in a trance, 'until I was wounded.'

'Of course,' said Beaconsfield, nodding, 'and I trust you're fully recovered.'

'I am. Thank you.'

'Excellent. From what His Royal Highness tells me, you have performed a double service for your country: first by your acts of valour during the fighting; and secondly by exposing the inadequacies of the military command in South Africa. My instinct on hearing the news of Isandlwana was at once to relieve Lord Chelmsford of his duties. But the duke argued against this, as did Her Majesty the Queen, on the grounds that it would be unfair to condemn the man before the full details of the battle were known. Well, now they are, thanks to you, and a few days ago Her Majesty finally sanctioned the Cabinet's recommendation to replace Lord Chelmsford with Sir Garnet Wolseley, who will leave on the SS *Edinburgh Castle* tomorrow. I gather you're booked on the same passage?'

'Yes, I am,' said George, barely able to conceal his delight that Chelmsford had finally received his come-uppance. He was anxious to return to South Africa for various reasons: not just to avoid being implicated in the Plymouth killing (a danger made all the more real now by his encounter with Thompson's brother), but also to take revenge on his Zulu cousin Mehlokazulu for killing Jake at Isandlwana; to settle scores with Sir Joshua Harris, his former CO, for drumming him out of the 1st King's Dragoon Guards; and, simply, to get on with his military career. But the one thing making him uneasy had been the thought that he would have to serve again under Chelmsford and his evil deputy Crealock. That threat had now been lifted.

'I can see from your expression that you approve of the Cabinet's decision,' said Beaconsfield, leaning forward. 'Quite right. But I must tell you that you may not have the opportunity to make Sir Garnet's acquaintance, because we have in mind for you a quite different form of military service in another country that should suit your unique talents. Lord Salisbury will explain.'

Nonplussed, and not a little irked that his return to South Africa was in doubt, George swung round to face the foreign secretary. 'Have you ever heard of the Prophet's Cloak?' asked Salisbury, in a deep, gravelly voice.

'No,' replied George, 'but I imagine it has something to do with the Mohammedan religion.'

'Exactly so. Mohammedans believe it was once owned by the Prophet Mohammed himself, and as such is one of their most sacred relics. How it found its way to Afghanistan has never been properly explained. Some say it was given as a present to an Afghan chief called Kais who fought on behalf of the Prophet in the seventh century; others that it was owned by the Mughal emperors of India, who swept through Afghanistan in the sixteenth century. It now resides in a sealed cabinet in the Abdurrab Mosque in Kandahar in the south of the country. If we could be sure it would stay there, and never see the light of day, we would not be having this conversation. But experience tells us it can and will be brought out in times of national emergency. It was last donned by Dost

Mahomed, the late Amir of Kabul. Does that name sound familiar?'

'Of course, your Lordship. Every schoolboy knows of Dost, and how Britain was forced to restore him as ruler after the disasters of the Afghan War in the forties.'

'Quite right. Dost understood the symbolic power of the cloak as a means of rallying the faithful against the foreign invader. Which brings me to the point. While you were battling the Zulu, a quite separate war was being fought in Afghanistan. And like your war, it was launched by a pro-consul who exceeded his brief. When Lord Lytton took up his post as Viceroy of India in seventy-six, he was instructed by the Cabinet to find a way to prevent the ruler of Afghanistan, Sher Ali, from falling under Russian influence. One by one the khanates of Central Asia have fallen to the Russians, who now stand on Afghanistan's northern border. Our greatest fear is that they will continue their march south and use Afghanistan as a collecting point for an invasion of India. Lord Lytton's task was to encourage Sher Ali to accept a British resident in Kabul who could keep an eye on the Russians. What he was not authorized to do was to send a mission up the Khyber Pass without Sher's permission, which is what happened last September. Inevitably the mission was turned back by the Afghans and war was the result. It could have been avoided, but only if Sher had apologized and agreed to accept a resident. It was vital to our prestige that he agree to some form of reparation. He refused. These Orientals are very proud.'

George nodded in acknowledgement. The sequence of events was not dissimilar to the one which had preceded the Zulu War. Yet there was one vital difference, and he voiced it in the hope that it would end all talk of cloaks and holy war.

'All this is fascinating, your Lordship, but was not the recent Afghan War brought to a satisfactory conclusion, unlike the fighting in Zululand, which still goes on? That's certainly the impression one gets from reading the newspapers.'

'And newspapers never lie, do they?' said Salisbury, with more than a hint of sarcasm. 'But you're mostly right, Captain Hart. For once, our military operations went like clockwork – though the Afghans fought well against Roberts at Peiwar Kotal – and by January this year it was mostly over: Sher Ali had fled north and both Kandahar and Kabul were in our hands. Then in February we heard of Sher Ali's death and the accession of his son, and former prisoner, Yakub Khan, who had enough sense to open negotiations with us. The result was a treaty he signed last week at Gandamak, ceding a strip of Afghan territory that includes the Khyber Pass and the Kurram Valley, agreeing to our original request for a British resident in Kabul, and guaranteeing British control over Afghan foreign policy and freedom of commerce. In return, he will receive an annual subsidy of sixty thousand pounds and the promise of British support in the event of war with a foreign aggressor.'

Salisbury paused to let the details sink in, but George looked more confused than ever. 'Forgive me, your Lordship,' he said, 'but I don't see what this has to do with me or the cloak. Surely with the war over and the treaty signed you've got everything you want: a British resident at Kabul, a pliant amir and Russian influence nowhere to be seen.'

Beaconsfield could remain silent no longer. 'Appearances can be deceptive, Captain Hart. In truth, the situation in Afghanistan is far less satisfactory than the newspapers would have you believe. How do we know this? Because the Foreign Office has a spy in Kabul, and his last report warned that Yakub is despised by the majority of his countrymen for concluding such a shameful treaty, and that an extremist cleric from Ghazni, called Mullah something or other . . .' Beaconsfield turned to Salisbury for help. 'What's his name?'

'Mullah Mushk-i-Alam, Prime Minister,' said Salisbury, 'which apparently means "Perfume of the Universe".'

'Extraordinary! Well this "Perfume" fellow, according to our spy, is trying to rouse the faithful against our presence in Afghanistan and all who condone it, including Yakub. And the easiest way for the Mullah to do this is to don the Prophet's Cloak and declare himself the spiritual leader not just of Afghanistan but of the whole Mussalman world. It goes without saying that it's in our vital interest to prevent this happening – which is where you come in. We want you to travel to Afghanistan, locate the cloak and bring it back to Britain.'

Until now, George had listened to both men in respectful silence. They were, after all, the most powerful men in Britain which, by dint of the Empire's pre-eminence, meant the world. But this suggestion was insane; no, he decided, it was worse than insane. It showed that while they might be prepared to change commanders like Chelmsford, the rulers of the Empire were still acting with blind arrogance, learning nothing from their adventures in places like Zululand. What was more, this plan was guaranteed to get him killed.

'I'm flattered that you've considered me for such an important mission, Prime Minister,' he began, careful not to sound ungrateful. 'But, with all due respect, I fail to see how I fit the bill. I'm still young and learning my profession; I've never been to Afghanistan, and I've no experience of espionage. Surely it would make more sense to send an agent of the Indian government who knows the country and can speak the lingo?'

'You might think that, Captain Hart,' said Salisbury, 'but we and the Indian government don't always see eye to eye. For the last few years they've been pursuing quite a different—'

Beaconsfield interrupted with a raised hand. 'I don't think we need to go into that, Salisbury. Suffice to say, Captain Hart, we have our reasons. As for your fitness to undertake this mission, I can think of no one better. Yes, you're young, but you were the best in your class at Sandhurst and your feats in Zululand confirm that you're an officer of outstanding promise. You've shown bravery, endurance, resourcefulness and integrity, all qualities that are needed for the Afghan mission. I'm told you pick up languages easily, you're an excellent horseman, and you have one big advantage over just about any other British officer for an undercover operation of this type, and that's – how can I put this? – you're . . .'

'Expendable?' suggested George, one eyebrow raised.

'Why on earth would you think that?' asked the Prime Minister.

'I apologize, Prime Minister, I was being flippant, though it strikes me you'd be much less likely to send a titled member of the Brigade of Guards than a misfit like me.'

Beaconsfield smiled. 'You might be right, but there's a reason for that.' He turned to the duke, who was still standing by the fireplace, a glass of whisky in hand. 'Your Royal Highness, would you mind if I have a word in private with young Hart?'

'Not at all. I'll be next door.'

'You too, Salisbury.'

The foreign minister frowned. 'Is that really necessary, Prime Minister?'

'Yes.'

Once the pair had left the room, Beaconsfield turned back to George, a faint smile playing on his lips. 'You may be surprised to hear this, Captain Hart, but you and I have much in common.'

'We do?' asked an unconvinced George.

'Yes. We're both – how can I put it? – cuckoos in the nest: we may look the part, say the right things, but we don't really belong, do we? My father was a practising Jew who baptized his children into the Church of England so that they could get on in society. Did you know that?'

'No, I had no idea.'

'Well, it's true, and just as well for me because I couldn't have climbed the greasy pole if I hadn't become an Anglican. Until a few years ago Jews couldn't even vote, let alone stand for Parliament. But don't misunderstand me. I didn't always want to be a politician. Before I became an MP I tried my hand at business and writing novels. I wasn't very successful at either, and that mattered to me because I always want to be the best at anything I do, and I suspect you do, too. Am I right?'

George nodded. He hadn't given it much thought before now, but he couldn't deny he had always been fiercely competitive, and had worked twice as hard as his peers at Harrow and Sandhurst.

'I thought so. Truth is, Hart, people like us don't fit neatly into English society, and never will. They know it and, more importantly, we know it, which is why we'll move Heaven and Earth to prove ourselves superior. I was spared the torment of public school, thank God, though I know Harrow and Sandhurst can't have been easy for someone of your background. Yet you excelled at both, and clearly have determination as well as brains, the sort of combination not usually found in a pink-cheeked ensign of the Grenadier Guards. You think we've selected you for this mission because you're nobody and therefore expendable? Far from it. You possess a range of qualities that are rarely found in someone your age and with your education – not least a handsome figurehead, which is something, alas, I was never blessed with – and that's why we'd – I'd – hate to lose you.'

Not as much as I'd hate to lose myself, thought George, as he tried to read between the Prime Minister's honeyed lines. Did they really have that much in common? Or was Beaconsfield, consummate politician that he was, simply telling him what he wanted to hear? He couldn't decide. And there was something else about the nature of the undercover mission that was making him uneasy. 'I'm flattered, of course, my Lord,' said George, after a lengthy pause, 'but there's much to consider. I appreciate your intention is to avoid more bloodshed and turmoil, but would it not make more sense simply to withdraw from Afghanistan and leave the Afghans to their own devices?'

'And leave the way clear for the Russians to advance to the very borders of British India? No, we cannot let that happen.'

'But would it, my Lord? Surely the Russians would find the Afghans every bit as tough a nut to crack as we have? Is it not better to have Russians dying in the Hindu Kush than our own soldiers in the Khyber Pass?'

'Of course. But we can't guarantee the Afghans will win such a war. And if they don't, we'll face a mortal threat to our Indian Empire. No, Hart, the only sensible option is to have a British envoy in Kabul who can keep an eye on things, which is what we've done. But the position of our current envoy, Sir Louis Cavagnari, is in danger of being undermined by religious radicals, as I've explained, and the best way to prevent this is for us to get our hands on the Prophet's Cloak.'

George rubbed his chin. 'I see the sense of that, my Lord, but I can't help feeling uneasy. The cloak is clearly a religious artefact of great importance to the Afghans and removing it from them will surely make it harder for us to be accepted as an ally.'

'Of course, but only if they know we're responsible, which they won't if you're careful. Well, I've said my piece and now, I think, it's best if the others rejoin us. Andrews!' shouted Beaconsfield.

The butler peeked his head round the door. 'Yes, Lord Beaconsfield.'

'Be so good as to ask your master and Lord Salisbury to come back in.'

'Of course.'

Once the pair had resumed their former places, Beaconsfield continued: 'I think, gentlemen, that Captain Hart is ready to give us his answer. Is that right?'

'Not quite, my Lord,' said George. 'You still haven't explained what "big advantage" I have over my peers for a mission of this kind.'

Beaconsfield chuckled. 'I would have thought that was obvious. Why, it's the colour of your skin, of course. Put you in a native costume and you'll pass for an Afghan in no time. What say you, Salisbury?'

The foreign secretary nodded vigorously. 'I agree. They'll never know you're British.'

That's because I'm not, thought George, well, not entirely. But he was not about to tell these powerful men the truth – that he had a mixture of Zulu and Irish blood in his veins, as well as his father's British blood, if indeed he was British – what was the point? Far better to stick to the story his mother had told him as a boy; that she was of Maltese descent. That way he could continue the charade that he was an officer and a gentleman with only a slight touch of the tarbrush. After all, if Beaconsfield – the son of a practising Jew – could become Prime Minister, what was to stop him rising to the very top of his profession if he kept quiet about his African heritage?

'I am, of course, happy to second you to the Foreign Office for the duration of the mission,' interjected the duke, 'and if you're successful there's a good chance, a very good chance, that Her Majesty will approve your brevet to the rank of major.'

'So, will you do it?' asked Beaconsfield.

George paused before answering. Every logical bone in his body was urging him to say thank you, but no thank you. It wasn't just his unfinished business in South Africa; he was also looking forward to joining the 3/60<sup>th</sup> Rifles and becoming a proper regimental officer with men under his command. Yet, on the other hand, he could not help thinking that promotion to major would take him tantalisingly close to the rank of lieutenant-colonel and £5,000 under the terms of his father's bequest. Nor could he deny that Lord Beaconsfield had a point, and that he possessed many of the attributes required for such a mission. This gave him, he realized, a crucial bargaining chip that might help him solve his mother's financial worries. And there was something else helping to sway his mind, the same something that Beaconsfield had just alluded to, and that had enabled him to ignore his tormentors at Harrow, to pass first out of Sandhurst, and later to re-enter the military as a trooper after the humiliation of his brief time in the King's Dragoon Guards: a determination to excel at the only profession that interested him, soldiering; and, at the same time, to prove himself as good as, if not better than, all those officers who were unmistakeably 'white' and who knew who both their parents were. He could feel his heart thumping, more through excitement than nervousness, as he drained his glass of its fiery liquid and then set out his terms.

'I will, Prime Minister, but on one condition—'

'Now, Captain Hart,' said the duke, gruffly, 'I hardly think you're in a position to set conditions.'

'On the contrary,' said Beaconsfield. 'It seems to me he's in a very strong position. We need him, but does he need us? Let's hear what he has to say.'

'I won't go into the details, gentlemen,' said George, 'but for personal reasons I need a substantial sum of money by the end of the year at the latest. Therefore, I'll only agree to undertake the mission if you promise to pay me the sum of two thousand pounds.'

'*What?*' said the duke, red-faced. 'You have the gall to demand money to serve your country? Have you lost your reason? You're a British officer, not some soldier of fortune.'

'Your Royal Highness, please,' said Beaconsfield, his hand raised. 'Allow me to respond. Two thousand pounds, you say? That's quite a sum, but not impossible to come by.' He turned to the foreign secretary. 'Salisbury, could we procure this amount from the Secret Service Fund? After all, Captain Hart will be undertaking special duties for your department.'

Salisbury frowned at the irregularity of the request, but he knew Beaconsfield well enough to realize when he was being asked and when he was being told. 'I'm sure that could be arranged, Prime Minister, but I'd like to add a caveat of my own: that we only pay the two thousand pounds if Captain Hart's mission is successful, that is if he returns to this country with the cloak intact.'

'All right by you, Hart?'

'Yes, Prime Minister, that sounds fair to me.'

'Excellent,' said Beaconsfield, rising stiffly from his

chair. 'Well, I must be getting back to number ten. It's late.'

'I must go, too,' said Salisbury.

George rose to shake the politicos' hands. 'Good luck in Afghanistan, Hart,' said Beaconsfield.

'I'll second that,' added Salisbury, 'but remember this: officially, the government knows nothing of your mission; if anything goes wrong, you're on your own. Understand?'

'Yes, my Lord.'

'Good. You'll be briefed tomorrow at the Foreign Office, nine sharp. Don't be late.'

As the door closed on the departing politicians, the duke turned to George. 'You've made the right decision, Hart. You wouldn't have enjoyed serving under that pretentious snob Wolseley who, if it had been down to me, would never have been appointed. I wanted Napier, but the Cabinet said he was too old and that only Wolseley would do. Bloody fools! What do they know of military affairs?'

George raised his eyebrows, surprised that the duke was prepared to criticize openly the two men who had just left his house.

'Oh, don't get me wrong,' continued the duke, 'I admire Dizzy and his gang as politicians, and would see them in government before any of the ghastly alternatives, particularly that old prig Gladstone. They, at least, act in the best interests of the service and the Empire. And Dizzy clearly has a high opinion of you or he wouldn't have asked you to undertake such an important mission. But enough of that. You should be getting along, too. Before you go, though, I have a favour to ask.'

'By all means, your Royal Highness.'

'It's . . . um . . . a personal matter,' said the duke, colouring slightly. 'I know you'll be travelling to Afghanistan incognito, so to speak, and not in any official capacity, but if you do cross paths with my son Major Harry Fitzgeorge, who's serving on General Roberts' staff, could you give him a message?'

'Of course. What would you like me to tell him?'

'Could you . . . ah . . . ask him to write to his mother. An odd request, I know, but she worries.'

'Of course,' said George, with a smile. 'All mothers do.'

'Yes, but some have more reason than others. With Harry and his brothers it's one scrape after another,' said the duke, shaking his head. 'I imagined the military would straighten them out, but it hasn't made a blind bit of difference. They're constantly in debt and I've lost count of the times I've had to pay off their creditors. If they'd been anyone else's sons they'd have been cashiered years ago. But I'm convinced Harry in particular has goodness in him, and not a little aptitude for soldiering, and lately he's shown signs that he's put the wildness of his youth behind him. Why, only last week I received a letter from General Roberts complimenting Harry on his excellent intelligence work during the recent war. Naturally his mother is delighted, but she would love to hear from the boy himself.'

George nodded, though he could not for the life of him imagine why the duke was talking so freely about his errant sons. 'I'll be sure to pass on your message, your Royal Highness.'

'Thank you,' said the duke, his head cocked to one side,

'and the very best of luck in Afghanistan. I once met an officer who was on the retreat in forty-two. He couldn't talk about the horrors of the march, but he did say the Afghans were easily the toughest, most treacherous and pitiless foe he'd had the misfortune to encounter. So my advice is: expect the worst and trust no one. Oh, and one more thing, Captain Hart. You may not agree with everything we're trying to achieve in Afghanistan, but remember where your loyalties lie.'

George was already nervous about the task ahead, and this was not the encouraging chat he had hoped for. But he felt that the duke's sentiments were genuine, and marvelled again at the contrast between the public's perception of the duke as a cold, unimaginative bureaucrat and the warm-hearted family man before him.

'I'll endeavour to remember that, sir,' said George, trying to look a deal more confident than he felt.